T0354915

Arn OF CLAYHAVEN

Autumn's Lonely Road

GREYSON DE SAYE

Order this book online at www.trafford.com
or email orders@trafford.com

Most Trafford titles are also available at major online book retailers.

Printed in the United States of America.

ISBN: 978-1-4120-7364-6 (sc)

Library of Congress Control Number: 2011918388

Trafford rev. 12/16/2011

 www.trafford.com

North America & international
toll-free: 1 888 232 4444 (USA & Canada)
phone: 250 383 6864 ♦ fax: 812 355 4082

I would like to dedicate this humble work to the great Creator, without whose gifts I would have nothing. To my dearest Ann, who worked so diligently with me, thank you so very, very much. I could not have done this without you. To my father, a chronicler, and my mother, a teacher, thank you for all you gave me. My history, my heritage, my knowledge of who I am, all come from you. To my dearest William, without whose enthusiasm, great ideas and encouragement I would not have finished this book. He will be a great writer one day. To my Uncle Bud, for his great encouragement to read the classics, awesome knowledge of history, excellent grasp of world situations, fantastic artistic ability and unfailing kindness. I know you are in heaven's embrace, talkin' of ships 'n such, Cap'n, and whether Wellington should have stayed closer to the Prussians, and the composition of a Roman legion. Last, but not least, thanks to you dear reader, who have taken your hard-won coin and purchased this chronicle, inviting Arn and myself and the rest of the cast from Cast into your homes and hearts. We live in troubled times. Know that you always have a friend in Arn and in me. Keep fighting. Keep trying. May many blessings be with you and yours.

NOTE FROM THE AUTHOR:

My good reader, I have decided to place the history of the continent of Great Cast in the back of this chronicle. If you be a lover of history, I might suggest you read the fairly detailed accounts of Southaven's traumatic beginnings, along with a bit more about the place whence Arn came. If you be a lover of a story of fair flow, then read the story starting with chapter one. You might say I've put the foreword in the back. Take a glance at the map. It will give you some ideas as to where things stand on the Great Cast. Thank you! Greyson de Saye

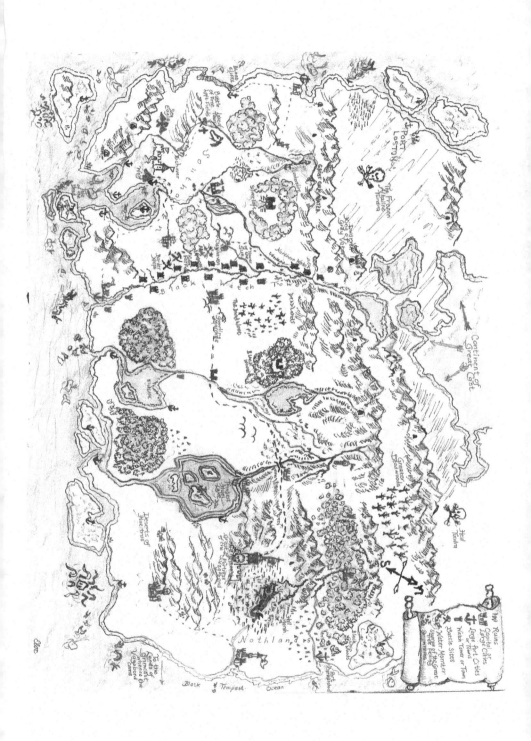

CHAPTER ONE

STRANGE TRAVELLERS

*O*ur *story begins on a cold, autumn day with that bright hint of crisp* fall air that reminds you that hot summer is over and the beautiful snow-blanketed winter will soon be here. That kind of morning makes you want to think that all the world is hopeful, and all is well. There was a sparkly dew on the ground and a spectacular, fiery sunrise that sent red and gold fanning out right before your eyes.

This is what Arn saw as he looked out of the window of the small room that Brother Kile had given him to live in. It was part of the stable, but with a lot of work and some nice goat's milk paint that Brother Clement was quite proficient at making, they had made it a very pleasant, though still small, room. And Arn cherished it dearly. It was the only real, happy home he had ever known.

The brothers were always quite nice to Arn. They treated him as if he were someone, an intelligent someone, and they never talked down to him, which was something everyone else did. Arn so detested being spoken to as if he were less than a slave. Arn was no man's slave, although he may have fallen on hard times, his family may be no more, and he might only have himself and his stray dog.

Actually, Arn was not quite sure if he was a wolf or a dog. The brothers could not tell him one way or the other for certain, but agreed he was an intelligent creature. Arn had named him Greymist, because he had found the dog one misty autumn morning like this one, outside his door, whimpering.

At first Arn had worried that perhaps he was going to attack the animals, but despite his large size, as they regarded each other, Arn had decided it was safe to offer his hand, and Greymist had touched it with his cold nose. The good fellow that he was, Arn had taken out a few meager scraps from his breakfast and offered Greymist some egg and a bit of the bacon that he cherished. The poor starving dog had hungrily devoured this great gift, and Arn had been very surprised that the next morning, he had been at Arn's door again. Arn had said, "I will call you Greymist."

Greymist had come many times periodically since then, and Arn had tried a few times to catch him, but to no avail. Greymist went his own way, and Arn went his. Arn always wondered what interesting life Greymist must lead when he was away from him.

Alas, it is morning again, thought Arn. Beautiful as it was, soon the sun would be up full, and he had many chores to do. Many stalls in the town to clean. Many chamber areas for the merchants in town, privies I should say. A terrible job. He wondered, as he looked at his filthy clothes and his grimy fingernails and hands, if he would always be relegated to such unpleasant tasks. *One day*, he thought, *I will be someone. One day everyone will respect me, and no one will ever ask me to clean chamber pots again.*

Time to see if Greymist is out there, he thought to himself, as he completely dressed in a coarse spun grey tunic that he liked. It was a bit chilly, so this heavier tunic on his white linen shirt would feel more comfortable.

The monks had, with some difficulty, built a nice, wee stone fireplace in his little room. *I will remember them kindly*, Arn thought, *one day when I am somebody. I will remember all the people who have been nice to me, and I will also remember all the people who have not been so nice.* He had a grim face at this thought, but then, opening the door, he saw his friend Greymist.

He thought, *Now there, there is somebody. He has a great life, no stalls to clean, no chamber pots, no one laughing at him, no one insulting him.* "Greymist, my friend, I am just going to breakfast and I will be back with a treat for you. You are like royalty to me. You should be bringing me something." He laughed.

Greymist just cocked his head to one side, with that funny kind of smile that he always had, at least Arn always fancied he had. He patted Greymist on the head. After their initial meeting, it had taken a long time for Greymist to let Arn get near him again. Finally Greymist had accepted him, not only as a feeder but also as a friend, and Arn considered Greymist his best friend, except for the monks. And Lady Hannah, who owned a small but nice house towards the end of town where she rented out four back rooms she had built on.

Lady Hannah was a widow, her husband having died in one of the many battles Southaven had fought in recent years with the evil empire. She had always been kind to Arn, and after he had done a little bit of work this afternoon, he would go and see her.

Sometimes she would even give him a treat. When she butchered, often she would give him the pig's tail, which for the children in town was a choice prize. She would make sure that he got it and he always enjoyed it as a treat. Sometimes she would bake actual cookies with sugar and shared them with Arn. He thought she must have been a beautiful lady when she was younger, because he could still see beauty in her lined face. *I will remember her too. She has been a dear friend, not like the others in this town.* Arn forgot his grim mood for a moment, and smiled as he walked to his breakfast.

Brother Clement was already setting the table. Arn smiled at him and asked, "Brother, may I help you?"

"No, lad, you just sit. I have a special breaking of the fast for you this morning."

"Really?" asked Arn. *What could it be?*

Arn smiled and suppressed a small giggle. Treats were something he treasured very much. The brothers had given him many in the years since his parents had died. He had learned much from the monks as well, but alas, they did not have much money, and coin was gotten from cleaning stalls and chamber pots around town. It wasn't a pretty job, but a hapenny was a hapenny, and money was money. Arn saved what he could.

One day I am going to buy myself out of this situation. I will be somebody, he thought again.

Greymist stayed at a distance. Arn could see him out through the small kitchen window, behind the main church and small building where the monks slept. The small kitchen and larger dining area also served as a meeting area for the priory, where feasts would sometimes take place. Greymist was just sitting, looking around; he was wary of the monks but he had grown to tolerate them as well. He just sat and panted a bit, looking happy, knowing that Arn would bring him a treat.

Father Kile and Brother Francis hadn't arrived yet, but Brother Clement brought out two steaming pots and one small cooking kettle, full of a delicious smelling aroma.

Arn asked, "What is that? Is that a soup or a stew?"

"Oh, it's stew, or you might call it a soup. Good question. I'll let you decide. There's a treat in there."

"Is there fish inside?"

"Nope, something a little better than that."

"Deer?"

"Nope."

"Is it beef, brother?" Arn asked, his eyes full of wonder.

"Aye, 'tis beef, lad, a real beef stew, a little thin probably to be called stew. Be that as it may, it's a special breakfast treat. And in this pot, I've prepared my skillet cakes. My special food item here, hmmm."

Arn sat eagerly, trencher in one hand and fork in the other.

"Aye, lad. You might even get to use that fork! There's big chunks of beef in there."

"I haven't had beef since, oh my goodness, since last Yuletide."

"Aye, this is a fine beef, lad. 'Twas given to the priory by one of our parishioners."

"Oh really," said Arn. "Was it Sir Ronald?" He was a knight of Lord Moresfield, the unpleasant lord of the area.

"Oh no," said Brother Clement with a chuckle. "No, he hasn't given anything to the priory since, well, I don't know when he ever gave anything to our priory. No, it was a new fellow who came to the church with his wife. They received a blessing, they said, after prayer, and they were most pleased, and they sent this nice beef. Father Kile has allowed us to have a little bit for breakfast."

"It smells so good. Are those potatoes?"

"Aye, and leeks, barley, big carrots and parsnips and my own gravy with just a touch of this and that," he tapped his finger to his forehead, "only I know."

Arn laughed. "You are the best cook in the world, Brother Clement. I hope that one day I will be as good a cook."

He said, "Oh, aye, you will. That's one thing me mum always taught me. Her brothers, you know, they lived alone as farmers, and all they could make for themselves, since neither one was married, was boiled potatoes if they had any, and oatmeal, and occasionally, they might try to cook a piece of fat meat in there."

"That doesn't sound very good," said Arn. "That's all they ate most of the time?"

"Aye, if they had any meat at all, and when they didn't they would just make gruel."

"I'm grateful that you have taught me to cook. I won't forget it either."

"Be that as it may, lad, sit and enjoy your food. I've got some work to do. The others had some work to do this morning. They will be back later. I hear ye have got a lot of work this day."

"Yes, brother, I do. The inn is really busy. There are several horses in the stalls over there, so I might come out with a couple of hapennies for the day."

"Hmm, you make a better living in a lot of ways than we do, lad," he said with a chuckle. "I wish we could pay you. You are a strong, smart lad. That's not a job for you. One day there will be something better. It will come along, you wait." Brother Clement sighed and patted Arn on the back.

"I know how it guiles you. It's not the life you dream of. But you know, this is not your lot in life. This is not your station. There is something great for you, believe me. You won't be the manure boy forever." Brother Clement's serious eye was upon Arn.

"I hope you are right, but I feel you are not," said Arn with a half-hearted smile. Brother Clement patted him on the back and left him to eat.

After Arn's grace he sat and gobbled down his delicious stew. The bread was so sweet, flour bread with oats mixed in. It was very tasty, for Brother Clement was a great cook. The cows and goats at the abbey church were great milk-givers. They had always given good amounts and the butter and soft cheese that Brother Clement made almost daily were excellent. Arn ate better than many in the village, and for that he was grateful.

He ate hungrily. He placed a few precious grains of salt from the salt pot over his food. Greymist is really going to appreciate a bite of this, he thought. He took out a few choice bits of meat and some potato then reluctantly lifted himself up from the table to begin his day. He wondered wistfully if he could just have one more bite. And at that Brother Clement stuck his head in and said with a laugh, "Lad, go ahead and have another bowl. You'll need extra for today. It's getting chilly."

Arn grinned, "Oh, you are most kind, Brother! Thank you!"

"Think nothing of it, lad, you deserve it."

Arn sat and devoured a second bowl. It made him feel almost full, not a common thing at Arn's breakfast, or any other meal for that matter. He spoke aloud into the empty room, "Aye, this is what it must be like to be royalty."

From the kitchen Brother Clement spoke out, "That's it, royalty we are. I'm the high priest such and such and you are Arn, Lord of the Realm."

Arn laughed as he pushed his stool back and put the bits he had prepared for Greymist in the trencher. "Now, don't you go feeding that friend of yours out of the trencher," warned Brother Clement. Greymist actually paid for his own by chasing away the odd fox or wolf that sought the chickens for a snack. Greymist was very good about paying for his suppers, and Brother Clement knew it.

"I won't. I have a bowl I made for him."

"Well, just be sure to bring that trencher back."

"I will. Thank you so much. It was delicious!"

As Arn went out to meet the day, he felt strangely happy, happy has he had not felt for quite a while. *I think this is going to be a great day.* He went out near the stables to bring Greymist his delicious treat. Greymist did not wait until the food hit the bowl. Arn laughed and said, "Back down, boy! I won't take it from you!" He patted Grey on the head and leaned down as he very occasionally did.

Greymist trusted him enough to let him lean so close. He kissed the top of the furry head, and said, "I hope you have a great day, Greymist. Stay safe, my friend."

Arn returned the trencher to the abbey and then went back to his lodgings to get his trusty pitchfork. He started quickly on the abbey's farm, mucked out the stalls, and tended to the three cows, the goats and the chickens and let them out for the day.

As Arn set off to town, he was whistling a little tune to himself, and singing a song that went something like this:

"A-lo I go, a-lo I am
Cleanin' stalls, I'm the cleanin' man
They laugh at me but soon they'll see
The cleanin' man is someone to be."

It was a little song he had made up for himself.

As he got into town he saw that there were many travelers' horses tied near the inn and store. He wondered if something was perhaps amiss. There were not usually so many travelers. Of course, it was getting toward fall, and plantings were coming in and rents would soon be due to the landlords, and such. But these did not look like landlords' horses. He wondered what might be going on.

Next to the Brown Pipe Leaf there were four horses at the inn, and one on the side. Horses were rare in Clayhaven. It took a man of wealth to have a riding mount. Usually in Clayhaven were cart horses or goats, or oxen, if any animals were involved at all. Most just hoofed it on the foot.

Arn always wanted to walk through the inn, but going through the inn, he had learned, would put him in a bad mood for the day. He was called manure boy, manure man, and various other less savory names. He did not relish the older peasants and minor nobles insulting him, the bar spiders. So instead, he went around to the back of the inn to start his morning tasks.

The small tavern had been much larger before a fire had destroyed it many years before. A pillaging army belonging to a neighboring noble had come through and damaged much of the town. The noble thought he had a grudge to settle and decided to make the town and all the poor people of Clayhaven suffer dearly for their lord's insult. That small war went on for seven months before the high king put an end to it by making the two combatants joust on the field of honor. Both had ended up with a lance through the chest. Arn thought it was a fitting end to them after they had made all the local people suffer so much.

All the stalls at the inn were full. He hoped the groom was there. He hated tending to all the horses as well as mucking out the stalls, and bringing the horses water by himself. Since it was third day, the groom might have drunk heavily in the night, but probably not. Arn went about his tasks, keeping an eye out for the groom, but saw the horses had not been tended to. So he continued as efficiently as he could, brushing each of the horses and placing bags of grain with the horses whose stalls were marked with a red stone. These horses' owners had paid extra for the grain, meaning they were of some wealth. They were fine, beautiful horses and Arn found himself enjoying their company until he came to one pitch black beast.

This one was tall, at least twenty hands, with large hairy hooves, and had a bad demeanor. *That one's a monster. I wonder why he is so unfriendly?* He let Arn tend to his tasks around him, but grunted and snorted and almost stepped on Arn's foot. He was saying as a horse does, "Boy, don't you touch me." Arn tried his best not to.

After Arn finished his tasks in the stable came the most unpleasant part of the morning, tending to the chamber pots at the inn. There were eight small rooms in the inn, and usually there were one or two guests, if any, but he had a feeling there would be many more this morning. As he slowly went up the rickety stairs over the kitchen to the servant's entrance, he saw to his dismay that there were indeed six chamber pots. *Could be worse, there could be eight*, he thought with a sigh.

Just as he said that, he noticed the door to room number five open. Someone had obviously finished with his morning business and a hand gently placed the chamber pot outside the door. Arn saw the hand was of an obviously well-to-do man, clean, with no blemishes, but the chamber pot certainly wasn't clean. *How unpleasant*, thought Arn. *Steaming and smelly.*

Oh well, could be eight, thought Arn again. Then he quickly thought, *I shouldn't have said that*, but fortunately the door to number three had not opened. He quickly went about his job with what the innkeeper laughingly called the "honey bucket," placing each chamber pot inside its own little slot so it wouldn't be broken. He took the large honey bucket by its two handles. It was quite heavy with all seven chamber pots. *Well, someone else will have to do that last one*, he thought.

Just then the door to number three opened and a grubby, dark hand appeared, and plopped the chamber pot on the floor. Arn approached the pot and saw the arm with the black nightshirt retreating into the room. The hand repelled Arn; he did not at all like the looks of it. It was long and gaunt with long, unkempt, dirty fingernails. Arn thought he would not like to meet the owner of that hand. Something was creepy about it. Arn picked up the pot and was surprised to see there was a very light greenish colored steaming liquid in it. Not what he was expecting at all. Oh, what had that one been drinking! He placed the pot gingerly in the honey bucket and continued down the hall and out back to the compost heap.

The inn had money all right. This was the biggest compost heap in town, and the smelliest. But the inn's garden was quite nice, consisting of many delicious vegetables and some that you could not get anywhere else in town. The green liquid from the last chamber pot actually smoldered as it went upon the compost heap.

Oh my, what had he been drinking? Ugh! Arn had to keep himself from gagging. It had the most unpleasant smell. Arn continued with the cleaning of the chamber pots, which consisted of dumping water from the buckets inside, and swishing it around. Then he used a bit of lye soap to scour the smell out and clean them as best he could with a tattered, old scrubbing brush. The inn was quite proud of its chamber pots. It was unheard of in most places to clean out the pots. Cantree claimed a sparkling, clean-smelling chamber pot once a day as one of the boasts he used to entice guests to stay. The guests did seem to appreciate it. Arn hated it.

Arn hurried to return the chamber pots to the rooms. He placed each pot by the door with the number that matched. As he got to door three, he saw it was slightly ajar, as sometimes happened since the latch did not always catch. Being a young man of fifteen, Arn had a curious streak, as any young man would. He listened at the door quietly, and did not hear any noises. He thought, *I'll just take a peek. I can say I was placing the chamber pot inside the room to be handier for him.* Everyone in the inn knew Arn, and they knew he was no thief, and he was curious about that hand now, and the unusual contents of the pot.

He gently pushed the door open, and all he saw in the room was a black trunk, about six hands wide and about four hands tall. Arn thought, as the morning sun crept through several cracks in the window shutters and hit the trunk, that it seemed to swallow up the light. It was strange. He peered into the room and saw that other than these shards of light, the room was extremely dark. The traveler had also placed a blanket over the window in an attempt to block the light, Arn supposed. But there were cracks, and the light hit the trunk, but no other parts of the room received much light at all. The shutters had been drawn. Arn thought the visitor must not like the morning sun. Perhaps he was a heavy drinker. Suddenly Arn realized he was standing and looking at someone's room way too long.

As he turned back to go, a face appeared before him, the most unpleasant face he thought he had ever seen in his life. The man was wearing a jet-black mantle with a shadowy hood pulled low over his face. In the dim light from the hall, Arn could see just a bit of a pale, white nose, pointed, and long, thin, colorless lips, and a pointy chin. The mouth barely moved, but he heard the words, "Can I help ye, boy? This is my room." As the man spoke there emanated from his mouth a hideous stench. There was some hint of mint about it, but the foul odor overwhelmed it.

The voice seemed to hiss and growl at the same time. Arn could not help but jump back. "No, sir. I'm sorry. I was just returning your chamber pot, sir. I noticed the door was open, and I was thinking I might put it in here."

"Do that . . . not."

"Yes, sir," Arn gulped. "I'm very sorry."

"Get thee away," growled the voice.

Arn could not help but brush past the man, and smelled a strong odor of sage, along with another awful smell Arn could not identify. He scrambled down the hall, placing the chamber pot beside the door. He turned his back and did not turn around to look at that frightening face again.

Arn had never felt such fear in his life. What was wrong with that man? Arn had seen dead people before, and this one looked not too far away from dead.

The door of room three slammed with a resounding thud. Arn truly regretted looking in the room now. Arn, you nob, why must you be so nosey? He derided himself. He had not seen anyone with that frightening a countenance in his life.

He hurriedly finished his tasks around the inn, including carrying in fresh water, and filling the old rickety wooden bucket they kept in the back of the kitchen. Arn was glad to be done with things at the Brown Pipe Leaf. He wouldn't soon, if ever, forget that face, or that smell, or that blackness, or the paleness. That was a very unpleasant man. That unpleasant horse must surely be his.

10

Our young worker continued his tasks about town, carrying water for Trast's small general items shop and the potter's shop. He would get to the blacksmith's later.

The next stop in Arn's day was at Lady Hannah's boarding house. He did her chamber pots and cleaned about the privy. He was definitely surprised to find that the plump, kind mistress of the house had prepared him a small noonday meal. Usually the noonday meal would be the biggest meal of the day, but Arn rarely ate with her. She knew that her house was usually his last stop of the day before returning to the abbey, so this she had obviously prepared as a special gift for him. On the spotless table was his usual hapenny, his payment for the last week's work. The lady said with a soft, sweet voice, "Arn my lad, there are a lot of strangers about town. Do you know anything about it?"

"No, my lady. I don't know anything about it, but I'll tell you one thing. There's one fellow at the inn . . ." Arn stopped short. He felt as if he did not want to say anything about that man. He shook his head. *That's strange*, he thought, *I forgot what I was going to say.* He said to Lady Hannah, "Anyways, a lot of strange folk in town. Don't know much about it."

"If you hear anything, would you let me know?" She was always nervous when strangers were about. Arn thought it was because her beloved husband had been whisked away when the lord of the shire had come looking for the men of the area. Her husband had been a miles knight, which was a poor knight. He had had no retainers or squire, but he had been a knight in his own right.

He had gone off to battle on a spring day many years past, never to return. She had always missed him and never wore anything but black clothing, never any happy colors. The posts at the door of her house still wore the black cloth of the widow. She had loved him greatly and they had hoped to have children. Now she was some fifty summers and would not ever have her own children. Arn always felt of her like he would have felt towards a mother, if he had ever known such a thing. She had always been kind to him. She pulled cheesecloth off of a brown crockery plate, revealing two boiled eggs, a nice piece of pork and four hearty scones.

"Oh, this is most generous, my lady! Thank you."

"Just a small way to say thank you, Arn. Don't let this interfere with your other meal," she added with a smile. "Lads like you never get enough food anyway, so you go back and enjoy your other noonday as well."

Arn said his grace and ate his surprise dinner. He was careful to mind his manners. The boiled eggs were delicious. Lady Hannah had a reputation for feeding certain greens to her hens that made the eggs superior in color and flavor. Arn thought he was exceedingly blessed to have the lady and Brother Clement cook for him.

"Thank you, my lady," said Arn, as he finished. He decided to save one of the scones for Greymist and tucked it into the pouch on his belt, with his coins.

"I have things to do, rooms to attend to. Let me know if you hear anything. There are so many strangers about this morning."

"I will, my lady." Arn went out into the street, running as he went, forgetting the unpleasant experiences of the morning, but not totally forgetting that face and that smell.

I'll be glad when these strangers are gone, he thought, and he quickened his pace to his friend the blacksmith's place. He was right. He recognized several horses from the morning at the back of the smithy's shop.

"Ho there, Gustavus," said Arn. "How are you this eve?"

"I'm fine, lad. Got a lot of work for you. They've been making a good many piles back there."

Arn was glad to do his work. His friend had always paid him well, with coin and with a few cherished items he now proudly owned, including the spork. Though the smith often paid him in items he had made, they were always worth far more than he would have otherwise been paid. "Aye, sir, I'll get right on that. Can I ask you something?"

"Aye, lad," said the smith as he pounded out a horseshoe he was making. "What is that?"

"Do you know anything about all these strangers?"

"Hmm, no, I can't say as I know a lot about them, but one of them is definitely the herald of the high king."

"Really?" Arn was amazed. "Why would the herald of the high king be in Clayhaven? We're not on the way to many places he would be heading, are we?"

"I don't know. I think he's come to talk to the townspeople."

"Really?" said Arn again. "Well, that's unusual. Do you think the king is going to levy a new tax?"

"Couldn't say, lad. That would really be a bad bit of luck. It is getting to be tax season though. You never know. Probably right."

Gustavus spat as he said, "Just get those stalls mucked out and we'll talk in a bit. I've got work to do here." Something about the look of disgust on his face lit by his brazier bore a striking resemblance to some of the dwarves Arn had seen traveling through town on occasion.

"Aye, sir, aye."

"I might have a special treat for you too."

"Really?" Arn was always excited with the smithy's treats. It would be unique and beautiful. His craftsmanship was sought out through much of the land. Not just the people of Clayhaven, but those in the nearby towns and villages thought much of it. He went to his task.

These horses have been eating well. As quickly as he could, he lifted the straw and manure into the cart that the smith kept there for that purpose, then replaced it with clean straw.

As he got to the last of the three stalls, he recognized the sinister black horse he had seen earlier. *He's got to be the horse of that smelly fellow. Let's just get it over with quickly. Steady yourself Arn, you can do it. It's just poop.* He went over to the stall and said, in his calmest and friendliest voice, "Now fellow, I'm just going to muck out your stall a little bit. I'm not going to hurt you or anything. Be calm. Be calm. Think of a nice mare, or a beautiful meadow or something pleasant." The horse turned, and seemed to glare at him. It was even a sinister glare, if a horse could do such a thing. "You've got to be the horse of Old Smelly, there. I'm sure of that," he said.

As he mucked around the horse, the horse did not bother him, but he did notice a strange scent around the beast. A scent he recognized from the morning, and had hoped he would never smell again. *Yeah, you're definitely his horse.* Out of sheer habit, Arn patted the massive beast on his flank. He realized his big mistake as the horse reared up and screeched an unpleasant sort of noise. Sort of a whinny and sort of a growl. Arn stepped back to get out of the way. *Can't be a very good riding creature with that temperament!* Arn finished mucking around as best he could and decided he was done.

He went around to the front of the shop, where Gustavus was still working on a growing pile of horseshoes. "Could you tell me, whose horse is that ugly black beast?"

"He's a nasty one, isn't he?"

"Aye, very nasty. Snorts, and rears up, and has like a mean look on his face, if that's possible."

"It's possible, lad. Horse ain't no good. If I know horse flesh at all, I'd say he's bad seed."

Arn laughed. "I'd agree with you there." Arn sat and, impatient as a child, said, "What do you have for me?"

Gustavus chuckled, "I've got something unique for you. Something I've been wanting to give you for a while, but I missed your birthday. Sorry about that."

Arn shrugged. "I'm not even sure it's the day I was born anyways."

"Aye. But I finished it and I wanted to give it to you. Here, take this." He wiped his grimy hands on his grimy apron, reached over and pulled out a piece of oil cloth and handed it to Arn. Arn opened it and could not believe what he saw. It was a beautifully crafted dagger.

"I've never, ever seen a dagger so beautiful! Is it really for me? Is this right? Do I need to pay you something for it? I do have some money saved up."

"I know about your money, lad, and I know you've been saving what you don't give to the abbey, but no. I made that for you. It's a gift. That's the way it is," he said with a gruff tone. Gustavus was not much for emotional shows. He went back to his work, pounding out horseshoes. "I wouldn't wear that around while you're mucking out stalls though, Arn. It's a fine blade."

Arn was still holding the dagger in the cloth, as if he were afraid to touch it. Gustavus laughed. "You can take it out, boy. Take it out and look at it. I wouldn't be ashamed or offended if you did. But I might be a bit offended if you didn't."

Arn smiled a big smile and proceeded to pick the dagger up from its cloth. The glitter of the forge and lamp above gleamed off the steel. It was not bronze, and not a child's toy, but a real man's dagger. Arn examined the blade. He wiped the corners of his eyes roughly with the back of his hand. Nobody had ever given him anything like this. It would sure be nice to have. He had always promised himself he would one day have such a blade. Although daggers were often used for eating, he would never do that.

This blade was so beautiful. From helping his friend Gustavus for many years, he knew the quality when he saw it. The balance was perfect, but he would expect nothing less from his friend. The cross guard was a beautifully wrought bronze with an intricate little edging that looked like a vine. The handle was wrapped with fine bright silver wire and black leather all the way to the pommel. The pommel was the most unique and beautiful to Arn. It was the symbol that Arn had confided to Gustavus he would use as his personal symbol should he become a knight one day. An acorn. Not only was this immensely pleasing to Arn, but also satisfying proof of an enduring friendship, and the fact that Gustavus had actually listened all those hours to Arn's talking.

Arn looked at his friend, who continued to work on horseshoes. He could tell that Gustavus had watched him during his tearful inspection of the beautiful blade, but now was focused on work.

Arn said, "I won't ever forget this. This is a grand gift! I'll muck your stalls for the rest of my life!"

Gustavus chuckled. "That won't be necessary. You've done a lot of things for me, and I appreciate it. It's a gift. A birthday gift. You don't work for a gift."

Arn had an impulse to hug the dwarven man, but knew that Gustavus was not happy with such shows of emotion. He offered his own grimy hand to the larger, blackened smith's hand. Gustavus eyed him for a moment, stopped his work, and wiped his hand on the apron. Then he gripped Arn's hand in a steel-like vise, and shook it three times, saying, "Aye, lad, that's a gift for you."

Arn fancied that his voice sounded gravelly, almost emotional. Then he smacked Arn on the left shoulder and said, "Lad, you may never get out of this village here, and you may always muck stalls, but to me you are not just a stall mucker."

Arn could not help the tears that fell as he said, "This is a wonderful gift, and I thank you very, very much. I won't ever forget it, and I won't ever forget you. If I should ever rise out of here, I would not forget you. One day I will come back and build you the best smithy ever," he added with a smile.

The barrel chested man laughed a great laugh. "That's not necessary lad. I built this place with my own hands, and I like it just the way it is. She's like a wife to me, curvy and plump and the smoke of the forge is like long, flowing black hair. That's the way I like her. You could never build me a smithy better than this. But," he added with a smile, "If you ever do become a noble or something, I will come up with a request or two for you!"

Gustavus picked up his tools and continued, "Now, I still have work to do. Pick up your hapenny over there."

"Oh, no! I couldn't!"

"I said, that's a gift. The blade is a gift. The hapenny, that's your pay. Just keep the blade sharp, keep her clean, and don't ever let me see you abusing the blade."

"No, sir, I already decided, I'm not even going to eat with this blade."

"You can eat with it if you need to. Just keep it clean, keep it sharp, and always remember your friend the smith who made it." He turned back to his forge. "Even when you're a high king and all."

"I'll give this hapenny to the abbey for you."

"It's your money, boy. I've had enough of tongue-wagging. That foul beast is fixing to throw a shoe."

Arn had no desire to say it, but offered, "Can I help you?"

"No, lad, I've got my helper, Sam, coming later, and we'll get him shoed. Fearsome beast or not, it's got to be done. Fair evening to you, lad. Tell the brothers I sent greetings to them."

"I will!" Arn ran up the street, excited to return to the abbey and show the brothers his new gift. *I'll have to show this to Greymist in the morning.* Greymist seemed to take an interest in whatever Arn showed him and discussed with him. Arn considered, perhaps during Yuletide, dressing in his finest tunic and wearing his blade right out front, walking through town for all to see. Nobody would claim he stole it. They could talk to Gustavus.

His route through town would take him past the inn, and he considered that since it had gotten dark, and the stranger seemed suited to the dark, he should beware. He ran as fast as he could past the inn, and did not see anything. As he slowed down, he felt a little foolish, as he did when he was younger and ran from the boogeyman, but after all caution was the same as good sense, Brother Kile always said.

When he returned to the abbey, Brother Kile was just entering for supper by the far door, and Brothers Clement and Francis were already there at the table. Arn smelled the great kitchen smells, smiled, and realized this had been a great day. *Aside from old Smelly Spooky, this was even better than my birthday. I had real beef stew, and I got this wonderful gift. And I get to have beef stew again!*

He eagerly stood by his chair as Brother Kile found his way to his chair, and requested permission to sit. Brother Kile nodded. "Brothers, I received a present from Gustavus today. Remember how you asked me if he had given me anything?"

"Aye," said Brother Kile. "I was a bit surprised that he had forgotten your celebration. He seems quite fond of you, and all."

"Well, he didn't." Arn brought out the oil cloth and placed it on the table. "May I show you?"

"Aye, show us." Kile called Brother Clement who had gone to the kitchen. "Wait until Brother Clement gets back."

Arn smiled. As soon as Clement returned with a large steaming bowl, he opened the oil cloth, eager to show off his new possession. The monks were astonished, not having expected to see such a beautiful piece.

"Aye, it's mine."

"That's indeed a beautiful blade," said Brother Francis.

"You are blessed indeed," said Brother Kile.

"There is a fine beef meal this eve as well," added Brother Clement.

"It's been a wonderful day," said Arn. "Except for . . ."

"Except for what, lad?" asked Brother Kile.

"Well, when I was cleaning the privy pots, I ran into this strange fellow. He gave me the creeps."

"He did?" Brother Kile looked at Arn intently and leaned towards him a bit. "Tell me about him."

"Well, he was dressed all in black, and he smelled like rue, and sage, and definitely mint."

"Really?" The brothers looked at each other, thoughtful for a moment. "What bothered you so much about him, other than he smelled?"

"He was pale, and his voice was hissy and unpleasant, and his eyes, I couldn't see them. But I could feel them staring at me. Intently."

"He sounds like one to stay away from," said Brother Kile. "I think I'd try to stay clear of him in the morn, if you can."

"Aye, his chamber pot was unpleasant to say the least. I'm not looking forward to that again!"

The brothers exchanged glances. Brother Kile leaned over, patted him on the back and said, "It's a living, lad, but be careful."

CHAPTER TWO

AUTUMN'S LONELY ROAD

The next day Arn woke to a dim, grey light, with a definite chill in the air. The coals in his small fireplace that had comforted him the night before had burned out. As Arn rubbed the sleep from his eyes, he had to feel beneath his pillow to see that the beautiful blade had not been a dream. It was still there. He smiled to himself and quickly went over and placed the blade in his hiding niche. He took out a small leather bag and had a brief visit with his few lead soldiers. Then he carefully returned them to their hiding place.

He donned his clothes, for he knew it would be a long day. As he unbolted his door and went out of the small room, he saw the sky was heavily laden, brooding, and dark. A thick, soupy mist was about in many places, and it didn't look like it would burn off today. It looked like it was going to be a chilly, dreary day.

He hated to muck out stalls in the rain. It was always most unpleasant. As he looked across the courtyard he saw his friend Greymist come out of the fog wagging his big, hairy tail. Greymist already had a thick winter coat and was himself dressed for whatever the winter might hold.

Arn quickly broke his fast and to his delight it was precious leftovers from last eve's meal. Brother Francis and Father Kile were not present at breakfast and Brother Clement seemed strangely quiet.

As Arn gave some precious scraps to Greymist, the big dog seemed to look at him with a bit of worry in his face, like perhaps he didn't like the fog either, or maybe he was just getting older and it was sinking into his bones. He patted the dog on the head and told him all would be well, and to curl up in one of the empty stalls to stay dry if it should rain.

Arn retrieved his pitchfork and went off to his daily tasks. As he approached the inn, he heard the town's bell, which was mounted up on a large post not too far from the inn. There were three gongs, a pause, and three more gongs. Arn recognized this was the signal that the men of the village had something to be discussed with the elders or perhaps the lord of the town. The time was near when the local nobles and landlords collected their taxes and fees. Perhaps they would start collecting these early.

Many men and some ladies of the town were going to the inn to hear whatever announcement was to be made. Arn, being a young man now of fifteen summers, also went to hear the announcement. He felt a queasiness in the pit of his stomach that he had only felt when he had been scared of the graveyard outside of town when he was a lad.

Arn quickly went to the large door of the inn to see that the fire had been stoked up in the center hearth and that many of the young men and elders, and some of the lady folk, had gathered around. To his surprise he saw that the one who seemed to be the center of attention was a herald of the high King of Southaven himself. Although this was unusual, Arn thought he would probably be announcing a new tax. He took a place standing near the doorway, because there was no place to sit, and watched quietly.

The men of the tavern had never been nice to Arn. Cantree had always been cordial, at least, but he had never done much about the taunting. Sometimes they would throw half-eaten potatoes and such at him, saying he stank, and shouldn't come into the inn stinking so badly. He remembered those events, and looked around and saw many of the faces that taunted him in the past. He tried to make himself as inconspicuous as possible by shrinking against a support beam. Feeling the beam and wall to his back was somehow comforting.

The herald cleared his throat, with a definite intent to get the crowd's attention. "Hear ye this. Hear ye," he said in a clear, distinctive voice.

"From his lordship the high King of Southaven, ye of the town of Clayhaven and the Lord Noble Moresfield of this region, are hereby levied to make available to his royal highness, as many combat-worthy men as possible. All who are of age from fifteen to sixty-two are hereby ordered by his royal highness to gather upon ye what ye need for travel and for warfare, whatever equipage thereof that ye have. His highness will see to it that all who serve him nobly and well will be compensated for their time spent in his majesty's army."

This announcement immediately caused quite a stir among the townspeople. Arn realized with a cold shiver that fifteen was his age, and levied he had just been.

Thought Arn, *What am I to do? This is most unexpected.*

He was quite shocked by the announcement, as were many of the townspeople. Perhaps some had had an inkling of it before Arn did. Arn, not being one of the tavern yokels, did not realize that a levy in all the towns had been raised because the armies of the north had attacked again. And it was not just a raiding attack this time, but a large attack.

Arn looked to old man Hayes, who had been somewhat friendly towards him. He was a farmer who had a bit more land to work than most of the peasants. Arn ventured to ask, "Sir, could you tell me what is going on?"

"Yeah boy, ya been put into the Army," was Hayes' reply.

"What . . ." Arn stuttered. Hayes said, "The borders have been hit hard by the Notherners, not just a probin' attack this time, or a raid, it's real. Seems like we're at war again."

War? Thought Arn. Real war? All the visions he had had when he was younger about being a knight flashed before his eyes. Then fear hit Arn in the pit of his stomach. Visions of war were one thing, but actually heading towards it was another.

Arn asked, "Do you think everyone will have to go?"

The man raised his bushy grey eyebrows, and said, "Aye, lad, if ya can hold a weapon y'are going. Ya heard the man, from fifteen to sixty-two. Often they don't worry much about checkin' yer age."

"All right, then, what do I do?" Arn asked.

Hayes said, "As that thar fancy speaker said, grob ye equipage. Get ye at least two pair of shoe if ya be havin' 'em for ya will be doin' much walkin'. Grob ye a good fightin' stick, scythe or pitchfork if ya got it. Ya will be reportin' back here to the front of the inn."

As there seemed to be no more announcements forthcoming from the herald at this time, the man stood up, as did others, to leave the tavern.

Some women who were with their husbands began to weep. This was indeed a bitter blow to the town of Clayhaven. It had had its share of bad luck in the past wars, being so close to the border with the Nothlund, and now it was surely to face bad times again. The women would be left to do most of the work, along with the elder men who were too old to fight, and the few boys who would be left behind. The hardships were going to be many indeed.

As Arn removed himself from his corner post, he spoke to Hayes again, "Sir?"

"Aye, what is it, boy?"

"This is fall, isn't that a bit unusual, for full warfare, I mean, sir?" asked Arn.

The man raised a bushy eyebrow, surprised Arn would know about such things. He said, "Aye, lad, it is. Fall campaigns be rare to none. Attackin' with a full army in fall just don't make no sense. Ye attack in spring, when ye have time to campaign all summer and into fall, not in the fall." The man scratched his head as he went out with his own worries in his face.

Arn went and quickly performed the tasks that he had. There were many horses, and he did the job that he had sworn to do around town as quickly as possible, explaining that he must be off.

The mustering was to be at noon in the center of the village. Arn wanted to be there without being late. He went to Lady Hannah last of all. She had quite a sad look upon her face when she saw him.

"Mistress, I'm sorry I can't stay for any vittles, or any sup, this day."

She said, "I know, you have been called into service."

She hugged Arn before he could say anything else, with tears in her eyes, and said, "You be careful, lad, be very careful. I have something for you and I want you to take it."

He looked on with a smile, but not a normal smile of a boy who was about to get a gift from a generous benefactor. A more serious smile of a troubled boy who was going away for who knew how long. She went into her house, and came back out, carrying hapennies for him, which she placed in his palm.

She said, "You might need to buy things from the commissary. But I want you to have this as well." She gave him a small silver coin.

"Oh, I can't take that," Arn said.

The lady's watery blue eyes were kind. "Hush now, boy. I give you what I give you."

"Thank you, mistress. I will return it," said Arn.

"No, it is a gift."

She also had a bundle folded up under her other arm that she pulled out, and said, "I think this might fit you. By the look of the weather, you might need it soon."

Arn looked in wonder at the lustrous, although moth-eaten and patched, grey woolen cloak. "That is indeed beautiful. Are you sure you want me to have it?"

"Aye, it was my husband's. I have taken the end off a bit, and I think it will fit you well. It's just a cloak, not a full mantle, but I hope it serves you well. I am so very, very sorry, Arn. So sorry you have to go to war." She began to weep openly, and Arn felt a sinking feeling he had not felt since Brother Arvon had died.

He hugged her and said, "Don't worry, I'll be all right. I'll be back to look after the stables, and take care of you." Even at his young age, Arn knew that her tears were not just for him, but also for her own loss.

She hugged him and kissed him on the forehead, and said with a smile, "Be well, lad. If I had a daughter, I'd marry her to you."

Arn was surprised by that. His station was by no means acceptable to marry the daughter of even the smallest landowner.

Arn couldn't say anything. He was too choked up.

"I know you will see us again, lad," she said, still smiling, trying to wipe her tears and be brave. "You be careful, and you mind your head."

"I will," said Arn sadly.

"And if you can stay out of battle, lad, you do it."

"I will," Arn said, and then he corrected himself. "I cannot promise that, mistress."

She looked a bit surprised. She said, "You are only a lad of fifteen summers."

"Aye, and I have been called by my high king, and as such I must do what a soldier must do," he said, stumbling over the words. They sounded absurd.

The lady nodded but could not say anything. She just put her hand upon her forehead and looked at Arn. She said, "God be with you, Arn of Clayhaven," and retreated into her home.

Arn was relieved that it still had not begun to rain. He thought he would put the fine cloak in his tube roll until he would really need it. It was too pretty to wear, and like his dagger, he was afraid it might be stolen from him at night while he was asleep. To lose it, what an awful thought.

He found that Father Kile was at the abbey. "Arn, is it true? Have you been called up for service as well?"

"Aye, I have," he said in a low voice.

The monk hugged him, and realized that there was nothing he could do. "I suppose I and Francis and Clement will be joining you in a couple of days, lad. We'll catch up with you, don't you worry. You just travel on with the soldiers for a little while and then we'll join you."

Arn said, "You mean, they called you up?" The monk laughed, "Of course they have. Monks we are, but men we are as well. We don't have much say in things such as this, and they have apparently broadened the levy to include older men as well as the clergy. But did you think we'd let you go by yourself anyway?"

Arn smiled a broad smile. "I'm very grateful that you are going, but I'm also sad. This is very much a surprise."

The monk looked grim and nodded. "Aye, it is. We have heard rumors but apparently they are not rumors at all. The northern borders have been broken and there's a war at hand. We will be coming with carts laden with bandages, ointments and poultices and such, in just a couple of days.

"Arn, I hate to say it, lad, but you'd best get your stuff; it's getting close to noon and you don't want to be late. They don't smile on that. Wouldn't do to be late."

Arn looked sadly around. He wouldn't see his little abbey for a time, maybe never again. The thought sunk to the pit of his stomach like a ball of lead.

I hate this, thought Arn. *Where is Greymist? Let me say goodbye to Greymist.*

He ran behind the sheds near the gardens, looking for Greymist, but alas, he was not there. It was not quite noon, and the dog usually came just about noon.

He went back to the eating hall where Brother Clement handed him a bag of rations. "There is some dried fish in there, and some meat dried, some potatoes down in there, and some way bread that I had stored away. That's enough to last you for at least five days, lad." Brother Clement also gave him a water skin full of clean water.

"Try not to eat too much while you're marching. Be careful with your water. And mind your shoes. You never know how far you might march in a day, so take care of your feet."

"Thank you for your advice and kindness, Brother." Arn could not help but hug Brother Clement and the brother hugged him back. Tears began to blur both their eyes. "Please say goodbye to Brother Francis."

"This is a sad event," said Clement as he pushed Arn away, "but the land's in danger and we must all do our duty."

"Aye," said Arn, "I will." And with that Arn shook hands and said, "I'll see you soon."

"You will, lad," he said reassuringly.

Arn went back to his simple quarters and took his two-tined pitchfork, realizing that was the only implement of war he might have, gathered up a few of his things and packed them in his haversack. Taking the brother's advice, he included an old, worn pair of leather sandals.

As he looked around the small room, he realized he might not ever see it again, and that was too much to think about. He quickly moved the stool over and retrieved his dagger from its hiding niche. He wondered whether he should put it on his belt as a man going to war would do, or if he should hide it, to keep it from thieves while he slept. Deciding on the latter, he tucked the knife into his belt and folded his long shirt over it.

He held his lead soldiers in his hand and looked at them. As hard as it was, he knew he would have to leave them here. He tucked them back into hiding, hoping he would be able to return and get them later, when this thing was over.

Going out, he looked again for Greymist, and with relief saw the big, friendly dog had come for his morning meal. Arn took a few pieces of the meat out of the haversack to give to his friend.

"I won't be able to give you any food for a while, boy. I've got to go off to war." The dog looked at him with sad, quizzical eyes but Arn could barely look at his friend.

It was all too much. After the wonderful day he had had yesterday, today was dreadful, dark and gloomy, and he felt sad and lonesome at that moment.

He patted his friend and said, "I'll be back. You'll see me soon, Greymist." He hugged his furry friend and kissed him several times on the head. The dog, which had very rarely ever licked his face, licked him several times before Arn released him. Standing up, Arn looked down at the big, wolf-like dog. A strange, sad look had come over Greymist's long face. Arn looked into his keen, intelligent eyes, and he saw wisdom in their depths. The tears were thick in Arn's eyes as he waved goodbye to Brother Clement and the only good home he had ever known.

"Goodbye, Brother Clement!" he yelled.

"I'll see you soon," called Brother Clement. "Don't worry about your dog. I'll tell the folks who will be looking after the abbey to feed him some scraps."

Knowing his friend would be looked after, Arn cheered up, and waved a sad farewell to his friends. It was close to noon and Arn reported to muster, as did the other men of town.

In this first muster of common soldiers, there were eighteen in all, some being about fifteen summers and the oldest being in his sixties. Most were equipped with farm implements such as billhooks, scythes, staffs, flails and clubs. Arn scratched his head and wondered where to place himself as they all started to form a rough line.

A man bearing the arms of the king came, carrying a beautifully wrought halberd and clad in the colors of the king, a beautiful depot grey and dark purple. He wore a splendid suit of chain mail and upon his belt, hanging from his sword ring, rode a fine long sword. In his left hand he carried a shiny acorn style helmet with a large, flaring nose guard. The man started to bark orders.

"Alright ye sod bustin' dogs, this is the way it's gonna be. Form a line here. I want to see the smallest man to the tallest man, understand?"

Arn wasn't the smallest, and took his place as best he could as everyone moved around in almost a comical dance to find their places. The tall sergeant shook his head in disgust. "You'll make a pretty sight on the battle field dead. I've got a lot of work to do with ye." He spat some of the brown leaf he chewed on the ground with contempt.

The women in town came out to say farewell to the men, and many of them were crying. He did not see the Lady as he had hoped. But he realized it was probably too difficult for her to see them go, knowing that on a day not unlike this her husband had gone off to die, some summers ago.

As the line formed up, the arms man yelled something about forming two ranks of a march column, which made no sense to anyone. The group fumbled around as the sergeant placed one tall man in front and another tall man beside him, yelling, "You over here, form a line on this man, and you over there, form a line on this man. Is that simple enough for you stupid sodbusters?"

He shook his head in anger and disgust. The sergeant glared at the two ragged lines of men, muttering, "Why am I with these fools of peasant stock?"

Just as he had formed his lines a very regal looking figure appeared on a great stallion. Instantly Arn recognized the local lord of the realm, the noble caretaker of Clayhaven. Lord Moresfield looked dignified and clean as he always did. The tall horse he rode had not a lick of dirt on it from the day, nor did his fine clothes, including his great cape. He had an aide behind him on a small pony. Behind his squire followed two pack animals, one with the noble's armor slung on it.

The arms man looked up to his lordship on the horse and asked, "My lord, would you like to review the men?"

Moresfield laughed, raising a handkerchief to his mouth as if he smelled something distasteful. "Certainly not. The real fighters of my domain have gone on ahead. And I hasten to join them. Woe to think I must arrive to our high king with this rotted bunch.

"But I need to go speak to the town elder now. Would you try to level this rabble into a line," he said with his head held up in arrogance.

"Aye," said the arms man, with an almost hurt sounding voice. "I will, your lordship."

Moresfield sneered, "Good, and do keep the men behind me. No one may walk in front of me. Do you understand?"

"Aye, my lord."

As Moresfield trotted off down the road, not turning back for a second glance, his retainer and second followed close behind.

Arn's column moved forward at a quick pace, and the arms man yelled to keep up. As they left the town of Clayhaven, Arn looked back over his shoulder, realizing he might never see his little town again. The terrible lead ball that had been in his stomach grew to twice the size, as tears welled up and fell from his eyes.

One of the men looked over at him and said, "What's the matter little boy, you crying?" The column of men joined him in laughing with glee. Arn shook his head trying to cast his tears away, looking aside so that the bully would not see him.

The man was a local brute who often insulted Arn. He had even struck Arn once. After that, Father Kile and Gustavus had each paid him a visit separately, and he never again had come near Arn. Arn had noted the next day that the bully's hand was injured. He had found out later that his arm and his hand had been broken. Arn had always suspected that either the monk or the smith had been responsible.

As they raggedly marched down the road, Arn was the butt of many jokes. They wanted something to take their minds off of leaving their wives and girlfriends and children at the edge of town.

Grandsires and younger boys were there to wave goodbye as well. Some were weeping openly.

In the crowd, Arn recognized a pretty blonde lady of fifteen summers, Jenny, to whom he had once given a beautiful wild rose, in an attempt to earn her acquaintance. She had cast the rose down in the dust at his feet, laughing at him.

Although Arn had bathed and worn his clean clothes, she said the beautiful fragrance of the rose was not enough to cover his stench. Arn still had the beautiful rose, pressed in a book at the abbey. It reminded him not to try some things.

Even now she averted her eyes from him as he marched past.

As the column wound its way out of town, Arn had a realization that he was a soldier, and he was on his way to war. Somehow this buzzed in his head, pushing out all other thoughts. The lead ball expanded once again in his gut.

Whatever might befall him was going to befall him no matter what, and it might end his life. He had little to no say in it.

As Arn moved out of Clayhaven with the column of newly recruited soldiers, the lord kept at a steady pace and everyone tried their best to keep up. It wasn't that difficult for Arn at first, but horses tire a lot later than men, and the lord seemed not to worry if the men needed a rest.

As the day wore on, a cold drizzly rain fell on the column. A few soldiers had been laughing and joking, but one by one, they became silent. There was no house to go into, no barn to shelter them from the weather. There was no bier, no shed, they were simply marching and they were no longer men of free will. They were now under the direct command of their lord and noble.

Arn still felt that sickening heavy feeling he had felt earlier in the day. As the weariness began to take his limbs, he realized that the path he was on was indeed a path to war. This was not what he had ever imagined when he dreamed of being a knight.

This nobleman in the lead had no great entourage, no fluttering banners or musicians playing. There were no beautiful maidens blowing kisses and giving him ornaments and tokens of their love and affection.

For Arn, war was not like that, at least not so far. It had been quick. He had awoken in the morning to do his normal tasks for the day, and was now leaving in the evening, marching off to war.

Arn's heart was heavy. He would never have dreamed he would be marching off in the company of men he did not like, ill equipped and miserable in the chilly evening rain.

As Arn marched in the column, if you could call it that, there were no paces, no regular intervals. Arn had seen soldiers marching before, through Clayhaven. They had marched to the beat of a drummer. What Arn heard now was the whistling north wind, the pat of rain upon his head and the splashing of hooves and feet through puddles of mud, along with occasional curses of men stumbling and trying to keep up.

He saw Lord Moresfield in the lead, his second upon a fine pony, the obviously well-conditioned sergeant arms man keeping up behind them, and the ragged column coming behind.

The sergeant would often step off to the side of the road, let the column pass and yell, and smash someone in the back or buttocks with the flat of his halberd and tell them to move on, you're going too slow. Move up. That happened to Arn once. He didn't care for it, nor this man.

The sergeant was a gruff, red-faced man of about 40-some summers. His limbs were definitely seasoned from campaigning with many bulging muscles in his scarred lower legs and upper arms. It looked as if he had probably been through many battles. Arn thought about asking him about it when they stopped to make camp, but he would just get angry. It seemed like he was angry most of the time.

The noble was enjoying a light banter with his comrades and chuckling occasionally. Arn had caught bits of the conversation between him and the sergeant and realized that the rest of his noblemen, his knights, had gone on ahead to meet the king, but he had been delayed by some errand in the kingdom. He was now annoyed by having this peasant rabble to escort him to the battle.

But be that as it may, he would have an escort. He would not be on the road without an escort. He was confident no highwaymen or brigands would dare attack so large a column. As they marched on, Arn thought about what it must be like to have the duties of a lord, and how a noble would always be at the sway of someone higher than him. Even the king must surely have responsibilities that make him obliged to do things he would not normally do, such as this war.

Obviously the Dark One, who had taken many lands in the past centuries, had left Southaven alone due to the large quantity and quality of the armies of Southaven. Perhaps now was the time he would turn his evil gaze upon this fair land.

CHAPTER THREE

A FLAME WITHIN

Arn wondered if he would be able to prove himself in battle when the time came. Perhaps he would see one of the Dark One's minions, one of the cold, jutted-jaw, hunched, grey creatures that he favored so much, known as goor. Arn did not care to at this moment for as the darkness grew, the thought of meeting one brought a greater chill to his bones.

He understood those gaunt creatures, seeming short in stature, were quite tall when they stood straight up. They had great strength and had earned some prowess in fighting, from the taskmaster's whip. Arn looked at his splintered, wooden, manure-encrusted pitchfork, and thought, *that will do against one of the nasty minions of the Dark One?* He almost chuckled to himself. He realized that if a fight came indeed, he might get lucky, but probably not.

The fork had grown quite heavy the longer he carried it, and he hefted it up in his right arm and switched it again to his left arm.

The march went on, and on and on. Evening became night, and the column still proceeded on. The sky opened up again with rain, and only the occasional jagged bolt of lightning. Arn stumbled many times, as did many of the column. He thought they might march on through the night and never stop. His arms and legs felt wearier than they ever had.

He wished he were back home in Clayhaven, back in his little room, back talking to his friends the monks, or Greymist, whom he already missed very much. Or the Lady. He wondered what she might be at right now. Perhaps praying, thinking about him. As were the monks. Of course the monks would be joining him soon, with their medical supplies and bandages loaded in carts.

He wondered if Gustavus would be coming as well. In a war you would need a lot of smiths, as well as baggage trains and such. Then he thought, *where is this lord's baggage, other than the one mule? He must surely have a baggage cart somewhere.* Probably it had gone ahead with his other soldiers.

As the night wore on, and they had been marching for at least an hour in the dark, the noble's horse seemed to be stumbling a bit as well. Arn could just barely see it occasionally, with the flashes of light. Many of the peasants were already mumbling about how they could not possibly go on, that this was too much to expect from them on the first day's march.

But Arn noticed one old man going on at a good pace, who did not seem to be tiring as much as the others. He recognized him as a man who had protected and spoken up for him a few times in the inn back home. He had not been a friend as such, but he had always been polite to Arn. He had occasionally, before the light completely faded, looked at Arn and given a reassuring nod that all was going to be ok. Arn realized he was probably the only one that would be polite at all to him on this journey.

He thought he would try to ask him some questions when they stopped for camp if possible. Another half of an hour passed. Finally the lord had had enough stumbling through the mud, and ordered the sergeant to get the men to the side of the road.

In the flashes of lightning, there appeared a clearing off to the side. Arn went with the rest of the men as the noble trotted into the field. He dismounted and yelled at the sergeant, "Have the men get that tent off of that beast, and put it here.

"Yes, my lord," said the sergeant, "Anything else?"

"That'll do. As soon as you can get that up, I'll have other tasks."

"Alright you grungy, smelly, peasant lot, move here! Get those packs off that pony and get them set up now!"

As the sergeant yelled instructions, the peasants worked diligently to put up this rather large pavilion-style tent in the dark with just a few lanterns. Sergeant seemed to know what he was doing, although the yelling of instructions in the dark to men who had never erected such a pavilion was frustrating all around. It was very difficult.

Arn could see that it had both the kingdom's colors as well as the noble's personal colors. It was quite a pretty thing, from what he could see. More like what he thought going to war should be.

Pretty colors and unique pavilion tents, banners waving. The nobleman's banners had been cased when the rain started.

Arn and the others continued to do various tasks for the noble, including bringing out food items that he had had his cooks prepare for the march. They smelled so good to Arn, who had not eaten since earlier that day. He realized there was going to be no tent for the men. The crude wool blanket he had on his back was what he would use. His food would be the provisions in his haversack.

Arn and the other men managed to get the lord situated for his evening's rest. As Arn sat by the dreary small fire that the men had started, he was still cold and wet. Lord Moresfield had a small camp stove of sorts, made of iron inside. He seemed quite toasty and warm.

The sergeant even ordered two of the peasants to guard the entry to the tent. Arn chuckled at this. One was armed with a scythe, for cutting wheat, and the other with a digging spade. Surely no goor would have much difficulty dispatching them with a wicked scimitar.

The older men sent him into the woods to try to gather some dry wood underneath the leaves, and Arn realized with disgust that he was going to be the fetcher boy, even here. Everyone would be asking him to bring things, or do something.

As Arn and his companions all tried to huddle close to the fire he ended up at the very back, quite far from the fire's warmth and light. He finally settled in for what sleep he could get, and decided to ask the old peasant who had been polite to him what he knew of war. His name was Hayes, and he was sitting, smoking a clay pipe with a reed stem. The bowl of the pipe was upside down, to avoid being extinguished by the rain.

"Sir?"

"Yeah lad."

"It seems that you know war."

"Aye, I do."

"Have you been to war many times?"

"Oh, aye. I have. I've been to war probably eight times."

"Goodness!" blurted out Arn, "That's quite impressive, and you lived all eight times."

Arn could just barely see him chuckle in the flickering firelight, a bemused look upon his old brow. Arn realized what a stupid comment that was.

"Aye, I would say with a great deal of difficulty several of those times. But I did live. War is not a pretty thing, lad," spoke the old man quietly. "It's not what you might imagine. As you can already see, it's dreary, it's lonely, it's hard labor, it's a lot of walking, and iff'n your noble ain't too lucky, it's a lot of running for your skin. And it's terrible food," he said with a phlegmy spit, as he pulled out some kind of cornmeal cakes his wife had made.

He said, "This ain't terrible food though. This is what the missus made for me before I left. It's delicious. I've got about three days here, then it's time for the terrible food."

"You mean, way bread?"

"Aye, way bread if you're lucky." He chuckled to himself. "Lad, you're going to be a soldier, but more than likely you won't have to fight, you'll just fetch things."

"Well, I guess it's similar to what I do back in the village."

"But you always had a nice, warm stall to get into when it was raining, instead of being out here in God's own with the rain pouring down on you in buckets."

"Aye," said Arn. "Well, do you think we will find the enemy along the road, as Moresfield talked about earlier?"

"Well, no. You never know though, boy. Things happen. I doubt we'll see any of the enemy until we get to the field. But I'm not quite sure where that is. When we get there his lordship will separate from us, and we'll be off to probably guard the baggage or something. I've done that quite a few times. That ain't so bad. You just kinda stand around and if any of the enemy gets near you, try to fight 'em. A couple times I went to war and didn't fight at all."

"Oh, that's good," said Arn, sounding relieved.

"But that's only because I was on the winning side, lad. Ye know, soon as the army falls apart, baggage is the first thing the marauding demons from the north will go after."

"You mean, we might actually lose?" Arn said, gulping out the words.

"Yeah, we might actually lose, lad. There's no guarantees in war. Somebody makes a mistake, somebody says the wrong thing, somebody charges too soon, somebody don't have the archers where they're needed. Anything can happen. If God's not with ye that day, that could be the end of ye."

"End of ye?"

"Aye, the end of ye. It's very easy to happen. Best thing to do, lad, if it gets bad, and ye can't outrun 'em, is throw the blood of a wounded man on top of ye and try yer best to look like yer dead. If they take anything off your body, let 'em do it. Don't breathe. Don't even think about it. Just sit there like yer in yer own tomb. 'Cause ye will be if they think yer alive. I tried that trick once and it worked. I highly recommend it," he said, chuckling a bit.

Arn watched Hayes as he curled up under his old wool blanket and noticed some sort of hard blanket over top. "What is that, sir?"

"It's my blanket treated with tar to keep the rain off. Works pretty good. Also I have cleverly cut it to be a poncho if needed."

"Poncho?" That's great, thought Arn. "Where could I get one of those? Will they issue me one of those? Or maybe a sword?"

The old man laughed. "Lad, ye got what ye got on yer back. Ye got what ye got in yer hands. Ye got what ye got on yer feet. Yer a peasant, lad, and ye'll be lucky if they feed ye, to keep ye alive."

This made Arn feel quite bad. He had hoped to allay some of his anxiety by talking to Hayes. He lay still, thinking. The old man looked at Arn for a while, not saying a word. He seemed wondering about something, lost in his thoughts.

Suddenly he slapped Arn on the leg and said, "Ye best get some sleep, boy. Yer going to need yer sleep."

"Yes, sir." Arn curled up under his now soaking wet, coarse wool blanket, shivering from the cold. Slowly his eyes closed. He had a dream of meeting a goor in combat and losing, trying to hide and pretend he was dead, but the goor pulling him up, laughing, saying with a hiss, "I know that trick, and you'll not be getting away with it!"

Arn awoke with a start some time before dawn, and was reluctant to stir because he felt a bit warmer. Looking down, he saw that the old man had covered him with the poncho while he had been asleep. He looked over at Hayes, snoring and covered up with his blankets. Arn smiled and realized he had indeed found a friend here. No one else would have done that.

Arn closed his eyes, hoping he could get just a little bit more sleep, but it seemed like the next moment that the sergeant was yelling and the camp was roused from its slumber.

"All right you dregs, get the lord's tent stored. Get his things stored and move it quick! We haven't got all day. We've got a war to get to!"

As Arn and the other men quickly went about their business, a dreary dawn greeted them, although the rain had stopped. Arn looked about with a shiver.

The old man had already gotten up and was tending to the small pony that was carrying the gear. Arn went over and was going to help him but was quickly dispatched for other duties by the men of the column, all apparently outranking him even though there was no rank system.

He busily went to work moving pieces of the tent back, and bits of the lord's fine porcelain service, that he was told to be very careful with, and placing them on the various places of the pack animal.

The column formed up and moved out, at about the same pace as yesterday. Arn's limbs felt yesterday's march. His legs were sore, and even his arms were sore from constantly switching the weight of the fork in his hands. Also his shoulders hurt where his pitchfork had been resting the day before.

As they walked, Arn occasionally spoke to the old man. He found out his first name was Bill. The others didn't tease him as badly today, although once about midday one of the brigands from town tripped him, and all of them laughed.

Once when he asked for permission to relieve himself, they told him to go right where he was walking. He stunk so badly anyway, nobody would even notice. That brought a great deal of mirth to the group.

At that, Bill spoke up and said, "Who amongst ye doesn't stink? Yer tongue in yer mouth certainly does. Have ye ever thought about inviting a polecat to live in there? Then perhaps your breath would smell a bit better." The other men in the column laughed, and the bully, realizing he had been shot down, mumbled under his breath.

Arn smiled at the old man, and the old man sort of smiled back. Arn thought, *at least it's not so bad; I have a friend here. Someone who is going to help me. I'll remember him if I ever become great. And the brothers will be with me soon.*

Once, when the march had gotten a bit ragged, the men strung out here and there, Arn had found himself walking almost abreast with Lord Moresfield and his horse. For that he got a sharp, painful bash to his right shoulder blade with the flat of the Sergeant's halberd. "Get your stinking carcass behind his lordship! You have no right to walk there, boy!" This made Arn feel very sad indeed. The blow hurt, but the words hurt more.

When he looked at the knight trotting before them, proud and regal in his fine clothing, with his fine sword and fine lance resting at the back of his saddle, he suddenly realized the knight was born a man of station, a man of purpose. And Arn was born a peasant. He would never acquire such a horse nor be the one sitting on it. He would never be at the point of commanding men or having respect.

Arn at that point began to cry. The whole past two days began to overwhelm him. He realized he missed his friends, his home. He was sore and he hurt, and he was going to be the fetching boy for everyone in the column.

What a dreadful thing this is, thought Arn, and he sighed. *I never imagined war would be like this. I just want it to be over. I want to return home and live out my life as best I can and stay out of the miserable rain, and not have to march everywhere. Throw a stick to Greymist every now and again.* He wandered off in his thoughts.

The column moved on and on, resting only occasionally. The lord spoke loudly some times, saying things like, "I have to get to my men! If they should attack in battle without me, that would be most unpleasant."

Then Arn started to hear whispering in the column that he hadn't heard before.

"Oh yeah," said one the peasants, "I heard he didn't go because he was trying to get out of trying to fight."

"I heard that myself a couple times, he's not one for fighting," said another. They all chuckled quietly.

Sergeant yelled several times to the men as they talked, "Shut up!"

As the column wound up the road, they came to a great path between two large hills on either side. One stony and shrub-covered, the other almost a sheer cliff, or bank, all the way up with sparse poplar trees and cedars.

His lordship turned around and said to the column, "We're not far now; it'll only be another half day. We'll march on into the night. I wish to join the king's entourage, as I should. You peasants had better keep up. I've been very disappointed with your lack of pace over the last day and a half, and I expect better of you. Do you understand?

"You have delayed . . ." and suddenly, the words didn't come out. There was a strange thunk, the lord got a strange look, and he just looked, and stopped talking. *Perhaps he was too angry to talk*, Arn thought. He started to have some kind of screaming fit, but he said nothing.

At that the second rode up closer to his lordship and looked, turned to the men with a look of horror on his face, and started to yell something. Suddenly a cruel black-shafted arrow went through his throat, from one side to the other, all the way through.

Arn gasped in horror, as did the rest of the men. The old man beside him yelled, "Ambush!"

He pushed the boy to the ground, as several of the peasants turned and ran back down the road. Arn lay on the ground trying to figure out what was going on. He could hear the hissing of arrows, hear the thunk. He could hear the men yelping in pain all around.

He looked at his pitchfork lying on the ground beside him, and looked for his friend, but did not see him. Suddenly, looking up towards the bank he saw Bill Hayes, billhook in hand, yelling a war cry. The sergeant had taken cover behind a rock. The old man was the only one charging up that hill, by himself.

Arn thought, *how brave. What is he doing?* With a yell and raising his hook just as he got to what turned out to be a concealed assailant, an archer, the archer rose up and put an arrow right through the center of the old man's chest.

But Bill didn't stop. The billhook came down, and a horrible shriek came out from the archer as part of the billhook bit deeply into his neck and shoulder.

But then Arn saw with great dismay and horror that his friend fell upon the archer, across the bush that had been concealing him. Arn realized he must be dead, or severely wounded. He thought, *I have to do something*, as several of the peasants followed their mates up the road. The sergeant joined them in their flight, but Arn kept hearing, "thunk, thunk, thunk."

One by one they were shot down by the precision of the archers. Arrows did miss here and there, but most found their marks. Arn realized these were men of skill, and obviously there were a lot of them.

At least they were fast. Arn looked at the abandoned horse of the noble, whinnying and trying to protect its master, who lay upon the ground twitching. His second, with a terrible cruel shaft through his neck only looked up to the sky, obviously quite dead.

As the last of the peasants were about to be dispatched, Arn thought, *what am I about to do?* Suddenly strength came to his limbs; suddenly purpose came to his thoughts. Suddenly a will he knew not himself to have stood him up with the help of his pitchfork. He looked around, realized the pitchfork was of little good against these assailants, and casting it to the ground he saw something else.

He saw something he had only held once in his life when the smith had crafted a beautiful one. It was Moresfield's sword. Still not loosened at his belt, but there, the white leather handle wrapped with a silver wire and a beautiful pommel shaped like an acorn.

Arn gathered his strength and his courage and dashed towards the blade. Several arrows thunked around him, none finding their mark.

He reached down and loosened the blade from its fastening and pulled. It was large, very large indeed. But it was a good weapon and now he thought, *what am I to do with it?* Just as surely as the notion that got him there had arisen, the notion to attack came to his mind.

He looked at his friend up there who needed him, and knew it was time to act. He said a very short prayer to God as he hid behind the horse for a moment, the horse not being a target because of its value.

He stepped out, and started to run up the hill, not knowing who he was. He, Arn of Clayhaven, a mighty sword in his hand, running up a hill towards archers? This was lunacy. He had very little training with a blade, though some he did have, with a wooden sword from the brothers.

He had no armor, but his friend needed him. And that was enough.

Arn did not feel the weariness of his limbs any more. He did not feel the cold dampness around him. He only felt a warm strength and vigor he had never felt in his life. It felt good. It felt very good. He might die this way, but at least he would not die with his back to the enemy, as many of the other peasants had done.

He yelled a mighty yell, the only thing he could think of, "Greymist!" It was a strange and crazy thing, but the only thing that came to his mind, and he yelled it indeed, with all his strength. And as he yelled, the archers stood up, and he saw that there were seven, not including the one his friend had hurt. They did not fire as he quickly made his way up the steep precipice.

But they trained their bows, and the one who was obviously the noble in charge of the archers, yelled, "Stop, boy!" Because the voice was so deep and authoritative, so much like what he was used to in his life, Arn actually did stop.

No archers released their arrows upon him. Several lowered their bows, obviously in their eyes having contempt for a boy with a sword.

The noble said, "Go back! Go back to where you came from. Tell them about the slaughter of this column. Tell them anyone who tries to help the high king of Southaven will pay the same bitter price. I'm letting you live boy; drop that blade though, as you go. And pick no weapon up. And hurry up that road as fast as you can go.

"You are lucky this day, boy." He chuckled. "A child with a sword! Lads, what is Southaven coming to?" All the archers began to laugh.

Arn looked at the sword in his hand, and looked at his friend, who lay gasping there on top of the archer. He could now see that the archer was dead, his eyes wide open and looking at the sky.

Arn thought there was no way he could do this thing. There were six men and a noble, and he had been given free leave to get out of this bloody place, this first battle field of his life. As the vigor and flame that had overtaken him dissipated, he saw there was no chance for him to make even one strike with the blade before they cut him down.

Arn turned and began to walk down the hill that he had just sprinted up with such determination, his eyes downcast. Terrible, terrible pain overwhelmed him. His friend was dying. He could do nothing. And now he was turning his back on the one chance he had to help his friend.

I wish I had never left Clayhaven. I wish I could just clean stalls for the rest of my life, he thought bitterly. *I just wish I were home. I'm only fifteen. What an awful thing,* he thought, as he went down the hill, the sword clanging as it dragged on several rocks.

He heard a voice again say, "Drop the blade, boy. Or we will feather you where you are. You will not take that from the field. This is our victory, that blade is our spoils. I gave you a chance. Drop it now, little boy." The archers began to laugh.

"He smells of dung, too," one of the archers yelled. "Are you dung boy?"

Another archer laughed, "Yes, it's dung lad, dung lad the hero with the sword."

Suddenly, Arn felt that flame again, stronger than he had ever felt it in his life, stronger than when he had felt it at the foot of the hill. It was welling up like a volcano about to explode. He had read about volcanoes with the brothers. They exploded fire and melted rock upon the earth.

Arn stopped in his tracks. As the archers continued to laugh and throw jeers his way, the blade did not fall from his hands. A little voice inside him said, drop the blade and go. They have given you leave, you should go.

He thought to himself, *no. What waits for me there is nothing. What waits for me here is certain death. But I'll not leave my friend there. And I'll not suffer the barbs any more, of sharp-tongued devils like that.*

Arn grasped the sword like a man grasping an axe. He had that determination of a woodsman about to fell a great tree. Arn smiled to himself, not the smile of a boy, but the smile of a man about to make the decision of his life.

Again he heard the man ordering him to drop the blade and move on, but he could just barely register the warning. The energy, the zeal, the power he had felt a moment ago, had returned tenfold. Arn turned and one archer actually almost dropped his bow, when he saw the look upon Arn's face.

Arn stood almost six feet tall and made an impressive figure with fire in his eyes. He looked at the noble and the archers and said, "No more. If God strikes me down this day, then so be it. But *you* will not."

The noble looked a bit shocked and moved his head back as if he was trying to contemplate this new situation. Arn did not give him or any of the others a chance to think.

He charged with a roar. He ran like he had never run in his life. There were only a few paces and Arn made those paces faster than he had ever made any run before. The first archer who had lowered his bow actually cast it down and turned and ran.

Arn had made a man run? This only increased his speed as he nimbly and expertly jumped from rock to rock, avoiding anything that would make him stumble, like a sure-footed wild animal. As the other archers who already had their bows bent let fly their arrows, Arn did not pay heed. But knew soon he might feel the horrible sting of those very sharp barbs.

But no pain came. Arn reached the first archer closest to him, who was fumbling desperately with his bow. As he looked up with a great deal of surprise on his face, Arn brought the blade down across his neck and in one moment, a crimson spray fell across the man and his vision.

The man dropped, and Arn could barely consider what had just happened as he moved on to the second archer, who was trying desperately to remove a knife tucked into his belt. Arn gave him no chance to free it, jabbing through the boiled leather hide that the archer wore, all the way through. He felt the blade going deep and quick and smooth. He never imagined the blade could go into a hard surface like that so easily.

Arn quickly removed the blade, leaving the archer gasping for air and falling to the ground. He moved to the next archer. The noble indeed looked shocked, and ordered his men to fire. Two more bolts flew, one actually hitting the archer in front of Arn, who was Arn's next target.

The archer collapsed and Arn sidestepped him as the man fell with a cold black shaft in his back.

Arn leaped forward to the next archer, dispatching him with the same ease as he had done the first. The blade across the throat. The last archers, seeing their friends dispatched so easily by the boy, and not seeming to be able to hit him at all, decided that discretion was the better part of valor, and immediately turned and ran away up the hill, as fast as they could.

Arn now stood at the man who had been jeering at him and mocking him so few minutes before. The noble fumbled desperately with his sword, trying to get it out. Arn thought, if he gets his sword out, that will be the end of me.

But Arn remembered something that Brother Francis had taught him, that a knight must always offer another knight quarter in a situation like this.

Arn thought, *I'm not a knight,* but with the great blade in his hands, he raised it for a deathblow and ordered the man to stop.

The man looked at him, eyes squinted, and spit, and said, "Curse you, boy." And added a rather profane remark.

As the noble started to slide out his blade, Arn quickly lowered his and jabbed with all of his might at the breastplate that the nobleman wore. His blade went through it with surprising ease, and it managed to go from one end to the other. Arn realized he had put this blade all the way through this man.

As the man looked at Arn in disbelief, and shock, he fell forward, the blade jabbing even further through him. Arn looked around, and the only thing he could think of was his friend. He didn't have time to think about what had just transpired. He ran to the old man, who was still alive.

Arn turned him over, saw the ugly black arrow sticking in just below his heart. He said, "Bill?" The man looked, his eyes flickered. He said, "Arn, is that you lad?"

"Aye, sir."

"Looks like I might have got this one, but who got them?" He blinked at the row of dead soldiers.

"I did, sir."

The man smiled, almost knowingly. "I knew you had something in you, boy. I knew you always had something in you." The man coughed, and spit up blood. Arn took out a cloth that he kept in his belt and dabbed away the blood.

"May I have a drink? Please?" Bill said, with a whispery breath.

"Aye." Arn pulled his water gourd and gave the man a long draught.

"Arn," he said at last, "ye were never destined to be a stable boy. Thank ye for helping. I guess this is the last war I'll ever be in."

He looked at the sky, uttered a prayer, and looked at Arn one more time. "Tell my wife I love her. And make sure she knows my last thoughts were . . ." He trailed off as the blood trickled from his mouth and the open wound.

Arn thought desperately for what he could do to stop the bleeding, but he knew it was too late. He knew that the archer had found his mark true and close. The shaft had gone deep. It was actually pushing through the back of the ragged cloth the old man wore.

Arn sat for a while and held the man's head in his hands, then crouched and put his legs under his head, as if to provide a comfortable pillow for old Bill to sleep on. Arn began to cry, looking at the wreck of humanity around him.

The dead soldiers that he himself had killed.

He cried and he cried. He knew not how long. He looked down at the peasants and the noble, he looked at the steeds running away. One running up the road and the two running down the road. He could do naught but look. And he cried bitterly.

The sun went across the top of the sky and down many hands, and still he sat with tears in his eyes. He realized he was not quite a man yet. But he had done this thing that men in warfare do.

It did not make him stronger, and it did not make him happy. It only made him sad. He could barely look at the dead faces looking at the sky, or the backs, or the blood splashed all about.

After a time, Arn managed to get a hold of himself. He lovingly crossed the old man's arms, took his old blanket and placed it over him. He went down and took a spade that had been thrown down by one of the peasants.

He thought the best place to leave him now that the horses were well gone, would be to make a grave at the top of the hill. Arn dug. The ground was soft from the recent rain, but it did take him a long time. He took the time to dig a nice grave for his friend, and he did.

As the day wore on, Arn managed to get a grave fairly deep, and he wrapped the old man in his blankets and several other old blankets, and he placed him in the grave. He covered it with sod and placed stones upon it. He had been one of the best men Arn knew.

He put a cross upon it with the words, "Hayes—He died with his face to the enemy." It was all Arn could think to scratch in with the rock he had. He took time and made it well. Then carefully stoking a small fire from dry tinder he found on one of the dead men, he heated the end of one of the daggers until it was glowing red. He burned the words that he had scratched in the cross, so it would be a fitting marker for the man whom he now knew was his friend.

Arn stood upon the hill and looked about.

This is war. There was nothing to do for all these men but to cover them. He grabbed as many blankets as he could. First he covered the people he knew from his town, and then the men that he had dispatched.

He thought about taking things from the men but he could not bring himself to do it. He could not figure why. There were indeed treasures. They would no longer need these treasures, and certainly they would not make it back to the men's families, but he could not take a thing from anyone.

But he went over to the last noble, the last man he had killed. With a sickening sucking noise Arn pulled the blade from the deadly wound. He could not bear to look at the man, so he found a blanket that seemed suitable for the noble, placed it upon him, and tucked it underneath.

He tucked rocks along the blankets as best he could. He knew someone would be along to loot them, but he could not dig graves for all these people.

He hoped honest people who really needed these things would come and take them. But he just did not have the stomach to dig another grave that day.

As Arn looked at the bloody blade in his hand, it felt light somehow. Indeed it was a sharp blade. It had made quick work of the boiled leather, and even the noble's breastplate, as if it were nothing. Arn just could not bear to leave the blade with his noble. He thought, *it will surely be stolen if I don't take it.*

So he loosened the scabbard from the noble's belt, and he cleaned the blade as thoroughly as he could, and placed the blade back in, thinking, *I will never pull this blade again. It's not mine. I will continue on to the field, as is my duty as a soldier, and I will give this to someone of authority, who will know what to do with it.*

Looking about him, he had many things in his mind. The deeds he had done, and the deeds he had seen done. It was quite a shocking thing, this introduction to warfare. He realized to himself, yes he had killed these men, but they were armed and attempting to kill him. Somehow that made him feel a little bit better.

He thought for a moment that he might wait for the brothers to come. Knowing he was only half a day from the King's camp, he decided to wait for them there. He could not bear to wait among the dead anyway. He slowly plodded up the road.

He was not sure exactly where he was going, but he just kept walking. He walked on into the night. As night drew on he saw lights over the hills, what seemed to be a bright glow. It could be the camp of a large army, with many fires burning.

He made his way through the night towards the camp, the events of the day constantly replaying in his head. He would occasionally finger the sword absent-mindedly, looking around in the dark, wondering if the great jut-jawed horrors would leap out upon him.

But none did, and he made his way. Arn realized he was no longer a boy. He was most definitely a man.

He wondered what would happen next. Perhaps he would be killed in a battle, as he had just killed in battle. Or maybe he would just be at the back guarding a baggage train as Hayes had said.

He did not know what fate would befall him on this new road, but strangely, as the day had worn on and into the night, he felt a comfort, the sadness had left him, and he felt stronger again. He had committed indeed a brave act, and he had done nothing wrong, as far as he knew the rules of war.

So now, this new path he was on, where would it lead? Who would he meet? What would happen? He didn't know. But he knew one thing. He had seen his first friend die before his eyes, and he didn't like that feeling at all.

CHAPTER FOUR

SAVED A SWORD, CONDEMNED
BY A SWORD

*A*rn *wanted get as far away from the scene of the day's battle as* possible before night fell. He had heard stories of the dead coming out of their graves, and as the sun waned in the autumn sky, he could not forget that he had dispatched people. Perhaps the newly dead were able to seek revenge on the living that had hurt them. He had certainly hurt those archers and that nobleman on the hill. These thoughts bothered him increasingly, even as he tried not to think about them.

He had not been able to lay to rest all of his comrades who came with him. Not that he liked them much, but he wished he had had the strength.

Night came quickly and he began to feel a chill, not just from the cold autumn breeze, but also from inside. He felt as if someone was watching him.

He found what could be a nice campsite. It was by a small stream next to the road, kind of open, and looked as if others had used it for a campsite. But it was just too close. He had not gone more than a league, he thought, from the scene of the day's horrors, and he just couldn't bring himself to lie down. He stopped to refresh himself in the stream and have a bite to eat.

Sitting on an old log, he had a very unpleasant feeling that he was being watched, a feeling of dread. He decided it might be better to go on up the road a ways, much farther, so he set out even though the last rays of the sun over the hills had just disappeared.

He wished for light to walk the rutted dirt path, but the breeze would put out his candle if he lighted it. His sense of dread pushed him on, stumbling, up the road. Surely the king's army would not be far ahead. He seemed to sense a glow from a large number of campfires, but he was not sure if it was his imagination.

He couldn't bring himself to stop and rest, and finally, after traveling another hour, stumbling in the dark, he realized the moon had not risen. A new moon. His dread filled his chest with pressure.

He wished he could just go home, and be in his nice warm bed, by his own little fireplace that he was blessed enough to have in his regular life. He never wished to kill anyone. He thought of those men, their eyes staring up at the sky. He had killed those men. They must have had families and children. Even evil people have families.

Maybe they weren't evil at all. Just because they are my enemy, does that make them evil? He stumbled yet again.

Too bad Clayhaven isn't more important, he thought randomly. Then they would have perhaps had stone or slate on the road, so that when it rained the wagons wouldn't so dreadfully disturb the roadway, leaving these big ruts which make it very difficult to travel at night with no light.

He felt he could not go on anymore. He said a silent prayer and stumbled off to the side of the road. The lights that he thought would be campfires didn't seem to be getting any closer. He decided to sit until morning with his back against a big tree. That way he wouldn't hurt his legs anymore, and his knees.

He wondered, *what will I see when I get there? The king's army, all splendid. That would have meant a lot to me a few days ago, before all this.* Those beautiful colors of the standards of the heralds, the knights in their full regalia of their family lineages, beautifully cascading, their hauberks shiny and polished, their lances with points gleaming off the sun, their personal pennants flowing. How that would have meant so much. The drums and the pipes playing. The wild men of the hills who were united with the king had a wonderful thing he wanted to hear, those strange pipes. He had heard almost mythical stories of great men with flaming red hair and long beards who played these great pipes.

But now it all seemed somehow inglorious, somehow sad, because all of these colors, fine horses, all of these grooms and squires, kings and nobles and knights, and the high king himself have all gathered for one purpose: to destroy their enemy on the other side of the field. To make them dead so that they do not become so themselves. Arn sat at the nearest big tree close to the path that he could find, and he pondered this for a while.

Only the stars twinkled in the crisp autumn sky. He looked at them, somehow comforted knowing he could see those same stars from his home so far away now. He had never been so far from home, at least that he knew of. At least when he was older, he never remembered traveling this far. Suddenly he remembered that long ago, Father Kile had let it slip that Arn had come from far away. He wondered from where.

They never would tell him much about his parents, and what happened. Just that they were gone. He never got a clear answer whether they were dead, or they had abandoned him. It saddened him greatly to think that they might have abandoned him. Perhaps they just could not feed an extra mouth. Perhaps they had a big family.

As his mind dwelt on these thoughts, he was wary of every noise. He pulled his birthday dagger from his belt, and clenched it in his hand. He kept the sword upon his lap but it was sheathed, because he could not bear to bring it out, even at the scariest of noises. Occasionally in the distance he would hear what sounded to be a great wolf howling, with a great fire and fierceness that he had not heard in a wolf before. It sounded large, frightening. He shuddered.

At the same time, the sound reminded him of Greymist. But Greymist's howl was a different kind, not with malice and twisted malevolence, but a softer, mournful yet beautiful sound.

A few times Arn drifted off to sleep but every time he did, he awoke to wonder if he had heard a branch crack or a leaf rustle.

One time during the night, about the fourth hour of the morning, he could have sworn he heard shambling footsteps on the road. He froze as his heart pounded. Was it the dead? The slain dead coming back to get him? To drag him off to a horrible demise? He gripped his dagger tighter, stood up and said, "I'm not afraid, do you hear me? I am not afraid!"

His voice sounded small and his very skin felt cold. He could feel the cold bumps all upon his body. "You stay back now."

He had stumbled over a small rock as he sat down at the tree, and now he groped for it in the dark and picked it up. Arn was pretty fair with a rock. The monks used to kid him that if he ever went out on the road, a highwayman would be sorry he met Arn, the dead-on rock thrower.

He felt a strange comfort as he gripped the rock. Distance would be better. If he could see one of the terrible distorted faces he saw earlier, if they happened to come out, he hoped he could throw the rock and not have to get close.

He thought the shambling noise was getting closer, and he could bear it no longer. He grabbed his small pack and placed it upon his back and tucked the sword into his belt. The shambling seemed to come from the direction that he had come, so he headed up the road as quickly as he could, stumbling many times.

He thought he heard running behind him, and that was enough. He began to run, blindly up the road as fast as he could. He fell several times, and finally fell very hard and hit his head. He heard a great thump and felt a warm sensation trickle down into his ear.

His head was swimming as he tried to rise, and he prayed silently, *oh please, send someone to help me. I did not mean to slay anybody. I only know what I was supposed to do, and that was to kill the enemy. That's what is right. I'm so sorry!*

He rolled onto his back, grabbed the dagger in his left hand and kept the rock still clutched out of fear in his right hand. If the dead had come he needed a way to deal with them. Groveling on the ground wouldn't be it.

The prayer had brought a fire to his heart, a warming, and he felt strength. *I will face them*, he thought with some bravery.

He tried to stand but fell back into a gully just off the road. He looked at the sky swirling above him, and did not feel very well. The blood that trickled down his face into his mouth was warm, and for a moment he wondered if it was warm water. But the taste was definitely his blood. He was not thinking straight.

He closed his eyes to stop the stars from swaying. He remained where he was, quite unconscious for many hours. He was protected there, quite safe. None would touch the boy, not a thing.

When he awoke it was full morning, and at first he felt refreshed. When he sat, his head hurt terribly. His dagger was still upon his chest, and the sword had fallen underneath him, safe. Then he remembered the events of the day before.

It must not have been the dead he heard or certainly they would have taken their revenge. Maybe it had been some kind of animal in the woods. The fear of the night before seemed silly in the bright autumn daylight.

His head had stopped bleeding, but it was throbbing, and as he looked up at the sky, his eyes filled with pain. He looked down and saw the stone that had put the gash in his head. It looked small to have caused him this much trouble, buried in the dirt of the road.

Arn would normally enjoy such a pretty autumn day. He tried to stand but felt a little dizzy. He sat and sipped a bit of his water and ate a small piece of way bread and some pieces of dried meat the lady had given him. He wondered how long he had lain in the gully.

He contemplated wrapping some cloth around his head, but when he looked through his meager possessions, nothing was very clean. He knew Brother Clement insisted on clean bandages. He used his handkerchief and some of his precious water to clean the wound. Maybe the air would make it feel better anyway.

He managed to get to his feet. He looked around but did not see evidence of anyone nearby. Weak-kneed, he walked through the area, and decided to get a bit closer to where he heard the footsteps.

He could see no evidence that any one had been there at all. Perhaps it had been just a deer or a rabbit. Sometimes they could sound like people walking. He wished his head would stop hurting.

It's time Arn, he told himself. *You are near the battlefield for goodness' sake; you have fought your first battle. You need to act more like a man.* Out loud he said, "I will be more like a man." He did not quite believe it. It did not sink in.

"I'm going to be more like a man," he repeated. "I'm going to go up this road and find the army and do my duty, then go home." The thought of going home warmed him for a second.

Arn hiked his belt up, and pulled back on one of his boots that had partially come off as he had stumbled to get up. He tightened the leather thongs upon his boots. This always made him feel better somehow, like he had more strength in his legs. He never knew why.

He thought, *I've looked for my pursuers and there were none apparently. Everything's ok Arn, you just fell like a silly doorknob and hit your head, running from probably a deer or rabbit, silly boy.*

He started to feel a bit better and decided he would head up the road. Slowly at first, he looked at the trees and listened to the birds singing, ones that had started to head southward for the winter already. He wondered what it must be like to be a bird, to fly free, free of worry and toil.

It was a pretty little blue bird on a branch that he saw as he walked down the road. He stopped a minute and looked; the little fellow was sitting there tweeting away happily. He thought, *that's the way I should be, I'll think of a song. That'll make me feel better.*

He sang these words to a little tune the brothers sometimes played: Along I go The path is long Along I go My legs are strong Along I go The path is long Long until I reach a place of rest I shall go along the path so long I shall go upon this path far I shall go along upon this path so well Until I reach its end And then I'll know my rest

He managed to pick up his pace a bit, heading up the road happily humming the tune as he went.

After he had sung this song a few times, he sang his own personal song. He was Arn of Clayhaven, on an adventure no less. He had heard travelers coming to the tavern when he was younger, when he had a chance to go to the tavern and people weren't being mean to him.

He remembered a one-eyed man that was very interesting. He had just dealt with brigands upon the road. Arn had helped sharpen his sword, no less. That had been a great thrill. That happened about two summers ago. He had been a big man, over six feet, and he had had a large horse, probably 18 hands.

Arn had loved the stories the man told, of adventure, beautiful women, treasure. He even mentioned going into the dark lands, but those stories he would trail off and he had not talked about the dark lands much. So that made Arn and some of the others in the tavern believe he really had gone there.

Without boasting, he said he had crept into the dark lands when he went there, on an important mission for the king. He couldn't say what the mission was, and he wouldn't finish the story.

Arn thought, *how far are the dark lands now?* His thoughts trailed off from the one-eyed hero to the dark lands, now perhaps not so far away.

He knew as he moved closer to the border, the lands became blighted. Trees, as the old one-eyed traveler told him, would become black, the bark and leaves blackened. Most of the beautiful trees would simply wither and die. There were flowers, but they were dark and unpleasant. Some of them would sting the very naked flesh of you if you touched them. *How could flowers be so villainous,* he wondered, as he looked at a few fall flowers along the path here and there.

How could flowers sting? He went over to a very pretty flower. He did not know what it was. It had a yellow center and white petals. Brother Clement had probably told him the name, what was it? Fairlady? Perhaps that was it. He picked three of them and placed them in his small jerkin pocket. He would look down at them occasionally as he walked. Somehow they made him feel better.

They didn't sting, they didn't bite, they didn't hurt and they weren't ugly. They were pretty and bright. Arn felt better since the morning. He had traveled well into the afternoon. His head didn't hurt near as much but still throbbed.

He thought in the distance he heard a noise, like a thumping. As he continued up the road, he was excited to think that it was the beating of a drum. He couldn't be far from the field now. He couldn't see where the fires of last night had been, but he could certainly hear he was nearing the camp. What was that? Was that a man yelling orders?

For a moment he imagined he would find warm food and somebody to take care of him, then his thoughts trailed off. Probably they wouldn't give him any warm food or comfort him in any way.

Villains, however, couldn't as easily sneak up on him if he was in the middle of an army. At least he would be off this road, and hadn't run into brigands, wolves, or goor or anything.

What should he tell them about the blade he was carrying? Normally a boy could expect to lose his head over it, but surely they would believe him when he told them the story of the ambush, and having to take the sword so no enemy could get the beautiful blade.

Arn cut through the woods to his right, where he heard the loud beating of drums, and a horn, and voices yelling. He could also hear some laughter, and that made him feel better.

By chance, he found a trail that seemed to wind its way towards the noise, and he took this path. Brush had grown in the trail thickly in places, but he hastened as quickly as he could through the woods. Most of the path was fairly clear and it was much easier than walking along the road.

The trail opened onto a meadow. There was grass blowing in the breeze, and a sight befell him he thought he would never see in his life.

Waving banners in gold, black, red, and blue, white, green and yellow. All the beautiful colors he had seen in his life in one place.

Arn was viewing the army for the first time. He forgot about the dull ache in his head. He forgot about the weariness of his body, and the terrible unpleasantness of the day before.

Drums were playing, men were laughing, archers were stringing their bows to the left, and squires were tending to horses to the right. *I'm on a battlefield, my first battlefield, and I'm a soldier!* These thoughts raced through his head as he looked around.

From where he stood, he saw no peasants as he thought he might. Apparently not too many of them had made it yet, if any. He looked at the beautiful pavilion tents. *Why, there were even women over there, some beautiful women!* They looked as if they were tending to different things in beautiful long dresses. This is more like a parade or something.

Where is the king's banner? *I have to return this blade, before I am accused of stealing it,* he thought. He turned his back to the spectacle, took out his ragged old grey blanket and wrapped it around the beautiful blade and scabbard. He tried not to remember what he had done with it yesterday, and tucked it into his tube roll, beside the beautiful cloak the lady had given him.

I'll just look for the king. He might even be grateful. Would that be so much to ask?

"Hey, you boy!"

Arn shook his head, his thoughts of meeting the king quickly dissipating. "Yes sir?"

"What are you doing there?" It was a man standing with a group of archers.

"I've come to join the army."

Oh, have you now?" One of the archers chuckled at that. He said, "Look at that little wee one, he's come to join the army, he has. Now we're in good military shape!" The archers laughed aloud. "Boy, you are better off if you go back in those woods and pretend you were never here."

"B-b-but I'm a soldier!"

All the archers turned at that, jabbing at each other and laughing. "You're a soldier now, are you? I didn't realize." The man gave a curt, mocking bow. "Your lordship, could I take you to the king?"

"Yes," said Arn, "you could. I want to see . . . ."

All the men laughed a great laugh. Arn could tell they were nervous and it seemed to help them greatly to laugh, so perhaps he was being some kind of benefit, although he did not like being the brunt of the jokes.

"I'll find him on my own, thank you."

"You do that, and when you find him, tell him that me, Darrin the archer, says hello, greetings, and I thank him for the fine dinner he gave me last eve." All the men laughed heartily and slapped Darrin on the back.

Arn said, "I will, sir, I will," knowing that this would perhaps bring more laughter and he could quickly make his getaway.

It did. The archers all laughed and pointed. "Tell the king," one of them yelled in his best nobleman's voice, "that his loyal servant, Belvon, says greetings and I hope he will visit my castle one day."

Darrin, not wanting to be outdone in his joke, said, "And you tell that king about these shoes he gives me, I would like a finer pair, pointed on the tips even, and with some bells."

All the men laughed at this, and Darrin wasn't outdone. They roared with laughter as Arn quickly made his way from these jubilant strange men of the bow.

He quickly got into other units. One unit appeared to be spearmen, all of them having grounded their spears. One of the archers yelled over, "Hey! He's a friend of the king! Give him leeway! Don't be in his way, bow!"

The spearmen looked with a bit of gruffness and mumbled to themselves; they didn't seem to be as jubilant as the archers. Arn knew that if all went well, they would be doing a lot of the fighting, while the archers would be standing off shooting.

Arn just nodded and smiled at the spearmen as he tried to make his way through their ranks as quickly as possible. None bothered him, although some mumbled a few things here and there.

He moved forward, towards the small hill where the king was, amazed at the different sights and sounds of all the soldiers. His eyes followed a particularly flamboyant knight who was riding up to join his unit, was not looking where he was going, and found himself bashing into a tall, bearded man in a rich, blue coat with metal buttons.

"Oh, forgive me, sir," said the tall man before Arn could say a thing. "I can see you are a most important man, on the way to an important appointment, perhaps with the king? I'm so sorry to have impeded you." He bowed mockingly.

"I'm very sorry," said Arn. "I do have an appointment. I do need to find the king, sir."

"Well by all means, don't let me stop you, young urchin. I should have seen clearly by the unstained finery you wear that you are obviously a young man of royal blood, perhaps a prince. I shall write of you one day, young prince, for I am but a humble scribe. Allow me to step aside, sir."

Arn did not know how to react to this strange man's sarcastic behavior but he passed aside, begging again the man's pardon as he went.

He encountered a group of sergeants, mounted men. He knew what they were, since they had come through the village a few times, and he thought he would try his luck. He thought, *I know what I'll say, it might not be exactly true, but I think the king will understand.*

"Um, good sergeants!" One of the men looked down at him impatiently as he was brushing his horse. "Aye lad, what is it?"

"I'm here . . . I have something to tell the king."

"Do you, lad? And who sent you with this message?"

Arn thought of the sword on his back and the nobleman he had taken it from. "A nobleman, sir."

The sergeant thought that was possible. He could be a messenger. Arn looked into his eyes and could see him considering this possibility as he scratched his slightly bearded face.

"Aye lad, I'll show you where the king's pavilion is."

"Oh, thank you my lord, thank you."

The sergeant chuckled. "It's alright lad, you don't have to call me my lord. Let's go." Speaking to one of the younger men, he said, "You tend to me horse." The young man came up and nodded, and immediately did as the older man said.

"So, what's the message lad?"

"Well, it . . . well, sir." Arn began to shake, realizing he did not know what to say next, and perhaps his sort-of lie would be found out and the man would be angry.

"It's not really a specific message. I'm from Clayhaven. The lord there, he . . ."

"Spit it out, lad! Or perhaps you should tell the king. Is it just for the king's ears, lad? Tell me."

"No, not specifically. We were coming en route from Clayhaven, we had been gathered up into a unit of militia, preparing to, you know, we went upon the trail, and as we were coming down the trail, the road, to join the king's army, we were ambushed, and . . ."

"Oh, ambushed," said the man. "Archers?"

"Aye, sir."

"That's not the first I've heard of that in the last few days. We've had many a soldier killed upon the route to joint the king or the other army that's further north of here."

"Aye sir, we were ambushed."

"Just tell one of the king's men."

As they arrived at the foot of a gentle but large knoll, towards the center of the meadow, Arn looked up and saw the great pavilion with the king's colors on display. He had never seen such a beautiful tent before.

"That is the king's tent, isn't it?"

"Aye, that's it. Look, lad, I've come as far as I can. You go up and tell one of those nobles in one of those smaller tents what you've told me. They are the king's aides and such, and they'll take your message and give it to his majesty."

"Aye, sir. Thank you for your help."

"Aye, lad, and good luck to you."

Arn was nervous as he started up the hill. He stared in wonder at the pavilion and the men around and the horses. He could just see the army and he could see the soldiers. As he climbed the hill he could see soldiers to the right and rear of the army, washing their aching feet in the stream. He could see soldiers tending to horses, some laughing, and some sitting upon the ground sewing. He could see ladies giggling and talking to gentlemen in fine regalia and thought perhaps there would not be a battle after all.

Perhaps I'll get to go home soon. That would be wonderful, Arn thought. *I just hope I can soon be back in Clayhaven.*

At that Arn felt a hard hand on his right shoulder. "Halt! Who is it that comes before the king's tent?"

"I'm Arn of Clayhaven, sir."

"What do you want, boy?" said the finely dressed guard.

"I have a message for the king."

"Oh, do you now, the king himself? Do you have a writ?" When Arn stood speechless, the guard continued, "Do you have something written?"

"No, I wanted to tell the king . . ." and just at this moment Arn saw a stately man dressed in beautiful purple robes come out of a tent, placing upon his girth a fine thick leather buckled belt. An aide tried to help, not very effectually.

"Who is this?" The regal man spoke out. He had a fine salt and pepper beard but on his head, flowing, greying brown hair with red streaks. And then Arn noticed a golden crown on his head.

This was the king. Arn did not know what to do. He fell upon his knee and said, "My lord!" The king looked over in surprise.

"Who is this, guard?"

"It's some boy who has a message for the king, he says."

"Really? Boy, look up at me. What is your message?"

"I'm uh . . ."

"Speak up, boy. I haven't all day."

"I'm Arn of Clayhaven, sir. We were . . ."

The king interrupted with tightly spoken words. "What is your message?"

Arn tried to speak but only stuttered some sounds.

"Clayhaven?" said the king. "Lord Warwick, did I not have Lord Moresfield coming from Clayhaven with the rest of his conscripts?"

"Aye," answered the aide, "He should have been here this day."

"Hm, what is your news, boy?"

"We came from Clayhaven and we were en route and . . ."

"How many were you?"

"About a score, sir. And we, um," this led to more stuttering, since Arn found himself extraordinarily nervous to be talking to the king. "We were mostly poor people."

"Peasants, yes, go on." The king's nobles and knights were already upon the field, and he was supposed to join them. "Where is Lord Moresfield?"

"Well sir, he . . . We were ambushed sir, my liege, my king." Arn stumbled over the words, not knowing exactly what to say to a king.

"Hmm," the king looked down and stroked his great beard. "This is bad. This is ill news. I was to have him at Yule with me. He was a good man. Ambushed by archers, were you? Were they men or goor?"

"Men, sir."

"How many?"

"Well . . . there were seven."

"His lordship's second?"

"He was killed too, sir."

"These are indeed grave tidings."

"But sir, my king, I killed the men."

"You what?" The king looked down, eyebrows raised. Arn began to see anger in the king's face.

"I mean," started Arn.

"Shut your stuttering, boy, and tell me what you just said," said the king in a quiet, tight voice.

"I killed the men who ambushed us, as I was supposed to, yes?"

"You killed that many men? You are but a boy, but now you are lying. Why have you brought forth this lie? Why don't you just say you were ambushed and you ran away, or perhaps you were let go by the men as in other cases I've heard, to tell the story of the ambush? Now you've come before me to tell your message."

"But that's not the truth, sir. I did slay the men; I slew the archers and a noble."

"You slew a noble? With what, your little knife?" said the king with scorn.

"Well the lordship, his horse, he fell over and he was there on the ground. His sword was there, and I picked it up and I ran up the hill."

"You what?"

"I ran up the hill, my lord, and they laughed at me, and I turned to go, I don't know. Then I turned back, and I killed several and I killed them, the archers. Some ran away, but my friend had been killed and I couldn't stand it, and I just turned and I killed the archers. I ran and killed the noble, with the sword from his lordship's . . ."

"You are a liar, boy! How dare you insult me by coming with your filthy presence upon my hill? And how dare you insult me by lying to me in the flesh!"

"But it's true! I have . . ." Arn reached behind his back, wishing he had never seen the sword, slowly pulled it over his shoulder, trying desperately to explain the situation. He saw the king's guard watching him closely.

"This is the blade." Nervous, he could barely unwrap it from his tattered blanket. "This is it."

"That is a nobleman's blade. You stole the blade and you lied to me and you insult me with your presence! I will deal with you, boy. Lying little peasant!"

"But my king, I am not lying!" Arn felt tears gather in his eyes.

"Quiet, boy." He snapped a finger at one of his guards. "See to it that this rat goes to the back, and does what he is obviously meant to do, tending to horses and such and see that he steals nothing else. See that he is kept for the end of the morrow and I will deal with him personally."

"Yes, sire," the guard said.

"You have had your last days upon this earth lying, boy. What was your job in Clayhaven? What were your duties?"

"I cleaned stables and privies," Arn could barely get out through his tears.

"Then a fitting duty you will have in your last hours. Take this rat," the king's men laughed at this, "and see that he is punished with work until I punish him with justice."

"Yes, my king," said the guard.

The king stood at least six feet high and weighed many stone. He was a man of strength, even at his age, and a man you did not want to anger. Arn had not meant to anger him. He felt so terrible. The great king he had heard so much good about was now someone who was going to slay him. What a horrible thought. The king reached down with his great hands, snatched the sword and turned his back upon Arn, not looking further at him, going back to his battle plan.

Arn began to weep bitterly. He had only done the right thing, and now this was his last day on earth. I don't deserve this. How can this be? A man as well thought of as this king. There are other kings who are tyrants, but I thought he was a good man.

He must not be such a wise man, or he would have surely realized that a liar and thief would never bring back such a valuable prize to him.

The men chuckled and pointed and whispered a few things Arn could not hear while the guard who was with Arn snatched his dagger away. "That's a fine blade for a thief," the guard said. "You keep moving, boy."

Arn put his head down and wept bitterly while he walked. Many of the men were laughing, but some who probably had boys his age tried to give him words of encouragement, not knowing Arn's true situation.

"There now, boy, it won't be so bad."

"Buck up. Stand to. The battle will be over soon."

"You'll be all right," said one kind man.

Another said, "Wipe your tears away, boy. It's a battle we're at."

"It's as fine a thing as any beautiful lady's hair," said one big-chested red-bearded man. He looked like a hill man.

Others laughed as Arn went, mocking him as he passed, crying as a boy for his mum. Arn could not look at any of them, but as he walked down the hill towards his duties in the back, he tried to wipe his tears away. And walk upright. He would not let these men see him cry anymore, nor mock him anymore. He would go with some dignity to his task. He tried not to think of the bitter end that would come soon. He kept walking but could not stop thinking how truly unjust this was. He had done the right thing; he was a hero after all.

Arn mumbled to himself.

"Shut up," said the guard. "Move." The man pushed him roughly from behind. Arn continued until they came upon the pickets of horses. Great pickets full of horses. Arn had never seen so many horses.

"These are what you'll be tending to boy, noblemen's horses, sergeants' horses, light horsemen's horses. You'll tend to all these horses, and pick up their poop like you're used to, and you'll be smart about it and quick."

There was a large burly man who had had many a good meal, Arn could tell, with greasy black hair and a filthy tunic and a smell Arn knew all too well. Horses. Squire looked up and said, "What's this?"

"He's a personal guest of his majesty. He is to be watched by you, and given the hardest labor you've got until the king sends for him, at the end of the day or on the morrow. This boy is to be given king's justice."

The man laughed and shoved Arn as hard as he could towards the fat squire.

Arn began to cry again, his will broken. He said, "I didn't do anything. I did what I was supposed to do. I did the right thing!"

"Shut up!" And with a whack, the man's big meaty left hand crossed Arn's jaw, pushing him off his already wobbly legs to the ground. Arn hit hard, with a thud, and his head hurt him again, while blood trickled from his mouth.

He thought, *it's not right!* Several of the other grooms laughed, pointing, as if this were great fun for them. One of them even managed to pick up horse dung with his hand and fling it at the boy.

Arn sat upon the ground and wept. He heard shouting, "Get up boy! You have duties until your day of reckoning, today or tomorrow as the guard said. Perhaps we'll come and watch you."

As poop landed upon Arn's head, he felt all the pent up sadness and all the years of torment he had suffered from people like this all of his life. Suddenly he stopped crying, he looked at the beautiful blue sky, he felt his head throbbing, but decided to try to stop thinking about it.

He thought the day would never end, even though at the end of it there might be something quite horrible waiting for him. The fear continued to bite at him, but not as much, as he tended to his duties of helping the squires and teamsters.

About eve time, another squire came and said, "You're coming with me, boy." Arn of course diligently went. He was still trying to think of a way to get out, to escape the unjust fate that awaited him. He looked around, wondering if he could run. *Maybe*, he thought, *I could lose myself in the crowd.* But there were so many people around.

As he walked back past the little knoll where the king's tent was, he looked up to his left and saw the majestic tents and the flags flying in the evening sun.

What a pretty sight, the sun setting over the king's standard. He thought, *this might be my last sunset.* Perhaps he would never see the sun again.

He thought about his little home, and realized that in his last hours, his yearning was not for that. He had always wanted something better than that, a place where he belonged and was not scorned by everyone he met.

Brother Clement had always told him, "You're always wanting to rise above your station, lad. Maybe you will and maybe you won't. But I wish ye the best. Just remember things aren't always as easy for others as you think. The life of a noble can be dangerous as well as fancy. In a battle, they are likely the first to die, because they have to lead men, often who don't care, who just want to go home."

Arn thought about that for a moment, about the king leading his army, and wondered what he was thinking. But alas, no such station and responsibility would be his, he knew. Soon he would be going clean to another place, a better place at least.

The monks always said heaven was a place where there was no more suffering and grief. A crisp, cool breeze blew across his face as he walked. He could smell the winter soon to come. He would miss Greymist, and the lady.

He approached a large baggage train, and was amazed at the goods spread before him along with all the pack animals and carts, for carrying so much stuff. *I wonder if I could find anything in all that stuff to help me get away.* He contemplated this. *At least I'll have hopes of getting away if I have the chance.* He could not fully accept the fate that awaited him.

The rest of the day blinked quickly into night, and Arn worked very hard under this new, unpleasant man. Though he didn't backhand him as the other man had done several times during the day, this was someone he did not want to make angry. Arn saw the way he used the lash on the pack mules and ponies. If possible, he might be a more unpleasant man than the last.

Arn put his head down and just worked, patting and soothing the poor creatures that had suffered cruelty under the hands of the taskmaster and the other teamsters.

He worked late into the night, and eventually, somewhere around midwatch, was relieved from his duties by an even younger lad who seemed to have had many dealings with the evil man with the lash. Arn could see the evidence on his face, and back, and his hands. He felt sorry for the boy. In the dim firelight, he could see no spark of hope or joy in the boy's face.

I suppose at least I'll be leaving this sort of life, Arn thought to himself. *But people are so cruel, so . . . so mean.* He was so tired, so very, very tired. It seemed like years since he had left his little village. *I just want my nice warm bed, and Greymist to say goodnight to, and talk to me as he always did.*

Arn was thrown, in a rough fashion, by one of the cooks, a bowl of some sort of gruel, with what looked like green pieces of meat. It did not look very good, but he was so hungry, he found himself devouring it before he knew what was happening.

Surprisingly, it didn't taste as bad as it looked or smelled. Arn was told he would stay there that night, and he would be watched. A gruff watchman walked up to him and said, "Lad, you'll sleep right there on the ground this night, and I'll have me eye out for you. You see this lantern on the pole?"

"Aye."

"I can see a long way with it, and I got good eyes at night, boy. You don't see me, that don't mean I don't see you. You run, I will catch you, and I'll make good sport of you!" He laughed aloud as another burly man came up and slapped him on the back.

Arn fell back where he sat, and tried to pull what meager coverings he had over him. It was getting quite chilly. Arn had not seen a battle this day, but now as he looked from the ground, just over the rise, he could see a glow that was not from this camp.

Could that be the enemy? Arn thought. *I wonder what they are doing. Why are we camping so close to the enemy? Can't they attack us at night? Can't the goors see at night better than we can? I wonder why we are just sitting so close to the enemy. What strange ways war has.*

Arn's eyes lowered, as he contemplated all the difficulties of war he had never thought of before. Baggage trains, tons of supplies, people who didn't seem to want to fight, and people who seemed to be greatly amused by it, all on the same side on the battlefield. How strange.

War is a complicated beast, thought Arn, as the exhaustion of the past days caught up to him, and his eyes found rest.

CHAPTER FIVE

ARMIES OF THE KING

Arn had no pleasant dreams that night. But he did have one dream just before dawn, a dream that shook him to his very core. It was a horrible dream, of a black steed, as black as night, as black as cave dark, and upon its back a creature clothed in dark colors with a stench that you could smell even in sleep. He even heard a low growl. The creature rode by on some dark road, as Arn was looking at him. Arn was hiding behind a tree and he hoped whoever the rider was, he wouldn't see him. There was a terrible evil in that man, beast, creature, whatever it was, that gave him a fright.

He woke with a start, to the noise of screaming and talking. He could still smell the horrible stench of that evil rider. He had never smelled anything fouler; it was surely the crypts of old, decayed and abandoned.

He scrubbed his eyes and saw moving fires and something else in front of him. Something . . . *What is that? Is that some sort of . . . ?* Arn reached out and touched it, and with a start, he gasped and pulled his hand back.

There were feet in front of his nose, horrible smelling feet. Is this man asleep? The man was quite sound asleep, snoring loudly, making a terrible growling noise.

Arn thought, *how could anybody be so unpleasant? I've never smelled anything worse in a stable.* He sat up and dusted himself off and pulled the blanket tighter around him. He hacked a vaporous cough in the cool early morning air, trying to forget the unpleasant odor as much as he could. He looked about, wondering what was happening. He could see men firing torches, and he could hear yelling and horses tromping in the distance.

The words became clearer, "It's a raid! We hit them with a raid and now they've hit us!"

A raid? What . . . The man ran off before Arn could ask any questions. Arn stood up and felt excitement in his weary limbs. He felt a bit rested, but not much. He probably had not been asleep very long. He managed to stretch and moved his aching limbs about to shake off the stiffness. He didn't think he would be going back to sleep. Arn picked up his things, still looking about at all the excitement, intending to ask someone just what he should be doing.

A few feet away he spied a man that he thought had to be the ugliest he had ever seen. The man was stooping over a bundle upon the ground, rummaging through it, obviously trying to find something. Arn thought he would ask him. Maybe he would know.

The man was wearing some sort of skins, and had a rough, squat stance. He reminded Arn of old Jake Peterson in the village, a squat little man who wasn't actually as little as he looked, but had bowed legs and could lift a mule, they said, over his head.

Arn approached the man cautiously, looking at his ragged clothes, his stinking fur and what looked like heavy sandals.

Arn said, "Excuse me, sir, I'm very sorry to interrupt your looking, but I was wondering . . . ."

The man looked up with a fire in his eyes, and Arn realized to his horror that he wasn't just ugly, he wasn't a man! Arn stepped back, his mouth agape. He had never seen a creature like this, but he knew what it was. He knew all too well what it was!

He recognized the grey skinned, black wrinkled depths of that horrible face, broken yellow teeth with sharp jutting edges, and what looked to be fangs. It had eyes like those of a pig but glowing red, a snout nose splayed out with large gaping nostrils, and black oozy hair upon its filthy head.

Arn was certain that the army of the king employed no such creature. He fumbled for his dagger, but it had been taken from him by the mean sergeant who had escorted him to the baggage train.

He could think of nothing else to say but, "Nice goor, I have to go over here." He quickly turned and ran as fast as he could in the other direction. The creature snorted behind him, and he knew in a second he would hear the bowed legs running after him. But to Arn's amazement, he heard no running.

He ran to the nearest pack mule, a little grey fellow who was braying and looking wild-eyed at Arn as he approached. The mule recognized the goor stench. Arn hid behind the mule, since he couldn't think of anywhere else to go, and there was nothing else to hide him. He stood behind the mule praying, wondering how he could fight something like that.

He watched the creature in the distant flickering of the firelight search through the packages, apparently find a few things, and place them in a ragged, black, coarsely woven bag. Arn thought, *he's looting the baggage! He's looting!*

This was a raid, and he was a raider, stealing things from the baggage. Arn had to take this in for a minute. The king's baggage. *What should I do?* Arn looked at the mule for an answer, and the mule looked at Arn. He seemed to be comforted by Arn's presence.

Arn had tended to him nicely several times in the evening, while others had not been so nice. Arn patted him on the head, and said, "What do we do?"

The mule looked at Arn with what seemed like wisdom for just an instant, and down to where Arn had been sleeping moments before, next to the sleeping, smelly man. Arn saw a dark bundle just beside the man's hand.

He's got a weapon; that's a club, thought Arn, as he looked at the mule and kissed him on his snout. *I'll wake him up, that's what I'll do!*

Arn ran over to the stinky man and prodded him with his feet. The man opened his mouth and let forth a horrible stench, a stench of really bad grog, Arn could tell, and Arn knew he wasn't going to wake up any time soon.

The grey mule pulled on its tether, trying to get further away from the villain who was pillaging the baggage.

"Help! Somebody help! A looter, a pillager, a villain, a raider! Someone!" Arn yelled several times, but nobody came. A sleeping man even yelled for Arn to shut up.

Arn could not stand by doing nothing, so he picked up the heavy wooden club at his feet, and looked at it. It was black wood, very strong. He knew of black wood. This was actually a pretty nice weapon for this burly, stinky and obviously not very wealthy man to have. It had been made quite well and Arn counted five notches in it. He wondered if this drunken soldier had busted five heads with it.

The grip of it in his hands was comfortable, though it was quite heavy. Maybe. An idea slowly came to Arn.

He had to do the right thing, and that was to defend the king's baggage. Whether the king would kill him later this day or not, that was up to the king, but he had to do the right thing.

He thought, he felt, the right thing would be to knock that creature in the head. Arn hefted the heavy club with two hands and slowly approached, as quietly as he could, slowly, step by step, and the closer he got to the creature, the more fear he felt.

Those creatures were so horrible; they were used to scare children. Stories of their brutality, their evil, their ugliness, their stench, all rang through his head as he remembered the monks and others of the tavern telling him stories of the wretched creatures with claws long enough to tear a man's throat out.

If you were bitten by one it could be fatal. Their saliva and their bodies in general were so filthy, the monks had told him. Their bites were like a poison that created a terrible illness.

Arn prayed as he crept closer and closer to the hunched, dark figure. He kept wondering, *why isn't anybody doing anything? Why is he looting so easily? And what is he looking for so intently?*

His steps faltered. *They are so strong, and they are fast. I'm not very fast and I'm not that strong either. If I can just get a little closer,* he thought, and he moved as quietly as a mouse.

As Arn crept, he intently stared at the back of the creature's head, which had no helm. The creature was intently searching through another bundle and throwing the contents on the ground.

Arn carefully made the last two steps toward the goor, but was not careful enough. He was not paying close enough attention to where he was walking, and stumbled on some cook pots that the creature had thrown out.

It turned upon Arn with its yellowish-red, hideous, glowing eyes, and almost seemed to have a smile upon its face when it saw the club raised in Arn's hands.

Arn barely recognized speech close to common, the words, "You are going to hit us with the stinkin' foul human stick." It laughed, a hideous hissing sort of noise, and Arn felt mortified. All the horror stories came washing back again, with all the fear.

Then a thought came upon Arn, *what difference does it make? I'm dead today anyway. I'm not going to be afraid of this creature. I'm not a boy any more. I'm not a little child.*

Arn managed to get out the words, "Flee, and I won't."

The creature actually laughed so hard it grabbed its sides and howled a hideous, screeching howl, lifting its head up in the air.

It shrieked, "You'll do what? You'll let me go, foul little stinkin' wretch of a human child? I'll eat you this night for my feast! Me and me mates will feast on . . . ."

And with that Arn decided he'd heard enough. With all his might, with all of his thought upon where the creature's mouth was, as it pulled a wicked-looking, curved dagger from its belt, Arn let the big club fall upon its broken-toothed face as hard as he possibly could.

The creature fell back upon the trunk, black blood oozing all over the place. He had broken the creature's nose and at least several of its teeth.

Leaning down, he bashed the creature in its left knee, which was sticking up, and thought, *at least it won't stand well if it stands up and tries to attack.*

He smashed the bowed leg quite well, placing its former knee joint in two different locations.

The creature did not seem to acknowledge the second blow. Arn looked more closely and saw that it had fallen upon something and hit the back of its head. In the flickering light of the watch fire, he thought there was black blood oozing from there as well.

Arn thought, *I did it! I got him. That nasty creature, the one I was afraid of when I was a little kid.* He lifted the bloody club in the air, and did one final blow to the creature, realizing he would prefer it did not get back up and speak again.

Arn shuddered. Even dispatching such a foul creature made him feel a bit unhappy. The creature had been quite helpless when he gave him the second blow, but then again he had never heard any fair deeds done by these goor.

Warped, twisted and evil, they had only malice, evil and greed on their minds. Arn had freed the world of one more tree-cutting fiend, one more dog-eating demon. He was satisfied after a moment.

"I got you," Arn pointed his dirty finger at the creature. "And that's because I was right, and you were wrong. Because my hand was guided and your mouth was foul!"

At least I did this and I'm a hero here. I can show anybody I did that. I did the right thing. Maybe the king will let me go, Arn began to think. *He'll see that I saved some of his baggage. This could even be the king's own baggage!*

He looked about for someone to talk to but saw lanterns flickering, torches going back and forth, but nobody close by at all.

I'll just stay here with it, he thought. *When it gets full light, someone will come over and see that I saved this stuff.* He looked at the things tossed around by the looter, and saw some cooking pots and some unusual things he had not seen before. One item, Arn picked up and thought it looked familiar. He remembered a visitor to Clayhaven, a journeyman, who used to mark out land for the king, having something similar.

It was a small black tube, about eight inches long, tapered at the end, with what looked like an actual glass front. Arn remembered how the journeyman had twisted his, and with a twist and a pop, out came a much longer device, now well over a foot. *Yes, it is one of those eyepieces, far eyes, I think he called it. Hand scope.* Arn looked into the smaller glass end and peered around at the chaos in the distance.

He could see men mounted on horses. They were looking around. It didn't look like any serious fight was going on. Perhaps here and there raiders had jumped into the baggage train. Maybe it wasn't even an organized raid. It could have been a few greedy ones who had sneaked into the king's camp for valuable loot, before the battle would come later this day.

Arn would really have liked to keep the scope, and in fact had dreamed of owning one, after seeing how it worked. He tucked it into his belt somewhat defiantly, thinking that he was going to be killed later on anyway. *It's right here for everyone to see, so they can't accuse me of taking it.* They hadn't believed him about the sword, though, and he knew he had to return the scope.

As the sky became a few degrees lighter, he realized there was a very faint, sickening noise in the distance. A most unpleasant noise. It reminded him of the noise made by village boys playing drum on the rotted body of a horse one day, when a bloated, horrible corpse had floated upon the Haven River.

Thum, thum, thum-thum-thum. It was quite far away. Probably the other army rising up for the day. Just then, closer, the horns of the king, and drums and pipes began to play. The day was dawning and battle was close at hand.

Some men passed close by Arn, but ignored him as he tried to get their attention to tell them of his victory. Absently Arn began to place the items back into the containers from which they seemed to have come.

The drums of the king's muster were stronger now, from the left and right. Baggage handlers were stirring about. The sun began to rise over what would soon be a battlefield, and in the distant past had been a battlefield.

Arn wondered if he would see the end of this day. Surely it would be a day to keep the king exceedingly busy. Yesterday, he had had a sinking suspicion that at today's dawn he would suffer his fate at the king's hand, and would be the main attraction of the morning. Now he felt hope that the king would have mercy for today.

With much effort, he pushed the heavy, stinky creature off of the trunk over which he had fallen, so that he could pack away the items remaining on the ground. He decided to leave a few items out, in hope that nobody would doubt his story that the creature had been looting. Arn was quite proud of his efforts in protecting the king's baggage.

He took the scope off of his belt and placed inside the trunk, at the top, so it could be easily seen that this valuable item was safe.

Arn guarded his prize for quite a while before anyone noticed. Finally one of the baggage masters came and asked, "Boy, what is that?"

"It's a goor, sir."

"Yah, that it is. And what will ye be doing with it?"

"I slew it, sir," stammered Arn.

"You slew that, boy?"

"Aye, he was looting the baggage, and I'm guarding it."

The baggage master chuckled, "I don't believe it! You're awful scrawny to be doing that!"

"I'm not that small, sir, and he was looting. See the scope? He had that and some other stuff."

"Aye?" The man looked about appraisingly. "Hmm."

The man's keen eye took in the scene, as well as the black, gory blood spatters that were drying on Arn's tunic and brechs. The club Arn held also gave evidence with the black blood and hairs still on it.

The man clasped Arn upon the shoulder and said, "Well done, lad."

This was the first time since his conscription that anyone had acknowledged that Arn was indeed telling the truth. He was very pleased and relieved.

"That's a foul beast. You're very lucky, lad. Did you sneak up on him?"

"Aye, then he turned, and was drawing that wicked dagger there . . ."

"You keep that, lad, it's a fine souvenir," he interrupted. "It's not the best of steel, but it's a good dagger."

"But . . ." Arn stumbled over the words, "I'm a prisoner, sir."

"You are? Why is that?"

"They say I stole a nobleman's sword, but I didn't, sir." Arn's words rushed together. "I slew the people who killed the nobleman, and I was trying to return the blade to the king."

Arn thought the man showed the wisdom of his years as he scratched his head, considering Arn's words. Obviously he had a lot of experience, with pale grey eyes, grey hair, and a droopy white moustache. His clothing was quite a bit better than many of the muleskinners and teamsters. He wore a kindly expression, such as Arn had not seen since he left his friends from the village, and his kindness gave Arn courage.

"Sir, would you tell them I did indeed strike down the beast and protect this property? Maybe they will tell the king? Maybe he won't . . ."

"What's he going to do, lad?"

"Well, I think he's planning to . . ."

The man nodded. "Sorry about that, lad. Well, we've got a lot of problems today. The baggage was raided three times during the night, in this area alone. But you got one. I'm proud of you."

Arn said, "Thank you, sir, for your kind words. I'm just glad I could help."

"Well, you did a good job. I'll put in a word for you, but I don't know what weight it'll hold, especially with our high king and all, but I'll say it. Can't let you just take punishment when you done such a fine job protecting my baggage."

Arn smiled for the first time in a while. "You are most a gentleman, sir."

The man smiled a toothy grin. As Arn watched, the man fished about in a greasy, brown leather pouch. "Here." He threw Arn a piece of way bread and two small pieces of jerked beef. "Eat that, looks you could be hungry."

He fished in another pouch and brought out a very small, sweet cake. It looked delicious. It was frosted with white, and had a small, dried cherry on top. "I was saving this, but I think you've earned it." He patted Arn on the arm as he handed him the cake.

"Well, let's see if we can get this wicked creature out of here. It's starting to stink! Wait a minute, it was already stinkin', it's just stinkin' worse!" The man chuckled to himself. "This is going to be a bad day for the king, I fear."

"Why?"

"Why? We been raided not just here, but in other places during the night. That army, if those fires are true that we saw last night, we counted more than nine score campfires. That's a big army over there. It's not a bluff, say the scouts, but we been fooled before."

"Fooled, sir?"

"Aye, sometimes if you put in enough fires at night, have people change out pennants and flags and such, if you know where they're watching, you can make 'em think there's more of you than really are. That's what a famous raider called the Grey Ghost did. He would sneak into the Nothlands, and had a funny way of foolin', makin' the dark ones think there's more of his number than was. He often fooled 'em. The dark one uses that trick too now." With a sober expression, he shook his head.

"There are a lot of 'em, then," Arn looked serious.

"We're lookin' around at least seven, eight thousand, and it's been growin' all night. The king's army here, he can muster about twenty-five hundred."

Arn answered, "I'm not the greatest in math, but those are not very good odds."

"Aye, it's not. The great army up the way will do well for the king, but we can't join them, we're cut off, and they've another army facin' 'em. This is a full-fledged invasion."

Arn gazed across the field at the forest of trees. He could see nothing ominous but smoke of fires in the dawn light. He began to feel a chill he had not felt before. Receiving penalty of the sword from the king was one thing, but the thought of being chopped up by those creatures was quite another. A shudder went through his body.

The old baggage master observed this and reassured Arn, "Don't be scared, lad, don't think of it. I've been through many a battle. We'll save this baggage, that's my job, and let the king worry about his job. He'll take care of things, don't you worry."

"Aye, sir."

"Name's Cavanaugh. You know, I think that old king oughta listen to me when I say that I think you're a good lad. Of course, there's no guarantee, but who's to say what the day will bring. Troops are already mustering down. Come, let's watch. You've earned a view of the grandeur of war. You haven't seen it yet, have you?"

"No."

"It always surprises me. I still can't get over it. I used to be with those knights, until some things happened." He scratched his head and spit to the left as they walked to the top of a small knoll, not too far from the king's hill. They looked out at many troops mustering, and saw many colors of the king's army with purple, grey and gold predominating, those being the king's colors. The king's coat of arms, a medium blue wolf's head with a golden crown, was visible on two of the four quadrants on his standard. On the other two rested a silver and gold key, the keys to the kingdom of Southaven.

There were retainers, lords, nobles, and minor kings. They saw horses, squires, archers, men-at-arms, peasants, and knights armed with shiny steel-tipped lances, carrying colorful pennants that represented their lands. The king's personal royal guard, resplendent in purple and grey, was starting to mount at the foot of the king's hill, ready for battle. The squires were busily helping them to their steeds.

Archers nearby were checking their sharp-tipped arrows. There were strange looking, fine-pointed tips, and some with v-shaped tips. Arn wondered aloud, "What are those v-shaped ones for?"

One of the archers answered, "We use it for several things, cutting an apple from a tree, for instance." He laughed along with several of his friends. "But it's mostly meant for cutting rope, if you hit it just right, works pretty good."

"I've never seen one. That's clever," stated Arn.

The archers observed Arn standing with the baggage master, and invited him, "Here, take a look." With a quick gesture, and perfect precision, he threw the arrow so that it landed between Arn's feet.

"You must be good at darts, sir. We've played that at the tavern."

"Aye, I'm the best," he boasted with a grin and a raised eyebrow. "I've never been beaten."

"I believe it!" Arn picked up the grey and purple fletched arrow, and looked at the long, white shaft. "Is this white wood, sir?"

"Aye, from the elves. It's very uncommon."

"Wow, a beautiful arrow. You stuck it well into the sod."

"I don't miss."

"Good marks this day, sir."

"Thank ye, lad. We'll be giving them the two-fingers today."

"Two fingers? What is that?"

"That's an old gesture. It means, well, a long time ago, some of the better border watchmen, along the border of the Dark Lands, were captured. They were very good archers, and they worked with the elves. Now, the goor, they hate the elves. They despise their love of the trees and of the land. The grey watchers in the woods, that's what they're called, the king's watchmen, a small group, was surrounded and captured by the goor. Over a score of them. The goor had never had quite a victory like that. It was magic and guile that day helped them. The gist of the story, lad, they captured these men, and the high wizard ordered, just as a lesson, that their two arrow fingers of the right hand, that they had done so much damage with, should be cut off and fed to their mounts."

Arn could not control a look of disgust. "That's awful! What cruelty!"

"Yeah, and the fate afterwards was quite cruel as well." All the archers within hearing bowed their heads as if in prayer, and some crossed themselves as a warning. "But we, you might see later this day, in victory or in defiance, will raise two fingers to the air, high! A symbol of our keeping of our fingers and our never forgetting our contempt of our goorish foe." He showed the gesture to Arn.

Arn started. "Isn't that quite a rude gesture?"

"Aye, they'll find it rather rude when our feathers are in their throats." The archers raised their hands with two fingers up, and whooped and shouted. A group of archers yelled, "Vive le roi!" They must be from the Seine regions, where Arn had heard the ladies were most beautiful, with radiant fair skin and long, dark hair. They hit each other on the back, before turning back to their preparations for war. They had packed so many arrows, it seemed to Arn.

The old baggage master was smiling as he spoke, "Our mustering point's ahead, boys, about 200 paces. We'll see you, lads! Fair day! Good luck to you." He was starting to walk down the hill.

"Wait!" cried Arn, as he ran up to the tall archer with dark hair and keen eyes, to return his arrow. "It's a fine arrow, thank you, sir."

"I've cut many a rope with that, won some contests, even the kiss of a fair lady, once."

"Really? I've always wanted to kiss a fair . . ." Arn's words froze as his face turned red with embarrassment, and he looked away.

The man laughed at that, slapped Arn hard on the back, and said, "Don't worry, you'll have the kiss of many a fair lady yet, don't you worry."

"Here." The archer pulled an arrow tip from his pocket, quite sharp. "This is an armor piercer, lad. Goes right through linked chain armor quite well. You keep that."

Arn stared at the finely crafted tip. The archer said, "Don't have time to refletch it now, anyways. Make good use of it, lad. Kiss many a fair lady for me, if I don't come back this day!"

"You'll come back," Arn countered, turning away. "You're the kind who always does, and tells fine stories in the tavern about it all."

The archer's hair blew in a gust of wind and he added, "And wins many a dart contest too, don't forget."

Arn waved and ran back towards Cavanaugh, keeping his eyes on the activities of the archers.

They went forward to their starting point to the front and off to the right of the king's army. When they arrived there, they placed their arrows, and several long stakes they had carried on their backs, in front of them.

He asked Cavanaugh, "What are those stakes for? Are they for keeping the mounted beasts away?"

"Aye, very keen, lad. Who told you that?"

"Nobody did, I just know that horses and just about any beast fears a sharp point."

The man pointed at some men-at-arms nearby. "Look at those men there."

Arn saw them using spit stones to sharpen their halberds, military billhooks and military forks. "That's a fine unit. Is it from the king's castle?"

"Aye, they are his personal heavy men-at-arms. See that fine chain mail, those helms, those shields? They place those shields in the ground, and with some rope they can make a fine, knotted wall, and they fight from behind it. If the battle goes well, they take out those daggers they carry there, those short swords, you might say, hack down through the ropes and charge forth. Many a Nothlund regiment's been slaughtered under their might. You can see what happened to some of the Nothlund leaders slain upon the battlefield." The man nodded toward the regimental banners flying over their heads. Two skulls stared out from the tops of the banner poles.

"It's a fearsome unit, sir."

"Aye, one of the best. And look at those peasants over there, ready for battle too." The weapons were mostly agricultural implements, and the men dirty and disorganized, but most looked strong and ready to go.

He continued, "They don't even want to be here, they are afraid, but there's a lot of them. And they'll be fierce in a charge. As long as things go well, they'll stand and fight. Of course, they don't have any armor, and their weapons aren't the best. If things go bad, you'll see them goin'. But every one they kill is a dead one just the same."

The two stood watching the scene a moment, until the old baggage master quietly spoke. "It's time to get back to the horses. Remember I'll put in a good word for you."

"Thank you. That is most kind."

Cavanaugh turned to go, but then something caught his eye. He raised his arm and pointed down the hill, as Arn followed his gaze. The high king emerged from his tent. His armor was shinier than most of the other armor. The morning sun glinted off of it as if it were a clear lake in high summer.

"That armor is made by dwarves. They take from the earth and make such metal work as is God's gift to them."

"It's very beautiful, glowing practically."

"Aye, it's a different kind of steel."

They stood and watched the king walk towards a huge grey horse that was being led by a groomsman. The horse must be twenty hands high. He had barding of steel and felt about him.

"What an amazing horse," wondered Arn.

"Aye, he's supposed to be a smart one, too."

"Smart? I've heard of horses like that. Almost knows what you are saying."

"That's right, lad. Almost knows what you're saying."

The old man's arm went about Arn's shoulder and they stared at the king's entourage. There were many lords and nobles with different colorful standards fluttering in the morning breeze. The horns and drums began to play. Clearly they were mounting up for war. Arn thought a prayer of protection for the army this day.

Suddenly, a piercing, hollow, evil horn blasted from the other side of the forest. Many turned to look, along with Arn and the old man. In the distance, Arn could see the glinting of metal. "Sir, those glints of steel, are they . . . ?"

"Aye, lad, those are, well, looks like some are men and some are half-caste. Some are goor skirmishers coming out in the front of the wood."

The entire edge of the forest began to move, as far as Arn's eyes could see, and from the woods emerged figures, carrying glints of steel. Many were the dark, hunched figures of goor. As they moved forward details became more distinct, points of weapons, some shiny, some black, but all gleaming with hate.

A hot feeling washed over Arn and made him sick to his stomach. "I've heard of those cruel two-spanned arrows, sir. Some are tipped with poison and some are enchanted with evil magic."

"Aye, lad. Don't want to get hit with one."

More horns blew, and two ranks had stepped out of the woods, as far as he could see. There was a clamor of screeching and howling that was getting louder. Some figures were taller, dark-haired, wearing furs from the north. They were fearsome-looking men, howling like the goor who surrounded them.

"Why do those men serve the Dark One?"

"Who knows why men do what they do, lad. There's evil in a man's heart. If you are not careful and blessed, it'll take you over," spoke the wise older man. He gazed at Arn's face, and saw him shudder. "Don't worry, lad, they're just skirmishers. They'll fire a few volleys, try to kill off some of the higher ranks if they're lucky. They're not that good though. Our archers will make quick work of them. They'll break and run."

"Really?" wondered Arn in amazement. It was hard to believe that these fierce-looking, fiery creatures would run away from battle.

"Oh, aye, our archers hardly ever miss," the old man said with a chuckle. "The skirmishers will just fire mass volleys, but if anyone gets near them with a sword, an axe or a lance, they'll be turnin' on their heels."

Arn scratched his head. He could see the black banners, some with various markings, but all bore the red goblet of the Dark One. "That symbol is frightening."

The man knew about the goblet. "The blood goblet is a fearsome flag, lad. First time you've ever seen it, I take it."

Arn just nodded and swallowed.

Cavanaugh gripped his shoulder. "Steel, boy. Steel yourself. Ain't no good to worry. What is, is. What's gonna be, is that too. We got a good army here. The king and his counsel are wise and good. He's beat this number before, and three, four, even six times this number once on the field."

The king's army had formed several lines, stretched out in both directions as far as Arn could see. Some areas were two lines deep, some three. Behind the lines were units of men waiting.

"Who are the men waiting there?" asked Arn.

"Those are reserves. As the battle goes, and the king needs them, they'll fill in the holes, wherever they may appear. If there's a push that does well, they will join in the push and hopefully break the enemy. That's one of the ways a battle works."

Two armies, many, many foes facing each other on a sunny fall day. Arn knew in just a while blood would be thick across the field.

Dismembered limbs, men howling. He had heard the stories in the tavern, and they had never sounded good. Arn solemnly considered his first view of warfare. He hoped he wouldn't be one of those victims on the field this day.

He smiled a humorless smile at the man beside him. It seemed so remote a chance that this man might just save him from the king's wrath, and convince him Arn did not steal the sword. That Arn would not indeed die in battle this day, and that one day soon he would see his beloved Clayhaven again.

CHAPTER SIX

A BATTLE AND A NEW KNIGHT

*C*avanaugh *intently stared at the scene before them. The enemy's line* of skirmishers seemed to divide near the center, and Arn watched as three riders approached from behind. The center rider was stooped and dark. He was flanked by two equally dark and sinister figures. All three rode huge, angry horses. One of the beasts, black as a moonless night, reared up and kicked his front feet in the air, and a cold shiver fell on Arn. He stared at the horse and rider and the truth dawned. He recognized these two. "That was the horse! And that foul man who stayed at the inn!"

"Where, lad?"

Arn pointed at them in amazement. It was astonishing that he had himself been so close to such a creature and his revolting rider, and his horror was full to realize they rode at the center of the enemy's line. "A few eves ago, in Clayhaven, I saw them."

"Aye? That's a scout, I believe. I've heard of him on his monstrous creature he rides. He's a foul one. Not living, son."

"He's not living? But I was close to him!" Arn screeched as he felt his throat tightening with fear.

"Don't worry, lad. Unfortunately, you've probably heard, the Dark One uses the unwholesome dead to do his work. They tramp about endlessly, no rest. Frightening aspects of what was once alive." Cavanaugh took a very deep breath and let it out forcefully. "Some with the flesh falling from the bones, some are just pure bone. I've seen 'em, lad. He was in your town spying. Probably other towns as well, finding out what he wanted to know for his filthy master."

"Who's his master? On that large beast there? That huge man. He must be over seven feet."

"Aye, even at this distance, with his hunched frame, you can tell he's a tall one. Well, he's not a man anymore either. He's long since passed this world, flesh anyway. Don't know what he looks like under that cowl, don't want to know! Some men who've seen him freeze in their very tracks. He's right out of the pit, lad. Evil, greedy, full of malice. Cunning though, and strong. That's Angueth. And that snarly creature he rides upon is Blood Hoof."

The sun seemed not to even smile upon Angueth, for there was no gleam seen on him, or even the normal glistening of the horse's hair as he reared up and whinnied in anger. They were an incongruous black shadow on a sunny fall morning. Even at this distance Arn could feel their hatred, their desire for death.

"Angueth. And Blood Hoof," Arn whispered. "I've heard of them."

As Arn watched, Angueth on his horrible mount came forward of the line. Contemptuous in his carriage, he sat upright as if daring the archers to throw one arrow in his direction. The crossbowmen seemed ready to fire upon him at an instant's notice, but none raised their bows yet. They stared at the great rider as he came towards the king's army.

Without warning, a loud, booming, hissing voice issued from Angueth. "Who of this rabble dares treat with me? I am the servant of the Dark One himself, chosen this day to slaughter you pigs and foul, living filth. Who will come treat? Perhaps my kind mercy might shine upon you this day as this filthy sun shines upon this field. Come forth and speak." Arn was startled to his bones, and wondered what sort of magic Angueth used to make his hissing voice sound as if it were just in your ear.

By contrast, the king's voice sounded almost musical, while loud, powerful and full of courage. "I, High King of Southaven, do not treat with the filth of the earth. You are in our lands and this day our blades will send you back to the hell whence you came. Be gone from here! Be gone, and mayhap we will not follow."

Angueth's wheezing cackle sounded too close. "Oh, it is you! I'm so pleased. Oh great king!" he mocked. "I thought perhaps you were with the main host. How interesting! Oh, our plans are sweet and true this day!"

The king's counselors were deep in discussion with one another, and Arn could not tell if they were listening to these words.

"Peasant ruler of Southaven, know that thy time has come! My lord has sent me to slay you and put you up in a moldering grave, perhaps to be summoned later for my master's pleasure, to serve him!" There issued a dry, hissing cackle from the dark figure. "Your time is over, high king! Your lands are ours! Our victory is this day!"

Many in the ranks shuddered at these words. The sky above them seemed to darken, as if fear were a palpable entity coming to hover over the field. It was a darkness Arn had never seen before. There were indeed some black clouds, but there were also some flying things.

"What is that?" Arn wondered aloud, as all eyes on the field looked up.

Cavanaugh answered, "The caul. The black caul, as it's called. It flies over the dark army. Some are bats, some are demon birds from the very pit of hell, nasty creatures, sort of like vultures but at least vultures are doing honest work. These are frightening things, not living. They feed upon the field as the men lay dead and dying. Those clouds, they spit a burning rain that you'll want to cloak yourself from. It's ash from the burning mountains over the great northern lakes. I've seen it for myself, living maggots come in it, and feast upon the dead. You might have heard of it."

The sky became darker and darker. Arn heard distant squeaks, chirping, and the flapping of unwholesome wings. "This Angueth is quite high in the arms of his dark master," finished Cavanaugh quietly. "Just remember the king has beaten these and worse many a time, as his fathers have before him."

Arn's eyes found the king, standing above the battlefield on his hill. The king pulled a large hand and a half sword from its scabbard. His purple and grey mantle rippled in the crisp breeze that had arrived with the black caul. He made a magnificent figure, every bit the hero, as the last rays of the sun shone upon his blade. As Arn watched, the light multiplied as it shone and somehow fanned out over the king's ranks.

The high king spoke words, ancient and old, that Arn did not recognize.

Arn realized he was seeing, first hand, the high king of Southaven with the renowned Blade of Old. "The king hasn't ever brought that sword out before, has he?" asked Arn wonderingly.

"No, lad, he hasn't, not that I know, and I would know. It was in the tomb of his fathers. I wonder why he has brought it out this day, on this field." Cavanaugh looked puzzled as well. "Things must be dark indeed," he added, almost to himself, but of course Arn heard.

Despite his determination to be strong, Arn felt cold trembling start in his arms and hands. He felt very thirsty.

As if he realized this sight must be overwhelming a young man, his first time in battle, Cavanaugh continued, louder, "Just look at the effect that the Blade is having there."

The light that reflected from the Blade of Old washed out, down the ranks, and even up the hillock where Arn and Cavanaugh stood. The king's army began to cheer and yell their loyalties and promises to the king, raising their fists. As the light flooded over the hill, Arn's trembling vanished in an instant, and in its place he felt vigor, strength and determination to win this battle.

As the light fanned out and reached the terrible, black rider in the middle of the field, he emitted a sickening, hissing shriek, turned quickly about on his mount, and returned to his lines. Many of the skirmishers on the far side of the field actually turned and ran, to Arn's disbelief. The cruel taskmasters with sharp, barbed sticks and short whips chased them down and forced them to return to their lines.

Arn was filled with hope. "I think this day will go for us."

"Aye, lad." Cavanaugh patted him on the back. He glanced nervously around to the woods surrounding them. "I just don't like these woods off to the left, and right. Even though this is a field of old, where victories for the king have occurred, and we have skirmishers out in those woods . . ." He bent his head down and spit, and scratched the back of his neck.

Arn was thankful to Cavanaugh for his kindness, and told him so. "And thanks especially for the sweet cake."

"You might go ahead and eat it now. You never know what the day will hold." Cavanaugh started off to his work. "I'll be over there with that great lot of pack horses. They seem quite nervous."

"Thank you, Cavanaugh. You have been most kind, and I won't forget it. I never do."

"You do that, lad." He reached up and ruffled Arn's hair. Arn was not a short boy, but slight, and felt young as dirt and dust fell out around his eyes. "Have you ever heard of bathing, lad?" Cavanaugh teased with a grin. "It's not so bad as you've heard."

Arn smiled a sheepish smile. Just now his mind was racing with so much going on around him, he was too preoccupied to be offended. As Cavanaugh left, Arn was determined to take the best care of the animals he could. The raiders had come once; they might come again.

The king on his glorious horse went down to the base of the hill, followed by his entourage, perhaps to encourage the ballista crew to assemble the large crossbow-type artillery more quickly. Those could be used to good effect against mass troops, as well as fortified walls.

Arn worked diligently taking care of the horses. As more pack animals arrived, he removed their wet tack, brushed them down, and staked them in green pasture. His body was busy with hard work, but his mind was aware that neither army had fired an arrow, and he felt uneasy. He glanced over his shoulder many times, at the field and at the edges of the forest.

The dark figure remained sitting near the edge of the woods, with his growing host, gesturing in different directions. One of the minions gestured at one point to the woods on Arn's right, and Arn looked intently, wishing he could see through the trees. At times he could see some of the king's soldiers and spearmen walking in the dark, thick pine trees.

He was startled to see several small, hunched shapes moving very quickly from the great forest towards the woods on the right. They moved so fast, Arn couldn't be completely sure he was not imagining them. They reminded him of groundhogs, but they were larger than groundhogs. They waddled, but moved very fast. Perhaps they were some poor beasts scared from the forest by the black creatures. He lifted a prayer for the soldiers in the woods to beware.

His eye kept returning to the dark leader, like a moth to flame. The rider raised his full stature in the saddle, almost nobly, a reminder that he had been born and raised noble, human once. He raised his great, black-gauntleted hand high in the air, making a gesture with his hand that Arn did not recognize. His voice was not amplified as it had been in the field, but Arn could just hear him say horribly, "Now, my children, this time, this day has come at last! Fear not the foul blade of old, dead kings! Fear not the light of the sun, for it shall be vanquished! This day, your victory shall be assured! My children, now stand strong with steel in your spines and prepare! Those foul across the way will die and flee before you! Southaven is ours!"

His entire line began to yell, some of the creatures jumping and doing back flips. They seemed incongruously happy, with such a noble king upon the field, and the sun behind him. Something bad was afoot. Arn could feel it in his bones.

The huge arm swung down to his side, and pulled forth a blade that would be for two hands of a normal man. It was black and frightening, similar in size to the high king's sword, but not as impressive. Arn imagined how many innocent had been slaughtered with the point and edge of this sword. Many a story had been told in the tavern of this sword, which could hew a man or a horse in half with one stroke. Angueth wielded it with great skill.

With his left hand, the dark one pulled forth his staff of knotted, black wood. Even at this distance, about 700 paces, Arn could see the skull shape forged on the end of this mace of war. The mace was legendary, known simply as Skull. It was made of a knotted sapling of a tree from the dark lands. The skull had two red, glowing gems in the place of eyes. It was a great mace, and frightening in the wrong hands.

Arn could feel tension, and knew the time had come for something to happen. He gripped the goor sword in his belt with his right hand, wondering what might befall him and the other men this day.

Angueth called, "Move forward, to victory! Defy the fangs of death! My children sweet! Victory is yours!"

The black sword dropped, and suddenly a huge volley of black-feathered arrows arced high into the air. Arn's heart stopped as he saw this first volley fly. As the arrows came down, many of the men in the king's line screamed and grabbed their chests or limbs, wherever the cruel fangs of death caught them, and fell. A few broke off the shafts and cast them aside.

The king raised his blade, crying, "This day, my sons, evil has come upon our land! You know your duty! God is with you! I stand with you, to live or die!"

His words did not seem to have the heart they had had earlier. Arn wondered if the king had a suspicion, or knew something dire, or if he was just old for battle. He could not tell.

"To victory! For God and for Southaven!" His blade fell in a pointing gesture toward the dark ranks. To Arn's amazement, a bright light, pure as sunlight, sang forth from the blade with a crackling noise, slaying about five of the enemy skirmishers in its path. At this, Angueth skulked back towards the woods, along with several of his aides, away from the light. The men and creatures hit by the light literally burst into a flame of white light, grabbing their eyes, falling to the ground, and screaming. They didn't seem to be killed by the light, but lay on the ground screaming in agony.

Arn watched the scene unfold. If he lived, and had children one day, he would remember this day and tell his children and grandchildren about it. By then, the story would be entertaining.

Several screaming men ran from the woods, and just then, three large regiments of goor clad in black armor with black shields decorated with glowing, red goblets followed. One regiment had cruel scimitars and short swords, another carrying long swords and wearing black hides, breastplates and armor, all blazing with the red goblet. They were emitting a loud, guttural whooping sound in unison with each left step of their foot.

Another regiment seemed not to be men at all, nor goor, but tall, grey-skinned creatures Arn did not recognize. Perhaps these were the augerhul, nasty creatures akin to men, who lived in swamps and distant caves. They were cleverer than goor, but not nearly as dim-witted as trolls. They stood seven or eight feet tall. Some had no armor and Arn could see their rippling muscles as they crossed the field with halberds and billhooks. A few wore armor that looked like the scales of a fish.

The enemy regiments were closing the distance quickly, Arn realized, as he could see more details. Many were dropped skillfully by the human archers. The creatures were tall, lanky, and strong, with bulging muscles. They seemed to prefer smashing weapons such as maces and clubs. Some even wielded the huge balls on chains known as morningstars. They were not more than one hundred paces from him now.

The archers had taken a toll on the enemy, then moved back behind their protective wall of spearmen, men-at-arms and dismounted sergeants. It was the king's halberd regiment that engaged the augerhul. The grey creatures began bashing into the shields that were locked together with rope, cursing and howling in their strange language. The men did not seem to be afraid at all. They steadily, and with great discipline, managed to skewer and smash the augerhul with two-handed halberds. The beasts' necks were unprotected, and the men even cut through the bits of armor the augerhul wore.

Behind the augerhul quickly came a regiment of hunched, goorish archers, who let fly over the heads of the augerhul into the ranks of the sergeants, and even the king's own ranks.

As the battle raged, many other regiments came from the dark woods, hitting the king's men with all sorts of different weapons. One horrible unit moved very slowly from the woods, armed with great pikes, with shields locked together. They stomped determinedly, in heavy black and rusted armor, across the field. Their stomping kept time with their own drums and a strange, rhythmic horn. They had been men once, but now their very flesh had fallen, or was falling, from their bones. On most only the bone was visible. It was a regiment of the dead. They marched slowly, three ranks deep, holding their pikes.

One of the human units, upon seeing the skeletal soldiers, actually broke and many of them ran off the field, repelled by the horror of seeing human cadavers in battle. One man fell to his knees, and Arn heard over the din of battle when he screamed, "That's my brother!"

Arn had never seen such horror. A regiment of dead men, back from the grave! Or did they ever even have a grave? Did they just serve their dark master from life into death? Arn found himself feeling frightened at this ghoulish sight. He could not imagine having to be one of the men in the front, having to fight such creatures, especially when some of the men recognized the dead in the ranks. An unthinkable thing—to recognize your own relative or friend, back after death, to fight you in battle.

Arn's fear energized him and he felt he had to do something. He could not bear to get closer to the dead regiment, or the augerhul, with their howling and filthy, yellowish teeth. Arn stood frozen, staring at the specter of war. He remembered hearing stories about days like this in the tavern. He could not have imagined it would be this horrible.

Perhaps he could help someone who was wounded. Some were walking back past him, with fingers missing, a few dragging themselves along the ground, unable to walk.

He heard clanging and thundering without pause. Howls, of victory over one's opponent, and of terror and agony. It was almost too much for him. Whether in this time and place he was called boy or man, he was still very much a boy, standing on this hillock and watching this battle.

The king and his entourage were suited up for battle. Several squires assisted the king in his armor as he mounted his grey stallion. Even at his age, with heavy armor, the king was very graceful in his carriage. He was surrounded by a bodyguard detachment as he surveyed the battle to determine the best placement for his best fighters. He had but a score, but they were very strong, all endowed with the best equipment the king could provide, some of it quite magical, and all splendid in the sunlight that still fell on them.

The king spoke to messengers and raised his hand as he gave them directions, moving reserves forward and moving other units back that were being hard pressed, or had fallen back.

It reminded Arn of chess, a game he had learned to play from Father Kile. Arn had kept the pieces clean, and returned them to the stone storage chest in the peaceful abbey halls. But the screaming was all war, not a game at all.

Strange thoughts ran through Arn's mind. He would rather be cleaning chess pieces. Even cleaning privies would be better than this! Energy flooded through his limbs, and he fought the urge to run. He thought, *Nobody is paying attention to me. I could just leave!*

But if the king fell today in this battle, he would be free. The charge of stealing a sword would be forgotten. He could even go back home. If he did run, he would leave behind his beloved dagger, and risk the wrath of the king, if the king did indeed live.

Several men ran from the woods, and just at the edge of the field, fell to their faces with great black arrows placed precisely in their backs. Arn saw a young oak bend and touch the ground, shortly followed by a creature with slick skin emerging from the woods. It was taller than two men, and pushed trees aside as it strode to the battle.

It pulled a cedar up by its roots and used it as a club. The man he hit was knocked to the ground and let out a cry that Arn could hear from his position on the hillock.

It must be a battle troll! He had heard stories of these creatures, and had thought they were all dead. A brave soldier approached the troll with a long spear, and the troll howled and smashed him with the uprooted cedar.

Parts of the regiment that had been anchored to the woods began to break and run. The officer stood and yelled, "Refuse the right! Refuse the right!" Arn thought this was a command for the regiment to form some kind of defense to their right, but it was in vain. To his horror, in just four strides, the troll reached the leader, and picked him up. The leader jabbed at the troll's chest armor, which had no effect other than to cause the troll to bellow with laughter as he threw the leader back into the woods.

This creature had broken a regiment single-handedly as the men ran in terror. The troll clearly spied the king and his guards, and immediately, with all of its strength, began running towards the king. Bits and pieces of black armor that had been haphazardly applied to the creature flapped up and down and clanked as it ran.

Behind the troll in the woods appeared red, glowing lights, like the dying embers of a coal. From the woods men still streamed. Obviously whatever units had been in the woods were now breaking. Huge, black arrows thumped out of the woods and bit precisely into the men as they fled. The accuracy was unbelievable, as each arrow seemed to find a human mark.

The king gave no evidence that he saw the approaching troll. Arn took off running to warn the king. Surely the king must have seen the huge threat. Why was he not doing something?

Arn yelled, "Your majesty! My lord!" He did not think his cries could be heard over the din of battle. To Arn's relief, however, the king did look to his right, towards the troll. The king's face registered shock. He had not noticed the troll's lumbering charge. He had been preoccupied with a messenger.

As it ran, the troll pushed over a supply cart, smashing it to the ground and pulling the poor donkey down with it, onto its back. The creature did not slow down but smashed through the king's own tent.

The body guard turned towards the troll, putting themselves between it and their king. The troll touched its belt buckle and pulled a great, glowing war club from its belt and swung it at the king's men. They were knocked from their mounts, and the horses also were felled. In one stroke, the monster had broken a hole open and was approaching his king. The troll paused to howl. It smiled and touched its belt buckle again. It must have surely held some magic saved for this moment.

With great bravery, and his sword in hand, the high king of Clayhaven spurred his horse towards the troll. He approached at full speed, his sword held like a lance, hoping for a blow against the large creature.

The creature lifted the war club, and when it fell, the king's beautiful mount was struck across the neck, breaking its glorious neck and sending it to the ground at a terrible, rubbery, distorted angle. Horse and rider fell onto thick poles that had been supporting one of the king's large tents.

The great creature howled into the sky, a great howl of victory. Other bodyguards surrounded the beast, but it easily dispatched two more of them with its club. It snatched a man off his mount and threw him directly on top of the high king.

If the army was defeated this day, Arn realized, all of Clayhaven was doomed. The abbey, the Lady, the tavern and all the people would be in terrible danger from this evil army. Greymist! If this should come to pass in the next few moments . . . Arn wondered. But what could he do? He was just a boy.

The red glow was much brighter and clearer now, like a bull's-eye lantern. As the troll howled, more and more black goor exited the woods, carrying large black bows. They pulled and released a volley upon the king's guard on the hill. The red glow was coming from the helms of these goor archers! Each one had one glowing red eye.

At least eight more of the king's guard fell from the volley of arrows, all hit accurately in the necks and chests, from a good two hundred paces.

After these eerily glowing archers came many more goor, wielding great two-handed swords. They accosted the human spearmen who were trying to rally, and the remaining soldiers. There were still almost a score of these archers, even after the human archers felled several.

Almost the entire king's entourage had been either smashed by the great war club or hit by swift, deadly arrows. Arn found himself running. Without really knowing why, he found himself running to help his king, towards the troll.

Perhaps he could smash its foot, if it did not notice him. Perhaps that would give the army time to slay this titanic monster. He sprinted down to the edge of the field, past the toppled cart with the poor, toppled donkey braying and trying to right itself. Past several men who were running the other way, and others holding the wounds they had just received in battle.

Even as he ran like lightning Arn wondered what effect he could have. These men were seasoned fighters, trained and experienced in warfare. They knew what they were doing, and they were dying en masse.

He ran full force, holding his club. At least the king would know he was a boy of honor. If he were going to die this day, it would be with some dignity.

As he headed towards the monster's foot, he tripped over one of the king's standards near the king's trampled tent. He fell flat upon his face. The great beast never noticed Arn.

In front of Arn, one of the king's guard had been pierced entirely through with one of the long, black arrows. The arrow had done its deadly work on this man, and the arrowhead that had seemed black at first, Arn now could see was glowing red, even in the light of day.

From his position on the ground Arn observed the troll raising the war club, obviously intent on smashing his quarry, the king, to pieces. Though pinned down, the high king had raised his sword for one last defensive blow. His armor would not resist the club, no matter that it was the best, strongest armor ever created.

The arrow gave Arn an idea, inspired by the creativity of youth, and the genius of necessity. Once, in the tavern in Clayhaven, Arn had used a trick when two bullies accosted him. When one knocked him on the ground and turned his back, Arn had kicked him as hard as he could in the upper back. Then he had innocently said, "Why did you punch him," knowing that bullies tend to punch first and talk later. Those two bullies still carried a grudge to this day. And Arn had gotten away while the two ruffians had fought it out. The arrowhead was full of some sort of deadly magic. The back of the troll's upper leg was before Arn, completely unprotected.

Arn took up the three-foot arrow, and with all of his might, jabbed it into the troll's unprotected thigh. The glowing, razor-sharp barb penetrated surprisingly deeply into the strong muscle of the troll's leg.

The creature's howl changed, became even louder, and revealed the troll's agony and anger. Arn glanced at the king, and saw his king looking directly at him. In a minute gesture, the king nodded for Arn to run. Arn turned quickly, ran and leaped behind the overturned cart, flat on his stomach. His king was indeed a noble man, trying to save Arn's life.

Arn did not see what happened next. The troll turned and eyed the archers behind him. "Filthy archers! How dare you pierce my flesh with this foul arrow! How dare you insult the great assassin! How dare you bring this pain I have not felt in my entire life?" The creature reached down, pulled the barbed tip from the back of his leg, and howled an angry curse, the likes of which had not been heard yet in this battle.

He took off with great speed, pounding off across the field towards the archers, clutching his huge club. Arn peeked up as he heard the troll leave, and from his vantage point could see archers firing, surprised that the troll was charging them. One tall human with a black flowing cloak, perhaps the leader, raised his hand, as if to ward the monster away, or make him return to his quarry, but it was the last thing he ever did. With one great swoop of the troll's club, the man flew fifty paces and landed somewhere Arn could not see.

In the next instant, the creature was among the archers. Slaying, tearing, throwing, bashing, stomping, biting, clawing, cursing. Several of the archers, thinking clearly, pulled their great black-hewn bows against the creature as fast as they possibly could, but the battle did not last long. Soon the entire unit of archers lay dead, and in the midst of them, the troll stood. He grasped his broad chest and finally plummeted to the ground, his anger finally spent, as well as his life. The enemy army, now disorganized, ceased advancing, and many of them ran.

The king's army cheered. Arn pushed himself up and approached his majesty, who was still pinned down. His nose was bleeding and he had a dazed look in his eyes. His shield arm was twisted at an odd angle, with the broken remains of his shield still clutched in his hand. Arn offered his hand to the king, and when the king looked at him, his eyes were wise. There was a great deal more sadness and age in his face than Arn had remembered.

The high king said, with labored breathing, "Lad, this day you have honored yourself, your family, your nation, and your bloodline." Several of the king's men freed the king and helped him to his feet. He eyed the battlefield and saw that it was at a steady point and his men appeared to be pushing forward. He looked sadly down at his beloved horse. "He was a dear friend," he said, patting the beast on the neck.

He turned back to Arn, eyes piercing, and said, "You did not steal that blade, lad. And even if you had, you have granted me a second chance, and perhaps even Southaven as well."

He straightened himself, pulled his great blade with some effort, and said, "Gather quickly around me." A number of his guard and retinue stood with Arn before the high king.

"What is your name, boy?"

"Arn. Arn of Clayhaven."

"This day, let it be known that this brave young man, Arn of Clayhaven, from this day forward, shall be a noble knight of Southaven, he and his bloodline. Let none be in doubt of this."

Arn knelt and humbly bowed his head. His royal majesty touched Arn on the right shoulder, then his left, with his heavy blade. "I dub you a knight of the realm of Southaven, with all the honors, duties and privileges thereof. Upon this battlefield you are promoted, and later we shall formalize this in a proper setting."

Arn's head remained bowed as he spoke, "My vow to you is to always protect you and yours." His head was swimming and he felt a bit dizzy.

"May you serve nobly, wisely, honorably, as a knight of Southaven." The king held his blade with the cross-shaped pommel towards Arn, and whispered to the lad, "Kiss the cross guard."

Arn leaned forward slightly and touched his lips to the cross.

"You shall hold a shield in defense of Southaven, to take upon yourself the defense of the innocent. And you shall hold a blade, to deliver justice to the unjust, as needed."

The king's stern face softened a bit. He smiled slightly at Arn. Now speaking quietly, he said, "You saved me, Arn. For that I will never forget you. Lands and station appropriate to an honored one shall be yours."

Arn could do nothing but gape in amazement, for next the king, with some great difficulty, using his sword for support, knelt on his right knee before Arn. He said, "I, your sovereign, bow to you in thanks."

The men around gasped. The old high king, who was of high blood, and probably almost two centuries old, was bowing to a lad with manure on his clothes. "Will you help an old man to his feet?" murmured the king.

Arn rose and said, "Yes, sire." He extended his hand and the king took it, leaning heavily on Arn as he rose to his feet.

The king spoke. "Let no one challenge this boy's integrity. Whoever looks disparagingly upon this boy, looks down upon me." Arn looked around to see all the men around bowing down.

A stallion pounded up carrying a man wearing elaborate clothes in the king's colors. It must be a high official indeed.

"Father! Your majesty, are you well?" exclaimed the man. "I saw you fall from across the way! I left my regiment as soon as I could to see you."

"Yes, my son." The king smiled fully at his oldest son. "I am well, thanks to Sir Arn of Clayhaven here." He gestured with his unbroken arm.

The prince clearly did not take in that the honor of saving his father belonged to the dirty peasant boy standing next to them. He searched with his eyes, observed the men standing around, and realization dawned. "This peasant?" he said with disbelief.

"Yes," said the king firmly. "A peasant once. Now one of my most honored and brave knights."

The prince nodded his head, bewildered. Facing Arn, he said, "I owe you for the life of my father, which is very dear to me. Thank you," he paused, and then added, "Sir Arn."

Arn just nodded. The king gave attention to some of his advisers, who gave a battle update as they pointed to the field. Another man brought forward another fine, royal mount to stand ready for the king.

"That is the breaking point," stated the king as he pointed at the battle. There was a breaking regiment of halberdiers who could not withstand the strength of half-trolls. "If we break them, the day is ours."

The king made ready to mount his horse, but one of his aides, a rogue who carried only a dagger, spoke, "My lord, you are unwell. Your left arm is shattered. Let us retreat from the battle, and make plans away from here."

"Retreat? When we are so close to victory?" said the king. Arn thought he might become angry, but instead he patted his aide on the shoulder and said, "Parence, I appreciate your concern, but the battle is here, and we are far too outnumbered to withdraw. Since my men cannot withdraw, I will not withdraw. That grey-skinned demon band there, that is the breaking point. Those to the left, there, we hit them after we break the half-trolls. After that, victory is ours. I see no more enemy reserves in this area. It will be difficult, but we can do it, and we will save Southaven this day. To me, all about!"

Arn found himself stepping towards his gallant king. He had never been around such high nobility before. He had only seen minor nobles who had visited Clayhaven occasionally, and then he had not been allowed to speak to them, just empty their chamber pots.

He ventured to squeak out, "My lord?"

"Yes, lad," the king answered from atop his new horse.

"What am I to do?"

"Equip yourself as best you can, and do what you can. There are many a lass and many a gaffer, and many noble souls in Southaven who await what you do this day, Arn. Do what you have done by saving me. You will do no dishonor to yourself. I think there is no dishonor in you at all." The king whispered words to his steed, and patted its neck.

Quietly again, the king addressed Arn. "Never forget. You are someone noble, no matter what your station. You always were."

These words made Arn smile, grin even. The king with his kind, grey eyes smiled back. He lifted his great blade and his voice.

"To me, broken of Southaven. To me, and to victory!"

The men could not resist the call of their king, and immediately, obediently began to run towards the hill. The wounded walked. The second regiment, at the foot of the hill, was beginning to break. Many of the first regiment gathered around the king.

He lifted the blade and spoke regally to his men. "The half-trolls die! That is the key, and this day is ours! For Southaven, for my family, and for all we cherish here. To victory!" He commanded, lowering his blade and spurring his horse forward to the foe.

The men yelled oaths of loyalty and victory and ran forward. Arn had tucked the goor dagger into his belt and picked up a club, more suitable to carry into battle. There was a small helm on the ground, nothing fancy, but it had a nose guard. It was lying near the king's broken tent, and Arn did not feel it was wrong to pick it up and see if it fit him, which it did.

He was looking about for a sword and heard a great clamor from the battlefield. He could see the king and his new host doing well against the grey ones. Arn smiled. Even with a broken arm, the king was dispatching the evil creatures with great precision. Arn knew that victory would be theirs.

As he watched, the dark figure emerged from the woods, just behind the regiment of the dead, which was doing quite well where it was. He saw the black blade and mace, and knew it was Angueth.

Two more regiments of dead came out, quite sinister. One wielded halberds, the other swords. They were each equal in number to the first dead regiment, and stood in straight order. Arn watched in horror as Angueth lowered his blade towards the king and his entourage.

Arn could hear the words, as clearly as if Angueth had been standing near by, "Let not the villain of Southaven escape, for he is your goal! You will not let him escape!"

The two dead regiments turned to the sides and in their rusty armor clanged forward. The ones with halberds moved faster than the other regiment, but instead of meeting the king's entourage directly, they hit the regiment beside that was already hard pressed by the dead. With this added strength, the enemy pike men easily pressed through. The dead followed as fast as their beleaguered steps would allow, mindless but determined.

The dead halberdiers, with great precision, turned and slammed into the flank, and wrapped around the king's men. Arn realized the king was cut off, and looked desperately for a sword.

He picked up a small shield to go with his club. *This would have to do*, he thought. He would not allow the king he had just saved to be cut off, perhaps killed, by these villains of the grave. Arn said a prayer, and found himself running down the hill, not of his own willpower but having no choice, towards a foe that had long since gone from the cares of this world. It scared him greatly.

When he had been a child, he had sometimes imagined that the dead from the graveyard of the priory would walk. This had been a thought that had scared him, but now he was running with all his might towards them. They were armed, and armored, and he had no good weapon with which to challenge them.

Suddenly, just in front of him, stood a man, or what had been a man once. It was a white skull with hollow eyes, white bones, tall. This was the last thing Arn would see for a while. He did not notice the black halberd hammer coming down upon his new helm, denting it deeply upon his head. The grinning white skull swirled as if in a mist, seemed further away. Arn's last thought was a vain wish that he could smash the smile with his club, and then he thought no more as he hit the ground rather hard.

The battle was over for Arn of Clayhaven.

CHAPTER SEVEN

LOOTERS AND NOBILITY

*A*rn *felt cool fall breeze, with warmth from the sun barely touching* his skin as he walked forward. Up ahead, Greymist bounded down the path. He wondered what interesting thing Greymist had discovered. When he was barking like that, it meant he wanted to show Arn something. Up on a small hill, he could see what looked like a well. He walked towards it. When Greymist got close, he stopped cold, and began to growl. Arn looked around and saw trees, and suddenly there was mist rolling in, and a small village appeared around the well. It was all sort of strange, and his head began to hurt. Perhaps he should go back to the abbey and lie down.

He saw two strange shapes at the well, which resembled soldiers. Greymist's growl grew more fearsome, and the two figures seemed to be fighting. As he watched, bodies appeared in the mist, on the ground all about the well.

Arn wondered, *what in the world is this?* His head was aching terribly now. *Greymist, what is going on, boy?* Arn spoke to his dog without any sound. Who are these people fighting? Arn felt very peculiar indeed. He decided it was best to sit down for a moment. Even with the battle raging on the small hill, he could not bring himself to run, or move. He sat upon the ground. The pounding in his head increased.

I need to go back to the priory. Perhaps if I lie down on the ground a bit . . . He placed his head upon the ground, closed his eyes and felt a small bit of relief. He heard the clash of weapons and yelling of men.

He couldn't bring himself to open his eyes to see what was going on. If he could just rest for a moment . . .

The yelling was louder, and he felt so much worse, like he was lying upon a rock. What a terrible day this had turned out to be! The scene in his mind slipped away and the pain in his head grew. He felt warmth on his cheek and his ear. Greymist was giving him a kiss. He should wake up now.

He opened his eyes and saw cold mist swirling all around him in near darkness. As his head cleared, he could hear horrible sounds, moaning and wailing, as if all the sick people he had ever heard in his life had gathered around him in the mist. Confused, he sat up and immediately knew he was on the battlefield. His limbs were numb with cold. It wasn't the licking of Greymist on his cheek. He lifted his right hand to his face and could see it was dark and sticky blood.

He now remembered the grinning skull face and knew that its blow had put him out. His next thought was for the king, and he tried to rise to his feet, but fell back with a thump. His back hurt, and feeling behind him, he found he had been lying on a broken piece of shield, for how long he did not know. The shield piece looked like it belonged to the king's own shield, the one that had been broken by the great troll.

The gathering darkness was illuminated in the distance by some small fires, and it seemed to Arn that there were shapes moving about. He wondered who they were, and the voices calling out for water, for help, for mother.

He could not discern army campfires, or the presence of either army, evil or good. Who had won the battle?

He put his hand to his head, which was aching terribly, and recoiled in shock when he felt metal. Then he chuckled to himself, remembering the helm he had picked up. It was sticky too, with his own blood, no doubt, and was dented on the side.

He could barely lift the helm off of his head; it was so heavy. The pain was a bit better, though. He could definitely feel blood trickling down his neck as he removed the helm.

Arn began to wonder what the people were doing, moving around in the mist as they were. Were they wounded? A cackling laughter came, an evil sound. "Want water, do you?" followed by more cackling. It sounded like an older woman's voice.

Beside him Arn found a broken piece of wood, probably part of a spear or lance, and used this to help himself to his feet, stiff with cold. He thought someone was giving aid to the wounded, and he almost raised his voice to call for her himself, but something stopped him.

Through the dark and swirling fog, he could barely see a figure bent over, reaching down into the mist. As he hobbled forward, he could tell the figure held a water gourd, and he was glad someone was ministering aid. But still something kept him from speaking.

"Water you want, eh? Here, have some water," followed by the wicked old woman's laughter. He could hear water hitting the ground. *Could she be pouring it out? Right in the face of the wounded men? What kind of evil woman is this?*

It struck him like a blow, that these people were not giving aid or water to the men. They were scavengers of the battlefield. Stealing bits of treasure from the dead and dying. They were helping themselves to whatever could be found on the fallen—food, wine, gold or silver. When nobody was left on the field to guard the poor, helpless dead, these lowest of the low would come to victimize them again. They were looters.

His head clearing quickly, he began to run through his mind what he might do to make the looters leave. He reached to his belt for his goor dagger, but found it was gone. His broken staff was the only weapon he could easily find in the darkness. He was not sure who—or what—the dark forms were lying upon the ground. One of them could be one of the undead, still undead, and might be able to harm him somehow. He could not bear the thought of searching the ground for another weapon.

Some other shadowy figures approached the old woman, and one said, "Hey, Ma, ye gonna cut his throat, or what?"

"Nah, he's suffering enough. I'm giving 'im some water, I am!" This was followed by snickering from all sides, and commentary by coarse, harsh voices. "There you go, nice noble. You were always so kind to us poor and needy!"

There was a breathy response, "Lady, all I ask is for water, please! Please, mercy upon me!"

Arn had thought that stealing from the dead was an evil thing, but even worse, these looters were torturing their victims. The offspring of the old woman were nudging the fallen nobleman with their toes and taunting him.

The looters would be gone by morning. They rightly feared that someone in the light of day would run them down. So Arn knew that he must get them to leave this night, and then plan what to do next. Arn remembered the valuable items he had seen lying upon the ground where the king's tent had fallen. He was sure he had seen some fireworks, perhaps a rocket.

Arn saw the first moon up, a slim crescent rising in the east. Second moon would be a little brighter. He crouched down into the fog and with great difficulty, for his limbs were still aching and cold, headed away from the woods, he hoped back towards the king's hill.

It took Arn a while but he did find the large, round tube in the wreckage of the king's tents. He was not entirely sure how the great rockets were launched into the sky. Most noblemen had discontinued using them in battle, for their results were inconsistent. Only the king would have such items as rocket launchers at the ready.

He knew they lit some part with a flint and steel. He felt around for the fuse, and found it. Next, he looked for a torch, something to light it with, found a red-hot brand, and held it far away from the rocket.

There was fear in Arn. He did not know for certain how to fire the rocket, or if he would be successful in getting the looters to leave. It filled him with a sick feeling to see how close they had been to him, as he lay unconscious. He said a quick prayer.

He did not see any way to get the rocket to go straight up, could not figure out what would hold it. But there was a broken wagon, lying on angle, which would send the rocket up over the looters' heads, if all went well. He hoped there would be a great explosion, a display that would even make them think it was magic.

He tugged the cart into position, and set pieces of heavy metal and wood on the sides, so that the rocket would go out into the heavens over the field. He decided that he would get quickly away after lighting the fuse, and pretend to be one of the dead, in case his plan did not work, and the looters came to investigate. Even if it did work, perhaps they would figure out someone was alive up on the hill.

One of the rhymes with which he used to busy his mind while doing his mindless work in Clayhaven came to his tongue, and he whispered, "Arn he was, and iron he would be." He steeled himself. He could not allow them to continue.

He placed the burning brand to the fuse, and stood back to watch. He would face the evildoers and make a stand.

The fuse lit and sizzled, growing louder when it entered the end of the tube. Then *whoosh*, like lightning, the rocket went off the ramp, almost straight into the heavens. It reminded him for a moment of a celebration day in Clayhaven, when they had seen several rockets and fireworks. He had been forgiven of his work that day, and played long with Greymist, and even eaten a small pie. In the evening they had listened to Father Kile playing the lute. It had been a great day.

Up in the sky Arn could see the patterns of the stars. All of them had names, he knew from the monks. The one directly above the rocket was the Great Warrior, fighting an eternal battle with a fiery blade. It was a good sign, Arn thought.

The looters let out startled cries. Some began to run. One yelled from the darkness, "Wizard!"

Wizardry! That's it, thought Arn. Just as he began to wonder if the rocket would explode at all, there was a tremendous boom and a shower of blue, red and white sparks that lit up almost the entire field. There were bits of yellow as the sparks fell out of the sky, very beautiful.

Quickly, Arn grabbed up a piece of the king's shredded tent, and used it to cover himself like a cloak. He kicked the glowing pieces of wood from the fire in front of him to make it seem he was surrounded by light. He held the burning brand in one hand and the staff in the other, broken end down, and stood up as authoritatively as he could manage.

The terrified screams continued, "A wizard's come to guard the dead!"

He lifted his arms with staff and brand, but could not speak. He knew that his voice would sound like a youth, no matter how hard he tried to sound like a wizard. Instead, he grabbed up the helm that had saved his life and spoke into it. It was a trick he had played on the monks. Such a thing changed one's voice.

"You! Leave my wounded!" he yelled with as big a voice as he could muster. He did not think he was very loud, but many must have heard, including the old woman.

She yelled, "Ahh! It's a wizard, it is! I told you, you fools!" She picked something up from the ground and began to beat her two figures next to her. "These are not good pickings! Run for your lives, you filthy urchins!" She followed them as they departed, slapping them with some kind of stick, and cursing.

Quite a few of the brigands ran, but some stood in amazement, just watching. So Arn, in a louder voice, yelled, "Flee this field, and you shall live, and not feel my wrath!"

As Arn watched with great satisfaction, they all began to rout, their morale broken, fear and uncertainty overcoming them. They had never seen a rocket before, and such a display, combined with such a threat, was enough to send them running.

After a time, Arn sat upon the upturned cart. He began to hear the voices of the wounded, "We're saved!" His heart sank, as he realized this adverse repercussion of the trick he had played.

He heard a weak voice over to his right, not too far from where the king had fallen. It was that man whom he had bumped into earlier, the one with the seafarer's coat. He was lying with blood trickling from his right arm and a wound near his upper right chest. The coat had been pulled back to reveal a thin, very finely crafted breastplate. At his belt, strangely enough, he had two corked inkwells in a leather holder, a pouch of quills beside that, and a case with several parchment papers that had come undone. The big book the man had coveted so now was quite dirty from battle. He held a broken mace still in his right hand and a small dagger in his left.

Arn heard him ask for water again. He found a dead soldier's gourd canteen and swished it. There was still a good bit of water inside. Quickly he went to the man. There were three dead goor at his feet and one of the undead also. He had obviously gotten the better of some of them, before one got him.

He bent down and lifted the man's head gently. The man looked with surprise up at him. "You're that boy. I recognize you. The boy who crashed into me earlier," he said in a whisper.

Arn said, "That's right, sir. Just be quiet now. I have some water for you."

"Be quiet?" he whispered. "You still don't know your place!" The man looked out at the blue sky, then at Arn again, with a bit of a smile, and said, "My goodness, 'tis I who do not know my place!" He sipped greedily at the water Arn gave him. "Forgive me, lad."

After taking several long draughts of water, he said, "I offended you earlier, and now you bring comfort to me. This battle did not go well for us. What is your name?"

"My name, sir, is Arn of Clayhaven."

"You saved us all from those filthy looters! There was one not far away that would have been the death of me and many others. You are indeed a very clever character! For a moment I thought you *were* a great wizard. That was most clever, boy. I mean, Arn," he said, correcting himself. "If I may have leave to call you by your name. Do you have a surname, young Arn?"

"No, sir. Just Arn of Clayhaven."

"Forgive an old fool's quick tongue, and rudeness. You are a man of quality, and I pledge that I will keep my word given earlier. I will chronicle your story, whatever it may be. I will give it to you and your family. Can you read, Arn?"

Arn said, "Yes, the monks in Clayhaven taught me to read, sir."

"These filthy scum won't be the death of me," said the man, kicking one of the goor near his feet. "I'll mend. I am the king's high chronicler, and I will come to Clayhaven," he said, coughing. "I will write your story." He began to cough fitfully. "My name is . . ." he continued to cough coarsely, and Arn could not understand the name he gave.

There was a bedroll not far from where he lay, and the owner would not be needing it. Arn placed the thinly rolled, grey blanket under the chronicler's head, gave him the gourd of water, and said, "I have to do something for these wounded." There were many yelling for help.

"Water! Help us, please!"

Arn felt discouraged. There were so many; he could not possibly help them all. He had indeed saved them from the looters, but now what was he to do? He would do whatever he could.

He walked through the field, picking up water skins and gourds from those who were obviously dead. He asked forgiveness as he cut the cords that held the water to the dead men.

He headed for the noble who had been tortured with pure cruelty by the old hag. He recognized one of the king's guard who had been there when Arn was knighted.

"Who are you?" the man croaked from his dry throat.

"I'm afraid I'm not a wizard, sir. I set off the rocket I found in the king's baggage, to get rid of the looters. I'm here to give you water. I couldn't otherwise get rid of so many looters."

The man coughed as he chuckled, "You are a very clever lad." He weakly raised one blood-covered hand. "Thank you. Might I please have some water?"

Arn had been well trained by the monks to care for the ill and wounded. He gave just a few sips to the guard. His thirst quenched just a bit, his eyes were empty. He stared out into the night sky. Arn recognized this look, and it was not good.

"What is your name, boy?"

"Arn of Clayhaven, sir."

"The king knighted you, didn't he, upon this hill?" The man coughed. "You were accused of stealing the blade of a noble. The king realized this was a mistake and gave you a knighthood. You are a knight of the realm."

"Aye, sir."

"A nobler knight I have never seen. I wish I had been half as noble as you seem, lad."

Arn could not speak. He was still so unaccustomed to hearing words of this kind spoken to him.

"It is quite cold," said the guard.

"I will get you a blanket."

"No, lad, I won't need it. There are many about here who will need your help. Go about your work, as a knight and a nobleman."

"I will, sir." Arn patted the man's bloody hand and placed it on his chest. "I'm sorry, sir," he whispered. The guard's wounds were too numerous and deadly.

"You have slaked my thirst and chased away my tormentors. You have brought me comfort in my last moments. What more could I ask?"

Tears fell from Arn's eyes. How many more times tonight would he face this?

"Don't cry. We do not cry but at joyous occasions, and then only rarely," he smiled faintly. "I go to a better place, far better than I have ever known."

Arn's heartbeat pounded in his head. It was like the sound of horses' hooves. After a moment, he realized he was hearing many horses approaching. It must be an enemy. No mortal men could see well enough in this dark and mist to ride their horses at breakneck speed.

He did not consider leaving the guard's side. He hoped if they were foes that his death would come quickly.

The pounding of the horses came to a stop, and men dismounted. "This is the king's second army! We've found it! We've found it!" the men yelled.

"Take this message back. We have found the king's army and there are many wounded here." One of the riders turned and immediately galloped back the way he came, as fast as he had come.

The men were well spoken. Could they be the king's own men? Impulsively, Arn yelled, "Over here!" They had not sounded like the enemy, and Arn hoped they were not.

"Who is it?" yelled one of the arrivals.

"I'm Arn of Clayhaven, a knight in his majesty's service."

A small group of men walked over. A very tall, strong man with a weary face spoke, "Who are you?"

"I'm Arn of Clayhaven."

"Are you a looter?" he viewed Arn with suspicion.

"No!"

At the same time, the guard upon the ground spoke, weakly, "Good Lord, Devlin! Can't you see he's rendered aid to us?"

"Sir Walter!" said Devlin. His stern face softened, and he bent down. "Are you well?"

"No. I'm dying. This boy has brought us aid, and he sent a great rocket into the sky and chased away the brigands who were torturing us!" Speaking thus seemed to drain Sir Walter's last remaining energy.

Sir Devlin glanced appraisingly at Arn. "We'll get you aid, sir."

"No! Tend to the others as you can. It's too late for me," said Sir Walter. He looked into Devlin's eyes and said, "I have bitter news for you this night. The king has fallen. And his son . . ."

Sir Devlin's face registered shock, as did Arn's.

After a pause, Sir Walter continued, "He fell this day and his body was carried from the field. By whom, I do not know, but you must find him!" He spoke with more energy than before. "If Angueth has him, and his evil horde, you must try to retrieve his body!"

"Yes, we will do what we can."

"Give this boy food, and all consideration, for he . . ." Sir Walter began to cough violently. "He . . ." Some of the soldiers knelt beside him. After coughing weakly, he looked up into the heavens, seeing no more.

The stern rider placed his hand on Arn's shoulder. Arn said, "I am going to tend to others, sir."

"Yes, you do that. You've done a good thing. But for that rocket, we would never have found you in the dark. We did not know exactly where the king had made his stand. This field has known bitter and good, but today will be the bitterest memory of all. The falling of Southaven."

These words renewed the chilling numbness in Arn's limbs. The defeat of Southaven. He had never imagined what that would mean for him, and for Clayhaven. He poured himself into his work. He managed to find some herbs, and with the knowledge the monks had given him about caring for the wounded, he tended to those who had fallen on the field. There was plenty of clawfoot, useful for helping flowing blood to clot, and sealing out impurities from a wound.

Others appeared during the night to help him in his efforts. There were two ladies, one noblewoman and one servant, who had been hiding somewhere in the baggage, who were helpful in tending the sick.

Late in the night, as he was far across the battlefield, he heard a dog yelping. Then closer, a growl. It was one of the dark wolves that had attacked them earlier. He did not have the heart to fight another creature, and certainly did not want to grapple with a wolf. After all, his best friend in his life was Greymist.

Arn turned away and joined a group of men who were still searching for the king's body. Some of the soldiers had moved out at dawn, and others were left behind to dig graves and take away the wounded on carts. He was surprised to learn that the chronicler had survived the night and left with them.

Arn left the cold battlefield with a wagon of the king's soldiers. He talked to them about having been knighted the day before, in the fray of the battle, but they only looked at him warily and said it could be discussed later.

Many more riders came upon them, and it was obvious that they were all heading for the rear of the enemy army. Angueth and his men had moved forward, fast, burning and destroying villages and leaving wounded behind.

The king's riders quickly dispatched the enemy wounded. Arn was very glad that this duty fell to Lord Devlin's men. He was feeling very weary indeed, but could not rest. His mind was numb, but his body was alert.

Much of the terrain through which the men traveled showed the devastation of war. But when they paused by a stream to water the horses, Arn thought how peaceful the scene was. Rustling fall leaves, cool fresh breeze, and autumn-tinted sunshine gave no indication of the evil that had befallen Southaven.

Some of the soldiers speculated that there had been two armies. The king's army had defeated what was perhaps the main force from the dark lands; at least several men claimed that is what it was. But some of the older, more experienced men said that the Dark One was about something different this time. Perhaps Angueth and his mob had been sent just to kill the king and his son, to bring terrible disorganization to Clayhaven.

Lord Devlin sent some men, including Arn, and several wagons loaded with wounded men, down another pathway, toward one of Southaven's great castles, deeper in the border. The little outfit surrounded two of the noblewomen, mounted on horseback. In fact, all of the men were riding, either horses or wagons.

Arn squeezed into a tight spot in one of the wagons, but soon the pounding in his head became unbearable when combined with the jarring and jostling in the wagon. So he got out and walked.

Arn had no difficulty keeping up with their pace, at first. He felt weariness and aches shake out of his limbs as he walked fast, or ran alongside the group. In their haste to get to the safety of the castle, they went faster than Arn could manage, and eventually he fell behind.

One of the sergeants, noticing that Arn was having some difficulty, yelled, "Don't worry! Just follow this path and you shall be safe until you arrive at the castle! You'll catch up with us soon enough!"

This is how Arn found himself walking along the pathway alone. He could still hear the procession of horses and wagons, at times, and see them in the distance sometimes as well. He slowed to a walk, and felt his energy dissipating.

His head, which had been bound expertly by a soldier healer, was throbbing with pain. He walked persistently forward, and as he walked he thought. So many things had transpired in the past few days, a lifetime worth of experiences, must be.

Far ahead in the distance, he thought he could just see what was probably the fortified castle where he was going. It was Lord Hamilton's keep. He had heard it was very impressive, but of course had never seen it before.

Closer to the castle, he passed through a little village, smaller than Clayhaven. The residents were gathering supplies, grain, animals, everything they could load on their wagons or backs, to carry up to the fortified keep.

Even if they were busily evacuating their village, it comforted Arn to be in a normal village with normal people around. He noted that most of the small huts were empty, apparently already abandoned. He walked past several fields that had already been put to bed for the winter, and stopped in front of a small, empty hut.

It was obviously someone's home, but the door was standing open. Surely the owner would not mind if he took a short break. He needed to rest for just a few minutes. He was quite close to the castle now, and would be able to get there quickly when he awakened. Maybe the throbbing in his head would improve.

Inside the house he found a full water basin on top of a small table. He used the water to freshen his face and hands, and used a cloth to wipe off some of the blood that had trickled down his face. He knew that wounds to the head always bleed quite a bit, and knew his wound would take some time to improve.

Ashes had been thrown over the fire, but digging down, Arn discovered some live embers. He poured some of the water into a small metal pot with a cracked rim and placed it on top of the coals. He looked through the few little pots lining a small shelf, and discovered some tea. He only used a few tea leaves, just enough to flavor the water. He thought if he were the owner of this tiny home, he would not mind a soldier making use of a few of his things.

He sat down near the fire and leaned his head back against the wattle wall. Immediately his feet began to throb with pain. His legs and feet were cramped and felt hugely swollen. He closed his eyes against the pain.

He decided he did not care if the tea was not very hot, and leaned over to pick up the barely warm pot. He poured some of the tea into his old gourd cup and drank it, and was glad for its warmth and mild flavor. However, it did not sit well in his stomach and he started feeling sick.

His feet near the low fire were getting warmer, or perhaps they were just numb; he could no longer tell. Arn closed his eyes again and fell into a deep, exhausted slumber.

CHAPTER EIGHT

SHUT OUT AND HERO OF SHADOW

*W*hen *he opened his eyes again, he had no idea how long he had been* asleep. There was a loud clanging and scraping noise, and it was not far away. He stood up slowly, because his body still ached and he felt queasy. It was dark inside the little hut, but he could see it was lighter outside. His breath made little clouds of cold before his face.

It looked like full noon outside. He must have lain there all night and into the next day. Indeed, the few embers from the night before were completely cold. It was a little alarming to Arn that he had slept so long. He was also anxious to know what had caused the clanging noise. He remembered Angueth's evil army with a sense of dread. His head and his back ached.

Again, he heard grating and scraping. It sounded like metal against metal, and it was loud. He stepped cautiously outside and looked up towards the castle, for this is where the sound originated.

He gasped when he saw the reason for the loud noises. The castle gate had been closed and now the portcullis was being closed, slowly. The huge iron grating was sliding down in its stone grooves, sealing the entrance to the castle!

Arn staggered toward the gate on his painful feet, crying, "Wait a minute! Please, let me in!"

From a very lofty perch on a high battlement he heard a coarse voice, "Who are you?"

"I'm Arn of Clayhaven!" He wished very much to be on the other side of that battlement. "I'm a knight of the realm!"

He could barely hear the laughter, and it sounded very far away, but he did hear the rough answer, "What?"

"The high king made me a knight of the realm. I came with the party of wounded. Please let me in, please! Open one of the needle gates!"

Arn saw a helmeted head peer over the top of the wall, and heard a little clearer, "You? You are a knight of the realm?"

"Yes, sir. Please open the gate."

"Look, peasant boy. We haven't time for your foolishness. You should have gone in when the gates were open. There's a bad army hereabouts! They are coming, so you better be making your way somewhere safe."

"But, the castle, sir!"

"Sorry, boy. All the gates are barred, and everything is reinforced from the rear. You can't get in."

"Throw me a rope! I'll climb."

More laughter ensued. "Look, nobody is after you. Just run off to the woods there. Or go hide in one of the houses in the village. Find a cellar. You'll be safe enough. Now get on!"

Arn's hope fell. He was trying to find an answer when he heard, "But, that lie about being a knight of the realm, that one bothers me. You shouldn't be telling stories like that!"

"I am a knight! I helped his majesty, and . . ."

"You did what? Get thee off, boy! Before I tell the archers to use you as practice! More like a spy for the Dark One, says I!"

Arn could not believe what was happening. He had almost been to safety, only the day before. Now this cruel man would not let him in. If only he had not stopped to rest!

Arn tried again. "You open this gate now! I am a knight of Southaven, as declared by his majesty the high king just two days past!"

"Boy, the king of Southaven has been dead for three days! You are a liar, probably a thief, and definitely an idiot!"

"Three days!" breathed Arn. He was stunned. He must have been unconscious much longer than he had thought.

"Archers to the walls!" yelled the guard. Arn saw about twenty bows and arrows appear over the top of the wall. "You have the count of twenty before I order the archers to let fly!"

Arn had no idea where to go but headed away from the castle and back toward the village. He wandered through the empty village, and walked into the fields. He knew his body had taken a beating these past days, but he also knew that his memory was right. He had helped save the king's life, distracted the troll, and been duly knighted by the high king.

To be a knight had been a dream of his ever since he could remember. Of course, in his dreams it had been a much more glorious and happy event. His past few days as a soldier had brought him sights, sounds and smells he had never imagined before. Since he had become Sir Arn of Clayhaven, he had experienced and seen mainly suffering, pain and defeat.

He entered a wealthier house, not too far from the village. No one was in sight as he walked through the rooms, in search of a blanket. In the scullery, at the bottom of a wooden box, he found two turnips and a handful of barley, which he tucked into his pockets. The beds were stripped, but he did find a blanket just the size for one person inside a wooden chest.

He departed by the back door, and almost tripped over something that must have been dropped in haste at the last minute. It was a piece of salted pork, wrapped in a cloth. Heartened by these finds, Arn set off down the road, with his eyes and ears open.

As he left the town completely, he spied a piece of cloth near the edge of a field and walked over to it. Inside were some parsnips, carrots, and two small potatoes, probably the first ones pulled of the fall season. He imagined the farmer had planned to bring these home, but forgotten in the confusion of evacuating the town.

The best find of all, however, was the water skin lying next to the fabric bundle. Arn felt blessed to have found these items necessary for his survival. Adjacent to the field ran a little stream, where Arn filled the water skin with fresh, clean water. He was very happy to see that the water held. He had been worried it was discarded because it leaked.

He was still carrying his broken spear shaft. He did not know exactly where the enemy army was, nor from which direction they would come. Arn walked into the afternoon sun, warily, back down the road whence he had come.

Arn also did not know the location of the king's army. The castle was surely a target, and he knew he had to leave this vicinity, but he was not sure where he was headed. His shoes, with light leather soles, had developed holes, and his swollen feet hurt with every step.

He nibbled a little of the parsnips, turnips with their withered greens, and pork, as he walked into the night. Since he saw no evidence of the enemy's army, he was sorely tempted to build a fire and make the stew that was promised by the ingredients he carried. He had a bit of salt in his pouch, given by the brothers when he left Clayhaven.

As he kept walking, the stew began to be all he could think about. A little parsnip, a little turnip, a little water from a good, clean stream. He would shield the fire itself with rocks, so it could not be easily seen, then eat a warm meal.

The first moon came out, only slightly brighter than the nights before. His feet began to stumble. Not only was it now quite dark, but also he was exhausted and hurting from his recent ordeal. He tried not to think about his rejection at the castle wall, and think about the stew instead.

He knew he could make a delicious, warm meal. The brothers had acquainted Arn with cooking, and the stew would be the most enjoyable thing he had had to eat in the past week. Looking through his pockets, he happily discovered the small, white, cherry-topped cake, a bit smashed. He started a small fire with a flint and steel, and boiled the stew for quite a while. When it had cooled enough to try, he was very pleased with the flavor. The cake was the most delicious he had ever tasted, even if it was crumbled.

His head still hurt, but not nearly as badly as before. He could not believe he had actually slept for a day and a half. He had never slept that long in his life. He did not think it had been a restful sleep, considering how sore he had been when he awoke.

Arn settled into some leaves to rest with his little blanket, but kept the broken spear nearby in case it would be needed. He found a quite pointed rock, and worked on it a bit, and made it into a point, which he tied to the spear shaft. This spear and the little dagger he had taken from the battlefield were his only weapons now.

He knew that if he continued in the direction he was going, he would pass by the battlefield. But beyond that was the way to the border fortress, and Arn thought he would go there. By now, there would only be dead men remaining on the battlefield, and he promised himself he would go around it quickly.

Next, Arn tended to the cuts and sores on his feet. He trimmed some leaves from the leatherleaf plant, and used them to line his shoes. The underside of the leatherleaf was soft, even fuzzy, and felt good next to your feet. The top side of the leaf was tough and would endure a couple of days as the soles of Arn's shoes. If you walked upon layers of leatherleaves in the bottoms of your shoes, they stuck together forming a thick substitute for leather soles. He would keep his eyes open for more leatherleaf plants.

He was glad to be off of his feet for the day, and pointed them to the warmth of his little fire.

When he woke he was only slightly rested, but he was not as hungry as he had been the past few days. He finished off the cold remains of the stew, washed his feet again and put on his shoes, then gathered his things. During the night, he had heard some wolf howling in the distance, but had seen nobody.

He was careful to cover the few remaining coals of his little fire with dirt, and then quickly set off.

When he arrived back at the little stream where he had left Lord Devlin's party a few days before, he explored a bit, in case some forgotten, useful item could be found. Underneath a large, sprawling tree, he picked up several black walnuts. Getting the sweet meat out was quite a job, but Arn knew a trick with rocks that Brother Clement had taught him. He sat against the trunk of the tree, eating some bits he still carried in his pockets, and indulged himself in imagining.

Through the trees, just a bit distant from where he sat, Arn saw the tip of a spire. He had not realized they were very close to a town! He quickly covered that distance and found himself walking through the main street of a completely deserted town. The walls around the town stood strong, but the gate was open and the wooden towers empty. All the inhabitants must have escaped to a nearby castle.

They had evacuated in a hurry. Some of the doors stood open. Arn cried out, "Hello!" but there was no answer. He tentatively checked some of the buildings, but did not find anything of use. While walking back out of the little village, he heard a loud crack from inside a building. Not checking into the noise, he quickly left and went on his way.

The leatherleaf had done its job, cushioned his feet and covered the holes in the soles of his shoes. The herbs had done a wonderful job of making his feet feel better, and they were only a little sore. His head still hurt a bit, but he managed a fair pace.

Just about dusk, he came upon the edge of the field of battle. He had no desire to be there after the sun had set, so made up his mind to cross quickly, before darkness fell.

The battlefield was silent. He was aware of small and large carrion birds, and the scent of death in the air, but he kept his eyes down and skirted around anything lying on the ground. If he had arrived when light was full, he would have felt he should look around for a weapon. Perhaps a better weapon remained somewhere out here. But since darkness was falling, he only wanted to get through to the other side and away from here.

Suddenly he heard a sound that made his blood run cold. It was a shriek, or a howl. He began to run, and heard it again, a mournful cry this time. Was it a dog? He glanced around for anything moving. Could it be one of the evil wolves that traveled with the Vagabond's army?

Arn did not want to find anything, and the sound urged him forward. He only wanted to be gone from here. When he heard the howl again, it dawned on him that he had heard this sound before, a few days earlier, on this same field. Now he could hear, at the end of the loud howl, a whimper and cry. He stopped running. His heart felt pity for the creature that was crying thus.

Reluctantly, he walked quickly toward the noise. He tried to stay clear of the corpses, and did not look directly at anything that was lying on the ground. As he walked he thought, *what am I doing here, anyway? I am not experienced in any of this. Do I really need to be the one to check this out?* At the same time, he was strong and knew that there was a destiny for his life, that he would find guidance for whatever lay ahead of him.

Even so, every footstep was difficult and he dreaded what he would find across the field. Then he heard the wail and cry, and it was much closer. Up close, Arn was sure that some creature was hurt. The cry was mournful.

He steeled himself and crossed over a small rise. Directly in front of him was a large, black creature sitting on its haunches. It had the look of a dog but was larger than any dog Arn had ever seen. As he approached, he felt sure it was one of the Vagabond's large wolves.

He grasped his makeshift spear, and wished for a better weapon. He picked up a rock in his left hand. He wondered if the kind thing to do would be to put the awful thing out of its misery.

The closer he got, the larger the wolf appeared. In the waning light, Arn was surprised to see that the wolf was pinned to the ground by a great lance through its leg. The wolf saw him but did not growl or threaten Arn in any way. Its yellow eyes were tired and sad.

Arn stopped and stared at the creature from a distance. It was huge. There was no way he could easily fight this huge wolf with his spear and a rock! Even with the small dagger tucked in his belt. The wolf whimpered and growled quietly in its throat.

He could not help but feel pity for the beast. He walked around it. Every time the wolf tried to move, it cried out in agony. The great yellow eyes followed Arn, and the creature did not howl loudly as it had done before. The flesh around the lance was torn and bitten; obviously the wolf had tried to free itself, but the lance had pierced deeply into its leg, and was planted securely in the ground.

"Look here, foul creature," said Arn. "I believe we are stewards of all the creatures, even you. But I don't know how to help you."

The wolf growled low in its throat. Its eyes never left Arn. Arn knew he would not go any closer to the animal as long as it kept growling. Perhaps it felt threatened by Arn. He sat down on the ground and continued to speak.

"Now, I would like to help you. I only have this rock and this makeshift spear here, but I'm not going to attack you, fellow. I don't know what kind of life you have lived, but mine has been quite a trial. I don't think it is sporting for me to try to kill you just now while you are stuck like you are."

While he was speaking, the wolf was quiet.

"I could do this for you." Arn put his weapons down on the ground. "If you let me get closer, maybe I could try to do something to help you."

The wolf sniffed, yellow eyes staring, and cocked its head to one side. Arn felt surprisingly emotional, as the gesture was so familiar! This is exactly how his friend Greymist would look at him curiously.

"Look, no one should have to suffer like this." He inched a bit closer to the brute, and it did not growl, only whimpered. Its tongue was hanging out, dry. It must not have had any water for days.

Arn located a helmet lying on the ground and turned back to the animal, saying, "At least I can get you some water." He blew the dust out of the helmet, dribbled a tiny bit of water into it and swished it out. Then he poured in some of the clear, cool water from his water skin, and slowly approached the beast.

It crossed through Arn's mind that this might perhaps be some kind of trick, to lure him in close for an attack. But he was not afraid. Somehow, seeing the animal act so similarly to his dog friend, he did not think the wolf would harm him.

He carefully placed the makeshift bowl down before the wolf's mouth, as close as he dared. The creature lapped at the water without even glancing up at Arn. It drank just as a dog would do, and quickly emptied the helmet. Arn added a bit more water, leaving himself just a few swigs for later, and the animal drank that too.

The wolf looked up at Arn, silently. Its huge tail wagged and thumped on the ground. Arn took out a shred of his dried meat, and placed it in the bowl. The wolf ate it greedily.

Brother Francis had taught Arn that it was given to people to care for animals, and had taught him many techniques for handling them, and caring for them when they were ill or needed help. He prayed a prayer for protection, and reached down and held his hand before the wolf's face.

It sniffed, hard, and startled Arn. Arn thought this was one of the bravest things he had ever done, or the most careless. He could not help but feel kinship with the creature. It was strange to feel so familiar with a huge, black, enemy wolf.

When the animal showed no aggression, Arn said, "Let me pull the lance from the ground. It will hurt you, but perhaps I can free you. Do not bite me because it would badly hurt me."

The animal seemed to bow its head as if it recognized common speech. "You understand me, do you now? I hope so." Arn took a deep breath. He looked at the wolf's eyes and said, "Please, don't bite me."

Arn moved to the lance and upon closer observation could see that the tip was embedded deeply into a heavy wooden saddle, upon which the beast was lying, and then into the ground. For this lance to have traveled with such force, it must have been an enchanted weapon, Arn thought.

Arn grabbed the shaft of the lance and pulled, gently at first. The wolf made low whimpering and growling noises, but placed its head down on the ground and did not try to hurt him. This indeed was an unusual type of wolf. Nothing Brother Francis had taught him about wolves had prepared him for this.

He took the little dagger, and began to work on getting the broken splinters of wood cut from the lance, to free the creature from its tether. The animal occasionally made noises that sounded like the whimper of a puppy, but it kept its head down. It took Arn nearly half of an hour, but finally the wood of the shaft snapped from the buried end of the lance.

"Okay now, I'm going to pull this out now, get ready," he warned the creature. Arn started as the wolf's head turned and he could see its fangs, its mouth opening. He was still holding his dagger, but before he could do anything, the wolf did something that shocked Arn. It licked his hand.

It did not seem as if it were tasting him to see if he would make a good meal. It was as if he were saying thank you for helping me. As if Arn were the leader of the pack and this huge beast submissive to him.

Arn pulled, and easily the shaft came free. It had been lodged between two bones, and left a nasty wound. The creature did not try to run off, as Arn had expected. Instead, it placed its head on the ground and sighed. "You are like a big stuffed animal!" exclaimed Arn.

"Would you like me to call you Bear?" At this, the animal made a low noise in its throat. "Well, I expect you have your own name, and you are quite pleased with it." Arn dared to pat the creature on its matted head.

He sat for a while and watched while the wolf licked its wounds. It began to move its leg a little, although stiffly. Arn was glad the creature did not seem interested in attacking him, and began to search his things for long strips of linen. He had several, made ready for binding up wounds of men.

Arn knew that it was healing for an animal to lick its wounds clean. There was not a lot of bleeding. "It's a bad wound, but with some prayer and time, I think you will be all right."

The darkness was gathering, and Arn was anxious to be away from this field before full night. He put almost all of the rest of his water into the helmet for the wolf to drink, and patted the wolf on its head.

"I bet you do have a name. I wish I knew what to call you." The creature whimpered as if it wished it could speak. Arn continued, "You remind me of somebody. You even kind of smell like him. My friend Greymist. A very good friend of mine."

At this, the wolf's ears perked up and its eyes looked right into Arn's. "Do you know Greymist?" Arn knew this was impossible, but he could not shake the feeling he was having a conversation with this beast.

"I guess you are just trying to figure out what I am saying." Arn stood up and prepared to leave. "Try not to do evil, now. Remember someone has done you good."

The wolf shook his head. Arn said, "Do you mean to say you understand me?" It gazed at Arn with yellow eyes.

"Perhaps you are just meant to do evil, I don't know. I will call you Shadow." Somehow this name just popped into Arn's head. Shadow's head went up and down, just like he was nodding.

"You do understand me?"

Shadow just stared.

"All right then. I will call you Shadowfang." Arn knew his imaginings were getting the best of him.

There was just a little moonlight shining behind what looked like rain clouds. Arn took up his spear and tucked the dagger into his belt. He dusted himself off, and finished the last remaining drops of water.

A tear came to his cheek as he thought of the brothers at the abbey, of Greymist, of his home. He did not have very many friends.

"I will call you a friend." The great beast howled, and Arn watched with some sadness as the animal started to limp away.

Arn stood, and shivered from the cold. He began walking back to the path, and mumbled, to no one in particular, "I wish I had my nice, warm cloak the lady gave me. I wonder if it is on this dark, horrible field somewhere. I don't have the heart to go looking around."

He turned and sprinted to get back on the path and off of this battlefield.

He briefly considered just turning and heading for Clayhaven. But from what he could see, this war was going very badly. Life in

Clayhaven would possibly never again be his familiar life of before. The death of the king, and his first son, made everything uncertain. Was the king's youngest son even still alive?

Even if nobody else ever believed it, Arn was a knight of the realm. He had a responsibility to try to do something, whatever he could, to make things right again. Perhaps at the border fortress he would encounter someone from the king's army who could vouch for him.

"I was knighted!" declared Arn, and his voice sounded too loud in the darkness. Behind him, he heard the wolf howling. Surprised, he turned, and could just make out the shape of the big animal following him.

Arn was startled. "I didn't even hear you, Shadowfang! Do you want to follow me?"

It was moving slowly, limping on its wounded leg. It opened its mouth and lolled its tongue, seeming to smile, and wagged its tail like a lap dog. Arn shook his head and smiled. This large, black wolf looked almost cute. He said aloud, "You look cute, Shadowfang."

Shadowfang grumbled, tail wagging.

"You are welcome to come with me, Shadowfang. I sure wouldn't mind a traveling companion with your intimidation abilities!" The wolf sat and wagged its tail, sniffing the breeze. Then it turned its nose up and let out a long, soulful howl.

Arn hoped the wolf was not stalking him and calling its wolf friends to come devour him. The wolf turned away, but looked back at Arn, then again, seeming to want Arn to follow. Arn retraced his steps, deciding to try to follow Shadowfang.

Following an enemy wolf in the dark somehow did not seem foreboding. He would follow for a short time. Perhaps the animal would lead him to some food or water they could both share.

They skirted the battlefield, some way down the king's line, Shadowfang sniffing as he went. After a time, the wolf came to a dark shape upon the ground and stopped. Arn approached with some trepidation, looked down, and saw to his amazement and horror what remained of the brutal man who had taken his knife and cloak from him.

Shadowfang sat near the body, tongue lolling, almost seeming to smile again. Underneath the body Arn could see his cloak. He gingerly pulled the cloak out, happy that it was in good condition, and did not look directly at the man.

He considered looking for the blade his friend had given him for his birthday, but he could not bring himself to search the body.

Instead, he glanced over the body briefly. What he saw surprised him. Tucked into the left side of the man's belt, partially covered by a ragged brown coat, was his blade! Arn was so happy at his good fortune.

His wizard trick must have worked so well that the looters had not yet returned to finish their dirty work. The victorious dark army would have taken the armor and weapons immediately after the battle. Arn said a prayer of thanks that his blade had miraculously escaped being taken.

He looked at Shadowfang with wonder. "You understood me! You are indeed an impressive new friend. Greymist has a very keen nose also, but to understand my words! You are indeed a marvelous creature. Thank you, Shadowfang!"

Arn and the wolf walked quickly back to the path, away from the battlefield. Arn heard a noise behind him that sounded almost like a chuckle, and saw Shadowfang turning from the trail, trotting away with a limp. Arn felt sad. Even this scary companion was better than being alone here.

"Well, then," murmured Arn, as he sped up, in an effort to put as much distance between himself and the battlefield as possible.

Had the brothers arrived with the king's army at last? Arn hoped they were safely ensconced in the keep, along with all the others he was acquainted with from the ill-fated battle. The keep would be well prepared to endure a siege.

Arn had learned a little of siege warfare from Brother Kile. It involved ladders, and engines like the ones used on the battlefield.

As he walked, Arn prayed for the brothers and for the land of Clayhaven. He offered a prayer for his own safety, and that he would find someone who had witnessed his knighting by the high king. He thanked God for his new friend, Shadowfang, comforted by the fact that the wolf was strong, and far better equipped to deal with things than he was.

CHAPTER NINE
GREAT WIZARD, NEW FRIEND

*A*rn *moved as quickly as he could toward the border fortresses.* The road was very dark, and the trees were thick all around. Around midwatch, he thought he should stop soon, and walked as far as a slender beam of moonlight. At least the clouds above had not rained on him.

When he stopped, something happened that startled him quite much. He heard voices ahead. They did not sound friendly. It sounded like, "You stinkin', vile, little snake's belly! I told you this is the way to the battlefield. You'll listen to me!" Arn heard a louder whack, and was terrified. He was standing in the middle of a band of moonlight, but quickly ducked off the road. He knew how well the creatures could see at night, and hoped they had not seen him.

"Oh shut up! You two's always arguing and bitin' and snarlin'! I'm gettin' sicks of it, I am. The battle's up ahead, that's what he said! Let's go! I'm tired and miserable, and I wants to get there!"

Arn was sure the small bush he took for cover was shaking all about him. These were the creatures he had just fought the other day. The thought of fighting them with his broken spear shaft and his knife made him feel sick.

He was alone and scared. In the middle of nowhere, on a dark road, with at least three of them heading his way. Some of them had a very keen sense of smell. Arn hoped they would not detect him, and pass by, but everyone in Arn's life had reminded him that he did smell noticeably. He gripped the bush and closed his eyes in prayer.

The dark, shadowy shapes lumbered into his view. One stopped in the moonlight before Arn. "That's a bright moon now," one chuckled. "It's a good killin' moon."

"Aw, shut up!" The bigger one slapped a smaller one across the face.

"You filthy sow belly! You slap me again, and I'll . . ."

"You'll what?"

"Well, I'll . . . I'll slap him!" he cried, pointing at the smallest one.

"He's your friend, isn't he?"

"Yeah, then I'll slap you again!"

The middle-sized one seemed to lose this argument as the larger one breathed a deep breath. "There's dead ahead, and horseflesh, I smell 'em. Old Angueth's up there, and he'll be mad if he catches us!" chuckled the largest one. "Let's move on, see what we can find on the battlefield. If we's lucky, we might find some lootin' humans yet there. We might find silvers and golds!"

The two smaller goor seemed to concur with the larger companion's assessment of the situation, and they all quickly moved away. Just as they were almost out of sight, the smallest one stopped, sniffing the air. "I smells horse dung!"

"You do? Did you eat it?" The biggest one gave a resounding slap, and they all laughed.

"I'm tellin' you, I smells horse dung!" Slower, he added, "But it don't quite smell right!"

Arn could see the piggish, grey face approaching the spot where he hid, just a few feet from him. They did not seem to see him, amazingly, but they sure did smell him. *Arn the horse poop scooper*, he thought sadly.

"Aye, I smells something too," snarled the largest one, drawing a wicked-looking scimitar. "Smells like humans, it does." His big nose sniffed the air, and he approached the bush that hid Arn.

All Arn could think of to do was to run, so he turned his back and ran with all his might into the depths of the woods. He could not see in the darkness, and stumbled and tripped, but managed to keep to his feet.

He heard them crashing through the woods behind him. He ran for all he was worth. He ran for quite a long way until he heard them talking in the distance. The bigger goor said, "Aw, he's just a little peasant. Come on, you twos. We's got better things up ahead, and there's more of 'em where he came from. The battlefield's not far; let's go there. We can come back for him later if he's around. Maybe we'll invite him to a stew."

"Hey, little filthy human, you wanna be a stew?" yelled the little goor, while they all laughed and turned back the way they had come.

Arn ran forward through the woods, along what seemed to be a small path. At least it was clearer walking for a way. It led to a small clearing, which he crossed. To his chagrin, the next thing he found was a rather deep ravine, headfirst. He pitched forward about four feet. Perhaps it had been a dry streambed. He stood up, pulled the little dagger out, and waited. He knew the goor could be following him still. At least he could give them a surprise if they did come this way.

Nothing happened although he waited quite a while. It must not have been a trick, and they had gone on to the battlefield. The stench of death must have been a stronger lure than the stench of one stable boy, and for this Arn was glad.

Some night geese flew overhead. Arn wished he could lift up and fly away, out of danger. He hoped the wretched goor tried to mess with Shadowfang. He would make a quick supper of them, he thought. Arn investigated the stones beneath his feet and found three which would be good throwing stones, and put them in his pocket.

He climbed up out of the creek bed, and saw a big dark shape over to the side. Was it a cave opening? He cautiously approached, and could not believe what it actually was. It was a big barrel, in the middle of nowhere. Maybe this was an old road or something. It was a very large barrel, perhaps for wine in some large establishment.

He ducked down to peer into the opening. Why would someone bring this old barrel out here? The inside was pitch black and Arn could see nothing. Ever wary of snakes, and not wishing to surprise any of nature's inhabitants of the barrel, he placed his hand on top of the opening and leaned down to look inside.

What was this? Cloth on top here? Why, it was a flap of cloth, attached at the top, to form a cover for the barrel's open end. This was very curious. Arn quickly collected some tinder to make a small fire, and waited patiently while he lighted a small torch.

He looked inside the barrel and found there were many things inside of it. Someone must be living here. He saw a piece of paper on the wall of the barrel with a picture drawn on it. On the side a small window had been carved out, with a bottle fitted into the hole very cleverly. It was a nice little house.

"Someone must have abandoned it here. I wonder," said Arn.

"Wonder what?" said a voice from behind him.

Arn turned with a start and saw a dark-cloaked figure standing in the clearing.

"You are standing in front of my home!" boomed the stranger's deep voice.

"I didn't take anything!" Arn defended himself. "I meant no offense! I was just looking. I thought it was abandoned."

"Who are you?" inquired the man's deep voice.

"Arn of Clayhaven. I was chased here by three goor. I fell into that creek there. I don't mean you any harm. I've had a bad time. I was with the army, see, and we lost . . ."

The stranger interrupted with a loud, "I care not about armies! I am a great wizard and you had better run! Flee from me before I get angry!"

Arn saw a flicker from the stranger's left hand, as if a very small flint and steel had been set together to make a small candlelight. The tiny light sparked Arn's curiosity. "What does that mean?" asked Arn.

The dark figure moved his hand again, and again there was a small flame.

"I'll leave," volunteered Arn. "I didn't mean any harm."

"You had better!" The man made a grand gesture with his hand, which was followed by a puff of smoke, and another tiny light.

Arn stared in amazement. He wasn't sure if this person was trying to fight him, or entertain him. "I'm going to go now," said Arn, without actually moving away. Perhaps this was a crazy old wizard.

"I am Greygrim the Great!"

"I believe you. You needn't do the flame thing again. I'm leaving. I won't bother you again."

"Good. See that you don't," said the voice, cracking a bit. The booming voice didn't sound so deep any more. It almost sounded like a young man.

Arn peered at the man, trying to discern what he could in the darkness. "I don't mean you any harm. I'm not going to hurt you or take anything."

"Now see here, get away! Go away!"

Arn could definitely make out that it was a boy's voice, no longer deep or frightening. He approached the wizard and could make out that the robes were quite tattered, and a young face peered out through the hood. The boy appeared taller than he actually was by standing on a small stump, which was visible below the ragged hem of his robe.

"I'm lost and miserable, and I won't bother you anymore." Arn started to turn away.

The boy jumped down from his stump, and was in fact somewhat shorter than Arn. "I don't think that you do mean to harm me," said Greygrim the Great. He pulled his hood off and revealed that he was a boy of about fifteen summers at the most, just a little older than Arn himself. He had a little stubble on his cheeks.

"You are a wizard?" wondered Arn.

"I'm an apprentice wizard," he said, kicking a stone at his feet. "Nobody's ever found my hiding place. I thought it was safe. Well, I don't get visitors at all, so maybe you don't have to go."

Arn chuckled. "Okay. I don't have anything to eat, and I'm quite out of drink, or I would offer to share with you."

"I do. I have both. Come join me. It'll be nice to have some companionship for a change. This is my front garden," he pointed around himself proudly. "That there is my streambed, and if you dig in just the right places, good sweet water will come up."

"That's wonderful. If this is your land, sir, I should tell you I have taken three stones from that creek bed."

"That's alright. There are plenty. Come on in. I'll show you around."

Arn was delighted at this turn of events. Not only did he have someone to talk to, it was someone close to his age.

"You look like you've about had it!" said Greygrim, walking around Arn. "You look—and smell—terrible!"

Arn chuckled. "Well, I've been through a lot, as I said."

"I can see you have!"

Greygrim brazenly grabbed the little torch from Arn's left hand and used it to check inside his little abode. "Looks like nothing is stolen; that's good." He handed the torch back, saying, "Sorry, I didn't mean to snatch that from your hand. My manners are lacking out here, in the middle of nowhere. Don't have many visitors."

Greygrim lit a small candle and an oil lamp. "I don't usually use both pieces of light, but in honor of your visit, we'll make it cheery. Come on inside."

Arn stepped inside, and the two young men fit easily in the tiny house. They could almost stand upright. He said, "This is a huge barrel! Where did you get it?"

"Yes, it is! Thieves brought it here years ago. If you look closely, in the daylight, you will see there's a broken wagon that was carrying it. I think they stole it, dragged it back through the path, drained off as much of the wine as they could, and went on their way."

"It's a nice little home," said Arn warmly. "I like the window."

"Ah, you like that?" Greygrim pointed proudly at the amber glass that made up the small window. "It is a good house. It stays quite dry in here. And I can see out the window. I made a fireplace back here, out of stones from the creek. I don't think it is the safest, but it keeps me warm in the winter. I have to keep a watch on it, though."

Arn admired this abode with the appreciation only a boy or a young man could feel for such a small structure made into one's very own home. It was just the right size for one young man. It was private, and although it smelled a little dank, it was a great house. He found a little creepy stool and sat down.

"You like the creepy stools? I made them myself. Took me a long time to burn out those holes and get them made right. They keep me out of the smoke in the winter."

"Very nice," said Arn. "This cask was made well. Seems quite solid."

The boys sat and talked, and during their conversation, Greygrim worked over several pieces of fish, putting them into a small pot, along with some potatoes and some onions.

"Where did you find those?" asked Arn.

"Here and about," Greygrim smiled and gave Arn a knowing wink. Arn took this to mean that Greygrim gleaned whatever he could from travelers and homes in the area.

The fish stew smelled quite good as it cooked on the little fireplace. As the food cooked, and the boys talked, Greygrim gave Arn several large glasses of clean spring water. He was so achy, hungry and thirsty. It was very pleasant to quench his thirst, rest his body, and anticipate a nice meal with an acquaintance.

He told Greygrim he had been away from his home for almost a week. The story of his days was related in great detail, and Greygrim listened intently.

"Brother, you have been through a lot these days. We could make another bed of some leaves over there, and you could stay a couple of days if you wanted. You seem alright to me, neither thief nor crazy."

Arn chuckled, "No, I'm not. I try not to be. I try to be polite."

"You seem very polite. Maybe too polite." Greygrim slapped Arn hard on the shoulder. "Well, I need to get some shuteye. In the morning I can show you around my woods. For now, I'm just going to bring in some leaves."

The two boys carried in several armfuls of dry leaves and heaped them up for Arn. It was so comfortable to lie on a bed of sorts in a warm place.

Greygrim said, "Tomorrow we'll look around."

"That would be nice."

"Maybe we can find some more food lying around somewhere," grinned Greygrim.

"Is there a village nearby?" asked Arn.

"Well, there was. A small village, not too far away, but the people are gone. The war. I hadn't heard too much about it until tonight. Sounds bad."

"It is. It's bad." They were both quiet, and Arn felt relaxed on his leaf bed. "Thank you for your kindness, Greygrim. I will remember it. I will repay it somehow."

"Don't worry about it." The older boy sat and stared at the dying fire and stirred the embers with a stick, deep in thought.

"I ran away," said Greygrim quietly. "I'm not really a wizard. My master, he came from a long line of wizards. My father turned me over to him when I was only five. My father knew he was cruel, but said that I could learn a great trade.

"My older brother got the wealth of our household, what there was of it. So it was supposed to be a great opportunity for me, not to have to labor in the fields."

His face in the flickering firelight showed that the painful memories were still there. "He was cruel. I have the welts to prove it. He taught me many things, and I learned well. He didn't like it that I was a fast learner. You would think he would appreciate that from an apprentice, but he didn't. He was mean. And he was crazy. He began to delve into the black arts. I decided to leave, go back to my father's house.

"I learned a bit of magic, something he wanted to teach me. I was in the small study. I didn't often go to this place, but I was there practicing. I overheard him talking to the servant, his most trusted servant.

"He told him that he was not happy with me. An accident should befall me. At first, I didn't believe he was speaking about me. I knew he didn't like me, but—" Greygrim became quiet.

Arn sat up on his bed and said, "People can be very cruel."

"Yes, they can," said Greygrim. "I learned my father had died. My older brother had also succumbed to the illness. This wizard took great pleasure in telling me this, seeing my grief. The day I heard him plotting against me, I couldn't stand it any more. I listened at the door, carefully.

"The servant was to bring me my daily soup with poison in it, a very bad, quick poison. He was to dispose of my body 'as best he could.' How cold, how miserable I felt that day."

Arn nodded his head. He remembered being treated badly on many occasions in Clayhaven, but perhaps not as badly as Greygrim had been. At least he had the monks and Greymist.

"I was going to outsmart the old man. I sneaked into the scullery where the soup was laid out. I took a sample of the soup and an empty bowl. When they served me my bowl of soup, I substituted the soup I had taken for the bowl they served me. The servant came back and I greedily ate the soup.

"My master entered the room and watched me intently as I ate. He was unnerved and left, saying he was going to his library, so I followed after I finished eating. When I entered the door, his back was to me, and I heard him say, 'Is he dead?'

"Those words were like arrows. I stood there in the doorway and said, 'No, I'm not.'

"The old man looked up from his books, and I'll never forget the look of shock in his eyes. He said, 'So, you've heard of my little plot, have you? That's why you didn't die. Switched the soup, did we?'

"'Yes, we did.' I said. And with all my might, I hurled the empty bowl at his head, and darned if I didn't hit him, right in the head. He stumbled and fell; it knocked him cold.

"I knew this would be a very bad end for me. I gathered up what I could and I left. I ran all night. I wandered around these woods for probably two weeks before I found this place. I heard he placed a bounty on my head, claiming I assaulted him and stole many things from him.

"But truly, I only took what was mine, rightfully mine. He placed ten gold crowns upon my head!

"When I found this barrel, it was a miracle. And I have been here ever since." He looked at Arn intently, and Arn could see that there were unshed tears in his eyes.

Arn nodded. "I can't say that things have been that bad for me. But I'm glad that you are here and we met this night. I'm Arn of Clayhaven, knight of Southaven, and I call you friend."

Arn held out his hand. Greygrim seemed taken aback by this gesture. "Friend? I am Greygrim, to be a great wizard one day, or something," grinned the older boy. "And I call you friend."

He grasped Arn's arm in a great lion's grasp, hand to elbow. "Well met, Sir Arn," said Greygrim.

Arn said, "Well, I'm going to get some sleep. I think perhaps tomorrow we should see what's about. Maybe we might find you some interesting things if we went back to the battlefield?"

"No, no, I wouldn't want to go there." Greygrim shook his head. "We'll see what the morrow holds. I'm not that far from the road, really. We'll go up on the road and check in the village. We might find some useful things."

"Goodnight, Greygrim."

"Sleep well, Arn."

That night Arn slept better than he had in quite a while, and did not have any bad dreams. When he awoke just past dawn, it was chilly in the room. Keeping the blanket wrapped around him, he went over to the fire and poked around with a stick to stir up the embers. When the coals were going, he put in some kindling and started a small fire.

He lifted the old, heavy horse blanket that served as a makeshift doorway and stepped outside. The sky was clear and already bright with the morning sun. Arn's spirits were more cheerful today. The clearing that Greygrim called his front garden was very pretty. It reminded Arn of his home, peaceful and pleasant.

There was a small apple tree near the edge of the clearing and when Arn investigated, he realized there must have been an orchard at one time. There were a number of apple trees evenly spaced, and on some of the trees there were still a few apples. He found a couple that did not look too bad, and used a stick to knock them to the ground.

He scrambled down to the stream bed and found a couple of small pools of water, where he gathered some in an old bucket he found next to Greygrim's house.

"Awake friend, are you, already?" He heard Greygrim's voice behind him.

"I brought those two apples from the top of the tree. I hope you don't mind."

"Oh. I was saving those. Never mind, this is probably the best time to use them." Greygrim took the apples from Arn.

"I was going to make some barley and apples for breakfast."

"That sounds tasty! And, actually, I have a surprise to add to it." Greygrim smiled.

Arn mixed up the breakfast in a little pot and put it on the fire, while Greygrim rummaged in his things and brought out a tiny bundle. "It's cinnamon."

"Cinnamon! Where would you get that?"

"Found it. It'll make a king's breakfast."

The young men stirred their pot and got ready for the day. When Arn served up the porridge, he gave Greygrim the largest share. As they ate the hearty breakfast, they talked about their plans for the day.

Greygrim showed Arn many of the features in the woods, and Arn was amazed that Greygrim seemed to know every tree, every feature. In the village, they did find some evidence of looting. Most of the things had been carried away except for a couple of broken pieces of furniture.

They did find two ears of old dried corn, a potato, an old end of bread, and surprisingly, while kicking around in the leaves and dust, a bronze coin. In one tiny cottage, in the midst of what looked like broken bits of pottery, they discovered an intact small clay pot which contained, to their delight, strawberry jam.

Greygrim had Arn help him haul the broken furniture back to his house. He planned to make something of them, some other furniture to make his house homier.

By contrast with Arn's recent experiences, this day was so peaceful and happy that he planned to stay a little longer with Greygrim before leaving for the border. His feet and back still hurt, though not as much as before. Another day would help him get his strength back. He was afraid of the roads now, and he did indeed like the company of Greygrim.

They had had long conversations about the possibility of going back to the battlefield. The thought that they might find weapons or other valuable items was very compelling, and each boy could back up the other if they ran into any trouble.

Arn again gave some consideration to returning to Clayhaven, but decided he belonged at the border. Perhaps he could hear news of the brothers' whereabouts as they served the army in battle, and go find them.

Arn asked Greygrim if he wanted to go with him to the border fortress, but Greygrim declined. If Arn should come back this way, though, he was welcome to visit again at Greygrim's little house.

In any case, Greygrim had decided he would accompany Arn down the road part of the way to the border, about a day and a half. Arn was hoping that Greygrim might change his mind and go with him on his journey.

The two days Arn spent at Greygrim's were relaxing and peaceful. They gathered up the apples and stored them in straw for the winter. The boys did not see any other people.

In the peace of his own thoughts, Arn could see that he had indeed done some brave and useful deeds for Southaven. He replayed the words of the high king during his few moments of recognition for his efforts. He remembered the feeling of strength and pure, golden selflessness that had washed over him when he was doing the right thing, his duty for his land and for God.

Everything seemed different when there were no people poking at you and laughing, casting scorn and insults your way. Arn did not doubt that such derision would come his way again in the future, but he felt that he would not receive it as completely ever again. He imagined standing as a man, with his eyes open before him, not downcast ever again. He was a knight of the realm.

All of his experiences since he had left Clayhaven had changed him. Some of the memories were gory and terrible, and some were strong and happy. Arn felt he had grown up a lot in just a few days.

He would find the army and do what he could to save Southaven. If possible, he would find a noble who could provide him with a document of some sort to prove his knighthood. As a knight of the realm, he should no longer go hungry or thirsty, miserable and cold, or serve under mean taskmasters. He felt honorable blood beating through his heart, but he knew that his appearance was young, gangly, dirty, and that those he met would still doubt his courage and ability. Nevertheless, he would do what he could.

The boys' last supper together consisted of a stew containing parsnip, carrot, potato, and a small piece of pork fat they had found stuck to the rafters inside a smokehouse. For dessert they had crisp late-fall apples with a bit of strawberry jam smeared on them.

That last night, there was activity on the road. They heard in the distance what they figured was a band of goor traveling at a fast pace. Later, they heard the definite pounding of some horses galloping the road. Arn was reminded of his responsibility, that there was a war ongoing, and determined to make his way the next morning.

When they got to the road the next day, Greygrim found a broken spear lance with a broken steel spear point. They did not know if one of the goor had dropped it or perhaps one of the horsemen. It would be perfect to make a small throwing or stabbing spear. Greygrim weighed it in his hand and inspected it for quite a while. "It's quite a prize." He held the spear out to Arn. "I think you could use it in your journey more than I can. I've got magic after all," he grinned.

Arn smiled, "Thank you. That's very nice."

"Well, gotta be nice to you since you came to visit and all."

"Don't worry, I'll come and visit as often as I can. Don't know what the future holds though."

Greygrim gazed down the road thoughtfully, and spoke quietly, "We don't know what the future holds."

Arn now felt a sense of urgency to reach the border fortress. Each day that passed might be critical to the future of Southaven, and there might be something Arn could do to help.

Arn's friend had supplied him with some parched corn, a few apples, and a couple of large acorn cups which had been filled with the strawberry jam. They had pressed some wax into the top with hopes that the jam would keep a while.

As they walked up the road, they talked. "You know Arn, if you would just come back here, we could make this into a better place."

"You are right. Who knows what is left of Clayhaven by now." It sickened Arn to imagine harm coming to any of his few friends in Clayhaven, but he knew they all knew where to go in case of an attack. Arn winced at the thought of anyone looting his little room, or the abbey. He quickly rid himself of the thought that anyone might hurt Greymist, because he was confident of the dog's intelligence and loyalty. He hoped the dog's loyalty would not make him try to defend against any enemy that might come. He hoped his toy soldiers hidden in the rafters of his room would be safe.

CHAPTER TEN

THE MAIDEN

The boys walked for hours, sometimes conversing, sometimes in companionable silence, and each was glad for the other's company. Late in the afternoon, Arn said, "Did you hear that?"

Greygrim listened a moment, and said, "What?"

"Maybe it was just the wind."

A few steps later, "No, listen."

Silence was all they heard. "Wait a minute." Arn stopped walking, and Greygrim stopped also. They listened.

"It sounded like an animal? A girl?" said Arn.

"Oh—sounds like somebody screaming," agreed Greygrim. "Perhaps someone on the road needs help."

The boys rushed down the road, and Greygrim pulled his dark cloak over him. They approached a pathway that headed off the main road. They could now distinctly hear a girl screaming, "You filthy brigands! I'll kill you! Stay back!"

The boys crowded behind some evergreen bushes and listened. Greygrim hooded his face fully with his black cloak and peered around the bushes. "There's a girl over there, with three goor around her," he whispered. "There's one goor on the ground."

"Are they attacking her?" Arn whispered back.

"They have their filthy swords pulled," hissed Greygrim.

Arn parted the branches very slowly, and through the green needles he saw the prettiest girl he had ever seen. At least from this distance she seemed so. She had dark hair and stood a proud foot taller than the stooped goor surrounding her. She held a long knife and appeared prepared to use it. Indeed, her skill with the knife might explain the goor lying on the ground nearby. There was a tiny handcart a distance away that might belong to her.

The boys looked at each other. Arn hefted his little spear that they had found. "What do we do?" They quickly whispered a plan.

Greygrim said, "I will be the wizard, and you go around the back."

"Ok, you do the wizard thing and I'll try to get a jump on one." Arn felt the handle of his dagger at his belt. "Let's hope the one on the ground doesn't try to get back up. I guess the three of us can get the three of them."

"Count of thirty? Then I'll come out and show myself." The boys agreed to this plan, and Arn could feel himself breathing heavily as he nodded at Greygrim and headed back through the woods to circle around.

Greygrim very nervously began counting to thirty. His heart was pounding, and he repeated to himself, I've got to be intimidating, I am a great wizard.

It took Arn longer than the count of thirty. It seemed like every step was noisy, every dry leaf and twig crackled. It would be a miracle if he was able to get behind the goor without their notice. He was glad they were intent on their victim, and making all kinds of snarling and growling sounds of their own.

Then he heard a loud, clear voice from the other side of the group. "Halt, you demon brigands! Let the girl go!" Greygrim stepped out from behind the bushes, standing as tall as he could without the benefit of a stump. Amazingly, the flame-in-the-hand trick worked. He was a formidable figure, all hooded in black, standing taller than the goor and the girl.

The creatures were startled and two of them stepped back several paces, until they were behind the girl. Arn stepped forward, brandishing his spear, and it was enough to make his presence known. "We are a company of men who have come down the road, and we see what you have done. You have attacked one of our wayfarers, and now you will suffer our wrath."

The goor were startled, and began muttering beneath their breath, looking all around them. The girl wasted no time and sprang forward, jabbing something into the side of the hideous one nearest her. As Arn ran forward, he saw the eyes of the goor widen, then empty, as it fell to the ground.

Arn screamed as he rammed his spear towards one of the attackers. It parried the blow with its black scimitar. The remaining goor continually looked towards the wizard, obviously afraid. Greygrim began to make loud, howling intonations. Arn placed a blow with the wood of his broken spear on the creature's head. It screamed in pain.

The girl was a proficient warrior and had unbalanced the other goor. Arn recognized the disgusting creature, and realized these were the same three who had chased him through the woods a few days before. The realization gave him new energy as he fought the predators.

The goor on the ground was hissing and screeching at Arn, while holding onto its face. It landed a cut on his ankle. He brought the spear point down on the creature's back as hard as he could. He felt a sickening crunch as the spear tip pierced his foe.

The girl kicked the goor at her feet, separating it from its sharp scimitar. Greygrim ran forward and joined her in kicking it. The goor screeched and howled in anger, scrambled to its feet, stumbled past the handcart and ran off towards the road, screaming of treacherous humans.

The boys looked down at the unmoving goor on the ground, Arn checking to make sure that they would not get up again to bother them. The girl stood with her knife in her hand, then cleared a spot in the dry leaves and plunged it into the dirt. She did this several times, angrily, cleaning her blade of the sticky, black blood.

Arn spoke to her, "I'm Sir . . . I'm Arn of Clayhaven. This is Greygrim." Greygrim nodded when the girl raised her head to look at both of them. She looked surprised. Her face was wet with tears.

"I'm Anne. Thank you both." It seemed difficult for her to speak.

"You did well. You actually saved yourself more than we did," Arn told her.

Greygrim added, "Maybe we should get out of here. There might be more of them about."

"I ran into those three the other night, but I managed to elude them," Arn said. He had run from all three, but the girl had bested two of them. He extended his hand to help Anne to her feet.

"I am Greygrim the Wizard," said Greygrim with a small bow. "Did they loot your cart?" There seemed to be only some straw and some torn fabric inside it. As he gestured, some glowing embers were visible from the sleeve of his cloak.

"It's ok. What is that trick?" asked Anne.

Greygrim patted his sleeve and pushed the rod out of sight. "Oh, it's a powerful magical ability," he said with a grin.

Anne sheathed her blade at her waist, and the boys escorted her through the underbrush towards the road. She declined their help with her cart, and walked forward determinedly. The boys could see her hands shaking as she went. Greygrim offered, "Let me take care of your cart. I know of a place we can put it and come back later whenever we want it."

After gazing at Greygrim, Anne nodded her head and turned the cart's handle to him. He tucked the small cart under a bush and hid it with brush. "I'll be back later to take care of this."

Anne wrapped her arms around herself as if she were cold. These boys might not realize it, but Anne was not a warrior or accustomed to fighting. She would not have believed it if someone had told her she would be doing so now.

Sensing her discomfort, Arn tried to offer encouragement, "You can obviously handle yourself well. You took them out easily. You needn't be worried now."

"Thank you," she said quietly.

They walked along until they found a quiet site, off the road, for making a campfire. Greygrim made tea, and sweetened it with a bit of precious sugar.

Anne was surprised at the sweet taste. "Is it some kind of honey?" she asked.

"No, it's sugar!" grinned Greygrim.

"It's very nice," she said quietly, cupping her little bowl in her hands as if gathering the warmth.

"Where are you from?" asked Arn.

"I'm from Deladen, on the border."

"That's the border fortress to the northeast," said Arn.

"Yes, it was. I don't think it is any more. The dark army went through there." She shuddered, obviously remembering. "There were several dark armies, I believe."

"Yes, that's right, there were," said Arn. "I was in a battle with one of them, probably a smaller one. But very effective. Because they . . ." Arn's voice faded off. Greygrim looked away.

"What did they do?" prompted Anne after a pause.

"They killed our king. And his eldest son."

Anne gasped. Her face looked stricken. "This is terrible news! What are we to do?"

"The armies are still out. The lands are in confusion. The larger army was mostly victorious. This whole area is now mostly deserted. I was trying to get back to Lord Hamilton's keep. They wouldn't even let me in."

"They wouldn't? Why not? Did they know you were a citizen of Southaven?"

"They said I was a thief," Arn shrugged. "I'm used to it."

"*Are* you a thief?"

"No, certainly not!" said Arn with disgust.

"I meant no offense," said Anne, glancing down.

Greygrim piped up, "I'm not a thief either. I only acquire what I need to survive."

Arn smiled. Greygrim was quite good at finding things here and there. Picking up an unwanted or forgotten tidbit in a deserted town could hardly be considered stealing. Finding and making use of objects with no owner was a hard living, but Greygrim was an expert.

Arn stood up to go gather some wood. "Well, we should get a fire going."

"The fire magic is indeed a great talent," she said politely.

"I studied under a great wizard."

After a time, Arn returned with an armload of wood. The boys stirred up the kindling, added some larger pieces of wood, and scraped down to the dirt around the fire. Around the edges of the fire they placed several rocks to warm up for the oncoming night.

Arn had found an apple. Part of it was bad, and he cut that carefully away and handed the good piece to Anne. Their hands briefly touched and Arn watched in amazement as Anne looked down demurely, then back at him. Arn was surprised by his own reaction and made a point of not staring. He wondered if this was what the monks had spoken about, the wiles of a woman. It did make him feel funny. He couldn't help but smile broadly, and felt his cheeks burn.

The three companions settled in around the small fire. Greygrim rummaged in his pack for some supper. Arn looked up at Anne as she bit into the apple and saw what he had not seen before; the side of her face had an ugly red mark. Tomorrow it would be quite bruised.

"Did the goor do that?" he asked, pointing at her cheek. She nodded. "Those are rotten creatures!" Arn was angry at the wound the girl was suffering.

"Yes, they are," she agreed, "but at least two of them won't be hurting anyone anymore."

Greygrim set his little pot on the coals, admonished Arn to keep a watch over the pot, and set off, saying he would not be gone for long.

Arn found a small piece of cloth, wet it, and wrapped some of his precious herbs in it. After cleaning the wound with water, he handed the compress to Anne, saying, "If you keep this on your cheek, it will be much better by morning."

The girl smiled her thanks, and Arn found he could not take his eyes from her. He had spent precious little time around girls, but this girl intrigued him. She was beautiful, quiet and gracious, but also had fought a band of goor with courage and success. She did not speak much, nor even look up often, but she gave no sign that she thought ill of Arn or held any scorn for him.

Arn stirred the soup, which consisted of dried mushrooms and dried carrots from Greygrim's stores, and could not think of much to say. After a while, when Greygrim still had not returned, Arn served Anne some soup in her little bowl, and sat watching while she sipped it. Her eyes slowly blinked as she stared into the coals. It was hard to tell if she was awake or dreaming.

As soon as she finished her soup, Anne curled up on the ground by the fire and closed her eyes. Just then, Arn heard a cracking sound, someone approaching. Hoping it was Greygrim, he drew his blade and watched.

His friend materialized out of the darkness, hooded with his black cloak. "Well, everything is gone."

In a whisper, Greygrim related his tale of traveling back to the site of their encounter with the goor. Someone had already been there, and all the weapons, along with anything else the goor had carried, were gone. He had retrieved the cart and secreted it in a place he knew it would be safe. They could pick it up when they needed it. Greygrim was certain nobody could have followed him back to their camp.

The boys conversed in a whisper while they ate. Greygrim made a funny tale of their encounter with the goor, and declared he would make a story of it, or a poem, to remember it by. He was familiar with the terrain in that area, and described the cave where he had taken the cart. It was a dry, difficult place to find.

As he listened, Arn found himself watching the girl's sleeping face. Her rosy cheeks attested to the fact that she was warm despite the cool night air. Her dark hair was fluffy and shiny, not at all matted or greasy. He thought she was about his age, but he could not quite tell.

The boys talked about carefree things, like living a peaceful life in Greygrim's cask, or possibly making a home in the cave. They imagined what it would be like to be just a band of friends. "It is good to have company after so long," remarked Arn.

Greygrim noticed Arn's attention was divided. "You like her, do you?"

Arn laughed, "Not really. Well, of course. I mean, about the way I like you."

"I'm a bit older. I know a bit about these things," Greygrim smiled.

Greygrim and Arn started to settle into their places for the night. Arn found the smoothest warm stone and, watching Anne's face all the while, walked around to place the stone at her back. She startled when he was close to her, and in an instant she jumped up and drew the blade she had tucked in her waist. "Don't come near me!"

"Wait! It's just me!" Arn quickly spoke in calming tones, while showing his hands. "I was bringing you a warm rock for your back!" Arn was visibly shaken and surprised by her reaction.

Anne dropped her hand with the blade, smiled wearily and said, "I'm very sorry! I worked at a tavern. It was an awful place! People are horrible. They'll even take your place you're sleeping in if you don't watch out."

Arn understood this and answered, "Taverns can be unfriendly places."

"I'll take the rock," she told Arn.

"That's good, because this thing is hot!" Arn could feel the heat through the thick layers of leaves he had used to pick it up.

Anne lay back down in her spot by the fire, and allowed Arn to tuck the smooth stone in behind the small of her back. They left three stones next to the fire to use later in the wee morning hours when it was coldest and these warm stones would have cooled off.

"You have both been so kind," she said as she lay in the glow of the fire. "Heroes, you are."

Both of the boys grinned, and Greygrim piped up, "He's a knight, you know."

"A knight? No, you're not." Anne looked sleepy and doubtful.

Arn nodded his head. "I am."

Greygrim urged Arn to tell the story of his knighting, and Anne listened, eyelids low.

Anne slept until mid-morning. The boys woke up early, gathered up some wood for their fire, and found a few autumnberries. They were small, purplish berries with white stem ends. Autumnberries were quite a bit better if left on the bush until some frost should sweeten them. Arn remembered the Lady had used autumnberries to make tarts. He figured if these were left on the bush until now, that was proof that nobody had been here.

Greygrim had some ideas of where to look for forage, and sure enough, under his direction they found an abundant supply of hazelnuts for the picking. They spent a while gathering as much as they could hold, then went back to the camp.

Greygrim had decided that his best course of action would be to continue with Arn. He could always return to his home whenever he wanted. Their encounter with the goor the day before, and a rescue of a girl in distress, were enough to convince him that his friend would fare better with him along.

Who knew when they would need the services of a wizard? Or someone to find what was needed? They would need to ask Anne what she planned to do. They decided they could take her to the cave or to Greygrim's home, if that was what she wanted to do. Arn wanted to ask her if she would consider going to the border with them, since she knew the roads and pathways.

Arn prepared a cold breakfast, some of their oats cooked ahead by Greygrim. He added some nuts and autumnberries. They all ate hungrily. Anne even ate a second bowl. They wondered how long she had been without a good meal.

After she had finished the last mouthful, Arn said, "I'll be leaving later today, in just a while."

"Oh?" she said.

"Greygrim has decided to come with me. Do you know where you plan to go? We could take you to Greygrim's home, he said, or to a cave we know of."

"That road is quite unpleasant. Where were you heading? Were you going to Nordhold?"

"Yes, I was going to try. There is a nobleman there who saw me knighted on the field, I think, who is still alive."

"I would like to go with you. After all, you boys could get into a lot of trouble without me."

Arn and Greygrim laughed. "What if we got into a lot of trouble with you?" asked Greygrim, as he slapped her on the back.

Arn more seriously said, "I was thinking you probably would be able to help guide us, since you are familiar with the border areas."

"That's settled, then. What should we take along?"

Greygrim said, "We have picked up a lot of nuts and some berries this morning, and we have our provisions we brought along. Could you get the fire out? Things are pretty deserted around here. We will have to keep our eyes open for whatever we can find."

"Nordhold is at least two days' walk from here, and since I slept so late," she said sheepishly, "we are getting a late start. Shall we travel the rest of today, then into the night? That might be safer than traveling all days, or all nights."

Greygrim agreed he could see the logic in that. "This way if people are traveling during the day, they'll find us, and if they are traveling at night, they'll still find us."

Arn punched Greygrim on the arm. "It's a good idea. It's not raining, anyway. We should go."

They debated whether or not they would need the little handcart, but decided to carry their items with them. They gathered their meager possessions and what food they had and set off, determined to stay with the road, but not on the road. Greygrim wore his wide-brimmed, floppy hat and gathered his grey cloak around him. Arn carried his gear and makeshift spear, which he also used as a walking stick, with the air of a soldier. His eyes often traveled over to where Anne walked beside them.

They stayed in the shadow of the trees that lined the road, and watched for brigands in both directions. This was Greygrim's idea. Under the trees they would not be visible at great distance, yet they hoped they could see oncoming travelers before they themselves were seen. Greygrim seemed to have a bit of experience at avoiding unwanted eyes upon him.

The trio traveled many hours without incident. The afternoon was clear, lovely and cool. They almost forgot there was a war being waged in their fair land. The road was deserted, and it was difficult to imagine that they might easily see people fleeing conflict, deserters, enemies, army scouts, even armies at any time.

They were vigilant. Several times they quickly left the road, thinking one of them had seen or heard something, but no real problems materialized.

They played word games and taught each other songs to entertain themselves as they walked, and made good time. Arn thought this might be the most pleasant outing he had ever had in all his life. He allowed his gaze to rest on Anne's red cheeks and fair countenance often. A couple of times when she smiled, he found the sight almost too much to take. He did not understand why he would feel this twist of anxiety when watching her. He just knew he was compelled to do so.

The girl in Clayhaven had made him feel anxious. He had liked her. But that had been different.

They saw vultures and flocks of black birds off in the distance. As they went on they found debris along the side of the road. Things cast off in wartime as people left their homes hurriedly behind them. Some broken chairs, a small broken table.

Greygrim eyed these things intently. Arn asked him, "What are you planning? Redecorating?"

Greygrim laughed. "You never know. I have been thinking about hauling some of these things back home."

Arn was amused. When they saw broken crockery, he cracked a joke. Anything of true value was gone, however, which was too bad. On the other hand, if Greygrim had seen anything he really wanted, the temptation to take it back home might have been too great.

"What I don't want to find is any goor," said Greygrim. "It is getting dark.

"You are right," said Arn with concern. "Anne, what do you think? Do you think we should go on in the dark?"

"Let's go a little further. So far it has gone well. I've had a very nice day," she said, smiling.

Arn wished for more light. He could barely see her smile in the last rays of the sun and wished he could see more.

The three travelers went on into the dark for quite a while, until it got so dark. Then the full moon rose. They went over a rise, and ran directly into a broken cart, over on its side. On the other side of a cart was a dead horse, still hitched to the cart. Arn could tell the horse had been run until its heart gave out. It had not been dead very long. Arn patted the poor beast on its neck sadly.

They acquired some smooth spokes from the cart that would serve well as clubs. Arn kept his tucked into the back of his belt, extending just over his shoulder so he could grab it easily when needed.

They kept on going until their feet began to stumble. The darkness increased as the forest thickened, and they began to feel uneasy. Arn would have said it seemed there was an evil presence. The thing that had killed the horse and made its owner drive it to its death. It felt they were going towards this evil thing, not away.

Thoughts of things that had happened in the days before crept into Arn's head. As he observed Anne, she also looked uneasy. "How were those goor able to surprise you?"

"They seemed to be looking for something in the woods."

Arn was surprised to realize they very well might have been looking for him, or signs of him.

"An evil lot. I thought I was done for if you hadn't come along," added Anne.

Having made a great deal of progress, they stopped just about midwatch. They got well off the road and found a campsite that someone had used some time ago. Just then, they were startled to hear voices coming up the road. They ducked down, and Greygrim crept close to the road to see.

They were people who looked like refugees, but none of the friends said anything, not knowing what kind of people they were.

They slept without a fire that night. Arn took first watch, Greygrim second, and Anne watched over them in the early morning. She was used to rising early. There were no other travelers on the road during the night.

Since they were so close to the Nothlunds, they discussed it and made a decision to travel much more carefully. An encounter with the wrong group could be fatal. They got started just before dawn, staying closer to the edge of the road, and keeping the hoods of their cloaks pulled over their heads. When they came to an open field, they went as quickly as they could until once again they were bordered by the safety of woods.

There were a couple of parties that passed by them as they hid in the woods. Again, they looked like refugees, and were moving in the opposite direction. Greygrim ventured to talk to some of them, and he was told that the border fortresses were ready to fall.

Then a passing group of men explained that Nordhold was not under siege, but they feared it would not be long. The Dark One had isolated the border fortress for a time, then the watchers had moved on.

Arn, Greygrim and Anne were encouraged by this news. They had yet to see any groups of villains, since their encounter with the goor. They moved as fast as they could, and stopped again about midwatch. There were a lot more refugees on the road now, and they hid themselves carefully and slept without a fire once again.

Traveling was very exhausting as there were so many groups of people on the road that they had to hide and avoid.

Around midday, they began to hear a noise from the distance, over a rise in the road. It was the quick thumping of a drum, and the snapping of a whip. They took no chances, since this reminded them definitely of a goor troop. They quickly ducked into the forest, this time covering themselves with leaves.

The troop passed, and as Arn and Anne crawled out of the piles of leaves, they saw Greygrim had dared to watch the drumming goor pass by. He reported it was about a score, lightly equipped with bows, and one with the whip they had heard. He said one of the goor had a strange device strapped to his back that he had never seen before. The whole group had trotted down the road quickly, singing one of their foul marching songs. He understood the command given by the whipmaster, for his former instructor had taught him some vocabulary in the language of the vagabond. "Onde tighe, crawl doul!" which meant, "On straight, serpent boys!" The latter was meant to be insulting, that they crawl on their bellies like serpents.

Arn said a quick prayer for all the refugees they had encountered on the road, hoping they would not be overtaken.

After this, they decided to travel through the woods and avoid the road entirely. They thought they were not far from the border fortress.

In the middle of the afternoon they crossed a small road in the woods that led to a little village. They were happy to see it. Everything looked so ordinary and normal. Any minute they thought they would see harvesters in the fields and people going about their daily chores.

As they watched cautiously, the truth dawned on them. Things were not normal at all. There was not a single chimney puffing smoke from a family's fire. Nobody could be seen at all.

They approached carefully and saw the village had been ransacked and abandoned. They looked into the small buildings. Arn found a small piece of very white cloth, completely clean, which he tucked away for making bandages when needed.

Anne found an egg inside a chicken house. Arn and Greygrim both were delighted for her and insisted when they ate she should enjoy her find. Anne was quite pleased by this. She had not always been treated so well. Even though traveling towards Southaven's enemy made her anxious, she felt more secure with her companions than she had ever felt in her lifetime. She was much more accustomed to working bitterly hard, avoiding smacks and jeers and complaints of rude and hungry guests. Her uncle had treated her as though she was a slave, making her work from before sunlight to midwatch. She could not help but dislike him with all her heart. He had had a terrible, greedy disposition and she had not ever wanted to look at his face. One day she had simply gathered her few possessions and ran as fast and far as she could.

The boys suspected some of the difficulties she had endured but did not hear any details from her.

They moved up the road toward Nordhold. The town proper had been laid out on a hill, and there was an older town wall above, while the newer town wall stretched out around the bottom of the hill, with settlements scattered around beyond it.

The buildings at the bottom of the hill were deserted. Their objective was the fortress itself, at the top of the hill. It looked very formidable in the autumn rays of the sun, with six strong towers around the keep, all formed of grey and black stones. There was age-old damage to the stones from previous encounters. A very tall central wall led into the interior of the great castle itself. At the very top were four towers topping a central block structure.

They approached the gate cautiously, Arn bringing up the rear. He couldn't help but remember his last experience at approaching a fortress. Over the top of the twenty foot wall, they could barely see the top of a helm.

They heard a loud, "What's your business here?"

"We are travelers in seek of refuge," said Anne.

The gruff voice said, "Refuge? You should have gone south. This is a dangerous place to be."

"We did not know where to go," yelled Anne up the wall. "Our friend here," she pointed at Arn, "has an errand."

The guard spat off the wall and a thick brown spittle landed on the cobblestones beside them. Arn recognized this thick spit from cleaning many a chamber pot and spittoon at the tavern back in Clayhaven.

"Well, you don't look like trouble to me," said the voice, quieter. "Come in that side door over there. Be very careful. We might just have to send you packing back out of here if you look at us funny."

"Yes, sir," answered Anne politely.

The three approached the needle gate to the side of the main gate, and there the tall helmed man with brown spittle dripping from his chin met them, along with two other guards. "Are you carryin' any extra food with you that you will donate to the cause of defending the king's castle?"

"No, we hardly have anything left at all."

"Hmm. Rough times," he said. He seemed rough but strong and experienced, with forty or more summers. He did not search them but told them there was a wayfarer's kitchen set up by the brothers and sisters of the town, and that they would find soup there, and bread if they were lucky.

"Thank you, sir," said Arn. "You have been a lot kinder than they were at the last gate I was at."

"Oh? Trouble?" he asked curiously.

"No," Greygrim answered quickly, pulling Arn forward by the arm. "He fell and hurt himself on the cobblestones."

"Well, our cobblestones are nice and even. Least until the bombards knock them apart," he added with a grin.

The interior of the fortress was crowded with people. Several market places were set up, and they set forth, asking as they went for the wayfarer's kitchen. They came upon the station set up by the holy orders, and were greeted by a brother in brown robes who was washing wayfarers' feet, checking for sores and wounds, and binding them in salve and cloth. There was a sister of the order there who was helping. In the clay bowls beside her on a blanket were a number of herbs, many of which Arn recognized.

The brother asked, "You three look healthy. Do you need checking over? Is there anything we can do for you?"

"No," answered Arn. "We are just in want of food."

"The kitchen's over there." He pointed. "We have a good turnip soup."

That sounded delicious to all three, at this stage in their journey. Anne still had her egg, but everything else edible had been eaten. The steaming soup smelled wonderful, and they were glad to find little bits of pork cooked well into the soup. They filled their stomachs comfortably.

There was an aura of sadness and fear around them. They could tell that war had been on some of these people. There was a shelter next to the chapel which had been made into a hospital. Perhaps in other times outdoor services had been held here, or perhaps tables of food for some celebration, but now it contained a number of wounded being tended by brothers and sisters. From the shelter they could hear coughing, crying, requests for water.

Arn wanted to go help the holy people minister to the wounded. After all he had a small bit of experience and believed he could be of use. He decided the lord of the castle could wait, and told his plans to Anne and Greygrim. They too were willing to help.

After some discussion it was decided that Greygrim would scout around and see what he could find out about the lord of the keep, and try to find out if he would speak to them. "Do you really think he'll speak to us, Arn?"

"Well, he saw what happened. He knows that I was made a knight. If he is here."

"I can probably find out if he is here or not. If anybody will tell us anything. We are not exactly dressed as nobles!" Greygrim laughed.

"All right. We will help with the wounded and then let's meet back here in a couple of hours."

Arn and Anne tried to be useful in ministering to the needs of the wounded. Anne was quite unaccustomed to seeing such gory sights. Limbs cut off, fingers missing, ears gone, noses broken, gaping wounds of war. Arn saw a man with severe burns over his body.

The brothers were grateful for their extra hands and willingness to do whatever was asked. One of the brothers disappeared into the chapel and came back out with a piece of bread which he handed to Anne. He told her to keep it for the two of them. Anne felt that she should give it to some of the wounded, but the brother told her that most of the patients were not to eat anything solid.

Anne thanked the brother with a warm handclasp, and she and Arn went out to see if Greygrim had returned.

"I found out the lord is here!" Greygrim came running up. "And he is quite well. He wasn't wounded in battle or anything. We should be able to talk to him, hopefully. He should talk to one of the knights of the realm."

"Now if I can just convince the guards at the keep."

They hastened to the foot of the four great stone towers, and stood as if they were pebbles at the foot of a tall cliff. The gates were open, admitting supplies and troops as need be.

CHAPTER ELEVEN

THE BORDER

*A*rn *approached the guards at the gate and bowed low, saying, "Dear* sirs, is Lord Summerville in residence that we may speak with him?"

The guard was quite dressed for war with grieves, breastplate, and halberd with pennants of the kingdom. "Yes, he is here. Of course we will let you in." He addressed himself to the other guards. "These three urchins wish to see Summerville. Summon a white horse for them to ride in on."

The other guard, perched on a stool, slapped the first on his knee and laughed at the joke. "Yes, we will see that his lordship is informed of your visit immediately, sir!"

Arn began to speak but Anne interrupted, her cheeks flaming. "You are speaking to a knight of the realm!"

Arn rolled his eyes, and looked away, knowing the scorn this would bring.

"Oh, a knight of the realm, is it? That's an entirely different thing. If I have offended thee in some way, I beg thy pardon." His eyes hardened and he leaned slightly towards them and lowered his steely voice. "If you children don't have anything better to do than to bother the watch of this gate, I highly suggest you go out and find some goor to play with."

The other guard guffawed. "You're on a roll now, aren't you Ed?"

Greygrim spoke up confidently, "These are the guards for his lordship? He's lucky if he doesn't end up dead!"

155

Before Greygrim could finish his statement, both guards lowered halberds to his throat. "We didn't quite catch that, oh mighty visitor."

Arn stepped in, trying to bring calm to the situation. "Sir, I am a knight of the realm. I was made so by the king himself, at a battle, and Lord Summerville knows of it. I know that the way we are dressed, it seems unlikely, but what if it is true? If you do not allow us to be admitted, and Lord Summerville would wish to see us, do you think that . . ." Arn stopped.

The man glared at him, but was obviously thinking it over. "Well, I have seen strange things in times of war. I tell you what." He raised his halberd, and indicated for the other guard to do the same.

"If you are indeed a knight, we will find out. I will have a messenger inform his lordship that you are here. If you are not who you say you are, we will make sure you three are feeding dungeon rats by midwatch!"

"Thank you," answered Arn, knowing that now he had to rely on Lord Summerville. He motioned with his eyes to Greygrim and Anne, and they also reluctantly bowed their heads.

"You may wait in the guard chamber there," he indicated the small room just inside the portcullis gate. "We will call for you as soon as we can." He smiled a curt smile.

As they stepped away, the weary travelers could hear them speculating that Arn had come to bring harm to his lordship. Then one of the guards said, "but he doesn't seem crazy to me. He just might be what he says he is!"

Another guard said, "Well, you seem you judge people pretty well. You are a master at the card games. You win all sorts of people's money!" They laughed raucously.

"There is something about that boy. We'll find out. Either a knight, or rat bait."

"I'll go down there and poke him with some sticks, I will!"

"You do that, Ben."

"Now you watch them well, while I fetch the sergeant of the watch. And take care, because if it turns out to be true, he could have your tongue."

Ben eyed the guard chamber, and you could imagine the rusty cogs of his brain slowly turning.

Arn and his friends waited quite a while in the small, airless chamber. They did not speak much, and then only quietly. Arn was quite certain the lord would remember him. It was not a common spectacle that a boy, a peasant no less, was knighted upon the battlefield by the king himself. He wondered what he would do with his newfound position. Of course, he must defend the kingdom. That responsibility weighed even heavier as a knight than it did as a peasant.

As the waiting went on, he began to pace.

"Arn, he will remember you. Maybe he will even give us a room, and some clothes," offered Greygrim. Arn looked at him doubtfully.

"Well, can't I hope for some clothes?" Greygrim looked down at his ragged clothing with a crooked grin.

"I'm just worried, is all. I hope he will see us."

At that moment, the guard walked up to the doorway. It was the guard who had initially greeted them so unpleasantly. With a glimmer of hope, Arn looked at the man's face. He looked like he was about to be sick. It was not the scornful face of a man about to throw them in the dungeon for fun. He also carried a bucket of cool water in his left hand, along with a gourd dipper.

"Sir," said the guard hesitantly.

A flood of relief washed over Arn. He could not believe how good it was to be called *sir*.

"If you would like to freshen up with this water, and follow me . . ."

"He will see us then?"

"Yes, his lordship will see you as soon as he can. His affairs and preparations for siege have been quite taxing, but as soon as he can see you later this evening, he will." The man kept his eyes downcast. "In the meantime, he has authorized me to take you to an antechamber where you can rest and refresh yourselves with bread and some ginger beer, if you wish, or light mead."

"The light mead would be very nice," answered Arn. "Thank you." Things were looking up. "Did he say he definitely remembered me being knighted?"

The guard looked up. "No, he did not say that. But he said he would like to see you."

Arn's heart dropped somewhat, but he was still hopeful of the end result. They washed their hands and faces in cool water, and followed the guard to the antechamber where they would await his lordship's pleasure. Very shortly afterwards, a maid brought a tray with bread, cheese, and fine-smelling sausage. It must be a variety of sausage famous in the north part of Southaven. After a blessing, they enjoyed the refreshments.

To their shock, the maid returned a while later and asked them if they wanted more! Arn had rarely been asked if he would like more food. He said they would like a bit more. If they did not eat it now, they would have something to tuck into their pockets.

The sausage had been delicious, with a smoky flavor. It was a combination of pork, chicken and beef and had been smoked in a special way. The honey mead was delicious too. None of them had often had any drink other than water.

"Arn, my boy, it is fortuitous we met you!" grinned Greygrim.

Arn's mouth was too full to answer. When he had swallowed, he said, "His lordship must surely remember me."

"Perhaps you could appoint me your wizard to ride into battle with you!"

"Maybe," said Arn.

"Do you think it'll come to that?"

"No, probably not. I don't even know what a knight does."

"Neither do I," said Greygrim. "How about you, Anne?"

"Well, sometimes they have very poor manners indeed," she mumbled with her mouth full of sausage and cheese.

They did not eat enough to be actually full, for that would have felt very strange to them, but they were satisfied as they had not been in a long time. They felt relaxed and chatted together about their lives and experiences. They enjoyed hearing Arn talk about Shadowfang. They discussed whether he had gone on to do evil or good.

Arn was bothered to think that perhaps he had released a creature that he should not have helped. Deep in his gut though, he believed he had done the right. Many times in his life, when he had been alone, he had relied on his gut feelings. Most of the time he had been right.

The torches on the walls dwindled, and a servant came in to replace them. They asked if his lordship would see them, and the servant replied that he did not know.

Quite a long while later the servant returned, saying his lordship sent his regrets and would not be able to see them that night. He had left instructions for them to be taken to a sleeping chamber for the night. He inquired if they would be willing to share a chamber, due to the castle's crowded state.

"Of course," answered Anne.

The servant led the way down a narrow stone corridor, down a narrow stone staircase, to a lower part of the castle, near the ground level. There was already a fire blazing in the fireplace of a small chamber. There were three full piles of straw with clean linen on top fanning out from the fire. Against the wall was a small bed made of wood, support ropes, and some kind of mattress.

The travelers eyed the bed and each other. Arn and Greygrim in gentlemanly fashion insisted that Anne should have the bed to sleep in. There was a large bucket of clean water with which to wash up. Anne pulled over a tapestry screen for privacy, washed up and put on her slightly less dirty dress. The boys washed up and rested on their straw mattresses. They all talked sleepily of many things, late into the night.

Arn's imagination ran with what might be possible should Lord Summerville remember that he was indeed a knight.

The room itself was clean smelling, and there was a pleasant cool autumn breeze from the window, and the little fire prevented them from feeling chilled. No guard would be needed at the door. It was all soothing, and they drifted off into comfortable, restful sleep as they had not enjoyed in many days.

The morning light was bright and cheery to Anne, who was the first to wake. Arn's eyes opened, and she said, "You were having a nightmare or something. You were flailing around. Do you have nightmares often?"

"Sometimes."

"Do you remember them?"

"Sometimes."

"Do you remember this one?"

"No. And I'm always glad when I don't."

"I understand. I have them too, sometimes."

Greygrim piped up, "Can't you two be quiet?"

Arn kicked him in the foot. "Sure we can, as soon as you wake up and talk to us."

"That was a good night's sleep."

"I wonder if they will bring us breakfast in bed," said Arn with a laugh. It was something he had seen done at the tavern on occasion, a guest actually served his breakfast in his bed.

They got up and stretched, neatened their beds, and before long a servant appeared, announcing there would be breakfast gruel and bread served in a common room down the way. They thanked him and followed him down to the small makeshift dining area.

"This looks like it is a storage room."

"Yes, it is, but with the influx of guests we have had to make accommodations."

"Do you know if his lordship will see us today?" asked Arn.

"I'm sure he will," answered the servant. "Perhaps he will. He is very busy, of course."

"I understand," said Arn. "Preparing for a siege must be quite complicated."

"I can bring some more gruel if you require it."

The bread was a bit stale, but tasty, and they enjoyed their gruel. They decided to explore the castle. It took a while to find their way up to the upper levels, as they wished to walk the battlements. There were troops there but the three of them stayed out of their way. A servant showed them the way, and they were allowed to see the spectacular view of the town and surrounding countryside below them. It was practically deserted of all people.

The southern gate where they had entered was still open, but the northern gate, towards the town, was closed and barred.

They could see the small village they had passed through on their way to the keep. Arn could imagine really enjoying a visit here in better times. There would be bazaars full of wares, shops, lots of people. It was always interesting to look around, even if you did not have money to buy anything.

He knew that a boy of lowly position and ragged clothing was not always welcome in a market. In Clayhaven he had been able to wander through the shops and marketplaces, and had never been accused of stealing. He thought this was due to his home with the brothers at the abbey. The brothers had regularly supplied him with newer, cleaner clothes, but in his line of work his clothing had become worn and filthy very quickly.

Arn had rarely had anything at all that was new. He inspected the knife that had been given to him as a new gift from Gustavus, as he looked out over the battlements. He wondered if Lord Summerville would offer him entry to the armory, and equip him as a knight. That seemed unlikely. He chuckled to himself. This man did not owe him anything. It would be the king who should provide him with his equipment to serve as a knight. This posed some difficulty since the king had been killed, and whoever had succeeded him was unaware of his position as a knight.

"You are strutting about as if you are in charge of the castle!" teased Greygrim.

"No, I'm not."

"Yes, you are. Chin up, hands behind your back, walking back and forth like these are your soldiers."

"No, I'm not," answered Arn sheepishly, dropping his hands to his sides. "I'm just walking, that's all."

They could see many, many of bundles of arrows stacked behind the wall, ready for the expected siege. There were several big cauldrons set on stacked wood, ready to be boiled. Arn could not imagine what would be cooked down there near the wall, and ventured to ask one of the troops.

"Well, I suppose you could cook food. They probably have cooked something in those big cauldrons for festivals or such." He was a tall man, skinny, with several brown, broken teeth. Even so his smile was pleasant. "We put oil, pitch, or water even, and boil it hot as we can get it, then we pour it over the sides at whoever's trying to climb the walls."

"That would be very painful!" said Anne with a grimace.

"Indeed," said Arn. "I wouldn't like to be hit by that."

"No, you wouldn't," answered the guard. "And we have other choice things we like to put in there if we need to." He smiled.

Arn decided not to ask what the other choice things might be. The friendly cooking pots now looked like open black graves. It reminded him that his land was in the middle of a war. He would likely see more of the foul, black creatures that he had seen before, and they would want him dead. The walking dead, why they would not even be affected by boiling oil! It would probably just lubricate their dead, dried joints.

"Let's go," suggested Arn.

"I understand," answered Anne.

Greygrim stared at the cauldrons. Arn asked him, "Do you think you can fit one of them in your barrel?"

"Of course not!"

"Let's be out of here," said Arn, grabbing Greygrim by the arm.

As they headed towards the staircase, Arn said, "If I ever get rich, I will buy you your own black cauldron!"

"Really?" said Greygrim, poking Arn in the ribs.

"Boys, stop that!" urged Anne. "They will think we are children."

"We are children, aren't we?" answered Arn.

"I don't know," said Anne, smiling.

"What's that supposed to mean?" asked Greygrim.

Arn just shrugged, not having any idea what she meant, and not wishing to ask.

They descended the steps from the battlement. Arn considered the impressive domain that Lord Summerville commanded. It was awe inspiring that one man was responsible not only for the castle, the walls, but also the towns and land beyond. He hoped that if he ever had that kind of responsibility, he would be able to help people more than he had seen done.

"I think the high king tried to do what he could."

"Yes, well, maybe he didn't try hard enough," said Greygrim.

"Or maybe he did the best he could with what he had."

"True, true. I'm not going to talk ill of the man. He has passed on to his Father's."

Anne piped up, "He's probably looking down upon us smiling, grateful he is not here."

Arn looked thoughtful. "No, I think if anything he would be sorry he is not. He was the kind who would want to be in the fight. He would be in the front. I met him after all, and I liked him."

"Liked him?" exclaimed Greygrim. "He almost had you killed. That's ridiculous."

"Well, he was wrong. Even a king can be wrong, can't he? And he admitted that. I can forgive those who make mistakes, and I can forgive a lot." He scratched his head and wondered how much he would forgive.

They retraced their steps back to the small room they hoped would be waiting for them. It looked the same as when they had left.

After waiting for a while, Greygrim, who was restless, decided to go out and see what the local merchants had to offer. Arn grabbed his hand as he headed out the door. "Would you like us to go with you?"

"No," answered Greygrim.

"No five fingered discounts," warned Arn. "We don't need any trouble with a man who might help us."

"Me? Five fingered discount? I've only ever taken that which I need, and I've always left some sort of payment." Greygrim made a mocking offended face.

"Right," said Arn. "I'm sure you have. But let's just not do that here."

"Alright. Doesn't hurt to look though, does it?"

"No," agreed Arn, smiling and patting his friend on the back. Even though he considered Greygrim a friend, he wasn't sure he could trust him in this. "Maybe, if you don't mind Anne, you could go with him. I'll wait here in case anyone comes to get me."

"You are anxious, Arn, we can tell. Are you sure you want to wait here?" asked Anne, smiling.

"You're right. I am anxious. I want to see if he remembers me. If he doesn't we might have to pay for everything we just ate!"

Greygrim shuddered, visibly surprised.

Anne made a face. "You don't think so, do you? We don't have any money."

"If it comes up, I'll take responsibility for it," said Arn. "Because I brought you all here. I will work it off, and you two can return to barrel home."

Greygrim said, "Well, it hasn't come up yet, so let's not worry about it."

"Right," answered Arn. "I don't think they would have been as nice to us as they have if he didn't remember me."

"Well, we are off to look at the shops and things." Greygrim winked at Arn.

Time dragged by as he waited alone. He almost lost track of how long he sat waiting. Compared to the tired feeling he had had on days when he had walked all day long, this was a different tired feeling.

The door opened and his friends walked in. Greygrim carried a warm bowl. "Here buddy," he said, patting Arn on the back. "We brought something for you."

"What is it?"

"Beef broth." Greygrim reached beneath his cloak and pulled out some bread.

"Uh oh. Where did you get it?"

"Don't worry. We helped an old lady and she paid us with this." He handed over the small end of bread.

Nobody else had come to the chamber, although some had walked by and glanced inside. After eating, Arn took up a stick and began stirring up embers in the fireplace. Greygrim and Anne sat on creepy stools that had been provided. They decided it was best to wait because if Lord Summerville had time to see Arn, this room is where he could be found easiest.

Late in the evening, a servant came in looking very weary and dirty from the day. It was the same man who had helped them earlier in the morning. Behind him they noticed two guards in the hallway.

"Lord Summerville will see you now," said the servant with a bow.

Arn took the bow and respect as a good sign. He eyed the guards questioningly.

One of them spoke kindly, with a smile, "Don't worry, it's common practice for visitors to be escorted to his lordship's chambers, especially late at night. If you would kindly leave any weapons behind." These words put the three at ease and they made their way up and down winding corridors and stairways, following the guards.

They finally came to a grand staircase. Three abreast could walk the stairs at once. They climbed three levels and entered what seemed to be a private wing. The stone walls were adorned with tapestries and items of beauty. They could see down the long corridor for there were torches lit on both sides.

At the end of the corridor was a very large window. This must be an enclosed part of the castle where there was little concern about attackers. Arn knew from his education with Brother Francis, there was probably some way to seal this window should it become necessary.

There was a dank smell, similar to the rest of the castle, but also a strange smell noticeable in the corridor. It smelled of sage and rue, and possibly lavender. He was familiar with these herbs. Father Clement grew these in quantity and sometimes sold them to wealthy ladies in the community.

As they walked down the corridor, one of the guards asked, "Why isn't Jeffrey at his post?"

"I don't know," said the other guard. "His lordship should be in that room, so he should be on watch."

"Jeffrey's in trouble, I tell you. Last week, you know . . ."

At that moment, the door they were approaching flew open, and a dark figure emerged. They all stopped cold in their tracks, mouths gaping. A large black-cloaked figure stood facing them. They could see no face beneath the hood, but they could see the wicked looking dagger dripping with red blood.

Arn stood numb as he recognized the figure after a second. He could never forget that figure. It was Angueth! The general of the army which had killed the high king of Southaven. Shock and fright almost overtook him, as well as the others. The smell of rue and sage was almost overwhelming. There was another very unpleasant, rotten smell.

What a horror! To be so close to the source of the greatest threat to so many!

The guards loosed their swords while pushing the younger people and the servant out of the way, and then ran down the corridor. While they were yet a good fifteen paces from Angueth, he wailed with a hideous, shrill laughter. The guards stopped in their tracks.

Arn, by some twist of stupidity on his part, ran and pushed himself past the armed guards towards Angueth. The creature laughed again, and before Arn realized it, Angueth was upon him, pulling forth something from beneath his robes. It appeared to be a black ball of some kind.

Before he knew what had happened, Angueth had grabbed him around the neck, and asked him, "What do you do, boy? Are you going to stop me?"

The stench of death assaulted Arn and he felt faint as Angueth laughed again. The hand on his neck felt as if it were covered with crawling creatures. Arn could not answer.

"You send peasants to me? It's so nice of his lordship to send me so many nice gifts to accompany me back to the Dark Lands!" He laughed a hideous laugh that made Arn shake while he was held frozen.

The guards realized their master was surely dead or in peril, and saw Arn being held. The blade was no longer visible. Angueth had secreted it away when he pulled out the ball.

Arn looked down at the black ball. It looked very much like a pig's bladder, bloated with something black.

"Here is something just for you!" shrieked Angueth, hurling the pig's bladder at the floor, a few paces in front of the guards. The bladder exploded on the floor, and black, oozing liquid flew on the walls and on the stone floor.

The guards were staring at the black goo, perplexed. They were reluctant to fully attack Angueth for they knew his powers, that he was one of the right hands of the Dark Master himself. Anne and Greygrim stood terrified.

Angueth turned his attention to Arn. "You, boy. You have the stench of filth. I've smelled graves that smell better than you." He placed Arn against the wall. He hissed, "You filthy bug. How dare you approach me? Do you know who I am?"

Arn could not answer.

The foul grip was even tighter on his throat. His cheeks turned red and his eyes began to bulge.

"You filthy peasant! You are indeed an insult, but not worthy of my attention. I will not waste time with you."

Arn could see that his face was wrapped with black bandages, but he had eyes all right. If the color blue could ever be called foul, that would be the color of his eyes. They were like blue flames surrounded by oozy red meat. The stench was so overpowering, it was all he could do to breathe with the hand clutching his airway.

"I do my own assassinations, boy. I enjoy it. But you are not worth my time. I will let my pets do the work." With this he threw Arn back down the corridor.

The guards bravely stepped forward to help Arn, but stopped cold when they saw the black ooze was forming into shapes. Slithering into something hideous. "What's he done?" exclaimed one of the guards.

"You will see," hissed Angueth. "Good bye, dear friends. I will see you very soon." He turned and bolted down the corridor faster than they would have imagined a creature of his size and deteriorated state of existence could move. He moved quickly, like a runner, and leaped out of the great window, to their surprise, and disappeared from view.

The window was too high for a man to leap out of safely, but they realized that Angueth would have some means of escape.

The black ooze had formed into a mass of six slithering, red-eyed vipers, more smelly even than their master had been, if that was possible. Before he realized it, one of the guards had been bitten in the foot. The viper did not coil or give any warning, just reached out and struck. He screamed and hopped on his good foot. Before their eyes, the creature dissipated into black smoke, like in a forge fire.

As Arn try to catch his breath up against the wall, one of the black vipers slithered towards him. He heard Anne scream as from far away, and Greygrim yelling something while fishing something out from his sleeve. He could just barely see them through his glazed eyes. He wanted to push the viper off with his foot, but couldn't quite bring his foot to move.

The next thing he knew, Anne reached out faster than he could imagine, and snatched up the black viper, just within striking distance of his foot. Anne flung the creature against the corridor wall. It became black blood again, dripping down the wall.

To Arn it seemed as if he were in a dream, watching an interesting play. He wondered, *what are those black birds flying around in the hallway?* He realized they probably were not there at all, tweeting and swirling about. It was amusing as his eyes closed. He dreamed Anne saved him and kissed him on the cheek, as his head rested against the stone wall.

When he awoke, he found himself lying in bed and looked around, expecting to see his small bedroom in the stable. All at once, he remembered the scene that had unfolded earlier. He looked at his feet and saw no bite marks. His back, his neck and his head were in a great deal of pain. He wondered how long he had slept.

He saw two pleasant faces floating above him, one Anne's and one Greygrim's. "How did you survive that?" he asked them.

Greygrim smiled and shrugged.

"We were blessed," said Anne. "And a little trick from Greygrim."

"What was the trick?"

Greygrim smiled wisely and fished in his sleeve. "Snake sand."

"Snake sand? I've never heard of it."

"Sometimes called snake rock. Snake dust. I carry it because snakes like to use my home as their home. I was happy to find out it works even on magical snakes."

"What is it?"

He pulled out a small pouch made of coarse fabric and sprinkled some small stones and dust into his hand. "When the belly of a snake passes over it, it causes the snake excruciating pain and kills it. For these, they actually burst into flame and disappeared. I don't know if that was the blessing on the sand, or its inherent magic, but whatever. They burst into flames and dissipated. The guard that got bit wasn't so lucky. Anne tried though. She took the dagger off the other guard and tried to suck the poison out. It burned her mouth though, and didn't do the guard any good. She has blisters in her mouth."

Anne jabbed Greygrim in the ribs with her elbow. "There's no need to tell him that."

Arn noticed that she was talking funny. "It's nothing. I'm just glad you are all right."

"You saved me, Anne. I remember, there were some birds, and you were flying, and you grabbed the snake and threw it against the wall."

"Birds? Flying?" She smiled down at Arn. "You need some more rest."

"Probably," admitted Arn. "But you did throw one of those things against the wall, didn't you?"

"Yes. I have dealt with snakes before, but I don't like them. I couldn't let you get bitten after all."

"What happened to his lordship?"

Both of his friends looked down at the floor.

"He's dead, isn't he?"

"Yes, Arn," said Greygrim. "He and his guard. Let's just say they were dead and leave it at that."

Arn rubbed his face with his hands and looked at the ceiling.

"We've got a little something for you to eat," said Anne encouragingly. "It's a little stew from earlier."

Arn mumbled, "Well, I suppose he is with his Father now. I wonder what to do now."

"Don't worry about any of that now."

"Did they catch Angueth?"

Greygrim laughed bitterly. "No, there was no sign of him. Nobody even saw what happened. We were the only ones to see him."

"Was that really Angueth?"

"Yes, it was," answered Arn.

"They were just speculating. But you have seen him in person."

"Yes, I have, at a distance."

"He was an ugly thing," said Greygrim. "I don't ever want to see him again."

"Well, we're alive, and Arn is alive, and that is something. He obviously intended for us to die. What kind of evil magic was that?"

Greygrim answered, "It is a very frightening and bad kind. You don't want to know more."

"I'll just wait on the stew. Maybe some water," said Arn.

Greygrim went and poured from the water skin as Anne held Arn's hand, stroking it. Arn looked at her with a feeling of friendship and appreciation. His head hurt, he was dizzy and sleepy. He smiled at her and she smiled back sweetly.

Greygrim brought a wooden bowl with clean water and Arn drank thirstily. His throat hurt and he coughed some. "My throat hurts."

"That's probably from where he almost strangled the life out of you!" exclaimed Greygrim. "We're going to let you sleep and we will figure out more tomorrow. They said we could stay tonight, and tomorrow if need be. Nobody here knows that you were knighted. They were quite grateful we did what we could."

"It's been selfish of me to think of it anyways. Those poor men lost their lives. I have been lucky."

"Very lucky," said Anne. "He had you dangling like a doll. It was just like a puppet show I saw once . . ."

Arn interrupted her. "I'd rather not think about it now. I'd like to rest."

"We will go look about and leave you to rest. And no five finger discounts," smiled Greygrim.

Arn slept soundly, and when he awoke he felt better. He was able to get out of bed and move around. Although he was sore, he was definitely better. He was dismayed to find he had slept late into the day, until his friends informed him that more than one day had passed. He had slept again for more than a day.

Greygrim informed him that there were more and more soldiers arriving at the castle and requiring billeting, and that they would have to move from their room so soldiers could occupy it. They were offered quarters in a common room in the lower part of the castle.

"In the dungeon?" asked Arn.

"No, I don't think so."

"Well, I don't want to stay."

"Where will we go?"

"Let's just go back to the barrel." His friends could tell he was discouraged about coming so close to having his position verified by one of the few who were alive to tell about it, only to have the opportunity snatched away.

Arn decided to walk around. After a time, he ran across a sort of manager, an older man who seemed to know all about the running of the castle. He told Arn that Lord Summerville's cousin, who held stead over the other border fortress not far from here had also been at the battle. Arn wondered if he had possibly seen him knighted also. Arn told the manager some of his story.

"Well, it's possible he does know. I hope such good fortune does befall you." The manager was very kind to the three travelers, and grateful for their bravery in dealing with Angueth and the deadly asps. He prepared ample provisions for them on their journey back to Greygrim's home. Arn wondered aloud about returning to Clayhaven, and the manager told him that one of the dark forces might have passed through Clayhaven, and he was sure that all residents would have found refuge elsewhere.

"Are you sure you can spare the extra food?" asked Arn.

"Oh yes, we will be all right. We pray and things are provided. That's the way it goes."

Arn smiled at the man's confidence and his faith.

The trio gathered their meager belongings. They waited some time for a guard to come with the key to the locked box which contained their weapons.

They talked quite a bit about Clayhaven. Arn was obviously concerned about his family, the monks and Greymist, and the only home he had ever had. He wondered if his lead soldiers were still tucked away in the rafters of his room.

When leaving the protection of the city wall, they could feel a difference. They did feel unprotected. Several had warned them not to leave the fortress. "The Dark One and his armies are coming. He is not taking no for an answer this time."

Arn had smiled at the old woman who had issued this warning. "We will survive." She had smiled and walked away. He was surprised that the old woman was able to be comforted. He felt no comfort whatsoever. But the time to leave had come.

They made their way all the way around the citadel, out the south gate, and around the wall. As they went through the small town, Greygrim made a discovery on the sandy cobblestones. A small cobalt bottle, which appeared to be empty, but had a tight stopper made of cork. It was quite beautiful and valuable.

"I'd like to put blessed water in it," said Arn. "We can go past that church."

"That's a good idea," said Greygrim.

When they got to the church, they went inside and found a small bowl with a little blessed water remaining in it. They filled the little blue bottle, and also a small leather flask that Greygrim had with him. The church had been abandoned, and all the fixtures had been removed for storage. They still took time to pray, asking for God's protection on their journey.

When they left the little chapel, Arn decided to tell the others something that had been bothering him.

"What is it, Arn?" asked Greygrim.

"I'm not going back to the barrel."

"You aren't? Are you going to check the fortress near Clayhaven?"

"No. The folks there are tough. And smart. I don't think they need me there."

"Well then, where are you going?

"Eldross. We should be able to find help at Eldross."

CHAPTER TWELVE
SOUTHAVEN DAGGERS

They continued to walk on through the night, hoping to make Eldross some time the next day. Eldross was the oldest of the southern fortresses, also one of the largest, second only to Richaver's grand castle. The minor king of Eldross was one of the knights who had seen Arn be knighted. He knew surely this man would remember him, if they could just get there. Perhaps he could help defend the castle.

As the night grew wearily on, "Ow!" shouted Greygrim, falling once again. The wagon track rutted road being extremely difficult to walk down in the darkness. "Stupid darkness!" cried Greygrim. The small lantern that Anne carried was sheathed so that its light would point down and not out, to prevent the patrols of the Dark One from seeing it from far ahead. Greygrim arose, brushing his knees off once again. Arn and Anne understood his frustration, having both stumbled and fallen multiple times in the darkness. "I can stand this no more. Anne, shine the light down here," he said, pointing towards his feet as he stooped to pick up six small stones.

The road had been covered with stones a long time ago to ease the passage of horses, wagons and people, but had long since been covered by mud and neglect. The border road was fearsome to navigate at night, as any good trader or peddler would tell you. Greygrim seemed to be examining the stones in his right hand, passing his left hand over them several times, speaking words in a low tone that Anne and Arn did not recognize.

To their shock and wonder, all six stones began to glow in multiple colors. Anne pushed Arn aside excitedly, saying "Let me see! Let me see!" Greygrim smiled triumphantly as Anne bent down to study the beautiful glowing stones, one red, one green, one pink, one yellow, one blue, and one a delightful grey color. "How did you do that?" exclaimed Anne happily.

"Nothing any high level mage couldn't do," Greygrim said triumphantly.

"What are they for?" asked Arn, examining the stones.

"Well, like you both, I am tired of stumbling in the dark, so I got an idea." Lifting his leg and taking off one of his old ratty shoes, Greygrim took a red stone from the pile.

"What are you doing?" asked Anne.

"I'm going to put these on the tips of my shoes."

"How are you going to hold it there?" said Arn.

"Aha!" Greygrim said. "Something that I took from my former home." Digging through his haversack, he took out a small vial of what seemed like a yellow liquid, at least it looked that way in the light of the glowing stones. "I call it wonder stuck."

"Wonder stuck?" repeated Anne and Arn.

"Yes," answered Greygrim. Taking the liquid and placing a bit of it on the toe of his shoe, he placed the red glowing stone, holding it in place a moment. Releasing the smooth stone, he said, "and there you have it!" He shook his foot around vigorously. "It's a wonder it's stuck."

"Wow, you are amazing," said Arn, slapping his friend on the back.

"Now," said Greygrim, "we can see where we are stepping. It shan't be too bright at a distance for anyone else to see."

"Me next!" Anne said, as Greygrim adhered the yellow stone to his other shoe. She picked the pink and the green, leaving Arn light blue and grey stones.

They set off again in the dark, whistling and singing as they went. Anne had never seen such pretty stones and she enjoyed them greatly, even skipping in the dark as she sang a little song that went like this:

Oh glowing stones,
Lead me home

To clear waters
And fresh showers
And lovely spring meadows
Where I might roam.

The magical stones provided a lot of enjoyment and lightened their mood and made the darkness seem less sinister, until they came to a place in the road where great dark trees flanked the sides and steep banks with great, dark scrub brushes on either side. As they began to go through this narrow passage, Arn began to feel sick. It reminded him too much of the place of the ambush where he had lost a friend, and had had to fight for his life.

He could imagine behind the dark bushes and trees that there were dead archers he had slain waiting for him, their dead eyes full of malice, fixed on him and his companions. Waiting to step out at any moment, their faces fixed in death thralls, hideous to behold. But as they continued through the dark gully, just as they walked through what Arn thought might be the end of it, Arn thought they would be fine.

Just then, they heard a croaked voice yell from the darkness, "Halt or die!"

Arn almost leapt to the very stars, being scared out of at least one of his cat lives. They all froze as soon as they could, looking to either side, wondering whence the voice came.

"In the name of the king of Southaven, I command you to tell who you are!"

Greygrim spoke up, his voice cracking with fear and sounding small. "We are wayfarers on our way to Eldros for safety." They heard nothing from the darkness for many moments.

"Are you but three?" yelled the voice. "Is there anyone behind you?"

"No," croaked Anne, frightened when it seemed Greygrim was not able to speak again. "We are friends. Friends of the high king, and this is a knight who knows his majesty personally."

"The high king of Southaven is dead!" cried the voice, angry.

"We know that, we know, but he knew him before he died. He was made a knight."

"Indeed." Then silence for a long time. The travelers barely breathed, looking side to side nervously, imagining shadows moving this way and that in the pale moon and starlight. Finally one of the great bushes on their right came alive with noise and brushing sounds, and then many more came to life. They could even imagine some of the bushes came to life for real.

Men came down from both sides, men in great cloaks, with faces shrouded, but men the same, not undead nor goor. One stepped in front of Arn, a bit shorter than he.

"My name is Peter of Richaver, of the family Carville. I am the captain of these men. You will follow me. Veer not off my path even a little for there are traps." With that he moved quickly off into the dark, so swiftly they could hardly follow, trying desperately to keep in his path. Four of his men followed and the rest seemed to blend back into the bushes. There had been at least a score and ten a moment ago, with great bows and crossbows drawn and pointed at them, and now there were none except the five.

They followed Peter as best they could, through pathways, through great bramble bushes woven or cut through great thorn rows. The huge bush was called Southaven Daggers. It was said to have helped many refugees and soldiers be saved in wars past. The soldiers of the Dark One hated these bushes and burned them on sight. Their cruel, three or four inch long bars pierced cloth and chain mail alike. It was said the bushes were put in place by a great wizard to protect Southaven on the border with the Dark One where no walls could be practically built.

Arn ducked low, being taller than the rest, trying not to hit the sharp barbs. After quite a while of twisting and turning and going through darkness they came to a large hill they could barely make out in the fading light of second moon, the Follower. It was the smaller moon and followed the first across the sky.

They came to a cave hidden behind one of sharp brambles, difficult to see even from ten paces, for the entrance had been hidden by rocks and a clever blind of woven wattle that blocked the entrance. Inside they were surprised to see a fire blazing and men cheerfully laughing and cooking a large hare and a wallop. Wallop were such strange creatures, standing about six hands, kin to deer and kin to rabbit but not like either. They got their name from sharp spiky horns which could give you a wallop if you cornered the creature for they were tipped with a sedative. Often rabbits and wallops were found in the same area guarding their less protected cousins.

The group of men stood to attention and became quiet as the captain and his prisoners came in. "You boys head out," he said, "take the fourth watch. Nothing but these three supposed wayfarers tonight, but you never know. I expect a supply column from Nine Tower to be coming through here for the Dark One soon. I want nothing left alive, and everything off the road as quickly as possible. We'll have warning to join you if the taletell birds come through. Be alert for any advance scouts. Leave them be, unless you have to kill them."

"Yes, sir," said a scruffy, short bearded man. "We'll take care of it, captain. Don't worry, captain," he said stooping and turning meat on the fire.

"We'll save you some tasty tidbits from the meal you started here," said the captain, chuckling to himself. "Sit," he said, pointing to the three companions, "and tell me your story. Wendell, serve us all up some food, would you?" The captain pulled up a chair cleverly made of woven wood closer to the fire. As he sat back, beginning to take off his boots, the three noticed his boots had the red goblet on the sides.

"Don't panic," he said. "I got these from a dead caravan leader, my boots having been worn out many days before, and they fit terrible. The Vagabond doesn't know how to make footwear," he said, shoving brown chewing weed into his mouth, staring into the fire. The three watched for a while. He spat brown juice into the fire absently, lost in his own laments. In time his glazed eyes looked up at the three. All except him had been served some of the delicious, savory meat.

"So, you are a royal knight of Southaven, no less. Tell me the story and leave nothing out."

Arn took a deep breath and began to tell his story from the time he left Clayhaven, up to the battle. The captain enjoyed the story, except the part about Moresfield, at which he spat into the fire and said, "I never liked the man much." In time the rest of the third watch gathered with their captain, partaking of their food and listening to the rest of Arn's story, some lighting clay pipes. Many of men, they noticed, looked quite ragged, wearing quite a few things from the Dark One's armies, particularly shoes, boots and sandals. Most of the shoes had iron pegs and heel plates that the Dark One loved to place on soldiers, to keep their shoes from wearing out.

Although their clothes were ragged, they were oiling bows and crossbows looking as pristine as the day they were made. Some were sharpening swords and long knives on rocks.

The captain took Arn at his word, to all their surprise. "I am Peter, captain of this road ward," he said, properly introducing himself. "We have been many months fighting the Dark One along these borders. We knew he was about to bring war again to Southaven. We thought it would be small spoiling attacks as he likes to do this time of year. But not this time. For some crazy reason he is attacking in the fall. It makes no sense to me. Who can figure out the ways of the Vagabond. The castle in which you seek refuge is under heavy siege.

"Our job is to break supply columns and reinforcements heading that way. I fear if Eldross should fall, most of the south will go with it. He seems to be making his way towards the coast. I suspect he wants a test run of his great black ships, and they will invade the coastal areas and attack Richaver from that way. Angueth is a clever war leader. I have heard tell of one of our fleets of the watch being burned in mooring in the harbor in the last weeks."

Arn felt relief that his little home was out of danger for now but he knew it wouldn't be for long if the Dark One succeeded in landing ships on the coast.

"You and your friends here have no chance of getting into the castle at Eldross. I suggest you go back the way you came and seek refuge where you might. How about Richaver? It is not under siege, that I know of. Perhaps you could get the recognition you need and the orders you seek there.

"I would invite you to stay here and fight with us, but my men are trained. They are good with a bow, and good with a blade, and masters of concealment. We wardens take pride in that. I would lend you horses if I could, but we only have a few in the back of the cave."

"I thought I heard whinnying," said Anne. "May I go back and see them?"

"Certainly, young lady. Terrence will take you. He tends to the horses. As did the holy knights of old, we must double up on horses. They did it as a sign of their vows of poverty, and ability for one to fight on horseback, one infantry. We do it of necessity.

"I can make you a map of a little known road that we use that will take you away from the main road. Not only the large supply column but also the reinforcements of the Vagabond use the road. You are blessed you haven't run into any.

"Rest here today and I will give you provisions and the map tonight. With your glowing shoes," he chuckled and pointed at their still-glowing stones, "you should be fine at night. The Vagabond has flying eyes in the sky during the day. It is better to move at night and stick to the map I give you."

"Thank you," said Arn, "for your help and the information. We are in your service. If we can ever help you, let me know. You can find me in Clayhaven."

"I will do that, and get a good meal, for Brother Clement is a wonderful preparer of food. I know him well from better days. Until later, then," he said, pulling a ratty old blanket. Saying not another word he put his head on a piece of cloth that had obviously been the mantle of a Vagabond soldier, and began to snore.

Arn and Greygrim were quite tired and fell asleep quickly. Anne continued to visit with the horses a while. Horses had been just about her only friends in past times of her life. Eventually they were all sleeping safely among these men of Southaven, and did not awake until evening.

The captain was gone, back on duty. Another band of men were in the cave, having been watchers of some other place during the day. A few they recognized, and one was Sergeant Edward. They broke their fast with cold meat and some beans, for the fire had dwindled.

Sergeant Edward spoke, "Here are your provisions and a map. I am to escort you almost to the castle to keep you safe."

"Thank you, sir."

"It is my honor to help you, sir knight. The captain sends his regards. If you are ready, shall we go?"

They followed Sergeant Edward up an unknown route, happy to have such a brave and experienced escort. He carried a great halberd, a fine crossbow, a sword and two brace throwing daggers. All these men were very well equipped for fighting in different situations.

The three felt safe on the road for once, as they headed back down autumn's lonely road.

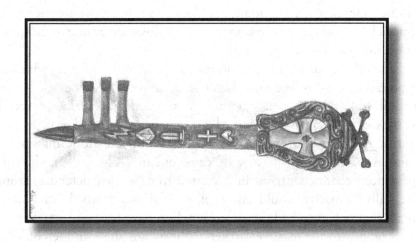

CHAPTER THIRTEEN

THE KEEPER OF TALLS AND TALES

"*G*reat heavens!" *exclaimed Arn. The entire trio were in awe. As they* approached the great city of Richaver, capital and seat of the high king, they could not believe the huge stone walls and towers that greeted their road-weary eyes.

"Look at the size of those walls!" said Greygrim. "Those towers, so many of them."

"The Dark One's army could never get through there," said Arn aloud. Arn looked at the great fortifications with a keen eye. He had always hoped to see the great capital one day. Several layers of walls and towers protected the main citadel, high atop the craggy peak of a small mountain called Greyston. Flags and banners flew from many of the towers. The beauty of the great grey fortress of Southaven was awe-inspiring.

Arn stood for a moment, looked up and down the impressive stonework, then thought of what Brother Kyle had once told him: even the greatest of fortresses can fail. He had said that a fortress could either be a place of offense or a place of defense, but its one true weakness can be to surrender the initiative to the enemy, for it cannot move. In time, a large and clever adversary can think down every one of the great protective barriers of your castle.

The three companions continued their way up the winding cobblestone road to the great outer gate, known as Archangel. It was as beautiful and fair, as fair as they say the dark gate of the powerful fortress of the vagabond, named Engluf, was dark and evil. It was craftily hewn by the dwarves of the north and the stone masons of Southaven. The first gate cleverly came out from the walls itself with great deep channels carved in a slanted roof, so that defenders from the walls themselves could easily roll great stones down the channels. Some channels even had ramps to launch stones out at any attackers at a fair range, for the massive earthen pathway was sheer and fell off to a precipice on both sides, which ran into a great chasm filled with dark, brooding water, encircling the entire outer works. After this, there were a series of seven more gates within this gate structure alone.

At this gate there were three great towers that guarded this formidable entry point. Arn knew that the towers were named. It was said that some knights of the realm quoted the names aloud before they went into battle. The first tower was "I." The second tower was "Trust." The third tower was "Faith."

The travelers were glad that they did not have to go through a lesser gate, and that the great gate was still open to wayfarers and refugees. Arn again marveled as they went under the great portals one by one, all amazing, all different. One was a solid portcullis of iron sheathed in copper. This great barrier was known as the Copperhead. As the companions went through the pass they were amazed at the sights and smells that met their senses.

This last outer ring of the citadel was known as the Farfields, for it was naught but a sawed-half century ago that these outer works were put over some of the small fields to give growing time during a siege, as long as these outer works were not taken, though most of these fields were quite hilly.

As they were looking about, a strange one-eyed old woman with a feather patch over her left eye came up with a bundle which she carried like a baby. "Have ye any extra food, ma'am and sirs, for me little one? He's just a bit whelpling." Arn reached in his pouch, almost empty from the long road, and gave her half of the crumbs he had left.

"Oh, thank ye, kind sir. Ye be a true gent, says me." She took the crumbs in her gnarled hands.

"How old is the little one?" said Arn, peering down.

"Oh, just nine weeks," she said with a toothy grin and bad breath. "Would you like to see him?" Arn peered down at the cute little fellow as she opened the folds around the face, and out came, to his horror, a snotty black snout with pointy teeth. He could not believe his eyes; it had long pointy ears, greasy black fur, some of which was curly, some of which was pointed straight up.

"It's a boarwolf!" said Arn in surprise, as he and the other companions stepped back.

"It's a pigdog whelp!" said Ann, laughing, her shock quickly overcome by delight.

Greygrim said, "Oh, yippee. Those things are ugly."

"It's me baby!" the old woman exclaimed in a singsong voice. "'E's natural ugly and all."

Arn and Ann began to laugh and pet the little googly-eyed creature to the chagrin of Greygrim. "No, he's not ugly, ma'am. He's a handsome little guy," said Arn, as the old woman finished feeding the scraps.

Ann even bent down for a kiss. "Kissy, kissy!" she said, to the disgust of Greygrim. A little pink, gooey tongue came out and kissed her on the nose.

"I never want to kiss you," said Greygrim to Ann.

"I don't want you to kiss me anyway," she laughed, looking at Arn.

The old woman leaned the little piglet thing towards Arn, repeating the words, "Kissy, kissy! 'E wants ta thank ye for ye kindness! It's good luck." Arn leaned forward and the little pink tongue gave him several licks on the nose. "He is kind of cute," said Arn laughing along. "This is indeed a good sign. You should get a kiss, too, Greygrim."

"No, thank you. Can we be off now please?" he said, marching up the path stiffly.

Arn smiled and said goodbye to the woman and the pigdog, wishing them farewell. The old woman quickly grabbed Arn by the arm, and said, "Kind sir, ye good heart will not go unrewarded. Mind ye the key. It's much more than ye think." Arn wrinkled his brow and looked strangely at the old woman, thinking she was crazy. He nodded politely, and stated that he would.

Arn and his companions made their way up the cobblestone street. The smells of delicious food were nearly overwhelming to the weary travelers. They had little rations left. But they also had no money to pay for the delicious wares, either, and really nothing to trade. They had been told by refugees and soldiers that ration stations for the needy had been set up inside the fortress. There were many granaries and food storage cellars within the capital.

It wasn't long before they found a long line of people holding trenchers and many makeshift tables set in a field from which the grain had already been harvested for the winter. The two boys were made to share a trencher and the young lady used her own cup to receive a ration of soup. It was a thin chicken stock with barley, cabbage, nuts and a few carrots. They were even given seconds.

As they sat, they looked around at the many displaced people who were also looking around in wonder at the capital city, many laden with heavy bundles, pushing carts, mules and pack animals. Some were streaked with soot from fires, possibly in their villages.

Arn wondered if he could really make a difference as a knight. Could he find a weapon to kill the demon Angueth? He knew he had to do something, whether he liked it or not. He felt duty-bound to do something.

Having rested their weary legs, they pressed on, into the city of Richaver. They were almost overwhelmed by the many crowded passageways, and did not have a good idea which direction they should be taking. Suddenly, Arn's eye stopped on a storefront containing many items beautifully made of metals.

The items that fascinated him were finely detailed miniature lead soldiers. Some were mounted on tiny lead horses, and they were fitted with all manner of tiny military gear. Through the old, diamond-paned window, he saw a glint coming from a little knight on a horse who was fighting what looked to be a great dragusin. He was so well-painted that he looked real.

He realized instantly that this was a great artisan of metals. There were a great many wondrous things other than the lead soldiers that he saw and liked in the window. There were also some suits of armor and chain mail, leather with iron strips, scale mail. Swords, quite a few maces. Spears. But there were things other than weapons here, such as lamps, sconces, and belt buckles with fine leather straps.

He barely noticed his friends entering behind him. He found his way over to the lead soldiers that he admired.

"Sir," Arn said.

"Yes," answered the man gruffly. He was of short stature, with a very long beard, hands black with soot. He reminded him of Gustavus. Obviously there was a forge in the back.

"What is the price of these fine figures here?"

"I cast these from a mold given by a friend of mine. Some of these reside with the high king himself."

"How much would they be?"

"You don't look as if you have the money, son."

"I don't, but things can change, can't they?"

The older man slapped Arn on the back and chuckled. "You are right about that!" He picked up a nicely detailed soldier mounted on a horse. "This one here, for instance, half gold." It was not as nice as the one in the window, but still a beautiful piece.

He examined a few of the pieces, mentioning prices Arn of course could not afford to pay. He wished he could add one or two to his collection and wondered if he would ever have money to spend on such a thing.

The man seemed to enjoy showing off his work, and they continued to examine things in the shop. There was an excellent chapeau de fer. "That one is worth a gold."

"How about this chain mail?"

"Oh, that is a lot of work. I made that for a man who's dead now. Most of what I make is custom for the buyer. Most of what you see here made was made for those who won't be coming back for it."

Arn and his friends were silent at this. His mind returned to his real mission. "Sir?"

"Yes, lad."

"Can you tell me, if one wanted to find a weapon . . ."

"There are plenty of weapons here."

"Well, let's say . . ." Arn hesitated, searching for words that wouldn't sound crazy.

"Spit it out, boy."

"If you wanted to find a special weapon, say, to kill someone . . . Have you heard of General Angueth?"

The man raised one of his bushy black eyebrows. "Aye, heard of him."

"If one wanted to find a weapon to kill a creature such as he is, not alive any more, but not exactly dead either, what would you use to kill someone like that? A regular weapon won't destroy him, I understand that."

"Now, why would you be wanting to know something like that?"

"I just, well, it's a long story. I would just like to know, I'm curious. He's our enemy after all."

"Hmm. That he is. An evil one, at that. An assassin, and a good one. He served the Dark One for many years alive. One of the old blood. Somehow after he died, the Vagabond managed to keep him around through evil magic." The man crossed himself as he spoke. "None of these weapons would do much against him, I'm sure. I imagine the high king would have some things like that in his armory."

"What if someone might, like me, maybe, and my friends, wanted to acquire something like that?"

"What?" said the man, laughing. "You and your friends want a weapon to kill Angueth?" This was a cheerful man and he smiled a great big grin at the trio. "Well, I guess I'd ask the records keeper. He'd know. In the great hall. I bet he would be able to tell you. He would know about those buried in the ground and such. Buried in mounds. Yeah, he'd be the one to ask. I've heard tell he knows all kinds of things. A magic user of some sort. He is able to see things, near and far. They say he can even see into the future. He knows lots of people, lad, lots of people. If anyone knows where you might find such a weapon, he would. Being that you have a humble purse, so to say, there might be some adventuring you could do to acquire it."

Arn, Greygrim and Anne exchanged glances.

"Then if you manage to slay Angueth and all . . ."

Arn interrupted, "Oh, I wouldn't slay him. I would give the weapon to a champion of the high king."

"Oh, good. I'm sure then the king will give you a fine reward. You come on back here and you can have your pick of one of these fine things. I'll even give you a discount."

"Thank you, sir. I would like that very much. Could you tell us where the records keeper is?"

"Not far at all. Just go through the next gate, and the second ring around the citadel. There you will find the big building, right on this road. It's marked Richaver Great Hall of Records. If you can read. If you can't there's a big scroll on there, can't miss it. It's huge. Three big columns on the front."

Arn nodded. The directions sounded easy enough.

"If you do talk to him, though, be wary. That fellow is a bit peculiar, to say the least."

"Thank you, sir." All three nodded their thanks to the older man. "And if you still have that knight in the window, that'll be the one." Arn smiled.

"I hope I do, lad. Business has not been that great, never is during wartime."

"Thanks for your help. I help a smith back home, you know."

"Ah, what's his name? Maybe I've heard of him."

"Gustavus. In Clayhaven."

"Hmmm, you know, I think I have heard of him. Quite a blade smith."

"Yes, he is. He made this." Arn pulled out his little knife and showed him. The man examined the blade in his hand, checking the balance and workmanship. "Quite a smith. This is an impressive piece. Perhaps I'll meet him one day. Give him my regards. I'm Donick."

"I will," said Arn.

"And good luck on your quest," added the man, chuckling. "And jab Angueth one for me!"

Arn just gave a goofy grin, and he and his companions left the shop, and headed up the road. They walked quite a ways through the crowded streets, wondering at all the sights of a great city, but not stopping, because they did not have any more time for looking. They needed to find someone to help them with their mission.

They reached the second battlements, just before the citadel, and encountered an old, large, stone building, with three huge pillars supporting the front. Arn recognized the styles from his education with Brother Kile. One was ionic, one was dorian, and one corinthian. The great scroll at the top of the building announced that this was a library.

Arn had a chill in his heart as he faced the doorway. The place was foreboding, dark. The tiny windows were all very dark. As they approached the great stairs, they could smell moldy cloth and parchment. They pushed on the left hand door, which was cracked open, and walked through the great doors hung on massive hinges, directly under the words *Seek Wisdom, Find Wisdom.*

They went inside and were quickly greeted by a wizened, balding, short, ugly little man wearing grey robes. "What can I do fer ye masters and lady?" he said in a creepy voice.

"We are here to see the records keeper. Would that be you, sir?"

The man cackled a high pitched laugh. "No, that wouldn't be me." He smiled a broken, yellow-toothed grin. "But I will go see if he'll see ye. May I give 'im yer name?"

"I am Arn of Clayhaven. This is Anne, and this is Greygrim. My companions. We seek an audience with him."

"Oh, ye seek an audience, do ye?" he cackled yet some more, and pointed his finger into Arn's chest. "You three sit there," he indicated a long stone bench. "I'll see if he'll speak with ye or not." He turned to go, then called back over his shoulder with obvious contempt in his voice, "Don't touch anything!"

The trio obediently sat, and watched him as he disappeared, hobbling down a long hallway. They did not wait long, surprisingly, before another short, wizened, even uglier man appeared through the same hallway. He had stringy, grey hair on his balding head and a paunch that proved his sedentary life. He had small spectacles crammed on his pointy, bent nose.

"Yes," whined the old man. "What can I do for you, Arn of Clayhaven, Anne, Greygrim?" He pointed at each of them.

"We came to ask a question. I don't mean to interrupt your day, sir."

"Well, the day is almost over, lad. I am always willing to help one of the king's good subjects." His voice was whiny yet whispery, and they strained to hear all of his words. "What can I do for you?"

"Well," began Arn, before the old records keeper interrupted.

"My name is Himmel," wheezed the old man with an obsequious tone and a leer. "You look weary. Perhaps we could get you something to drink? Come with me." He gestured, and out of nowhere the servant appeared and began to follow also. He moved with surprising agility and speed, with his gnarled, bent body.

They proceeded through a huge maze of stacks and piles and bookcases jammed with scroll cases and scrolls. The dust was thick on everything, and the smell of mildew was almost overpowering. They felt like their lungs would work hard to deal with the bad air in this building. There was a grand skylight overhead, but it admitted almost no light, for it had been mostly covered by a cloth tacked to the ceiling.

Anne pointed up at the skylight, and asked, "Wouldn't it be better to uncover that lovely skylight?"

The old records keeper stopped abruptly and spit out, "No, it wouldn't. We wouldn't want our fine works to be exposed to *light*. Besides, light bothers my eyes!" He squinted and pointed at Arn. "I am not a great fan of light. As old as I am, I feel it has detrimental effects on this old frame. Mord," he gestured to the strange servant, "please get our guests a drink, and bring it to the fourth room."

"Yes," replied Mord, bowing and shuffling off.

The trio followed the old man through many rooms, all darkened, with only a candle here and a sconce lit there. They finally turned left, and entered a huge, dusty room with a window at the far end. That window too, had been covered with black, dusty cloth. There was a long table set with many, many chairs, and one small candle illuminating stacks of scrolls and old tomes.

Greygrim especially seemed ill at ease, looking around nervously.

"Greygrim," Arn asked quietly as he entered, "Does this remind you of your master's place, somehow?"

"Aye, Arn, it does," whispered Greygrim, "and so does he. He's a bad one, I can tell."

Anne agreed. "There is something unwholesome about him."

"He smells even worse than you even, Arn," said Greygrim with a grin.

Arn hadn't noticed. "Ok, thanks for noticing that. I couldn't smell anything in here but that mold."

Greygrim winked at Anne when Arn turned away, and she smiled.

The old man walked to the far end of the table and took the seat at the head. The back of the chair extended over the top of his head, and was carved with designs that included a skull, a scroll, and what looked to be a baby's cradle.

Arn was at a loss as to how to converse with this strange man, and they all struggled just to see in the dim lighting.

"Is that a skull, and a baby's cradle?" asked Arn.

"Oh, aren't we perceptive," hissed the old man.

"I just wondered, what do they mean?"

"It means, from the cradle we learn simple things, then your life span, the scroll, the lessons of life. And the skull," he affectionately stroked the skull, "the end of our lessons on this great cast."

As he spoke Mord approached carrying a tray with four goblets. One was ornate with some kind of stones embedded on it. The other three were plainer but still beautiful.

"Drink, drink," said Himmel with a grin, as he reached for the ornate goblet.

Each of the three took a goblet from Mord as he passed them around. As they did so, they exchanged glances. They were actually tired and thirsty, but very reluctant to drink anything this weird man provided.

Anne politely lifted the goblet to her lips, but tried to hide the fact that she did not drink from it. Arn and Greygrim followed suit.

The old men were watching intently, strangely, and Himmel smiled when they seemed to be drinking. "Drink, enjoy, and I will take you to show you what you want to know."

Arn said, "But, sir, we have not said why we are here."

A wheezy cackle erupted from Himmel as his eyes glittered. "Yes, yes. Drink, and tell me what you are looking for."

Greygrim started, "We are looking for a very special weapon."

"Yes, we were told that you might be able to help us," said Arn. "We need to know how a person might go about finding a certain kind of weapon."

"Yes, yes, go on," said Himmel with a grin.

"Well, a weapon that could be used against a foe neither alive nor dead. For instance, to kill one such as Angueth."

"Oh yes! A certain kind of sword, useful against one such as Angueth," repeated the old man. He chuckled. "Yes, Arn, there is such a weapon. However, the acquiring of it would be a great task, far beyond your capability, I fear." His voice faded into a whine, while his eyes never left Arn. Himmel never let his grin fade, as if this were very enjoyable entertainment.

The three friends were not sure how to deal with this strange man, but continued to pretend to sip their drinks.

Himmel seemed not to like Arn's momentary silence. He added, "On the other hand, with the three of you, yes, you might be able to do it. You just might." He stroked his dusty beard with one hand, eyes glittering at Arn. When Arn did not answer immediately, his smile faded. He seemed almost desperate to keep Arn's attention. "I can tell you where it is and how to find it."

Arn and his two friends looked up.

"Drink, drink. Yes, why don't you bring your goblets with you while we proceed to the information you require." He smiled again, and stood, and indicated with his hand the direction they were to follow, towards a very dark staircase.

They descended for many steps. The echoing sounds of their footsteps drowned out the splashes they made pouring their drinks into a spittoon along the way. The cavernous room was very dark; the torch just barely lit the darkness. All the walls they could see were lined with stones. Himmel proved himself to be quite spry despite his limp. He seemed to know exactly where he was going.

Soon they saw many, many stone and wood shelves covered with books, small scroll cases, boxes and chests. Arn had never seen such wealth in one place. He could still smell the same odor as upstairs, together with the musty odor of wet stone and soil, quite pungent. He passed many large shelves. Some of them were numbered in the ancient numeral system, which Arn had learned from Brother Kile. At the end of each shelf was a desk with either a candle or a lamp upon it. For a place equipped with so much expensive lighting, it was dark and oppressive.

The companions glanced at each other. They felt a strange chill emanating from the place, an unpleasant feeling that made the hair stand up on the back of one's neck. Arn was grateful, not for the first time, that he had his friends with him. He could tell they were nervous as well.

Himmel went down the aisle numbered "Seven", glancing again at the paper he held in his hand. He made some indecisive noises, wheezing a bit from his exertion. He climbed a small stairway that had wheels attached, quite an ingenious invention. "That would be fun to ride!" whispered Greygrim.

In a few moments Himmel said, "Aha! There be it." He pulled down a small wooden box with iron banding.

Himmel hobbled to the desk at the end of the shelves, placed his torch in a sconce above the desk, and sat. He reached into his long black frock coat and pulled out a heavy set of keys, some black iron, some brass, others of silver. He located the key he wanted, just smaller than a man's thumb, and placed it in the lock. The key didn't seem to work and he cursed to himself. He reached into another pocket and pulled out another set of keys. After a bit he found another small key, this one of polished silver, and this time the lock clicked.

With a gleeful cackle the old records keeper slowly opened the dusty box and rummaged around. He pulled out something heavy wrapped in cloth, which he plunked upon the desk. He also removed a scroll about two hand-spans long. "Here's what we were looking for," he said.

He looked up at Arn and smiled. "How are you feeling? This damp air can get to you." He eyed the others as well.

"I feel fine, sir," said Arn. The others nodded.

"This air might get to you in a little bit. Don't worry if you feel dizzy," he said, grinning, showing his filthy, brown teeth.

Himmel took out a small piece of parchment from yet another pocket and began to write. He looked up at Arn and pointed at the cloth-wrapped item, and said, "Take that." Arn picked it up.

The old man continued without looking at Arn. "You'll need that if you are going to kill Angueth at all." He dipped the quill into the inkwell on the desk and continued to write.

"Go ahead, open it. It won't bite," he mumbled. "Unlike some things."

Arn unwrapped the oiled cloth and was surprised to see it held a very ornate key of brass, iron and copper, touched with some silver. It was quite beautiful, really.

"That," the old man continued to murmur, "is a key."

"He's right," chuckled Greygrim. The old man glared at him. His eyes were menacing in the dim torchlight.

"I don't like jokes from upstart mages, or street tricksters, or whatever you pretend to be!"

So frightening was his countenance that Greygrim could not help but step back, saying, "Yes, sir."

The records keeper cleared his throat. "As I was saying, that is the key to a very special place. It's a crypt. You'll find that crypt . . ." He unrolled the scroll and pointed a gnarled finger. "You'll find the crypt here."

"The Isle of the Dead?" exclaimed Anne.

"That's right, you can read, little peasant girl!" spat the old man. "I admire the ability to read."

Anne just nodded and looked away from the man's gaze.

"Perhaps your friends could go on their quest and you could stay here and help me, since you can read and all." The old man leered, and offered an unwelcome smile.

Anne said quietly, "My friends will need me, if you don't mind."

"They probably will!" cackled the old man, as he turned back to his map. He directed his next comments to Arn. "Did you learn anything from the monks about the Isle of the Dead?"

"Also called Isle Macabre," spoke Arn.

"That's right!" said Himmel.

"How did you know about the monks? I didn't mention them."

"I told you! I know a lot of things." He lowered his voice and said smiling, "Like who you really are."

Arn looked at Himmel in wonder. "Who I really am?"

"Yes, well, that's not for today! Perhaps I will tell you more about yourself, things you do not know, when you return from your journey." His ensuing laugh definitely sounded sinister. The three friends exchanged looks, each silently wondering what they should do.

"Regardless of all that," continued Himmel more quietly, "the Isle of the Dead was a place of great wealth. Years ago, a man named Benito Morte, a great designer from the kingdom of Iletia, decided there was too much robbery of the sintul." He glanced up at the three, realizing this word was not familiar to those in fair Southaven.

"Oh, I meant to say grave. And there was. Neither rich nor poor was safe from the spade of the grave robber. The Red Prince sent his minions to the border towns to steal the bodies of the dead for his soldiers macabre.

"Engineer Morte devised a way to protect the dead, mostly the wealthy dead. He bought the island from the high king, for he had a great deal of money. With the high king's blessing, he took a group of dwarven engineers and some of the finest stone crafters to the island, which contained three stone mountains.

"He began to excavate deep into the side of the center mountain. From the beginning there was much trouble with this excavation. There were many deaths, for it was said that the isle was cursed.

"In the distant past a dark tribe had lived on the island who practiced great evil. They had been dead for many years, but there was still talk of the curse.

"Morte worked hard, with great determination, and dug deep into the mountain, creating many vaults of varying sizes. Finally his work was done. He returned to Southaven and announced he had the safe place for your loved one's remains. He guaranteed the safety of all that were entombed on the isle, and their possessions. He even claimed his vaults were safe against the Dark One.

"In time, many wealthy nobles of Southaven began to inter their loved ones on the isle. Some even bought land from Morte there to build vacation homes near the ocean in which to stay when they visited their dearly departed.

"Before long, the island became a sought-after vacation spot with beautiful fruit trees, unusual animals for hunting, and white sand beaches as well as some blue sand beaches. There were natural hot springs and Morte built magnificent hot baths with all the luxury you could imagine.

"The vaults began to fill and Morte and his workers dug more crypts. There was only one entrance to the burial facilities and that was heavily guarded at all times. To enter and pay respects, visitors had to possess a key, and their names must be listed in the great book Delmorte.

"It was said that some greedy ones who were buried there also had servants, family members, even animals interred with them, and those not necessarily dead when they were buried."

"Oh, that's awful!" exclaimed Anne.

"That's true. I've heard that before," said Greygrim. Arn nodded in agreement. Much of the story was familiar to all raised in Southaven.

"In time," said Arn, "the agents of the Vagabond brought corruption to the isle. Isn't that true?"

"Yes," answered the old man, clearly enjoying this tale, "and Morte and several of his family died under mysterious circumstances.

Some said they were murdered. A strange nobleman with a great deal of gold, several different kinds of gold—which should have been a giveaway—bought the island.

"The new owner quickly made claims that some lucky ones might be able to keep their wealth with them in an ethereal world, a purgatory, where they did not quite have to go on. There were a few greedy, wealthy people who bought into this lie and purchased special death privileges.

"In a few years the isle was covered with vice and corruption and greed, and sinister connections to the Evil One.

"One day, it is said, one of the sons of the throne of Southaven, along with his sister and their friend, a monk, traveled there. The boy was not well and wanted to bathe in the healing waters. As they stepped onto the pier, the monk who accompanied them found he could not step on the pier. He fell back into the boat and declared that before the next planting season, the island would be dead. Everyone who stayed would die. Everything would die.

"As the story goes, before the next planting a great storm swept over the island. No ships could near it and those who tried were lost. For seven days the storm ravaged the island. A black, brooding fog was all that could be seen from the sea. All that could be heard were wails and moaning. No one lived to leave the island and tell what happened under that black cloud.

"On the eighth day a ship managed to near the isle and actually docked. Sixteen members of the crew, and a great captain, went onto the island and disappeared.

"From that day on, only fools ventured to the island. Occasionally a lucky pirate or thief might venture there and return with just a few trinkets. Most of the great wealth is still there." The old man paused and squinted as he eyed the three. "All the gold, silver and jewels you could want." He focused his eyes on Arn. "Some very fine weapons, too."

Himmel looked down at his feet and said, "I don't feel very well. Enough about the isle. You know the dangers." He slid the quill over to Arn and said, "Sign this."

"What is it?"

"'Tis a promise, to return this key and map that I give you. They are property of the Records Keeper of Southaven. And the high king," he added.

Arn read and signed the paper. Himmel pushed back his chair and rose, wavering a little as if dizzy. "I have something else that might help you on your quest," he said, again smiling his sinister smile. "By the way, I have done everything I was supposed to do as the records keeper of Southaven to help you in your quest, Sir Arn of Southaven."

"Sir? You know I am a knight?"

The old man just chuckled and advanced into the darkness with his torch.

Arn quickly asked, "Can't you tell people I was knighted if you know it?"

"That's something that is your own task, boy, not mine." Himmel rubbed his head with his free hand as he walked. "You might want to acquire a ship at the Fish and the Crow. It's full of pirates and brigands. There you might find one brave enough to drop you on the one standing stone pier. No one will take you on the island itself unless he is quite mad."

Anne was the first to realize, as the old man's speech slowed and his step faltered, that he had indeed placed something in Arn's drink. She felt sorry for him and wondered if it was sedative or poison. Still, he had tried to hurt Arn. She decided to wait and see what happened. Perhaps it was a sleeping draught and when he fell asleep, they could escape the hall of records.

The old records keeper went past many shelves and several stairways, twisting and turning until none could be sure of retracing their route. This place was much larger than it seemed.

They followed his torchlight to a very small door in a natural stone wall. The old man again jangled through his keys before finding the right one, a small key with a great skull on the end. "Come on in here. It won't be long until you are on your way. Just a few things to help you."

They all stooped to enter a dank room, sixty spans across and deep. There were piles of clothes, blankets, packs, weapons, water skins and gourds all along the walls. As they advanced they could see in the center was a large hole carved deep into the floor.

"Let me go over here and get you some things. While I am digging through these piles, why don't you look into the hole. You'll be quite amazed." He handed the torch to Arn and stepped towards the edge of the room.

Arn, Greygrim and Anne stepped near the edge of the pit and Arn held the torch up over the opening. They peered down and could see white things lying deep in the bottom of the pit. It didn't take them long to realize the bits of white, some draped with ragged cloth, some even with armor, were the strewn remains of many people.

From behind them they heard, "Goodbye, Arn, Knight of Clayhaven! Now I do my bidding for my new master."

They quickly turned to see him pulling a wooden lever. "Look out!" yelled Greygrim, grabbing Anne, who was nearest to him, and slamming her out of harm's way and to the stone floor.

But it was too late for poor Arn, whose reflexes were not as quick. Down from the ceiling above the door flew several long wooden beams. They swooped just over Anne and Greygrim's heads and caught Arn full in the side and sent him flying.

He caught one of the beams with his left arm and hung on for dear life, suspended over the pit.

"You are all supposed to go in!" shrieked the old man. "My dear pet's hungry! Needs flesh and blood, you know!" He grabbed an old rusted spear from the wall and lunged towards Anne and Greygrim. Greygrim leaped up and easily parried the rather drunken blow, cutting the old man's arm as he did so.

"You old traitor!" cried Anne. "I knew you were trying to poison us!"

"I was going to tell my pet to spare you, you silly little wench! But no longer." He jabbed at the floor near where she lay, wobbling on his feet and with poor aim.

Anne rolled away, rose to her feet and recovered the spear.

"Now for you, mage boy!" The old man stepped forward and lunged towards Greygrim, but the drug had taken its effect and Himmel stumbled and plummeted 20 paces to the bottom of the pit, screaming a curse.

Arn had watched suspended by one arm. He had never been a great climber, but just as he began to slip, he said a prayer and pulled with all his might. With a couple of pulls fueled by fear, he climbed up on the beam. "You can do it!" screamed Anne.

Greygrim ran around the edge and helped Arn work his way across to the stone floor.

Just then came a terrible scrabbling and squeaking from the bottom of the pit. They looked down to where the torch lay, still burning. From a hole in the side of the pit came a very large creature, the size of a very large bear. But it was no bear! It was a giant spider, no, a rat! A twisted horror no one could imagine, a spider-rat! Something created by a conjuring of darkness.

"No, my child, it's me," declared Himmel weakly, in a pleading voice. "Don't come near me, I'm your master!"

As the spider-rat approached him, he spoke faster. "Don't come to me, my pet. The Dark One gave you to me!" The creature with its bulk lacked the speed of both rat and spider, but gradually came nearer to Himmel, as he began to drag himself away. No whining slowed the progress of the red-glowing multiple eyes as they were fixed on their next meal.

The old man, gasping, looked pitifully up at the trio, staring aghast, not knowing what to do. They barely heard his plea, "Arn, noble knight of the realm, save me!"

Arn, being the kind of young man he was, had already been trying to figure out how to help the old man. He grabbed a spear from the wall. Brother Francis had taught him to throw a javelin and spear quite well, and he had many years of coaching and practice.

The spider-rat seemed uncertain about the still-burning torch, and with one of its many hairy limbs pushed the torch aside. It was approaching Himmel, intent on devouring its master.

Arn threw the spear, and it landed on one of the legs, but the creature moved forward with more determination, as it emitted a screeching howl. The old man shielded his eyes with his hands and yelled, "Forgive me, but I deserve this."

Greygrim had grabbed a large-headed mace, and Anne had a broken dagger in her hand. Arn, using another spear from the wall, took better aim and sent it straight into the beast's head. The monster realized pursuing this meal would mean its demise, turned, and shambled away as quickly as it could. Anne's dagger thunked just behind its neck, doing more damage. It let out a loud shriek just as another spear from

Arn hit it in the back. Black goo oozed from the creature's wounds, and it stopped shambling.

In a few moments the sounds of distress ebbed away, and the monster only twitched. They could hear the faint sounds of the records keeper's breathing. Greygrim threw the heavy mace onto the spider-rat, and it did not move, or make any noise.

Anne sorted through the piles of implements along the walls and found a wooden ladder that still seemed sound. "I think we can go down and get him."

Arn went first. Picking up the dagger, he sheared off one of the bulky creature's legs to see what it would do. Sticky dark blood came out but there was no further movement. "We've killed it," he hollered up to the others, as he walked over to the old man.

Anne threw down something that landed with a thud. "This has some wine in it," she said.

Arn picked up the wine skin and bent down over the old man. The bleary old eyes were looking up, not seeing. He was severely injured from his fall. Arn gave him a sip of wine.

"These were people," began the tired, old voice. "Soldiers of his majesty. They were getting suspicious about me." His voice became fainter. "I killed them," he whispered. "I murdered them. You tried to save me, you and the others."

Greygrim was now standing beside Arn, weapon in hand, with an eye on the creature in case it made any new attempts at life.

"Why would you try to save me? I tried to do away with you."

Arn looked at Greygrim. Greygrim said, "That monster was more monstrous than you. We couldn't just let it kill you."

"I had succumbed to madness these last ten years," spoke the records keeper, more coherently. "I slowly gave in to the Vagabond. I betrayed his majesty and all of Southaven and everything I stood for!" He took Arn's hand in his one good hand. "Forgive me, young Arn of Clayhaven, for you are of noble blood. May God and the high king of Southaven and all the innocents I have killed, and all I have betrayed, forgive me! You keep those things I gave you, Sir Arn, and go on your quest. Please don't tell anyone of my betrayal. If you do, you will be delayed and you may never get your weapon! That key is a special one. It only works . . ." He began to cough.

"It's special to fa . . . only fam . . ." Coughing stopped his speech. Taking a deep breath he continued, "Go to the Fish and Crow. Look for a captain with a gold patch, Trent. I think he'll take you." He reached into one of his frock coat pockets and took out a black leather bag. He grabbed Arn's hand and pressed the bag into it.

"I know this can't make everything right between me and my oath breaking, but here is to buy your passage to and from the island. I hope it's enough," he said gasping. "I give it to you freely. Fare thee well, Sir Arn." With these words the old man passed from this world.

Arn and Greygrim could not help but shed a tear, and looked away from each other to wipe their cheeks. They were, after all, supposed to be men. And why cry over this old man who had tried to kill them and betrayed all of Southaven? They could not help but have compassion for him. They understood the wily ways of the Vagabond, and the pressures he could bring to bear on even the noblest citizen.

With difficulty they extricated the old man's body from the hole and placed it in one of the empty chests. Arn carved some words into the side, "High Records Keeper of Southaven. May God forgive him."

They decided to heed the records keeper's advice not to talk to anyone about what had happened, but instead go on with their journey. They might be accused of some wrongdoing, and definitely would be delayed on their mission.

Although most of the supplies in the melancholy room were broken and rotted, Anne had uncovered two good water skins, and two good knives. Greygrim found a hand axe that he tucked into his belt.

As they ascended from the dark cellar, they felt a strange sense of peace they had not felt on the way in. They traced their way back out and left the building without seeing the servant, or anyone. When they reached the streets it was well into the night.

CHAPTER FOURTEEN

FISH AND CROW

*I*t was clear that they were not the only travelers in the fortress. There were many displaced people looking around in wonder at the capitol city. Some were laden with heavy bundles, pushing carts, having mules and pack animals. Some were streaked with soot from fires, possibly in their villages.

As Arn looked at these sad refugees, he wondered if he could really make a difference as a knight. Could he find the weapon to kill the demon Angueth? He knew he had to do something, whether he liked it or not. He felt duty-bound to do something.

Night watchmen were busy lighting the tall street lamps. They stopped to ask one of them the way to the Fish and Crow. "That's a pirate's den," was the reply. He gave directions to the port. "You'd better be careful there. If you don't read, the sign shows a fish and a crow. If you do read, there's also letters. Mind your purses and your goods. There's more cutpurses out than we've had in a long time," he warned.

"Riffraff from other places, I suppose. Rats fleeing the falling border fortresses." The man spit down on the ground beside them. He picked up his bell hook and his small torch and headed down the street.

They moved through the crowds cautiously, minding the watchman's words and sticking together. They made their way down to the port, where they could smell the salt water and hear seagulls.

Arn was actually excited to see the ocean for the first time. He had always dreamed what it would be like. If were only daylight. It wasn't long before they spied great masts of ships bobbing in the harbor. Green moon was out tonight, and with its smaller but still adequate light they could see white sails, ropes, and shrouds attached to the ships.

They found themselves looking in wonder at what they could see of the dimly lit bay. Squawking fat seagulls and crows, even at night, squabbled over fishermen's leftovers and tavern refuse. There were a large number of taverns and storehouses along the waterfront. They could see dockworkers loading ships with all manner of strange things as they walked.

They managed to find their way to a mid-sized tavern at the end of a wharf where they saw upon a swinging sign a symbol of a fish on one end and a crow on the other. A number of long benches were situated outside, upon which some men were seated, talking and smoking. Some were missing limbs.

The smells of pipe tobacco and stale beer and ale combined with the salt air and rotting fish to form a pungent impression on those unaccustomed to the seaside smells.

One old man with an arm and a leg missing held out his remaining hand to Arn. "Alms? For a poor disabled man o' the sea?" Looking Arn, Anne and Greygrim up and down, he laughed a hearty laugh. "Ye're pardoned, boy. You don't look like ye have an alm to spare. If I had an extra, I'd give it ye." He laughed as they passed. Arn and Greygrim laughed also, and tried to look tough to hide their nervousness.

After walking through the door, Arn noticed Anne was not with them. She was standing near the old men on the benches, staring into the inside of the busy tavern, with an obviously unhappy look on her face. The boys went back outside.

"What's the matter?" asked Arn.

"I hate these places. They are all alike. And hold bad memories for me," she answered with a sad look.

Arn looked at Anne, and at Greygrim, knowing he had dragged them here on his quest. Not theirs. He reached into his pocket and pulled the pouch out containing their money. They had already counted thirteen gold, four dark, one silver and one copper. He turned his back carefully to prevent eyes from seeing.

"You've been very good companions, and friends. I can't ask you to go with me any further. Let us split this pouch. Surely there is enough for you to find lodgings at a better inn. And I think my passage alone won't be that much, I suppose."

Greygrim and Anne simultaneously reached for the pouch. "Put that away," they urged him, looking around.

Anne whispered through her teeth, "You just don't do things like that in places like this, Arn!" Greygrim nodded in agreement. She grasped his hand and pushed it back towards his pocket.

As Anne touched his hand, she looked him in the eye, and he felt a strange warmth in his heart. He was amazed at how very smooth and warm her hand felt. He thought, not for the first time, how dear and beautiful this young maid was. At that instant, for some mysterious reason, Arn thought about all the suffering and grief the young lady had been through.

A part of him that stood taller, that was so much stronger, that was not a boy any more but that was every bit a man and protector, wanted to take every moment of pain, every ounce of suffering, every sweet tear she had ever spilled in her young life into himself and hide the grief from her. He actually felt like hugging her to comfort her. But he realized he could never take her pain away. He could never really be a hero.

He wondered why he was leading these two dear people to their certain deaths along with himself. He looked from Anne to Greygrim. *These are my true friends.* He felt weak and dizzy all at once. The pouch secure in his pocket, he sat on an old barrel cask off to the side of the walkway.

"Are you all right?"

"I'm all right," he answered. "You really need to take some money and find yourselves lodging. I don't want," he hesitated. "This quest of mine is madness," he added in a whisper.

Greygrim and Anne looked at each other and then at their friend. Both moved towards him and placed a hand on Arn's shoulder. Greygrim spoke first. "I don't have anyone, Arn. And I don't have anywhere to go but back to my barrel. Couple of squirrels I call friends," he smiled. "A brave little cardinal and his wife I like to give some seeds. That little black wolf pup I've seen a few times. Other than them I have nobody in my life. No, I'm happy to continue with you. Can't speak for Anne though," he added with a grin in her direction. He nodded at Arn. "But you two have become my friends. Sort of like, well, family," he mumbled. His words trailed off and he looked away.

Anne looked at Greygrim and then at Arn. Her look was so soft and sweet it caused Arn to look away. "I've only known sadness and hard work, and loneliness. You two have in this short time been more like family to me than anybody has. Don't think for an instant," she added sharply, "you're going to go off and leave me just because I'm a girl! I'll go where you go," she added, smiling sweetly.

She used her fingertip to turn Arn's face towards her. Arn gazed at her as someone seeing the night sky alight with stars for the first time. She reached gently towards the tip of his nose, then suddenly grasped the end of it and pulled, hard. Arn yelped, the introspective moment completely gone.

"Don't try to leave us again, Arn of Clayhaven. There's gold and treasure to be had and I for one want some."

"I could do with some of that," laughed Greygrim. Leaning towards Arn he said, "I've heard you can buy nice things with gold."

Arn smiled. Looking at his two companions he realized they were determined to stay with him. They were old enough to make their own choices and they had. Arn looked over at a knot of people leaving the tavern and saw a face he had seen before. He couldn't quite place it. They were all looking right at him and at his companions. The person had a friendly face, and was almost smiling. Almost. The crowd moved out into the night and the face disappeared. "I know them from somewhere."

"Who?" asked Anne. The crowd disappeared down the walkway, laughing in merriment.

"Oh, just somebody," answered Arn, watching. He stood up and brushed off the back of his britches. "Well, it's getting late. Let's see if we can find this sailor seadog with the patch." He stood straight and took a deep breath, looked at his two friends and walked forward without another word to the entrance of the tavern.

A cheery song played on a pushenpull, and as they approached the tavern entrance, many men and ladies began to sing. There was a warm central hearth, and the smell of food and smoke were heavy in the air. There were sheafs of tobacco hanging from the rafters, herbs, flowers of all kinds, dried meat, fish and seaweed over their heads. They took their seats at a small booth in the corner.

Everyone seemed quite merry. Perhaps spirits were flowing readily. Directly over their heads hung large bundles of sweet lavender. Anne ran her hands over the fragrant spikes and smelled her hand. "Doesn't that smell wonderful?" She held her hand before their noses and they agreed.

"I hate taverns normally, but I kind of like this place." Some folks had begun to dance to the pushenpull's music, to what was obviously a seafaring song. They managed to catch some of the words, something like this:

> "Me cap'n says go
> Oh dear, me ladies, no!
> One more kiss 'n one more dance
> For poor sailor Joe.
>
> Me money's all gone
> Me hat's put on wrong
> To go, I say no!
>
> Happiness be here
> A lovely wench and good cheer
> Ol' cap'n, ol' cap'n, don't shed a tear
>
> Dry clothes I got clear
> Fine noggin lubber shoes I have here
> Haven't gone yet for beer
>
> Me buckles they were fine
> On me buckle shoes a-dancin' time
> Though ahoy one be gone for good wine
>
> So I'll dance right now with this fine lady Min
> Ho diddly dee, ho diddly ren
> Ah, does that be ol' Ben?

From my fine ship o' forty good men
Oh what's that? A ship's pin
This poor sailor can't win!"

At this the singer jumped in the air, and hit his head hard with his hand, yelling, "Clonk! Me head's in a dark spin, of my song this be the end, good night sweet lady Min!" All laughed and clapped as this silly little jig ended. It wasn't too long before a middle aged woman in a rough-hewn dress, with curly red locks and bright green eyes smiled and asked, "What ye three be wanting? We got a fine mutton fish stew this night, or the cook's mutton pie."

Anne chose the stew, while Arn and Greygrim decided to split a trencher of the mutton pie. To drink they all requested kinder dry grape juice. Arn asked, "Milady, do you know . . ."

She interrupted, "My! Well aren't you a sweet one!" She tweaked his cheek. Arn did not notice the two dagger holes burned into the woman's forehead, but she saw Anne's glare and pulled her hand away quickly.

"Do you happen to know a pir . . . a sailor, a gentleman of the sea with a golden patch over his left eye?"

"Golden patch?" she laughed. "There's about five in here tonight with a golden patch. That's like askin' to see if the tax collector's pouch jingles. Do ye know his name?"

"Yes, it's Captain Trent."

"Oh, aye, he be right in front of ye, that booth there. Are ye friends, or are ye doin' business?"

"Business," said Arn.

"E'll be thar a while. Why don't I get ye grub. Eat up and drink up and ye can talk to 'im after he be done with his current business."

"All right," replied Arn.

"Sounds good," said Greygrim. "I'm hungry."

"The food sure does smell good," added Anne.

"Never talk ye business on an empty stomach, says I," said the server, walking off smiling.

As they waited there was quite a bit of good cheer and liveliness in the tavern. Arn wondered, "Is it like this all the time?"

"Probably is," said Anne. "Taverns are used for a lot of things. I've even heard of church being held in them, being they are the biggest building in some towns."

"Heard of town meetings and things being sold in a tavern, but never heard of church," said Arn. "Sounds like a bad idea to me."

"You can hold service anywhere," said Anne, "if the people are sincere."

"Lots of intrigue goes on in towns," said Greygrim. "A lot of political intrigue, lot of foul business too. My old master did many dark deals in a shadowy back corner booth." His face wore a look of anger for a moment.

Just then the server brought their drinks and food. It did smell good. She placed the edge of the great wooden tray on the edge of the table. There was a groove on the edge of the table and a notch on the tray so she could easily balance the heavy load with one hand and serve their trenchers with the other.

"That's clever," noted Arn, nodding to the tray. "I'll have to tell the innkeeper back home about that one."

"Yep, never spilt a tray since the owner did that 'n." She placed generous portions of food and drink in front of them and quickly moved on her way. They crossed themselves and spoke thanks for the provision, then began to eat heartily. The food was so good, no wonder the place was full of people.

As they ate, they looked around. One booth looked unusual because although there was not a great deal of light in the tavern, this booth was exceptionally dark. Arn watched the dark cloaked figure eat slowly. He was not an unpleasant-looking fellow, about midlife, with a small, well-kept beard and dark, flowing brown hair. What caught Arn's eye also about the man was that he was eating a delicious-looking jarg of meat, very undercooked. The man did not partake of the meat directly, but tore a piece from the large loaf of bread, sopped around the piece of meat, then ate the bread.

The man was very pale. His pallor reminded Arn of the horrid man he had seen in Clayhaven. The dark character did not take much note of the people around him. He seemed intent on his meal, though he did watch the door.

The three enjoyed their meal very much, and after a time the maid approached, saying, "The cap'n says he'll talk with ye now." The person who had been dining with the captain had gone. They could now see the captain was a man of gaunt proportions, with long brown hair and a great bushy beard. He nodded as the three of them approached.

"Greetings," he said. "I understand you three wanted to speak with me."

"Actually, we wanted to deal with you, if that is possible," said Arn, speaking for the companions.

"Well, dealin' means money, boy. Dealin' means life for a sea captain like me." He smiled charmingly at Anne. Anne couldn't help but smile back. He had made the effort to stand as they were seated at his table. "Mind if I smoke?" He pulled out a grey pouch and a very ornate bone pipe. It had been carved as a sea serpent with its mouth opening as the bowl of the pipe.

"Quite a nice piece." Arn had never seen such carving. The captain packed his pipe and they were surrounded with a fresh cherry aroma and sweet wafting smoke, pleasant for tobacco.

"What's the business deal?" he asked, wiping his face and rubbing his eyes.

"Well, sir, we would like to be dropped somewhere and picked up if that would be possible."

"Well, if it be somewhere me ship can get to, that might be possible if the money's right, boy. That's the key. Where would you like to go?"

Arn pulled the old parchment from his pocket and, after looking around, placed it on the table. The captain noticed his wariness and asked, "Are you worried about someone wantin' to know where you're goin'?"

"Well, sir, you never know. Anyways, we'd like to go here." He jabbed his finger towards the center of the island. The captain's eyes grew wide in the lamplight.

"Yah, I know exactly where that be. It's a fool's errand, boy. Why would you three young 'uns want to go there of all places? Perhaps instead of there we could just go directly to the black port. Might be safer," he said, sarcastically. "Ye haven't enough money for me to take ye there."

"Well, sir, I know it's a hard thing to ask of anyone, but I'm a knight of the realm and I must undertake this errand for the king." Arn was unwilling to give up yet.

""Ye be a knighted sir? Oh, I was not aware of that. Of course I'll take ye. And your friends. Free and all." He looked up in exasperation.

Arn's face was downcast, and Anne spoke up, batting her pretty eyes. "Sir, couldn't you see your way clear to take us? Just close by and let us off by boat."

The captain regarded Anne and Greygrim. Greygrim said, "We have money. We can pay you." The captain just stared with his one good eye. He looked at Anne longer than anyone else.

"Why are you three wantin' to go to the Isle of the Dead? Ye know it's not fit for man nor beast, nor blade of grass even. I'll grant ye once in a while some lucky seadog will get off it with some trinket, but most who go there just never come back." He puffed on the great sea serpent and sent up a series of larger and smaller smoke rings.

"Well," said Arn after a time. "I really am a knight, though I may not look it. And I'm determined to go there to get a weapon of power to kill the assassin of our high king. It is my duty, since he had just knighted me and all, before he died."

The old captain looked at Arn for a moment and puffed on his pipe. "So you're going to slay this, this Angueth the Assassin."

"No, sir, I don't think I could kill him, but I could give the weapon to the high king and he could find a champion to do it."

The captain stared intently at Arn for a few moments. His one-eyed gaze penetrated right to his backbone. "See this patch?" he said, pointing to the golden fish-scale patch on his left eye. "This here patch has a way of seein' the truths of things. Ye ever heard the story of the patch?"

"It has something to do with the fish and the crow, doesn't it?" asked Greygrim. "I've heard something about it." Both Arn and Anne nodded. Various versions of the story of the fish and crow had been told to children in Southaven forever.

"One day when our kingdom was younger, one of the kings of old had a great son, a fine seafaring boy. The king loved the ocean himself, very much. He's the one who started a lot of the improvements on the port here. He's the one that came up making notes of marquis against the Dark One's shipping and those who deal with him. Even in Southaven are those who will deal with him. Darklands does have some tempting goods I must say," he smiled.

"But anyway, this king had his son under the best captain of Southaven's royal fleet. One day the fleet of the watch was out doing its job, watching the dark waters for an invasion fleet. Sure enough, this day a dark sky came upon the fleet. Under the sky came a fleet like never had been seen before from the Darklands. It was believed the Vagabond had finally finished his cherished black fleet to return whence he came to take revenge on those who had cast him out, and he was going to use Southaven as a testing ground. He was going to destroy us from the sea, once and for all, as he had not been able to do from the ground.

"The captain of the watch's flagship gathered his host of carrier pigeons and set sail away from the dark fleet to give warning to the fleets of Southaven. But the black clouds of the fleet came and swatted as a great hand all of the beautiful carrier pigeons down into the great drink. The Dark One used carrion hawks, evil and cunning creatures from the Darklands to hunt down the pigeons.

"Finally the old captain had no pigeons left and three of his ships suffered torn sails. The other three ships were missing. He was desperate, and had one chance left."

"It was the crow, right?" chimed in Greygrim.

"That's right, boy." The captain smiled and nodded at Greygrim. "'Twas the crow. Its name was Tallorman. Said to be the last of his kind. The Dark One hated the smart crows when he could not bend them to his will, and had chased them from the Darklands and killed many. Old Tallorman was strong, with keen eyes, and he could talk to the captain. The captain knew what was left of his fleet would soon be lost, though he did have sweeps, and he pulled them out, trying to make way. He might lose the king's only son.

"So he gave his trusted friend Tallorman a note, wrapped it tight around his right leg, for not all could speak Tallorman's language. Then old Tallorman with his precious note and great bravery took to the air, saying goodbye to his trusted friend.

"But the Dark One, by evil magic, saw the bird. He threw wind, lightening, and breath of the very sky at Tallorman. The bird was smart. He darted in and out through all the Vagabond could throw at him. He almost outsmarted the Dark One. But he got injured just as he passed through the last of the storm. His left wing was hurt bad.

"The feathered hero flapped for all he was worth but he would not make it back. There was a small island not too far from the royal port. He just managed to make it there. He could go no further. There was no one around, no boats, no pigeons. Ol' Tallorman was sad, for he thought he had let his friend and the kingdom down.

"But his keen eye spotted a golden fish leaping from the water and dancing in the afternoon sun. Tallorman's race was quite wise and could speak many languages, including Ceylon, the language of the golden fish. Placing his long beak in the water at a calm spot, he managed to bring the gold fish close to shore and he spoke with him. Musta been a sight, a crow talking to a fish, squawking and dipping his beak in the water, getting wet and all from the surf.

"With some difficulty and time he managed to tell his desperate story. It just so happened that the golden fish knew the king's daughter, and knew her well. For almost every day, the beautiful princess went to a special place on the beach not far from the castle and fished. Her father had taught her and she had been fishing since she was six. She was now fifteen summers. The golden fish would tease her. He thought it was fun to barely touch her bait and dance around above the water. He swore no fisherman would ever catch him, for he was the prize.

"The fish considered how he might deliver the note to the princess. It might not work to deliver it to the shore, for she might not notice the note. The fish thought about it a while. At first he could not be convinced to deliver the note. It was too hazardous for him. After all he was still a young fish and wanted to have a family one day. He would miss his school. By far he was a bit of a loner and enjoyed his days in the ocean. He loved everything about the ocean, and the thought of being caught and possibly eaten was too much.

"Then he thought of the beautiful princess and happy, smiling people he had seen on the beaches. Even the worst people of Southaven were nothing like the evil men and monsters who fished off the coast of the Darklands, brutal savage creatures who would not only hurt the people of Southaven but all the fish if they won.

"So he decided with determination to take the note for the crow. It was getting late in the day and the princess would be leaving, if she was fishing this day. So he took the note in the side of his mouth and swam as fast as he could to where the princess liked to fish with her entourage.

"He arrived just as the princess was getting into her carriage up on shore. *All is lost*, thought the little fish. *What can I do?* As some of the sun's last rays hit the water, he got an idea. *I'll thrash about and jump and dance as I never have before.* As he did this, the princess saw him and yelled down, 'Silly fish! Another day!' But the fish continued to dance as never before. The princess was so intrigued with all of his flashing, she decided to throw out her line one last time. She had never seen him behave this way before. She baited and cast her line, and to her shock, the fish leaped upon the bait and she pulled him in.

"She could not believe this, for she never thought to catch him. 'Throw him back,' suggested one of her maids. 'Keep him in your pond," said another. They all admired the beauty of the golden fish. While they debated what to do, he gasped for water. The princess noticed the parchment sticking out of his mouth. To the fish's delight, she pulled and read the note.

"She quickly realized the situation, boarded the coach, and rushed to her father. It was the salvation of Southaven. The great naval battle began that day, with every ship and every coastal fort involved. Enough warning had been given. They even managed to save the prince, and the captain, and what remained of his fleet.

"After the battle Old Tallorman was rescued from his island. Brashfin, for that was the name of the golden fish, was taken to the little pond the king had built for his daughter and was fed the very best food. A great tree was specially brought in from Tallorman's home land. Gilded platforms were placed in the tree. Tallorman was thrilled with all the shiny things.

"The princess could not bear to see Brashfin confined in the pond. She would take him in a great bowl and set him in the ocean. In time the waters became darker. Ugly deep creatures crept closer to the shores of Southaven. One day Brashfin brought his wife from the ocean and they decided to live in the extended sea ponds built by the king. The Ceylon were quite amazing. They were able to swim in rivers as well as oceans.

"Of course the fish and the crow were great friends. Some of Tallorman's eyries were above the ponds and they talked. Eventually Tallorman found a lady crow of his kind and both raised their families. The royal fish and crow lived very long lives.

"One day old Tallorman lost what he called his favorite seein' eye to old age, and his little friend Brashfin could not bear to see his friend so sad. To the Ceylons' reckoning, he was still quite young and strong. So he went upon an old treasure chest at the bottom of his pond and brought forth his favorite and largest shiny, golden scale and presented it to his dear friend.

"From that day to the end of his days Tallorman wore the golden patch proudly. He claimed it brought good fortune to his family and that he had special ability to see with it.

"To this day seafarers of Southaven wear it as protection if they've lost an eye and good fortune. If ye have a special maker," here the captain pointed to his own golden patch, "ye have special abilities. Mine, I can see truths. And I can see a lie," he said smiling. "And I'll be hanged, yer not lying! How much gold have ye, boy?"

Arn pulled out his pouch and gave it to Trent. After eyeing it, he said, "Ye know there's four dark coin in here."

"Thirteen gold," answered Arn, for he had already taken out the others. "Four are Darklands gold."

"I can see that," said the captain. "Tell me how you came about this gold. I can tell yer not the types to have it." So Arn told the tale. The captain sat quietly and puffed thoughtfully on his pipe while he listened to their adventure. When Arn was done, he sat in silence for a bit then simply nodded his head.

He pocketed the pouch and its contents. "Neither by blood nor spit nor writ, but by our oath we make this contract between us. I can find somebody to use those four extra coin. This would be a fair amount to take you just about anywhere but the Isle of the Dead. But I'll do it for our fallen king. Also because you three show great strength, like the fish and the crow in my story. That's a good omen, says I," he added, pounding on the table with his fist.

At that, he said, "Let's be off." They followed the captain out onto the wharf. They walked past many ships and boats, great and small, until they came to the pier with a small boat and two ships.

"Is one of these your ship?" asked Greygrim.

"Aye, all are mine," answered Trent proudly. "That little coastal hoy is mine," he said, pointing at the smallest sailing vessel with one mast. "That be me sloop there, and the South Wind, that one there is me carvel we are shippin' out on tonight."

The carvel was quite larger than the sloop and the smaller hoy. She was a powerfully built ship with a fine wooden figurehead of a lady in a long dress, holding a dagger and an urn. "That figurehead is well made," commented Arn.

"Aye, that's the great lady. She watches over us. Ye'll see every ship in this harbor has eyes of some kind in the fore. To guide the ship, to keep 'em straight and true." As they approached the ship in the moonlight they could see crewmembers loading supplies and offloading empty casks and boxes. They walked up the gangway to the large ship and someone yelled, "Captain on deck!"

All the crew stood to and said, "Ahoy there, cap'n!"

"Ahoy," answered Trent. He went over to a middle-aged, skinny, balding man with bare feet, short grey pants and a formerly white shirt. Even in the dim lamplight they could tell he was tanned very brown from many long journeys on the open ocean.

"This is old Slimbones, my second and keeper of the canvas." Slimbones nodded in greeting, and they said hello in return. Arn noticed in his white blousy shirt he had a great needle with a grayish thick thread wrapped around it over his left breast.

"Is that for sewing something?" asked Anne, for she had never seen a needle that large. It resembled a small spike. Anne herself was quite proficient at sewing, having done a lot of it for former tavern masters. She had once had a nice collection of needles of her own, with pins and even thread, before they were stolen by an evil wench in one tavern where she had worked.

"Aye, it is, little lady. It's for sail keeping. And sail making. Though it's not special I keep it here in honor of the first revolt against the Dark One." Turning to Trent, he asked, "So what's the three young 'uns about?"

"Slim, they are honored passengers. We need to make 'em as comfortable as we can. This'll probably be their last week or so on earth."

Slim looked at them in wonder and scratched his head, giving a two-fingered salute from his right brow, murmuring, "Aye, sir."

"You lads continue loadin' the ship up. We must make sail about midwatch. They'll be changin' out harbor watch around that time. I'd like to ease on past 'em with no complications," he winked at Slim.

"As ye says, cap'n."

Captain Trent motioned the three to follow him. "Let me show ye yer quarters for yer journey." They followed him past the dark, open hold where men worked stacking crates below, down a set of stairs, in what the captain called the aftcastle. It was quite prominent and did look like a castle, with crellations along the top. There was also a smaller castle-like structure called the forecastle. They went down into a dark hallway.

"Meow! Hissssss!" they heard along with a loud thump. They all jumped, and the captain laughed.

"That just be old Patch Cat catching her a rat," he explained.

"Sorry, Captain Trent, we were just a little nervous of rats lately. And spiders." Arn smiled at his two friends.

The captain stopped at the second door on the right, and opened the door onto a small room about fifteen spans squared. There were six hammocks in the room, two laden with heavy burdens which looked to be some casks, old bundles of cloth, and an old pair of shoes. For a moment Arn thought someone was sleeping in one hammock, but it was just filled with junk, as was most of the floor. There was a tiny window in the back.

"This be yer quarters til we get to yer horrible destination."

"Please don't say that," implored Arn, "if you wouldn't mind."

They could just see the captain smile in the dim light. "Well, truth be truth but if yer not likin' it, we won't talk of it. I think I'd feel better if we didn't anyways. I'll have ol' Darby bring ye some water to ye. He'll place it outside the door there. There's a chamber pot neath the hammocks there." He pointed to the three empty hammocks on the right.

"Ye three look tired. Just sleep. Sleep as long as ye want. Nothing ye need do on me ship. Ye've paid yer fare. Unless I need ye. I got two rules. Don't bother the crew while they be working. And if I tell ye to do something, ye do it, snappy-like, ye see? Cause there be a good reason for it." The captain reached out the door and pulled a small covered iron lantern from the hall. "This is all closed in nice," he said, pointing to the lighted candle inside. "But ye three be extra careful with fire on me ship, ye got that?"

"Aye, sir," answered all three, in unison.

The captain smiled. "Good. Ye're already learning seafaring language. That's a plus. We'll have ye three working the rigging before too long," he added with a grin. "Well, a fair night to ye," he said smiling, placing the lantern in Arn's hand. "I've got work to do. Sleep as long as ye want. I'll make sure they save ye some food in the morning."

With that, he stepped out into the corridor and ducked out under the short wooden doorway, slamming it behind. The tired travelers carefully undid their bundles and pouches, placed them all together in the farthest corner from the door, and put their shoes in the corner. They climbed with some difficulty and amusement into their hammocks. They allowed Anne the bottom, Greygrim climbed into the top, and Arn took the middle. They chatted sleepily for a while about their adventures and speculated about adventures yet to come.

It wasn't too long after the captain left that a short, dark-haired man with a long dark beard brought them a bucket of water. It looked like it was good enough to drink. Anne twirled out of her hammock and handed each boy a cup of water in turn. They used the tin cup on the side of the bucket and slaked their thirst. Greygrim promptly fell asleep. Anne washed her face and hands and combed her hair with her old wooden comb. As she stood looking at a small copper mirror, combing her hair, Arn watched for quite a while, amazed that so fair a maiden would call him friend. He had two friends now. He could hear Greygrim quietly snoring above. He hoped he was not leading them to their doom.

Arn fell into surprisingly peaceful slumber. He and Greygrim slept late into the morning. When he awoke to the sound of the door opening, he saw Anne coming in with a smile, holding six freshly boiled eggs in a small basket. After giving thanks, they partook of the eggs with some water from the bucket. It wasn't too hard to rouse Greygrim from his sleep once he knew there was good food to be had.

They decided to go explore the ship in the daylight. Anne said it was a beautiful day out. Once up on the deck, it was amazing to see they were quite far from the shore. They could very distantly make out the shore on the left, and on the right all they could see was water. The crew were busily working rigging and singing a fun tune. They tried very hard not to get in the crew's way, as the captain had requested, but in time, Slim the deck master came over and smiled, particularly at Anne.

"You asked me a question, young lady? About this pin?" Anne nodded. "Grab a cask," he said. There were three casks tied to one of the wooden posts sticking up from the center of the deck.

"What's this post?" asked Greygrim.

"That's a keeping post, handy in case we want to lash something to it." The man leaned against the main mast, looking about, breathing the air. He was quite pleasant to the trio, his demeanor calm. He closed his eyes as if he were listening to every word the men on the deck were singing, and trying to memorize them. He smiled a toothy grin at them when the song was done. "That's purty, isn't it?" He had a big gold tooth in place of one of his front upper teeth.

"You said something about the needle?" asked Anne.

"Aye. I don't usually talk to any passengers much," he said, rubbing his clean-shaven chin. "But the captain told me last night what you're up to." Greygrim looked around nervously. "Don't worry," he said. "I'll not be telling anyone your intentions. Nobody would believe me anyway. I'm gonna tell you three a story—you like stories?" he asked, raising his bushy eyebrows. "About how seafaring men helped get us all out from under the claw of the Dark One. It has to do with this needle," he declared, pointing at his shirt. "This here is a sail making needle, and as I said before, I wear it here to honor those who brought us freedom a long, long time ago."

"'Twas a time when the five great tribes and all the lesser tribes had been bent down to where they thought they couldn't get back up. All of man had been enslaved by the vagabond with his filthy taskmasters and his goor. Men had lost, I tell you. We were on our way out. Women didn't even want to have babies no more. Wasn't much hope at all. As ye probably know, the old Vagabond had him a score to settle way across the waters. A place they say is called Grimcast. We'd been working over two hundred summers to make that demon something he wanted real bad: his great black ships. And his well-equipped soldiers. Both men and goor to take the Vagabond's war back to his enemies. Wasn't much hope. And 'twas in the great sail makers' hall of Narafell that an old, poor man was being beaten one day, worse than ever.

"A strong sail maker by the name of Godfrey couldn't stand watching the taskmaster any more go about his work. He was surely hurtin' this old man, bad he was, with a big stick with nine small black chains barbed with little black sea urchins all up and down its length. Godfrey couldn't take it no more. He took his sail needle out, long like this. Took his old leather seamer palm, placed his big sail sewing needle in his palm, went up behind the evil goor who was beating the old man and told him with the force of a king to stop.

"The foul creature turned about in disbelief, for no one ever stood up to him. He was one of the higher ups. It snarled and snapped in their foul language at Godfrey, telling him of the woe he would inflict when he was done beating the old man. Godfrey couldn't stand another word from the demon, and with all his might he slammed the needle into the beast's head, killing him instantly.

"Godfrey couldn't believe what he had done. He looked about to see if the other taskmasters in the hall had noticed. They were busy screaming and beating others. He raised his needle into the air, looking at the other sail makers, some chained and some not. He said with a great voice, 'This was our land! By God, by blood, by bone, by oath, it shall be again!'

"So the great war of rebellion began. Godfrey gathered up those near him and rushed the evil taskmasters in the hall, dispatching them quickly. He knew soon the Dark One's patrols would come by, well-armed and armored men on horses, who had sold out to the black master. They traveled about the various industrial places of importance to the Dark One, keeping order. To safeguard against just such a thing as revolt. Godfrey had a plan, a plan to destroy this patrol.

"How would Godfrey and his comrades take out these armored juggernauts? For they were well-trained in the art of war and well-equipped. He planned out an ambush, a deception of great cunning. They took the black sails that were laid out upon the floor and the ropes of hemp, and the shroud netting of the masts to use as nets. They raided the sail making hall next to theirs and took out those taskmasters as well. But Godfrey did not dispatch all of the taskmasters this time. He left alive one weak, cowardly taskmaster that he knew well. He knew by bells the patrol would be coming, so they tied a strong hemp line around the sniveling goor's left ankle and bid the creature to lead the riders into the sail making hall, telling them it was an emergency. They warned the goor that if he even hinted of the ambush they would pull him back in and kill him. If he helped them, they would harm him no more than tying him up.

"The bully knew it was his only chance to survive and agreed. At eight bells, the patrol came as usual, the officer bellowing requests for reports of progress. The little goor did his work and howled for them to come. He said two of the workers were beating a taskmaster at the end of the hall. 'Run them over! Run them over!' he laughed, quite convincingly. For the patrols loved to run people over with their heavy-hoofed horses. The ten riders laughed with glee at the prospect of riding down these two slaves. All the other men and women in the hall pretended to shrink away. The riders did not notice the taskmasters had been propped up and were not moving. For they did so enjoy the brutality of their work. This would be the last night of these things' brutality. Godfrey would make sure of that. For as the evil riders pounded in to do their hurt upon the innocent, they did not notice the huge doors closing behind them. They were very intent on their poor victims, charging at a full gallop, no less.

"The lead riders could not avoid the hemp rope pulled taut at their neck level just before they reached their victims. The middle riders could not avoid the shrouding that acted as nets. The last three riders turned, realizing the bad situation that had befallen their comrades, but blackness in the form of a great linen sail came down like the cloak of night over them. Men jumped down with it to act as weights, and all ten were dispatched with great ease.

"The sailmakers realized this night the spark of life had returned to them. They could overcome the tyrant. Godfrey lifted one of the black shields emblazoned with a red goblet. He took the sailmakers' needle, grey thread dangling, that had started the revolt, and pinned it into the leather, right through the goblet. He picked up the leader's great blackened helm and his great black blade, and said, 'This night we begin the end of tyranny, of cruelty, and of subjugation. Let the Vagabond know that all who join in this revolt shall not surrender his will or the will of those he loves ever, ever again. We live or we die as free men of the great Cast! We will never again bow to a tyrant, or to evil!'

"And so, with that, the great revolt began. Godfrey would become the first king of Southaven, for his blood went back to the kings of old, who had lost their freedom."

Arn, Greygrim and Anne sat, listening intently to the deckmaster's story. They had heard a little of the story of the sailmakers' revolt, but this was the first time they had heard the whole story. Just then, they heard the cook hollering for them to come below to sup.

They had a meal of roast beef, potatoes, roasted squash, buttered bread and wonderful gravy. It was a fine meal. Greygrim could not remember ever eating so well.

CHAPTER FIFTEEN

A JOURNEY BY SHIP

The first day of life on the boat was pleasant, as were the next five. The travelers heard stories of interest from the deckmaster, who showed himself to be a talented storyteller. He took a liking to the three, and seemed to want to entertain them. He tried to dissuade them from their quest to the Isle Macabre, but the three were dedicated to their path.

On the sixth day, they were introduced to a rough fall storm at sea. They remained in their quarters while the ship was rocked by waves. The captain and deckmaster would pop in and assure them that all was well, although it was difficult to believe as the ship was turned at unimaginable angles. Arn and Greygrim suffered seasickness during the storm, but Anne fared better. She knew a strange technique of tapping on her body with her fingertips, which looked a lot like nonsense to the boys, but that she claimed helped to tame the nausea.

On the seventh day of their journey, the squall abated, the tempest subsided, and they enjoyed a calm, clear afternoon and evening. The eighth day at sea went nicely as well. They had lessons from the deckmaster. They learned to tie sailors' knots and about rigging and rat lines, the shrouds that served as ladders for going aloft and supported the masts. Greygrim, characteristically adventurous, actually climbed to the crow's nest. Anne said she would have joined him if not for her skirts.

The deckmaster showed them about the hardwood deadeyes that held the ropes in place. They learned to use a marlin spike and a fid. Also on that day they learned a bit about belaying pins, wooden club-like devices that held ropes in place.

The captain took Arn aside and asked again if he could dissuade him from his course, but Arn would not be dissuaded. The captain knew Arn and his companions were not well-armed, and gave Arn a belaying pin beautifully carved with images of a carved ship, a sea serpent, a cross and a whale. He told Arn this was one of the first things he had ever gotten on a ship when he was a lad. He wanted Arn to have it for being a brave man. The club was of ironwood, an exceptionally strong and resilient wood. It had a good weight to it. Arn had never seen such a skillfully decorated item before. A thin rope was coiled around the narrow end of the pin to act as a handle. It was twisted into a lanyard so it could be hung from a belt, thus preventing it from being lost at stormy sea.

He also had a gift for Greygrim, a fine sailmaker's knife, which he and Slim presented. Slim had taken a liking to the would-be wizard's tricks and took great delight in them. The knife was quite sharp. It had a hook along the back which could be used to cut herbs. Greygrim knew the making of many poultices and potions for sickness. He was very grateful, for he had never been given a gift this valuable. He wished for something he could give in return, but they just laughed and said he and his companions should return safely, that would be gift enough.

To Anne the captain handed an ornately carved, wooden box, quite beautiful. She gingerly opened it in wide-eyed amazement, and wondered if he might snatch it back as a cruel trick. "And to the beautiful maid who travels with you," he grandly stated, "something that might help you on that isle, if anything might." Anne blushed and smiled at the kind words and pulled out an ornately worked silver cross, about seven inches tall. She gasped, thinking *I can't take this!*

The captain said, "Don't worry, dear maid," as if he knew what she were thinking, "that might be the only thing that gets you and them off that evil isle, for it is thrice-blessed silver and has a couple of tricks with it, too, young lady." He smiled and pushed a small, raised decoration towards the top, and to everyone's amazement, from the bottom shot a silver blade, about three inches long. "It's got another trick, too," he grinned. Turning the main thick bar of the cross, he pointed out a catch and pulled. Inside was a small compartment, long and shallow, containing an amberglass vial and coarse salt. The vial was almost the size of Anne's little finger. Holding the vial, he explained, "That be holy salt, and this here's holy water. The walking dead like neither." He popped something on the cross again, saying, "One last trick." In the center was a small scroll of holy words, four tiny holy wafers and the tiniest of candles. "You can use it as a light if you need to."

The three laughed in wonder as they had never seen such a neatly packed device. "An old monk I did a favor for gave me that. It's polished fine on the back too. If you reflect the candle's light on the back of the cross, putting it here," he explained, pointing at a small notch for the candle to fit in, "it reflects a mirrored effect a few feet away of the image of the cross. Any evil will think twice about crossing that image!"

He gazed into the distance. "In a few more days we'll be close to that isle if the weather holds."

They marveled at their gifts. Arn noticed something about his club that the captain had not shown him. It too had a hidden compartment which held a spike-like blade of about seven inches long. The spike could be screwed into the bottom, making the club a fearsome weapon. Also, a map or something else small could be held in the empty compartment.

They learned that their captain had a fascination for hidden, concealed items and spaces. There was even a hidden room on the ship somewhere, "for special cargo," he would say, smiling.

All went well until the twelfth day of their journey. They awoke early to pounding sounds of running on deck, heard the ship's bell ringing, and the crew yelling, "Shipjack!"

They quickly exited their cabin and rushed up on deck. "Thar be!" They heard the lookout yelling as he pointed with a large wooden stick that had a shiny metal end. The stick was called the crow's beak and was used to point at distant objects, so those below on deck could tell which direction he was pointing. The captain was already on deck, talking to the deckmaster and planning a defense against what everyone was calling a large shipjack.

Arn hollered at one of the deck hands who was busy winding a coil of rope and tying it off to a large wooden pole with a sharp metal tip. "Hands!" yelled Arn. The deck hand was called Hands because of his excellent ability in tying things and making knots. "What in the world is a shipjack?"

Hands chuckled nervously as he continued his coiling. "It's a water serpent, boy, big enough to lift our ship up if it wants to. Storms in the fall often bring them up from the bottom, make 'em mad or disturb 'em or something, I reckon. And it looks like a big 'un! At the very least they like to pull people off that area near the gunwale, so stay away from the sides of the ship, or it'll make a meal of ye!"

Arn and the others watched as the crew quickly took up weapons, including bolts for the large ballista in the aft forecastle. Several of the crew threw over barrels with holes punched in the sides. When they hit the water they oozed red and green, unpleasant looking liquid. "That's pufferfish poison," yelled Hands. "Don't kill 'em but they hates the taste of it. Might send 'im packing if we be lucky."

Arn felt a sickening feeling in his stomach as the creature drew closer and closer, spewing vapor like great puffs of smoke from its two front nostrils, and something on top of its head. Arn had never seen a sea dragon nor a land dragon, nor had he ever wanted to. The creatures were all too real in the dark lands and Southaven. Some say the Vagabond made them, some say they were around before the Vagabond, but he made them worse somehow with his twisted, anti-creational magic, taking what was already there and making it distorted and hateful. For the Vagabond could actually not create on his own, but was a master of twisting and warping—some of his favorite arts.

As they watched with horror, the creature grew quite a bit taller, with its head sticking out of the water. Its head alone was frightening to behold, with a gaping maw and dagger-like rows of teeth. It looked as if it could devour two grown men at once. When the serpent hit the swirling water, it veered away from the red and green liquid towards the bow of the ship. Obviously the liquid had its effect.

The shipjack snorted loudly, almost like a sneeze, as its head dipped into the water. Its eyes were a sickly red color. To Arn they seemed windows to a heart of pure malice. The serpent seemed both hungry and angry, and it eyed the crew of the ship menacingly. The captain waited to give the order to fire all the arrows and harpoons, to see if by chance it would turn away.

The serpent shook its head as if to say no, it wouldn't attack today. Speeding to the front of the ship and beyond the bow of the vessel, it dove into the deep sea. A great fan-like tail smacked the water before it disappeared completely from sight. It moved in the water like a snake, with the greatest of ease.

Arn could see the captain had moved to the forecastle and was eyeing the water, all about, as the sea became eerily calm. He and the crew looked about with great anxiety, and seemed to be listening. The captain placed his hands upon the forecastle wall as if he were trying to feel something. His head shot towards port, for the serpent had come from starboard before.

"Look ye to port!" yelled the captain. Several of the men standing on deck with great harpoons in hand ran to the left side of the ship. At that instant, not ten paces from the ship, the great blue and silvery head rose up, spewing vapors in a great cloud. It lifted its head over the gunwale even further out than before. The serpent lifted its great bulk and dove down, snapping at Hands. Hands, being small and very agile, quickly dove and rolled.

Arn could hear Anne, and unexpectedly, even Greygrim behind him scream in fear. The serpent had missed its prey but Hands had not. With his very muscular left arm, he thrust his powerful harpoon into the left side of the serpent's head. To Arn's surprise the harpoon did not penetrate far. It grazed the serpent's cheek just below its eye, making the creature let out a tremendous, searing bellow of hot air. Arn could not move. He was overwhelmed with rotted fish breath, and the demon from the deep was a mere five paces from him. He had never seen a greater horror this close in his life. Its forward teeth were longer than his entire dagger. After all, these things hunted whales and other large creatures for meat, when they weren't feasting on unfortunate seafarers. What went through is mind was, *Greygrim's scream sounded like a girl.* It would almost be funny if Arn knew he wasn't about to die a terrible, frightening, sickening, disturbing, nightmarish death.

He could see into the serpent's dead-looking red eyes. The monster puffed a great puff of hot vapor from its nostrils and the blowhole on the top of its head. Then it sniffed as if savoring a roast beef. The seaweed smell engulfed them all and made Arn feel nauseous. From the corner of his eye he saw Hands pull back his harpoon for another blow. The creature raised its head for a strike. It could easily reach Arn. Its mouth was much bigger than two men. It could hold half-twelve, at least. There was a fish's skeleton lodged in its lower jaw.

Arn thought, *that must be painful. Maybe if I plucked it out he wouldn't kill me and destroy the ship.* In his mind he laughed at himself. He might have laughed out loud. These silly thoughts rushed through his head, since he could neither fight nor flee.

The serpent's head rose higher and higher, preparing to strike him down. He felt as if someone had nailed his feet to the deck. Or perhaps the tar used to seal the wood was holding his feet fast. He could not think of a prayer for protection, though he tried. He thought the serpent's head would soon strike him down.

This seemed to take a long time, but was in fact moments. From behind, he heard a loud *ca-whack!* An instant later a long, powerful steel and wood bat stuck out from the creature's neck, just below its head. A bluish substance gushed out and the serpent bellowed and howled, its vapor billowing the sails as it threw back its titanic head.

Bolts, rocks, axes, spears and harpoons. Some glanced off the hide, some stuck. The blue nightmare hissed like a cat caught by surprise, turned, then plunged into the water, rolling the ship hard as it did so. Apparently Arn was not glued at all, for he lost his feet and wound up in a pile under the stars to the forecastle, his two friends piled on top of him.

The ship righted itself with a great creaking sound. It took a few moments for Arn to regain his wits and realized the sea worm had not made a meal of him after all. In a few more moments the joy rose in his heart. Poor Anne and Greygrim were still dazed. The experience had been unexpected and unpleasant.

Arn helped his friends to their feet. After a few minutes, the crew had returned to their duties as if nothing had happened. A great hand slapped Arn on the back and clasped his shoulder. "So, ye wasn't a tasty meal after all! I thought ye was a goner there for a second. 'Taint uncommon these days. That's why I took the big carvel instead of my little sloop," explained the captain. "Smaller ships just disappear all the time. Cook'll have something soon. Why don't you three go below and get some food. Forget about what just happened."

The captain looked at Greygrim and slapped him on the back. "I heard two gallish screams, but we only got one gal on board as far as I know." He smiled and patted Greygrim on the shoulder as he went by. Greygrim looked quite embarrassed and didn't say a word.

"Don't worry, Greygrim," said Arn as they descended to the galley. "If I could have screamed, that's how I would have sounded too!"

They ate a hearty meal and stayed below deck the rest of the day, deciding they had seen enough of the open ocean for a while. The next day was a beautiful fall day, calm and peaceful. The weather was cool with a pleasant breeze. They spent some time listening to some seafaring stories from Hands and Slim. Not a monster in sight.

Dawn of the last day broke calm but not clear. It was as if the vivid fall day had never been. The water was brooding and dark, and the sky was the same. There was an unwholesome smell in the air. A wispy mist could be seen in the distance. There might be land there.

The captain said, "Ye're up, are ye? Well, brave adventurers, that be the place." He pointed to the shadowy island in the distance. The trio noticed the sails did not seem to have a gust of air in them at all, but they were still moving forward. "Captain, sir, your sweeps aren't out, and the sails aren't moving. Is the island drawing us forward with some sort of evil magic?" asked Arn worriedly.

The captain let out a great, bellowing laugh that broke the stillness. "No, lad. I've got me a couple of current paddles."

"What are they?" asked Arn.

"Just basically big oars under the ship with the current washin' 'em back and forth. I had to let 'em down. It's hard to get near that island. She don't like visitors. Let's go to the forecastle." Looking out over the bow spurt, they all watched in silence as the slow current paddles brought them closer. They began to see a line of jutting black stones along the coast. "We're gonna sail right through there," said the captain. "Slim! Go to me quarters and get the offering."

"Aye, sir."

It wasn't long before Slim was back with a jingling pouch. "Hold yer hand out, boy." Arn cupped his hands together as the captain poured out some coins, fifteen silver pieces and one gold. A strange fish symbol was imprinted on the coins.

"What are these?" asked Arn.

"For the blue skeer."

"What's a blue skeer?" said Anne.

The captain squeezed two coins in his hand tightly and looked at Anne for a second. "Well, that's a good question, says you. They say the blue skeer, they are creatures, man-like things from the deep. Foul blue they are, with flowing white hair about. They're big. Some of 'em be bigger'n four men stacked on each other. The leader, he's over six men tall." The captain gazed out at the foggy coastline. "They came to be in this channel after the island turned. Some say they are the sixteen men who landed on the pier over there, the first to touch the isle after her black nightmare. It's said that cap'n and his fifteen men didn't get far before they jumped and howled with a blue flame all about 'em and jumped into the water. Never to be seen as men again. Might be true, says I. Be hanged if I know for sure. I think they are men still, in a way. Greedy. Like all us poor children of the cast. Born with a tich of greed."

After a pause he continued, "A league afrom the dock over there. 'Tis a stone carved, ye'll see it here in a moment." He took out his one-lensed scope he carried with him all the time. "There she be!"

It wasn't too long before Arn saw a skinny stone rising to starboard. It looked like one of the natural rocks had been carved. At the top was a skull with four faces. On the foreheads of the two skulls they could see were carved an N and a W. The captain pointed at the jutting stone. "Noth, west, south and east," he said, then raised his voice to the wheelman, "Bring 'er alongside—easy!"

"Aye, captain," was the response. The boat came within twenty paces of the strangely carved totem. Many more symbols were carved over the stone. One they could clearly see was a scythe, dark grey and covered with bits of seaweed.

"A fair number of adventurers come this way for reasons other than yourn." Near the bottom of the pillar was a stone bowl about twenty hands across. It looked to have some holes to drain off sea water. The captain grabbed a large pike from a rack on the heavy wood crellation wall. He pulled a heavy linen pouch from his pocket and gently placed the coins in it, as if he did not want to make any jingling noise with them. He wrapped the tie of the pouch around the pike and pushed it out towards the bowl.

In a very loud voice he yelled, "Blue skeer of the deep! Here be our humble payment for passage through yer fine waterway! Let the waters be calm and let your thirst be slaked!"

After the captain had placed the coins down in the bowl, a crewman brought out six casks of rum, each with a little rope looped around it. The captain carefully placed each cask on the giant bowl using the pike.

Josias was there with a wonderful smelling whole ham. "Everything a good seafarer needs. A good drink to slacken his thirst, a jarg of meat to sate his hunger, and a fine bowl of tobaccy after a meal. Though I ain't sure they lights it but I've seen 'em smoking. And of course a jingle in yer pocket. They must have a dragon's worth of treasure down there."

Arn was thinking about the cost of all these items, quite a bit of money. What he had given the captain would be just over his expenses for this trip. "Captain," said Arn. "This must surely cost you a fair amount. If I'm able to get coins later, sir, I'll pay you extra."

The captain smiled a toothy grin. "Yer a good lad. It's not necessary. I do what I do and make my own decisions. I'm my own man. You and yer friends come back safe with that weapon, and that'll be thanks enough. You've got the hard part, Arn!"

Greygrim, who hadn't said much for the past days due to bouts of seasickness, noticed the captain had the routine down well. "You've been here before, haven't you, captain?"

"Aye, this strait here is calm sailing if ye pay. I always like to leave a little extry for the sixteen blue fellas," he said, pulling out no fewer than sixteen white-bowled clay pipes with reed stems from his coat, along with a pouch of tobacco. "These blue skins have been good to us. They tore up a black corsair at the other end of the strait that was chasing us once. These old water boys are mean like ye wouldn't believe if you don't pay them. They'll shake yer ship apart, drown yer men, strand yer captain on the Isle of the Dead, take all yer coin and jewels and sech. That be a fate worse than drowning. But they hates the dark 'un, won't take no coin from him or his minions. They have to sail around that way," he added, pointing out to sea past the great jutting rocks.

"There's a great many rocks aneath the waves that way. Look right o'er there," he said. "See that fluttering bit? It's the sail from one of the dark one's ships. She didn't make it. Twixt the isle and mainland that way there's a great many reefs and rocks. Hard to navigate even for the best captains. But this strait is fair clear, good sailing, if ye pay." He was smiling as the ship eased past the marker.

Arn, Anne and Greygrim could see the wreckage of many ships out by the rocks and others near the shore. Anne said, "Look! What is that? Someone needs help!"

"Oh no," answered the captain. "One of the blue skeer watches makin' sure we paid our due." The trio stared in wonder. They realized if it were closer it would be many times bigger than a man. He had a shock of white flowing hair, like the caps of the waves. Indeed his skin was pale blue, a contrast with the dark water.

As they sailed closer to the docks, they occasionally spied a head popping up from the water. They were definitely being watched. It sent chills up Arn's spine to be watched by these eerie creatures.

"Lower the ship's boat!" yelled the captain. "Slimbones!" he yelled to the deckmaster. "Get that supply from below that I prepared!"

To Arn and his friends, he said, "You three go back and get yer gear. It's already mid-morning. I got ye plenty of provisions there. Enough to last ye two months if yer careful."

Old Slimbones threw off some mast shrouding that had been made into a ladder, and the three carefully climbed into the boat. An old sailor named Isaac, Hands and the captain himself were going to row them to the dock.

"Couldn't we just sail up to the dock?" asked Arn.

"Nar, nar, too many dead ships down there, and other things. Parts of buildings that have fallen in. Lot of stone. Old days this was a fine port. So my father's father said. Beautiful to behold. Wharves, jetties and sech. That's the old port city there of Cardeth, the old waterfront. Used to have beautiful inns and taverns, fine watchtowers, well crafted. Fancy people. Great bath houses, luscious smells. 'Twas said you could drop a pouch of gold there, and someone would tell ye not to litter," he laughed. "Now look at it! Dead."

As they rowed towards the dismal port, they could see dark windows in stone buildings that were still standing, many black windows. They looked like eyes watching them, waiting, hoping for someone to set foot on land again. There were gaping doorways with broken railings, which in places looked like teeth standing in great black mouths, ready to swallow them up with an unsatiable hunger.

The closer they got, the quieter they all were. A feeling of absolute dread came over the entire party. Arn thought, what have I gotten myself into? He wondered if he could follow through with his mission. All he could hear was the smack of water upon the boat and oars. No seagulls, no sea shanties. Just eerie, cold wind whistling through broken masonry.

The captain must have observed Arn's consternation, because he said, "We can still bring 'er about, boy. You and yer mates don't have to do this. I'll give you yer money back even. This is indeed a terrible place yer headin' to; very few ever come back. Them with jist a few trinkets. Jest enough to get the next fool comin' back. This island is alive, with evil. Don't do it. Let me take ye home."

Arn did not answer, but gazed out toward the island, for he had had his head down most of the trip, hoping not to catch a glimpse of the sinister place. The boat moved slowly but surely toward the one good pier that still stuck out. For that pier was mostly made of stone. He looked back at the ship that had brought them so far.

He wondered once again why Arn of Clayhaven was here. A young man of no great birth, no great standing. Someone who had worked hard most of his young life, cleaning privies and stalls of the refuse of others. He looked at his two companions, who looked to him almost as if he were a leader. Arn surely felt like no leader at this moment. He just wanted to go home and see his friends again, taking his new friends safely with him. He could not answer the captain's question. Part of him just wanted to say, *surely this is a fool's errand. Let's go home, captain.*

But the other part, the part that had always been with him, the part that had always done the right thing, that had always stood while others threw rocks and insults at him and had taken it with grim determination that he was somebody no matter what they said, that part said in a strong voice, *we will go on.* "I must go on, Captain," he said, looking at the island without really seeing it.

"Aye," was all the captain managed to say. He patted Arn on the back and said to the rowers, "Put yer back into it boys! Let's get this brave man and his friends there while we still have some light!"

All Arn heard was the word *man.* He looked down at his hands, still full of youth. They were very much still a boy's hands, yet they did kind of look like a man's, in the calluses and rough skin. No one had ever called him a man before. He wondered at that for a moment. He said a silent prayer of protection for himself and his friends, that he would not fail them, nor the high king, nor his country.

Then for some reason he thought of men going off to war with beautiful maidens wrapping ribbons or scarves about their necks. This was surely as great a challenge as that facing a knight going off to war. Today there was no cheering crowd, no favor or lock of hair for Arn or his friends. Just the slapping of the oars. There would be no riches at the journey's end. But there was a fire of determination building in the young man's heart. It was like that day on the hill when his friend had needed him and the archers had thrown jeers and insults at him. That feeling of energy was returning. He almost felt as if he could take on the entire Isle of the Dead by himself. He felt strong, almost giddy. He knew he and Greygrim and Anne may not all make it out, but they were determined and would do their best.

Then a strange word drifted into his thoughts. *Enough.* He found himself saying the word aloud with determination. "Enough."

Then he found himself smiling. Not the cheerful smile of a boy, but a man's. A warrior, no less.

"Enough what?" asked the captain.

"Oh, nothing," replied Arn, smiling at the captain. "Do me a favor," he said in a voice that surprised the older man. "Tell the brothers and the lady and my friend Greymist and anyone who asks of us that we went forward with our faces to the enemy this day." Arn felt a chill as he said these words, more meaningful than any he had ever said. The captain looked surprised.

"Are you still with me, dear friends?" Arn looked at Anne and Greygrim.

"Aye," they both said aloud, with determination. They could not help but feel the power of his words, as if they were charged with energy.

It was not long before the boat bumped against the stone pier. Arn grabbed the mooring line and to his own surprise, without a thought, he leaped onto the low pier to tie off the lines. The vigor he felt was still growing in his heart. His friends climbed much more slowly upon the pier. But they were every bit as determined as he was. The three could not help but smile at each other.

"This may be our doom," said Greygrim, patting Arn on the back, "but I have to say I would follow you anywhere, my friend. You've been more like family to me than I've ever had."

"Me too," added Anne, taking Arn's hand in hers, an act that surprised him. As he looked up into Anne's eyes, he felt to his amazement as if one hundred maidens had tied favors about his neck. *Her eyes are so beautiful,* he thought to himself. He could barely take his eyes away.

He murmured, "Thank you, my friends."

Greygrim said, "Let's take these things off the boat so the captain and his men can return to their ship."

They unloaded four medium casks of fresh water, one cask of salt pork and two linen haversacks filled to the brim with dried fish and sea biscuits. The captain also threw out a very nice coil of hemp rope with an iron grappling hook tied fast to the end.

"Ye might need this, boy."

He also cast a small cloth bag, a smaller haversack, stating, "There be sob bandages, thread and bone needles for bad cuts, and a little bag o' herbs, that's right, for making tea and giving strength. It's for helping yer head and giving ye strength. Also in there, a clean blade for a-burning yer wounds closed. And an extra flint and tinder box. May ye not need 'em." The captain stood on the bank and looked at the three. He would not set foot upon the stone pier with them. His hand merely touched the pier and he crossed himself. Arn could tell he had had some dealings with this place before, but he did not want to ask about it.

"I'm not so happy with yer errand, boy. But be hanged if I've ever seen a braver man. Or men," he added, smiling at Greygrim. "Or lady," he said, bowing his head at Anne. "Ye three take the cheese from the rat, I tells ye." He smiled broadly.

"On this where ye go, I canna go, for I swore never to come here again, myself nor my men. I'm afraid yer on yer own until we return a fortnight hence. Fourteen days and nights hence ye be here. But ye have my word as captain that come hell or high water I will be back fer ye. If I do not see ye when I return upon this pier, please leave a sign that ye been here and I'll be back next day. Pile a set o' rocks here in the center and I'll know there's been a delay and yer returning.

"I've given ye all the help I can. God speed to ye all. May his angels put shields and swords about ye in this evil place. Fare ye well, Arn of Clayhaven. If ye die here I will never forget ye, nor any of ye. Miss Anne. Greygrim."

The captain took off his large, black, broad-brimmed hat and bowed, hat in hand, upon the gently rolling boat.

"Farewell, captain. It has been our true honor to have met you. God bless and God speed to you and your crew, wherever you go, if we don't make it." At Arn's words the captain looked sad for a moment.

"Ye'll make it, lad. If ever I've seen heroes, it's ye three. Ye'll make it," he repeated, more weakly this time, as if he didn't quite believe his own words.

At the captain's last words, the crewmen stood up in the boat and bowed to the trio. Each said God speed, and Hands added, "Take good care of yerselves. Don't take nuttin' from this place of evil. They want you to, though. That's the trick o' the place.

Slimbones was the next to speak. He looked up at them and scratched his head. "I'll be flogged if I know why ye three be doin' this," he said. "But I'll be keel-hauled thrice over if ever I've seen a braver three."

Anne smiled at Slimbones and said, "Thank you for the wonderful stories you told us while we were on the ship."

"Yer welcome, little lady."

"'Twas an amazin' thing," said the captain, slapping Slimbones' angled shoulder. "He never talks to strangers."

"Well, they reminds me a bit o' me own young 'uns, I reckon," answered Slimbones.

"Ye three have been fine guests on me ship. Good fortune to ye and fare thee well," said the captain.

"Fare thee well, captain," they said. Greygrim untied the boat and threw the lines down. The captain sat down and stared at the friends on the pier as they rowed away back towards the ship. Arn, Greygrim and Anne watched for quite a while, until the captain and his crew were back on board, and the ship was underway again.

"Well," said Greygrim, "let's get this stuff somewhere safe. Maybe one of these buildings would be good shelter."

CHAPTER SIXTEEN

ISLE OF THE DEAD

*T*hey *walked into the dark port town. Even though they could see all* around that the sun was shining elsewhere, it was not shining in the town. The sky was dark and broody. As they looked around in the port city, they wondered at the beautiful, elaborate stonework. But they were very uncomfortable in the dark, winding streets of the port. Fortunately they were not far from the western edge of the city. They found not too far away, near the edge of the water, a small cottage with a portion of its roof intact. They did not feel so ill at ease here and decided to make this their base camp. Even though they knew there were no living thieves around, they covered their supplies with pieces of strong old cloth they had found. The captain had also included a cooking pot and a frying pan. They had had a good meal before leaving the ship so they decided to do a few hours of exploring with the daylight they had left.

They still felt quite vigorous and talked quite a bit to ease the stillness and foreboding they felt. They had seen nothing directly evil, but kept thinking they saw someone just out of the corner of their eye, or someone walking near them, or a face in a window. But when they looked directly, they could see nothing menacing.

Fortunately Slim and some of the other crew had prepared them a bit for what they would find here, so they were not surprised at these eerie sensations. They did not feel it from the water at least, but from every other direction.

There were two tall hills adjacent to the port where they thought they might get a good view, so they decided not to enter any of the tall, tall towers or buildings that still stood. They walked towards the higher hill, hoping to look out in all directions. As they came through the city and approached the hill, Anne's keen eyes began to make something out. At the summit of the hill stood a very large tree, with long horizontal spreading branches. There were a great many things hanging from the branches.

Before long, they approached a sign near the foot of the hill. Gallows Hill. To everyone's horror they realized what must be swinging from those many ropes tied to the tree's low branches. They did not want to continue their trek up the hill. Instead, they made their way over to the smaller of the two hills.

The only thing visible at the top of the hill was the almost-leveled ruins of some old building. From the summit they could see a fair distance. The great forests that were visible were made of dead trees. Not any green thing was to be seen. All the trees were grey, brown and withered. A few leagues from where they were, they saw a great, long lake. It stretched for miles in both directions. Though the lake was very long, the ends disappearing into the mist, they could see the opposite shore across the way. In the distance, across the lake, were the great Stone Mountains. Their destination.

If one thing stood out on this island more than any other it was the lack of color. As if a great bucket of ash had been dumped here, hiding all the colors that must once have been vivid and happy. The little structure still had a few good stones standing atop each other here and there. Although it was probably just over a league from their first camp, they decided to make this their second camp. Perhaps they would spend the night here.

They took a few of the old stones from the ruins and made a fire pit. The captain had told them that the island did not have much rain, even though it always looked as if it might rain at any moment. They did not feel they needed much of a covered shelter for the night. They gathered bits of dried wood and boards. There were still some furnishings, some still beautiful, standing in the ruins, even in the streets of the town.

At one point, Greygrim yelled out, and all three gathered to look. They had found their first evidence of the great wealth that was here in the middle of the main cobblestones of the port. Right at their feet was an old rotted sack made of painted canvas, like a sailor's bag. The contents had spilled out the sides. It was a great wealth of gold and silver coins. None of them had ever seen so much wealth in one place. They knew they dared not touch it.

Anne said in a quiet voice, "I wonder what happened to the sailor who gathered that up." It was quite a sobering thought for them as they regarded the lost treasure. They wondered if he had dropped it running, trying to get back to his ship perhaps. They decided not to dwell on it and went back to their task of gathering wood for the night.

Greygrim asked, "Do you think that taking just a few of those coins would be greedy?"

"It only takes one," answered Anne.

"Well, we heard that others have gotten treasure off," said Greygrim.

"We didn't come here for a swag," added Arn. *Swag* was a word they had learned from the captain to mean treasure. "Would we be the ones, Greygrim, they let get treasure out of here? There's very few that ever get anything off, and not that much."

The company gathered supplies from their first camp. As it got dark they decided to light a great fire, just to make themselves feel better. They had gathered plenty of dried wood. They knew that whatever dark presences dwelled upon the island were well aware of their presence. They made a good meal of some dried potatoes, salted pork and sea biscuits. As it grew darker, they told each other they would talk as long as they could into the night.

As the shadows grew longer, so did their apprehension and dread grow. And, yes indeed, they did see some of the shadows moving. Nothing was close to them, yet they could feel they were being watched. They were glad they were on the hilltop. They had toyed with the idea of barricading themselves in one of the port buildings. But the gaping stonework, twisted chimneys, narrow streets and dark, close alleys made the thought of sleeping the night there too much to bear.

The first, smaller, grey green moon came out to lighten the night somewhat with its pale, green light. The friends talked, but their sense of dread grew by the hours. Arn stirred the fire and placed more wood on it. He could feel the hair on the back of his neck stand up as if he were being watched close by. He looked out on the old abandoned fields, fallen or dilapidated structures and rotted old forests. The greenish moonlight gave all of it an air of desolation and sadness, tinged with horror.

They talked about all the people who had lived here once. The happiness, children playing in the streets, people dining in the great inns, sick folks washing in the healing baths, all the great works wrought here by the hands of men, and some dwarves and elves. Beautiful stonework, wondrous devices, grand decorative furniture, all for naught. Greed had taken these people, one by one, family by family.

A lot of them were still here. Just not alive. Nor were they still, as the dead.

Greygrim spoke up, as they sat next to the roaring fire. "Hey, Arn, Anne! Do you get the feeling this is just one giant graveyard? This whole island?"

"Please don't speak like that," pleaded Anne. "Isn't it enough that we are here? I don't want to dwell on what's out there."

"He's right though," said Arn. "Sort of like a graveyard or one giant, empty, howling soul of a giant that is no more."

They were all keenly aware of the wind whistling through the trees and broken masonry as if it were some giant struggling in his last thralls of life. They could feel the unearthly cold, as if one thousand pairs of eyes were watching them. Arn began to wish again that he hadn't come on this quest. Then he chased these thoughts away. Dwelling on them would do no good.

Greygrim spoke again, "Do either of you know the darklands word for gravestone?"

"Must we speak of this?" asked Anne quietly.

"It's just a stone," said Greygrim.

"Well, I don't know it," said Anne, putting another log onto the fire and pulling her blanket tighter around her.

"I don't know it either," added Arn. "What is it?"

"It's *sintelston*," said Greygrim in the Nothlund tongue.

"Darklands is a terrible place," said Arn. "Even their words for simple things are harsh."

"Aye," said Greygrim. "Did you know they have what's called a burybill there?"

"I've heard of that," said Arn in a quiet voice. "A terrible thing. They say in the last days of this foul place there was a buryman."

"Since I can't get you two to stop talking about this, what's a buryman?" asked Anne loudly, looking at them across the fire pit.

Arn answered, "In the dark lands, the people are so poor and there is so much tyranny the people cannot ever have a plot of land to be buried on."

"Aye, the people must save towards the end of their days if they have any guess when that will be," Greygrim continued. "If they have not saved enough to buy a piece of earth, terrible things could happen. It's considered a curse to be above the ground in that foul land. They seek permission for burial and when they don't have money that's when they call on the buryman. He comes to the village and dices bones with those who would have a plot of earth. Sometimes the players might win but mostly the buryman's game is fixed, and the poor player must sign on for servitude after life. A terrible fate. Weary in life, weary in death."

The three stopped talking a while and stared at the fire, listening to the wind and watching the sparks fly. They decided two would stay on watch and one of them rest. The two who stayed awake would sit back to back at the fire. Anne tried to rest first but it was no use. She heard her name whispered on the cold wind many times during the night. It was a nightmare.

I will not narrate this night to you, for there is no need, except to say the night passed horrifically and long. About midwatch, Anne found the cross she had received as a gift, attached it to a wooden pole, and staked it in the light of the fire. The normal glow from the fire reflected on the cross, then grew brighter and fuller, until the cross was bursting with light, not a normal reflection. She sprinkled some of the blessed salt in a circle about their camp, and after that they managed to get some rest in turns. I will leave it to you, dear reader, to ponder that night. Dawn came cold and grey, much as the day before.

Although they rested, they had slept very little in the night, and that sleep was uneasy. The shadows had kept their distance after the cross had been hung but there were still many unpleasant things just out of the firelight. Once dawn started, the tormentors disappeared one by one, into the shadows.

Anne spoke, "I do not know if I can stand another night like that."

"I know," said Arn. "I am so weary. Naught we can do until the ship returns. We must focus on our mission. If we can free our land of the villain Angueth we can prevent all of the kingdom from becoming a nightmare like this place."

"It's true," said Greygrim. "The dark lands are not much better than this place. At least tonight we will know what to expect."

Anne was walking the circle around their camp, retrieving some of the larger salt crystals and returning them to the precious little she had.

Arn said, "We'll leave some of our supplies here. We need to find a way to get to those mountains as soon as possible. As soon as we get that part done, the sooner we get the items we seek. I have an idea how we can spend our nights more comfortably until the ship's return. Slim told me the spirits do not venture out onto the water. There's that old stone building standing on the pier. We could make a camp there, put the cross and the salt and the wafers, and maybe some of that holy water at the start of the pier. Then wait there for the ship."

Anne's countenance lifted. "That's a wonderful idea!"

Greygrim added, "Yes, it is. Let's get this key so we can head out there."

They gathered up the belongings they would take with them and enough food and water to last about four days, and trekked off towards the grey, sinister mountains in the distance. There were not a great many hills. Most of the isle was flat. There were many good roads and trails. They quickly located the largest road, stretching from the city and headed to the mountains. They moved swiftly on the well-made, cobblestone road. It was good time they made that day. It wasn't long before they arrived at the bank of the dark lake, water slowly lapping upon the shore like the flicking of a snake's tongue.

Greygrim pointed and said, "I'm sure that used to be a ferry house."

"Aye," said Arn. "Sure looks it."

"And there's part of the ferry sticking out of the water," said Anne, disappointed.

"Oh, horse biscuits," said Arn. "That would have been handy."

"Horse biscuits?" mocked Greygrim with a grin. "No need for such strong language!"

Anne began to laugh. "I guess you see a lot of those in your line of work, eh Arn?"

Arn twisted his face in annoyance but couldn't quite keep the laughter back. The laughter somehow made the place less foreboding. "Is there any wood around here? We could make a raft or something." They looked through some small buildings. All the wood was in a state of decay here by the water. Some looked intact but crumbled into dust when they tried to pick it up.

"Wonder what makes all this wood so bad? There are no insects alive," said Anne.

"I think it's something to do with the curse," said Greygrim.

After searching for quite a while they found only three fair-sized pieces of wood. "Maybe we could use these as floats and try to swim across?" said Greygrim doubtfully.

Arn looked at the water apprehensively. "The land is cursed. Is the water cursed as well?"

Anne approached the water and said, "There are shells in here. Looks to be a salt water lake? I can't tell for sure, but is that seaweed out there? Maybe it's fed from the ocean." She dipped her fingertip in and tasted it. "Definitely salty." She walked farther down the shore. "Look here!" she said, pulling out a skeletonized fish. That's not that old."

"I wouldn't pick up a skeleton here," warned Arn.

"Ooh, you're right!" She threw it back into the water. "Anyhow, I don't think the water is as dead as the land is."

Arn walked closer to the waterline. "This goes on for many, many leagues. We can see the shore over there. It's not that far but I'm not that good a swimmer, and I don't see sticking my feet in this water anyway."

Arn and Greygrim stood discussing things that might inhabit the lake. Anne wandered down the shore and over a small rise. The boys decided they should walk around the lake, which would add a couple of days to their journey. The thought of the extra nights made both boys feel very grim inside. They would have to go back and get more food and water. "Anne!" yelled Arn, thinking to get on the way.

Then they heard Anne let out a shrill yell, "Arn, Greygrim! Come quick!" The boys glanced at each other and took off at a breathless run.

Arn muttered as he ran, "I didn't think these things were out during the day." He pulled the ship's pin that the captain had given him with his left hand, and his dagger with his right. Greygrim pulled the staff off of his back. Both were ready for anything. They ran over the rise, expecting the worst. Arn was angry with himself for letting the dear Anne out of his sight. *Please be alright*, he prayed as he ran.

As they reached the top of the rise, they were shocked by what they saw. There was Anne lying in a field of green and orange. To their joy, it was a great patch of giant pumpkins. Anne smiled and patted an extremely large pumpkin. "I tripped on a vine. Isn't it amazing? Maybe the island is not as cursed as we thought."

"Pumpkins aplenty," said Arn, as he slapped Greygrim on the back in relief. "At least we can eat as needs be. I like pumpkin!"

"So do I," said Greygrim.

"Brother Clement used to take the skin off, cut it up, boil it, mix it with butter and salt, and sometimes a bit of bacon. It was delicious!"

"We have salt," offered Anne, "and pork. We could cook some up."

Greygrim rubbed his stomach. "That would be so good."

"I think we should take a couple of the smaller ones," said Arn.

Anne was running through the patch, thumping some huge pumpkins. "I've seen these used before in a way that might be an answer to our prayers."

"What do you mean," asked Greygrim. "I don't remember praying for a meal."

"No, no, just listen," advised Anne. "Many years ago I worked at a tavern called the Pumpkin Tankard Inn. The owner there, old Ben Mead, was kind of a nice guy. Once a year he always got a big smile on his face, in the fall. Old Ben was the kind of a guy who liked to invent contests. One of his favorites, which he liked to run every year . . ."

"Go on, go on!" urged Greygrim.

"It was a race," said Anne, grinning and patting a giant pumpkin. "He gave a prize of a full week's food and drink to the winner."

Arn still didn't see quite where this was going. "What kind of race?"

"A pumpkin race! The Inn was right beside the Shen River. It was wide and calm and about a mile down the way was a fair-sized lake. What they'd do is find the biggest pumpkin they could, hollow it out, some would even decorate the sides, and off they'd go with paddles. From tavern to lake."

"Is that right?" asked Arn, laughing. "That's clever. Could we do it?"

"Sure," answered Anne. "I could help you."

Greygrim said, "You mean, hollow them out, and row over to that shore? We wouldn't have to put our feet in that water. It's not that far. I'm for it! Much better than taking the extra time to walk around!"

"I'm for it too," said Arn. "That's a great idea, Anne!"

"Let's do it then. This one's mine." She smiled and patted the large one she had tripped over and fallen beside.

They set to work and found four pumpkins that were just right. One for each of them, and one for their supplies. In a few hours the large gourds were ready for their trip across the lake. Greygrim worked on some of the wood and fashioned four crude paddles. One for each and one extra in case of emergency. They placed a sharp stake of wood in the supply pumpkin boat and tied a tow line.

Anne wanted to go first. She had not stopped smiling since they had started on this endeavor.

"Have you been in a pumpkin boat before?" asked Greygrim.

"I was," said Anne. "I won second, and old Ben gave me two whole days off, not having to work but still getting my meals. I actually slept late," she added, smiling to herself.

Anne's skill in carving the pumpkins had produced balanced boats. She placed hers into the water and slipped inside it. It floated perfectly.

"This is a great idea. We'll be across in no time. We can beach the pumpkins over there. They might just last long enough to get us back across. You are a genius, Anne!"

Anne looked away, blushing but smiling. "I'm not a genius," she said. "I'm just smarter than you two!"

"All right. Let's just get on with it," said Greygrim. The older boy placed the supply boat in the water and then his own. He climbed in while Arn checked the tow line. They had placed two spikes in each pumpkin in case one of the spikes gave out. Then Arn steadied his boat.

He looked at it with some apprehension. Now he was thinking about the sea monster and how he had almost lost his life in the water.

"I'm ready," declared Anne.

Greygrim said, "It's up to you, Arn."

Arn stayed on the bank, bowed his head and prayed. For some reason he was now quite nervous about crossing the dark water, much more nervous than his friends seemed to be. He had brought them on this journey and did not want to show them he was afraid.

"I'm ready," he said, pushing the great pumpkin into the water. The water was deeper here. As he stepped into the floating craft, he almost overturned it and landed in the water. Feeling awkward, he took up his paddle.

"It's a bit tricky," said Anne. "Just do what I do." She began to paddle, first one side, then the other. Greygrim followed, less skillfully. He watched Anne and tried to follow her example. Arn, however, was quite slow. It was cumbersome to row over the bulky sides of the deep boat. He was grateful Greygrim had the tow line.

Anne seemed happy and even began to hum a tune as she went. Arn was glad to see it. Watching her distracted him from thoughts of deep water.

> "Come what be, come what may,
> It's autumn pumpkin racing day.
> I'll paddle real fast,
> I'll paddle real hard,
> In me great orange gourd.
>
> I'll win me reward,
> Here and now moving forward.
> There be a great crowd,
> They will soon all be wowed.
> With me great orange gourd.
>
> As I win this race,
> In me small pumpkin space.
> No need for a boat,
> My pumpkin's afloat!
> It's me great orange gourd."

Slowly they made their way across the lake, Anne skillfully leading the way and happily singing. Greygrim caught on quickly to the ways of his pumpkin and he was doing much better. They had outdistanced Arn by quite a bit. In a short while, they were beaching their orange boats on the other shore and waving to Arn to hurry up.

Arn's crossing had been fraught with difficulty. Just as he was getting the hang of it, he noticed a bubbling in the water over to his left, about two hundred paces. He stopped rowing and watched. The water had been quite calm so far, except for some floating seaweed, no obvious signs of life in the lake. He wondered what this could be. The bubbles became larger and moved closer, and he began to paddle for all he was worth.

Ideas went through his head, of the sea monster. The size of the sea monster. The bubbles got larger, then up went three spurts of vapor in jets.

"What is it?" yelled Greygrim from the safety of the shore. Arn did not answer. He just paddled faster. *It can't be another one!*

To Arn's gut-wrenching horror, a huge greenish-blue head popped out of the water just in front of his boat. Arn looked up with sheer terror on his face. In the back of his numb mind, he could hear Anne and Greygrim screaming from the beach. It was indeed a shipjack, although not as large as the first one they had seen from the ship. Arn stopped paddling. Being in a small pumpkin boat instead of a ship added to his feelings of vulnerability.

This beast had a greener hue to scales and flesh than the bigger one had had. Although its mouth was much smaller, it was plenty big enough to gobble him and his pumpkin in one swallow. And pumpkins are edible. Its head swaying, it stared at Arn with keen blue eyes. It had probably never seen prey like this in its murky home. The monster came closer and emitted three more great vaporous spouts of water from its blow hole. Arn's mind calmed as he said his last prayer, asking for mercy from God.

The shipjack made a noise, not the fearsome growl the other had made. It seemed to have more interest, more intelligence in its eyes. Although loud, the noise sounded almost like a woman's laugh. He froze as the creature's head dipped down towards him. It sniffed him. Through his terror, he thought he heard it say, "You have the stink of the dark dwellers on you."

Arn blinked and watched as its head retreated. Its mouth opened, and he heard, "Join your friends, human child. I'll not hurt you."

With that, the great head slowly lowered into the water only a few paces away. Despite the shipjack's size, the pumpkin barely rocked. He recovered from his horror and began to row rapidly and more skillfully now. He reached the shore and quickly pulled his pumpkin up to land.

"What happened?" asked Anne.

"You wouldn't believe me if I told you," said Arn, looking pale. He wondered if he imagined the shipjack's words. He looked back at the dark lake and some small ripples out in the water. All he could think was that on returning, he would make another trip across the lake. The thing really spoke somehow. The sheer fright and lack of control over the small, tippy boats made him not wish to do it again.

They put their gear on and split the supplies amongst them. Greygrim had rigged a sling for himself and Arn to carry one barrel of water each. They made their way to where the ferry had once docked, and rejoined the cobblestone road. They continued on their way as fast as they could. The road headed towards the misty mountains in the distance.

They passed a cart, and the remains of what had probably been a mule, heading away from the mountains. Inside the cart they saw rotted, rolled remains of a tapestry, broken urns, and a few copper and silver coins in the bottom of the cart and spread out over the ground. There were picks and shovels in good condition. This was probably from a few years before, and the cart and poor animal had belonged to some looters. Something had obviously happened to interrupt their plan. They decided not to dwell on the fate of the looters.

Arn said, "I think these tools belonged to grave robbers. I think we'd be safe to take them up to the crypts. They will come in handy." Arn hefted a pickaxe and saw words burned into the handle, Lady Vain. He held it up for the others to see.

"See, definitely a looting party." He handed a shovel to Greygrim to carry and a small hammer and chisel to Anne. "These could come in handy." The thought crossed his mind to take the coins, but he was careful not to touch them.

They made good time for about three more hours. The mountain loomed larger in the distance. The sky was still brooding but not one drop had fallen. They interrupted the eerie silence with whistling, songs, and conversation. They knew in a few hours it would be dark. They all wondered to themselves what they would do, but did not talk about it.

CHAPTER SEVENTEEN

A CASTAWAY AND DARK PLACES

*T*he road led them to a great dead forest, full of oak, yew and ash trees. First they saw a great many stumps, evidence of timbering long ago. Then they saw trees, many, many trees, some with dry, brown leaves still hanging on them. Leaves that must have been hanging for a long time, well after the poor trees had stopped their reaching for the sun's light.

They walked with purpose through the woods. Although the trees were nothing but skeletons of their former selves, it was if a dark woods were pressing about them. Though they had not seen the sun itself since they had arrived on the island, here there were actual shadows, from what little light remained, and they felt the chill of every shadow that crossed their path.

They decided to stop for a good evening meal. They had been walking and working all day without much rest. They came to a great clearing in the woods, a meadow covered with dead grass, and a stream running by the foot of a hill. At the top of the hill stood a little cottage, quite inviting. The cottage was still quite intact, to their surprise.

It was an hour or so before sunset. Arn decided this might be a good place to spend the night. At the side of the house were many old, dried bits of pumpkin shell and stems in a rubbish pile. "These cannot have been here that long. Someone else used the pumpkins well, I see," he said.

Anne wondered, "You don't think someone could still be here?"

Instead of opening the door, Arn rapped loudly three times, and said, "Hello! Is there anyone about?"

There was no answer. Arn swung the door open and looked inside. It looked as if someone had been here quite recently. Many things stood against the walls of the cottage. Barrels had been turned up and placed beneath a table as if used for chairs. The table itself was quite crude. Several seashells held wicks and what was probably fish oil. But that was not the most amazing thing. The walls had been white washed, quite white, and upon it were some very good drawings of mountains, caves, rivers, tunnels, pickaxes and what looked to be dwarves, mining dwarves.

Very prominent looked to be underground rivers with dwarven people on boats and on the ocean in ships. Many, many places on the wall held images of crosses, angels and swords, with holy writing he could not make out. There were lines of hash marks. Many hash marks in a row.

From outside, Anne said, "Arn! Out here! Somebody's already put crosses. There are quite a few of them."

"In here, too," he replied from the doorway.

Greygrim said, "This will be a good place for tonight's lodgings. Let's look and see what else we find. Might be a bed, I'd like that!"

"That'd be MY bed and I'll be hanged if anybody else will be a-sleepin' in it!" A loud voice boomed from behind Greygrim. He leaped at least a foot in the air and tried to come down cat-like. With the reflexes of a two-legged cat, he tripped on his staff and fell flat on his face before the person with the booming voice.

"Never had anybody bow afore me," the voice said, chuckling.

Arn came out of the house, weapons drawn, and Anne ran to Greygrim to help him to his feet. Fearing the voice had belonged to an evil spirit, they were surprised to see a not-very-tall, but very stout, long auburn-bearded, obviously dwarven fellow standing before them with an axe over one shoulder and a bundle of wood over the other.

"I'm Rand Stoneanchor. And who be you?" he asked, pointing his axe at each of them. "Ah, wait. Ye must be the fools who lit that beacon on the hill yonder on other shore, anear the port." He laughed aloud. "So aside from you three kinder, where's the rest of your people?"

Recovering from surprise, Arn spoke first. "We are everybody, sir. And we are very sorry to have disturbed your home. We didn't think anybody lived here."

"Are you alive?" asked Greygrim, pointing his finger at the dwarf. To the others he said, "Could be a trick."

"Are ye blind, and a fool? Don't I look real? These other things don't look anything like me. I'm as real as they come," he declared, thumping the back of the axe on his broad chest. "Are ye three shipwrecked?" he asked, raising his bushy auburn eyebrows. "Surely if ye'd come to loot ye wouldn't have made it past yer first night just the three of ye."

Anne said, "No, sir, we haven't come to loot. We've come to aid the kingdom of Southaven." She tried to sound friendly and smile.

"Is that right?" he said pointedly, suspiciously eyeing the digging tools they carried.

"She speaks the truth," said Arn.

"So ye three younguns have come here to help the noble kingdom of Southaven." He laughed aloud.

"That's right." It was Arn who walked forward and leaned towards the dwarf and whispered, "The Dark One has come to invade Southaven with many armies. A full-scale invasion, sir."

"If that be so, bad tidings indeed." He thoughtfully stroked his beard. He studied the three for a few seconds under his bushy eyebrows. They felt nervous under his piercing, stony gaze. "Unless ye three are scouts for more thieves, or tellin' me a lie, I have no reason to doubt ye. Ye three come on inside," he said.

Walking to his door, he slung his bundle of wood into a small bier attached to the house. With one hand, he crashed the axe into a log, splitting the stump. He went over and washed his face and beard with water from a wooden bucket beside the small cottage. He took a wooden comb from the windowsill and combed through his beard. Walking in through the door, he said, "Follow me. Forgive me my ill manners. I haven't had guests for a while."

They went inside and Stoneanchor began to stoke up some burning coals and expertly placed pieces of wood to begin a fire. He pulled off a medium sized black kettle from the crane on the fireplace, and put it on a small wooden table just under a window.

There were so many pumpkin items. Storage containers made from emptied and dried large ripe pumpkins, and many small ones next to the door.

"Were those your pumpkins we saw over there?" Anne asked.

Stoneanchor turned around and raised an eyebrow to her. "Why do ye ask?" He sounded suspicious.

"Well, would you mind terribly if someone used some of them, maybe four of them, for something?"

"I'll be hanged!" he boomed, while slamming his fist on the table, hard. The noise made the friends jump to their feet.

"We are very sorry!" apologized Arn. "We will gladly pay you. I have some coins. We did not think they belonged to anyone."

"Just tell me they weren't the four great big uns," he said, lowering his head and looking very sad.

"We are all so sorry," offered Anne. "We did not think there was anybody alive on this island to own them." Her voice was soothing.

He looked at the three unhappily and asked, "What be ye usin' em for?"

"Well, sir," explained Anne, "it was all my fault. We used them to make boats to get across the lake."

"Boats?" he exclaimed in surprise. "And that worked?" The anger was gone from his voice, and he seemed curious. "Ahh, those poor lads. They'd have made good food for a while. One I was going to try to make a barrel out of." He looked at his visitors and smiled broadly.

He slapped his knee and exclaimed, "I'll be hanged! I'd never thought of usin' em that way. And me a lunker! Well, nothing much to do about it now. Wished I coulda seen that though. What about ole Lulubelle? She let ye cross the lake that way?"

"Aye," answered Arn, "If that's the monster you speak of, she did."

"Ahh, but if I'da only seen that! Musta been a sight. Well naught to do for it now. Here boy," he handed the kettle to Greygrim. "There's another bucket around the back of the house with good water in it. We'll have a fish and pumpkin stew." He pulled down some dried fish that had been tied to the rafter. He chopped up some pumpkin and fish and some other ingredients, including seaweed and sea salt for flavoring.

"I sure have missed butter and cream a few times, and cheese. Oh my, and beef. You wouldn't have any beef on ye?" He looked up at them.

"I think I do," said Greygrim. "Kept it from the ship when they gave us a bit extra."

"Ahh, give it me! That'll be fine." He took a bite of the dried beef, chewed it and savored it, and carefully stored the rest in a small pumpkin bowl. "That sure be good. Real beef. And bacon. Got any bacon?" Stoneanchor looked up hopefully, but they had to shake their heads.

Their host put the kettle on to cook.

Anne asked, "How long have you been here, Mr. Stoneanchor? Were you stranded?"

"Aye, lass." He gazed into the fire. "Been stranded in this evil place three long year, thereabout. I came with a ship, the Westward Star, along with Cap'n Rutger and eighteen other men. We came on shore armed to the teeth. Ol' Cap'n had even gotta couple magic weapons as worked against the dead.

"Well, we came, and first few nights nary a thing happened, just a few scares here and there, nothin' serious. Cap'n swore the curse was an old sea gaffer's tale. We made our way to the great crypts. We got into several. Some were open, swag likes ye never seen, just sitting, ready to be taken away. On our fifth day, we'd loaded up good, I tells ye. We'd brought some carts, coupla ponies, plenty of packs. We were so heavy with treasure it was late on fifth day we left the crypts.

"Just when headin' out the great gates, they struck. I was with the last men in the group. We heard the howlin' o' something, and screamin' of the men. Cap'n Rutger sent the armsmaster and another crewman back with one o' the magic weapons. They didn' make it back but we sure heard 'em screaming, and the horrible howling again.

"I grabbed me packs with treasure, filled with plenty of booty, gold, silver, daggers, even a beautiful war axe encrusted with jewels, made with magics. Great magics, dwarven made, ye know." His mind obviously wandered, remembering.

"The Cap'n yelled to run fast as we could to the boats. We ran, ponies, carts, all of us as fast as we could, down the pass. Moon blue was coming up, and first moon was out in full. Gettin' near the bottom of the pass, we saw 'em. Hundreds of shadows. Hundreds of white shapes moving towards us. They had trapped us good.

"What a horror to battle these, the angry, hungry dead comin after us. Cap'n Rutger was a man to be reckoned with, a powerful, strong man, with a will the likes ye never seen. Him and his magic cutlass fought his way through the crowd, cleared a path for some of us.

"Several more men fell there. Some began to drop their treasures, many hung onto some as we really took a fancy to. I dropped some gold and jewels to set me up the rest of me life. But I kept me pack and the axe I fancied. Down the mountains the path joined up with the big road, and we kept a-runnin'. Thought we might make it.

"At the edge of these woods here, more men went down. They leaped out from trees at us. Left me, Cap'n Rutger and two crew left, Old James and Salty Dog Pete. I watched while we ran up the path and there blocking us, probably another score of 'em, powerful ones at that. Cap'n charged 'em full on.

"I's about unslung the axe and was set to join 'im in death, for they surrounded him. Death he got quick. Pete grabbed me on the shoulder and pulled me into the woods. We ran along a path, with James lagging behind, exhausted. I yelled, 'James! Drop some! Ye might make it to the boats if ye drop some!'

"'Are ye daft?' he yelled back. Could see in moonlight, he was a madman intent on his treasure. See it in his eyes. I watched in horror while a large shadow came up behind James. The shadow wrapped around him and tore him off into the woods, fast as ye ken say 'all aboard' he was gone, treasure and all. Screaming.

"Never forget his wild eyes, him reaching for me. Couldn't do nothin'. Too quick. Pete and me continued up the trail, prayin' they hadn't noticed us." At this Stoneanchor closed his eyes and chuckled.

"Twasn't the case though, no matter where we were. Pete still held a scepter in his hand, had a backpack fulla loot and pockets a-bulging. I was first up the trail and he was losin' ground, from the extra weight. Heard Pete scream, I did. Turned about, determined to do something this time.

"I ran with the magic axe in me hand. I'm proud to say I cut down that demon shadow that had hold of Salty Dog Pete. That were the best axe I ever seen and magic as they come. Worth a king's ransom, it was. I'll be harpooned if I wasn't going to keep it. Pulled a knife from me belt. I was gonna cut the backpack straps. It was too heavy. He was exhausted.

"'No, ye fool! It's a life's fortune here!' he cried. I looked into his crazy eyes, heard somethin' me mama told me, loud in my head, just the way she used to tell me. Full blown greed'll cut dwarf, man and elf right down at the knees, and they won't get back up.

"I realized at that moment I couldna save old Pete, but I thought I'd try one last thing. Cut the shoulder straps to me pack and let it fall to the ground so's he could see. To my horror Pete screamed and went to the ground grabbing for it. I hollered, 'Ye dang fool! Ye'll be dead in a moment! Fergit the gold and come with me!'

Just as I said that, three great specters appeared, intent on swallowing me and Pete up. Turned about and ran fast as I could. Heard Pete screaming behind me. Weren't nothin' I could do for him. Ran quite a ways and grew weary. Could still hear 'em behind me, like a howling wind. Knew I couldn't outrun 'em. Saw a tree with a gap in it. Ran in there and put my back to it, I did. Hefted me axe, ready to sell me life dearly. As the three great specters approached, they were horrible to behold, I tell ye. Twistin', angry and hungry. It was gonna take me very essence of me life out any second.

"I thought about what happened. Emptied me pockets, threw out all gold and jewels at their feet. They came closer and looked at the axe in me hand. *Least I'll die with this dwarven-wrought beauty*, I thought.

"In me mind, me ma came again. She had a big boomin' voice when she was mad, I tell ye. 'Ye dumb hammerhead, put that down!' And I did. Threw it at their feet. They swirled around me and that tree for a while, sniffin' at me, pawin' at me. Didn't really hurt me, and after a time they just left. 'Twas greed kills ye quick on this island. Stealin' from em. They don't like that. All their fine treasures is a trap.

"Next day I came out of the tree, what passes for a day here. Hadn't a crumb of food nor drop of water, as I'd dropped it in the caves to carry more loot. Only thing in me pocket, five pumpkin seeds. Thought about eatin' em but somethin' told me to plant em and I did. By golly, they came up! Got three patches now. Living on fish from the lake there when Lulubelle isn't splashing heavy, pumpkins, occasionally supplies from fools that come on the island.

"Yer not the first since I been lost here. Tried me best to work a deal with the first few lots who came. Tried to tell them the folly of takin' treasures. Nary a one has listened. All offered me a ride, mind ye, as long as I carry a share of the treasure." He laughed heartily and spit into the fire. "Watched death take a great many of them."

The dwarf looked into the fire and pulled out a small clay pipe with what looked to be seaweed tobacco, lit it up and puffed a few times. "My little kingdom here for some fine tobacco. Wouldn't have any, would ye?" They shook their heads. "Well, ate fairly good tasting soup. Ye'll sleep here tonight."

Arn told him about their quest and he seemed sympathetic though doubtful they would be able to take even a weapon to be used for good. But it was the most noble endeavor he had seen come on the island since he'd been here. With not much other hope of rescue he promised his help to them.

He got up and drew heavy canvas curtains over his windows and bolted the door heavily. "This was one of the least ruined buildings. Don't know why. Perhaps someone with a good heart lived here. It's served me as a good home. Two year goin' on. Used to live down by the port. There's a great hungry specter as calls that home. Was always trying to find a way to devour me until I found this place. Ye'll hear clawing and knocking on the door, thumping on the roof. Whatever ye do, don't open the door, and don't ope them curtains!"

The dwarf lit quite a few fish oil lamps before going to sleep, and stoked up the fire quite nicely. "They don't like light." The three weary travelers lay down close to the fire that night. Though they did hear howling and scratching, they managed to fall asleep one by one, thinking of the day's events. Nothing bothered them. Stoneanchor slept in his bed, snoring loudly. It was quite comforting. Arn thought, *He's a tough one, to have spent three years here night after night.* As he drifted off to sleep, he was glad Stoneanchor was here with them.

Just after dawn Arn awoke to a delicious, savory smell, of fried fish. He looked up to see Anne's pleasant smile. "I've got some boiled pumpkin and fried fish," she said.

"Where is Stoneanchor?"

"He went for water and wood. He said we would be safe. They only attack in the day if you've stolen something from them."

"Is that fish I smell," grumbled a sleepy Greygrim.

"'Tis," said Anne. "And some pumpkin."

"Smells good."

"Aye. Let's eat," said Arn. The stumps upon which they had sat last eve were still at the table, so they gathered there for their meal. "Here's a bit of leftover seaweed from last night. Pretty good once you get used to it."

"Well, I guess this is the day. We are not far from the crypts," said Arn as they broke their fast after a morning prayer of thanks.

Just then Stoneanchor opened the door, and carried in a large bucket of fresh water and two more fresh fish. "It's a good ways to the lake and quite far to the ocean. How did you get the fish?"

"I have me a pond I made. I stock it regular with caught fish. I keep 'em 'til they grow a bit and it's not so far to the lake."

"But isn't it salt water?" asked Arn.

"Aye, it is."

"How do you keep them alive?"

The dwarf raised his eyebrows in surprise. "You're a clever one. It's an old lunker trick. Maybe someday I'll tell ya."

Anne said, "I have some delicious fish here for you, Mr. Stoneanchor. Will you sit and break your fast?" He placed the bucket on the floor and looped the cleaned fish over a wooden peg near the door, then took off his old worn out and patched cloak, which was soaking wet.

"Is it raining?"

"Spirits are worse on days like this, I tells ya." The old dwarf sat at the big chair that was his. He said a quick prayer and crossed himself, then began to eat heartily. "Would you tell us about the lunkers?" asked Anne. I've heard a little bit about them."

"Aye," said the lunker with a mouth full of food, and crumbs in his beard. He mumbled past the mouthful, "The lunker are a separate group of dwarves, proud workers of boats 'n ships. Unlike our cousins in the mines, who prefer delving in the dark with picks 'n shovels than wind in yer sails.

"In the beginning the dwarven king Farbeard Stonefist decided he was tired of the humans who came up the rivers to trade in the caves. Men that came upon the rafts, he believed, were stealing things from his kingdom. He placed them under heavy guard when they were there. Brung much friction between him 'n the human traders. So, he picked what he called dwarves less 'n miners, as he put it, and made us build great rafts and ports here 'n there so we would tote the goods out of the mines 'n out to trade. Then on it was rare to see either human, elf or any other race than dwarf in the mines. We never forgot that slight to our ancestors," the dwarf added darkly, skewering a piece of pumpkin with his two-pronged fork.

"But now we are the best waterfarers there is. We go where the stoneheads in the mines are afraid to. And we can swim!" he added, smiling. "And, we loves to fish, and we was the first to make a stone clad warship for Southaven." He finished his last few bites and pointed over near the door. "Got me gear ready. Ye'll be wantin' to go today."

"Didn't you say they were worse on days like this?" asked Greygrim.

"Aye, that I did, but that's the ones from the cities 'n towns and such. The ones in the crypts, they likes to come out 'n they follows a pattern, they do. A bad day to be down near port city, I tell ye that. Now, learned these lessons the hard way." The dwarf closed his eyes and put both hands to his long, auburn beard, and pulled it as if remembering unpleasantness from days past. "These hear greys in me beard, plain ol' fright's given em me."

"You didn't sleep much," noticed Greygrim. "I saw you get up not long after we went to sleep."

"Aye, don't sleep well here. Haven't since I been here. Besides, since you three were here I wanted to make real sure they didn' get in. Nothin's fer sure in this place," he added with determination. He pushed his chair back. "You rested good. Yer belly's fed. It's time to go and face the dead."

He chuckled at that. He could tell his little rhyme had made them nervous. "Lunker, like our cousins the stone dwellers, are a straight forward bunch. If there's somethin' to do, ye'd best do it. If there's somethin' to do that you don't like, best do it fast. And be ye done with it."

The three adventurers gathered up their gear. Stoneanchor had quite a few good lanterns and things, tools and such. "Hey, where are our digging tools we got from the cart?" asked Greygrim.

"I returned 'em. Right back where they were. That's what took me so long. I got plenty of digging implements and such here. Ye was carryin' enough beacons with ye like light houses. Glad I recognized 'em from that cart. Those owners be dead now and they might come lookin' fer their things. They likes 'em to stay right where they was. I manage to get a few things now 'n again from fools who come here. If they be given to me, they don't belong to this island, and occasionally some shipwrecks wash up. Get a few things from them if they are not claimed right away."

"Shipwrecks? You mean the looter ships get shipwrecked? I thought they mostly get away," said Greygrim.

"Oh no. No, sir." Stoneanchor stroked his beard. "Never forget when I got back to the port that day. Saw me ship, the Westward Star, drifting away. Not a sign of life on her. I yelled for hours. I swear I saw the dead a-mannin' her. Sixty-seven souls on me ship, including me. Sixty-six dead, and greed killed all. That's enough of that." The dwarf looked grimly away. "Let's be off. Daylight, what there be of it, it's a burnin'."

The three followed Stoneanchor down the path and headed through the woods to the Stone Mountains they could barely see in the distance. While trekking through the dark, dreary woods, they could feel eyes staring at them. Every once in a while, from the corner of their eyes, they could catch a glimpse of a shadow or what looked to be a person.

They exited fairly quickly from the woods, and walked through an expansive meadow with rolling foothills, many leagues across. It would have been beautiful in the past, all green, but now had the look of eternal winter bleakness. The dwarf moved very quickly, not stopping to rest.

Some time after midday they approached the foot of the road that winded up some foothills to the great stone mountains. Occasionally they saw more evidence of looters: bits of old barrels, backpacks, tube rolls, some still containing obvious treasures that had not been reclaimed by the owners as yet. "Why do they leave pieces of their treasure around, instead of taking it with them?" asked Arn.

"Don't know, an enticement to grab it? Never know what's lurking behind that rock. Don't take nothin' meself. Though by golly it is tempting, even now. I seen many a king's ransom. But ye can't take it. All uphill from here. Good road though, very inviting." He chuckled. "That's what they want, visitors." He gazed down the cobblestone road, his eyes following the way up through the hills.

"Day's wasting. We may not come back down, that's the way it is. If there be a good part to any of this." He finally stopped and sat on a stump. "Let's take a wee breather," he sighed.

"What is the only good part?" asked Anne. He sipped water from his waterskin.

"If you are right in your soul, iff'n ye die but yer right in yer soul, ye don't have to become one of these. These are all greedy, evil dead, says I. Ye won't have to linger with 'em." He looked intently at Greygrim, who had sat on a fallen tree. He didn't say anything for a while, but after a time he said again, "Let's be off."

"Well," said Greygrim, "One good thing. You said they're on rounds. How long before they return?"

"Oh, they're not all on rounds, just some of 'em." He headed up the road at a fast pace. They walked in silence for many leagues, passed through the foothills and began their climb up the great mountain itself. The grey stone loomed above them like a tomb marker.

They pushed uphill for another hour to what the dwarf said was an old resting station. Many old broken carts and several carriages, long since fallen out of use, stood before an old stone building, quite large. It looked as if it had been a tavern.

Stoneanchor looked at them and quietly said, "Ye'll want to rest here, but don't do it. There's a tricky spirit in there. Likes to make ye think yer safe. Got some of the boys from the last ship's crew that came up here. He's a tricky one, he is. Don't even look over there," he added, nodding towards one end of the building.

"Is that food I smell?" asked Anne.

"Smells like baking bread, and meat," added Arn.

"Aye, that one's got ye a feast prepared in there. If ye go in, ye'll see it all laid out nicely, but ye'll end up being the feast! I calls that one Mr. Hungry. Let's hurry along." As they passed the rest station they heard a loud banging, then hideous wailing, as if someone were very disappointed they had not stopped. It made the hair on the back of their necks stand up, like someone pulling on it.

They moved more quickly. Another half hour passed. The weak sun, what there had been of it, was now very low in the sky. They arrived at a strongly made wooden gate, with powerful iron bands, standing open. To the left were the remains of a guard house. Although the building was small and full of holes, and light should have easily reached inside, there was an unnatural darkness within.

Stoneanchor stopped and turned towards the guard house, and with a voice that made the others jump, said, "We come not for greed's sake but for the innocent, and for the kingdom of Southaven!" He stood straight and strong, like a representative of great importance making an announcement to a real person. "Oh lost, dark watcher within, I come as a representative of the dwarven king Kar Rune Talkin Drey Mort Dau." He bowed his head slightly, and looked at Arn and others, and said even more urgently, "Let's be to it."

Arn thought there was more to this dwarf than met the eye. Stoneanchor turned and started through the massive portal.

Just as they had started through the door, a frightening whisper came from the guard house. "You dwarf, have lived three summers. None ever fared so long here. There is much hunger for you." At the word *hunger*, Anne, Arn and Greygrim felt a chill of fear. "The cursed cannot partake of your warmth, your life essence. You have brought three children here," the voice added, hissing. "These I do not know, but honor you speak in the old dwarven tongue. Honor you have. I once served the king of Southaven. I anguish," the voice hissed creepily, "for those days of warm flesh again. My post I have held with honor. I grow so weary of this place. Know that you are not to take of what of value that is within. But you may enter."

To his own surprise, Arn spoke up at that. "But sir, we come for a weapon that we must take to defeat a powerful enemy of Southaven."

"You, key holder, enter the first large tunnel to the straw foot. One score and seven to the side of the hay foot. Now go!" the voice said in a whisper that sounded as if it were accompanied by pain.

"Thank you," stuttered Arn. They proceeded inside. As they entered the massive first chamber, the dwarf took his lantern from his pack and lit it with a flint and tinder. The others took out their lanterns the dwarf had given them. Each bull's eye lantern had tin plate in front, replaced by a cross, so that after lighting the image of a cross was cast upon the path.

"These candles are holy, blessed. They will help keep back the lesser of the dead. If ye feel a presence, shine the cross upon the creature, and it should shrink away. Iff'n we're lucky. If it be one of the more powerful ones, everybody together place your lights upon 'em. Hopefully a lot of 'em are still makin' a tour of the island. Still rainin' a bit."

All parties stood and looked about the large room. There were great marble pillars, finely wrought. It would have been beautiful. Much dwarven stonework was evident. Immediately when they went forward, they could feel the most unwholesome cold they had ever experienced. The kind of cold no clothing could ever keep out. It sank right to the bones, to the heart.

Arn was very grateful at this moment for the dwarf. It was like his power and presence comforted all his companions. Surely they would have not come safely this far without his help.

"Who's that?" shrieked Anne, shining her light into the corner at an old, broken, overturned table. As they watched, a tall, skinny man stood up from behind the table. He had white, glowing eyes, most frightening to behold. As he raised his arms toward the group, Anne shone her cross of light directly on him. He lifted his head and released a shrill scream of pain, and then poofed into nothing but an orb head. He then bounced off into the dark, still screaming.

"Aw, nothin' to worry about," said Stoneanchor confidently. "Jest one of them little ones." Anne crossed herself and whispered to Arn, "I don't know if I can do this, Arn." Arn placed his arm around her and kissed her on the top of the head. He didn't know why he did it.

"You can do it."

"Thank you," she said. "You are my friend and I will go on."

"I don't know if I can go on," said Greygrim to the dwarf. "Are there many like that? I don't know . . ."

"Well, I ain't kissin' ye boy. Buck up!" Stoneanchor lightly punched him on the shoulder with his great dwarf fist. Then in the dim light Arn could tell Greygrim was embarrassed.

"I don't need any kisses!" protested Greygrim. "Unless it was from dear Anne," he added, smiling, trying to joke in order to cover his embarrassment.

Anne punched him in the other arm. "Let's go."

"This ain't a place fer fun 'n games," the dwarf added gruffly. They continued down the large corridor.

"What did he mean, first large hay foot tunnel?" Arn asked the dwarf.

"Well, he's an old military man. It's the way they do cadence when a farm boy don't know his left from his right. Hay is left. Hay foot, straw foot, hay foot, straw foot." He shone his light ahead and kept walking.

They passed several smaller portals and soon came to a large tunnel on the left. There was a portcullis at the entrance to the tunnel, held open with many piled up stones.

The dwarf shone his light down the long passageway. They followed this tunnel quickly past many vaults. At the beginning the old vaults had been numbered, starting with number one, on the right. "These be the greater vaults of the dead, the whole reason for this whole wicked island," he explained. "Let's move fast, but careful. These 'uns can grab three people at once, easily, and drag 'em in. I've seen it fer myself."

They could hear whispering, crying, wailing and clawing at the doors as they continued into the dark tunnel. Even pounding. But some of the vault doors were open, obviously having been looted by grave robbers.

Here and there upon the stone floor they saw flashes of white, dried bones. They tried not to look at the unfortunate victims of greed. Probably looters who failed to make it out. Some of them still clutched chests and broken coffers of coins.

If it were not for the steadfastness of their strong dwarf friend, Arn was not sure that he could even have continued on this dreadful quest. Stoneanchor could tell they were unnerved. Occasionally he would look back at them and smile, though for a dwarf to smile was an odd occurrence.

"Don't listen to 'em, says I. We haven't looted a thing nor do we intend to. So you 'ens in the vaults, quiet now! Go back to yer cursed rest, what there is of it. There's nothin' fer ye here!"

Looking at a door, he said, "One nine. Almost there. One score and seven, says I. Here we be."

They could see several of the vault doors nearby had been pried, smashed, and broken open. "Let's be quick! Ye got the key!"

Arn pulled the leather thong with the heavy key that had been under his shirt from around his neck. Stoneanchor shone his light on the key, which seemed to have a bluish-green glow to it.

"Look!" Anne exclaimed. "It is glowing too."

"No doubt about it, lad, ye've got ye the right key! I've heard a wee bit about these vaults and how they worked. Ye told me the story how the records keeper gave it to ye. There's somethin' about ye bein' the one to ope it!"

Arn looked at Anne and Greygrim and at the large key he held in his hand. "All right. It's mine to do." He took his old handkerchief out of his pocket and placed it on the back of the key.

"Nar!" exclaimed the dwarf. "Take the cloth off. Gotta be flesh on metal. That's the way it's gotta be."

Arn did as Stoneanchor directed, carefully and firmly grasping the key, flesh to metal. Just as he was about to place the key in the lock, they all heard shrill screaming from behind them.

It was Anne. Clutched about her ankle were four grizzly, white-boned fingers and one large bony thumb. On the grey stone floor behind her lay the bones of what had once been a man, clad in rags, a simple, rusted pot helm on his head. On his back was a big leather pack laden with gold and silver which could be seen through rotted tears in the fabric. The pack so weighed him down that he could not stand.

Behind him stood his three grizzly companions, one armed with a cutlass and boiled leather breastplate, the black patch over his left eye emblazoned with a faded red goblet. One was armed with a ship's pin and a crowbar, and the other with a rusty old dagger. A sun cloth wrapped around his head, he had only one arm, the other having fallen off either in life or in death. He had three gold teeth shimmering in the light of the few holes pricked in the backs of the tin lanterns.

Before the companions could react, the leader with the cutlass had knocked down Anne's and Greygrim's lanterns from their placement on the floor. Anne tried to pull her ankle from the fierce skeleton grip which was cold as ice and very strong, considering the hand was naught but bones.

Greygrim hauled back his foot and with all his might attempted to kick the skeleton off of Anne, but in poor light caught the treasure pack and hurt his foot. He fell ungainly over the crawling skeleton.

Anne began to bash at the skeleton arm with her pickaxe.

The skeleton leader with the cutlass spoke in a raspy voice, "Looky 'ere lads, we've a been waitin' fer hours to get in 'ere. And 'e's got the pretty key, says I. An' they feels all warm, warm like the sun."

With those words, Stoneanchor surprised them with his agility and speed as he leaped over the twisted duo on the floor.

Anne began to cry, screaming, "It burns! It burns!"

"Ol' Tom, ye won't be needin' that pry bar. I'll catch us this key 'ere quick after I cuts out this lubber dwarf."

"Lubber!" roared Stoneanchor. "Who ye callin' a lubber! Ye dang fools don't even know how long ye been dead." With great strength the dwarf brought a mighty blow with his pickaxe on the breastplate of the old corsair captain. The pick stuck deep in the breastplate and slammed the villain against the broken door frame behind him.

"'Ere now, that be our cap'n!" yelled one of the undead, slamming the ship's pin heavily on the dwarf's head.

"A fight! A fight, oh what fun, a fight!" exclaimed the fourth skeleton. "I loves a fight!"

Arn did not know exactly what to do. He pulled his own ship's pin from his belt and charged rather clumsily at the one who had just hit Stoneanchor in the head. By this time Arn saw Stoneanchor hit the floor rather hard. The skeleton captain had fallen on the ground with the heavy pickaxe in his chest, yelling, "Get it out!"

The one with the ship's pin and crowbar turned on Arn before his blow found its mark. He parried Arn's ship's pin quite easily and jabbed full force with his own pin, striking Arn in the cheekbone, hard, sending Arn tumbling to the floor.

Arn thought dizzily. He wished he had minded his head like the woman had warned him. He wished he had gotten a great helm like some of the knights had on the battlefield. As things went dark, Arn had a sad thought that this was the second time a bone man had knocked him in the head. He heard, "That'll be a fine ship's pin that'll be comin' with me. Ye shoulda learnt to use it, boy!"

He did have the satisfaction, as he went unconscious, of seeing a great dwarven fist coming from his right, slamming into the skeleton's head and sending it flying. The rest of the skeleton fell across him as he faded away.

"Pick me body up, ol' Tim, says I," said the skull as it hit the floor. "The mean dwarf be right, we didn' survive that thar fight with the one in this 'ere tomb."

"Don't ye worry, ol' Tom. I'll take care of dwarven boy."

"Get this 'ere pick outta me chest, ye snaggle toothed sea dogs!" yelled the captain from the floor.

Meanwhile, Anne managed to release herself from the bony grip by literally crushing and smashing the bones with whatever weapon she could grab. She could feel a burn on her ankle. It reminded her of the time an inn master had sent her to gather sticks in the snow and her ratty old boot had been filled with snow. It had caused her a great deal of pain later. She had almost lost two of her toes.

The skeleton on the ground looked at the others and said, "Throw down yer weapons and grab 'em. I'm feelin' much better now," he grinned.

"Not likely, says I. This dwarf got bite, for a lubber!"

"Who ye callin' a lubber?" yelled the dwarf again with a roar. "I won't be called a lubber, I'm a lunker! Seafarer of the great seas!" He spit a large wad of saliva and blood at the fourth, still-standing skeleton. He pulled his axe from the pack on his back. "This ain't a boardin' axe but it's a choppin' axe and I'm a-gonna chop ye!" he screamed, charging towards him.

"'Twas all them!" the skeleton yelled, seeming afraid if that were possible. He threw his weapons and retreated back into the vault as fast as he could go. But not fast enough. Another skeleton head went flying deep into the vault.

At that moment the skeleton captain managed to get to his feet, having pulled the heavy pickaxe from his breastplate and ribcage, with a clink and breaking of ribs.

Greygrim managed at that moment to bash the old gripper's head fairly well. The skeleton advanced on him with his cutlass.

"Well ye folks seems to like the takin' of heads, so I'll take me one." He raised his cutlass and was just about to chop Greygrim's head off.

Suddenly a bright white cross appeared just between his neck and broken breastplate.

"Tryin' to blind me with yer pretty light, ye foolish girl," he laughed. "I'll be finished soon wi' this tangle legged pretend wizard, then I'll finish ye!" At that moment Greygrim leaped back up, reached into his pouch and clutched an odd-shaped stone about the size of an acorn. He said three words and threw dust upon the stone, then shoved the stone in the old captain's good eye socket. The captain reached for the glowing stone in his dusty head, with a kind of comical look, if you can imagine it, on his bone face. The stone grew brighter, there was a blue and white flash, his head exploded, and his bony body clattered to the floor.

Anne proceeded to point the cross at all remaining moving skeletons, bits and pieces, silencing them.

"That's our Anne!" said the lunker loudly with a broad grin. "Good girl!" He pulled his pack from his back, reached in and pulled out a bottle of something oily. He began to apply it to her wounded ankle. She was now holding back tears.

"It still burns," she said.

"This'll hurt a wee bit. It's blessed olive oil." He continued to rub, causing her discomfort. "But in a moment it will start to feel better."

"Is Arn all right?" asked Anne.

"Here, Greygrim." Stoneanchor handed the little cobalt bottle to him. Greygrim looked skeptically at Anne's ankle. "Don't be squeamish. If you don't rub it on there good, she will lose her foot."

The dwarf went over and checked Arn. He placed his old cloak beneath the boy's head, then held a lantern close to his face and pulled up his eyelid with a dirty thumb. "He'll be all right," he pronounced, and splashed some water on Arn's face. "He got him a shiner there, though."

Arn's eyes fluttered as he felt water splashed on his face. He reached up to wipe water from his eyes. Looking about the hallway, he said, "I guess we won? Who were they?"

"Jest looters. Don't reckon they even knew they's dead, really. Well, they probably know it, jest didn't want to admit it.

Anne murmured from her seat on the floor, "I feel sleepy."

Stoneanchor stomped over, poured water out into his hand and threw it in her face.

Anne shrieked, "Why did you do that?"

"Need you to wake up. That skeleton boy was drawin' away some of yer life force. That's why he felt better he said, after grabbin' ye, and why they said we felt warmer. They didn' know what they was. They was basically like the specter that killed 'em. Speakin' of that, won't be long fore they're back. Let's get this thing if it's in here and be outta here! I'll be glad to get back to me house," he murmured.

Arn stood up, dusted himself off, and helped Greygrim to his feet.

"Ouch! I think I broke my little toe kicking that rotten pack." Greygrim grabbed his staff. Both reached to help Anne to standing.

"Can you walk?" Arn asked solicitously.

"I'm starting to be able to feel my foot again. I think I can manage."

"Here," said Greygrim, handing her his staff. "This will help you."

"You three did pretty good in a scrap," said Stoneanchor, shouldering his pickaxe. "I'm proud of ye. Ye even made me laugh a little. Yer fightin' methods were a bit comical, what with fallin' on the floor and tanglin' yerself up in yer opponents. Well, first workout we had in a while. Let's git back to the door."

Arn found the key on the floor where he had dropped it in the scuffle. He gingerly pushed away some bones that had fallen in front of the door, steadied the key, and for a moment he hesitated.

"Lotta power there, boy. Ye can see it in the key and the lock," observed Stoneanchor as they both glowed. "We'll just stand here outta the way whilst you do that.

"Oh thanks," answered Arn with a wry smile. "That fills me with great confidence."

Stoneanchor winked, and spat, and said, "Think nothin' of it."

Arn lowered the key towards the keyhole. The pointed spike at the end of the key shot out even further. Four more smaller teeth were now visible. He was amazed how fearsome the key looked now and his hand began to shake a bit. The skull-like end he held in his hand did not make him feel any better.

He slowly pushed the key into the keyhole. "Boy, whatever ye do, don't let go the key. Whatever happens, ye gotta keep a hold of the key. Might even be a bit painful, ye understand?"

"Painful?" asked Arn, as he yelped in pain. Three vicious needle-like points shot out from the key, jabbing his fingers. It was all Arn could do to do as Stoneanchor warned and hold onto the key. Though he watched, no blood could be seen falling to the floor. Arn's blood instead flowed down the grooves of the key. As it hit each of the green glowing runes, they turned purple, one by one. At the end was a lightning bolt.

He turned the key, and as he did so, the pain went away. The entire key glowed with purple light in the dimness. Though the vault door was ancient, to everyone's amazement there was a clear clicking of the tumblers. CLACK. CLACK. CLACK.

The great oak, brass and stone door opened quietly, revealing blackness within.

"I knew it would work!" exclaimed Stoneanchor from behind, excitedly. "That be a special key, boy, very special." He smiled. "Ye go in first, boy. Ye must say this."

Stoneanchor began speaking, slowly, words which Arn repeated inside the chamber.

"Oh reverent sleeping child,
Forgive us this intrusion,
Blood of my blood,
Bone of my bone,
Flesh of my flesh,
Dust of my dust,
We enter not for greed's sake,
But our time of need is great,
That we may take that which is lawful,
We pray ye have gone on and are at peace."

With that, Arn walked forward, followed closely by Stoneanchor, then Greygrim, and Anne with her walking stick. They shone their lanterns about. The place was filled with more treasure than they could imagine. Gold, silver and weapons. To the right, twenty paces down, was a great beautifully-wrought sarcophagus.

Sconces and several candles were near a small stone desk. Stoneanchor began to light these. Not far from the coffin stood an entire warhorse, standing proudly erect on all fours, with steel barding. It was supported by wood and copper bars. The mane and tail were jet black. Without doubt it had been a magnificent beast in its day.

Beside the horse stood a great shield with a coat of arms and quadratic field. One quadrant was black with an ornate cross of the hospice, one with a gold field with a wondrous blue fleur de lis, surrounded by three white acorns. Below on the opposite gold field was a bull's head, and the other black field contained a red lion rampant. Above the shield was a great helm with the design of the hospice cross surrounded by fleurs de lis in the corners. Above this was an ornate silvery bull's head, similar to the one on the shield.

A suit of armor chain, with steel breastplate, steel shinguards and arm guards stood to the side. Above this hung an ornate lance with black and gold pennant, similar to the shield as well.

A larger pennant of grey and purple, the royal standard, hung on the wall.

Unaccountably, Arn thought what a splendid miniature this knight upon his horse would make. He also held his helm, an open faced helm with a simple hospice cross at the top.

Arn was almost overcome at the sight of such splendor. So much wealth in one tomb. Why had the owner buried these things with him? Why had he not at least left the coins for his family?

"Yuck," said Anne in a too-loud voice. The room sounded hollow. "Why are these in here?" She was staring in the corner, where there was a pile of skulls, but not human as far as they could see. There were several score goor skulls, piled with their broken black blades. There was a very ornate, though badly torn, standard of the red goblet on a black field. Behind stood many black shields.

"Those'd be foes he vanquished," whispered Stoneanchor. "Morbid to bring 'em along to yer final rest, but a lotta yer fancy royalty did that. The dwarves like doin' that too." He continued speaking quietly. "Me, I'd jest like me a nice river painted in the back of me tomb. Fish, ducks a-swimmin'." He stroked his long beard.

"Let's go to it, let's find that weapon."

Arn pulled three withered flowers from his pocket, the petals falling, and placed them on the stone desk. He had brought these with him, thinking they would be a symbol of respect on the island here where such flowers could never grow.

"That lance looks could be magic, but it's too big fer us to carry," said Stoneanchor. "I hate to say it, but that sword's shinin' in the lamplight. That's probly it."

Arn carefully began to remove the sword from its belt, careful not to dislodge the dagger also in the belt. "Should we take the whole thing? I don't know if I feel right about this."

"Owner's in paradise, boy. He don't need these anymore."

Arn took down the belt, sword, scabbard and dagger from their place on the wall. He was stunned how light it felt. It was a hand-and-a-half sword, also known as a batard, good for a mounted knight.

Stoneanchor said, "Ye'll be the one to pull that."

Reverently Arn pulled the blade from its scabbard. Though it had been there a long time, it slid out easily and silently, as if recently oiled. The blade was etched with argent, a magical form of silver. There were at least seven runes of great power etched on the blade.

"That was made by dwarves, boy. Powerful blade. That's the one. I'd bet me a ship on it if I had me one."

"Aye," answered Arn. "I hope they find a worthy champion to wield it."

Greygrim and Anne stared, openly admiring the great wealth in coffers, chests, and weapons racks. There were shelves stacked with armaments. Some white falconers' gauntlets sat next to a grey velvet pillow, upon which rested the remains of a falcon, laid out with honor.

"We had better be going."

"Aye, lad, ye've done a good thing."

"Maybe we can return it here one day, after the war."

They turned to go out the door, and the door slammed shut. A deep, mournful voice said from behind them, "Who dareth take that which is not his?"

Arn could not find his voice. Stoneanchor answered instead, "We are friends in need." Arn and the dwarf turned to face the voice.

A great, cloaked, ethereal figure at least six and a half feet tall stood holding Anne tightly in the grasp of his right hand, and Greygrim in his left. The bony, ethereal fingers clutched their throats. Their faces showed a look of horror such as is difficult to describe, and which one would never wish to see on one's friends.

"You, looter boy." Slowly, without removing his grip from Anne's neck, he pointed a finger. "You, Anne and Greygrim." He put his head between Anne and Greygrim, staring directly at Arn. "Rest until I feast."

With that their eyes rolled back and they fell to the floor with a thump when the specter released them.

"Ye leave those kids be now. We came with good intentions. Yer a-makin' me mad! Yer not a-feastin on nobody!" Stoneanchor had pulled his great axe from his pack. "I'm gonna chop ye down to size. Maybe ye'll think sensibly then!"

Stoneanchor charged the specter, wielding the axe. He couldn't get within three paces. The specter pointed both hands at the dwarf, then blue and green power surged from both his hands, blasting him back several paces before he fell unconscious or dead.

Arn stood, mouth agape, holding the sword in his hands. What a terrible fate he had brought upon his friends and himself! He stuttered, "We've come in our time of need for the king, the high king of, of South . . ." He could not remember the words he needed to say.

He was terrified. He found his hands and feet did not work. The specter from the grave approached him. "Come closer."

He knew he was the only one who could act now. His dwarf friend was not moving. He found the strength to draw the blade. There was a glowing cross rune on it. He lifted the sword in a defensive movement. "Please, stay back."

"You dare draw my own sword against me, then you have the audacity to tell me to get back? Thief!" The specter raised his right hand. Then Arn heard a sinister whisper, "That is mine, child!"

The sword was pulled from his hand, as if someone had tugged it away. The specter was still many paces from him. In horror, Arn pulled his own knife from his belt with his left hand. With his right, he pulled his ship's pin. He backed up against the wall, remembering the tomb robbers in the hallway and thinking there might be more. He murmured a prayer for protection, for himself and his friends, as the grave dweller approached.

"You die now, little fool." The specter's eyes glowed piercing white. "For daring to touch my blade."

Arn was ready to parry the blow as the weapon came slashing down towards his head. He knew likely it was all over, but he would die with his face towards the enemy as he promised himself he would. Instead the blade tip dug deep into the wall behind him and stopped just over his head.

He jabbed upwards with his dagger, full force, into the arm, or what would be the arm of his attacker. He struck something within the folds of the burial shroud. The creature brought his hand down, tossing Arn across the room, where he crashed into several chests containing treasure. One smaller box fell onto his head with a thunk, but fortunately it was a glancing blow. Arn's poor head! He thought he would be addle-headed at the end of this if he lived at all. He thought there was not much chance of that.

Before Arn could regain his feet, the effigy pulled his blade out of the wall. He pulled back and aimed deadly for Arn's chest. Arn had dropped his weapons. He tried to roll out of the way but was too late.

The blow was true and quick, until the last six inches, when it veered hard to the side, and lodged deep into a treasure box, and the stone wall beyond.

Arn thought the old villain's arm was terrible, for all his years in a tomb. He must get to a lantern. One that still sat on the stone floor shone its cross brightly on the far wall. This was his last chance to resist this monster out of the grave. Or still in it.

As the specter struggled to dislodge his sword from the wall, Arn scrambled and grabbed the lantern. He thought he probably would not win, but he would at least hurt this one. At least he would have that satisfaction. Stoneanchor had said it took three to hold off one of them.

The villain released the great sword from the wall and sent crumbled stone and wood flying out into the chamber. One coin had been cut directly in half by the sword. "This time, you die, little thief."

Arn pointed the lantern directly at the villain's chest from only a few paces away. "Why dost thou point a holy symbol upon me?" he hissed angrily, as smoke rose from the shadowy form. "I will kill you!"

With all his might, he swung an attempt to take Arn's head, but to Arn's absolute amazement, the sword flew up to the ceiling and stuck into the stone. "Cursed smith! What is wrong with my blade?" he screamed in rage. "I will kill you with my bare hands!" He walked towards Arn, hands outstretched, ignoring the searing flames engulfing his chest.

This was surely it. The two gauntleted hands tightened around his throat, and he prayed for protection for his friends, that they would awaken and flee, even as his life was squeezed from him. His neck felt searing, cold, terrible pain. He was sorry he would never see them again.

The specter began to laugh, and said, "You are very warm, little thief. Thank you for picking my tomb to rob!" Arn's eyes became bleary but he could clearly see the white glowing eyes. He would never see anybody he loved again. He would never have his dream fulfilled of having a love and a family of his own, a little home. He felt sad that he had led his friends on a fool's errand, to their doom.

CHAPTER EIGHTEEN

NEW FAMILY AND UNEXPECTED VISITORS

*A*rn's *eyes flickered in the dim light, and the light brought pain. His* limbs hurt, and he found he could not lift his arms. His head felt as if an anvil had been dropped on it. *Where am I?*

He heard a steady sound that he thought was someone breathing. The tomb specter sat about three paces away, against the wall, head bowed. Arn stared at him and remembered what happened. He couldn't move, but managed to croak out, "Finish it! I can't defend myself! Neither can my friends."

"I have restored what I have taken from you," the shadowy figure whispered. He looked up, his eyes visibly paler, and no longer bright white.

"Why would you do that?" His voice cracked.

"The sword was trying to tell me something. I should have listened, young sir. Your blood, your life force, is mine. For you are my great-great-grandson."

Arn processed this information and realized why Stoneanchor had him say what he said at the door, and why the key had not hurt him.

"You were not taking my possessions for self gain, were you?"

"No," answered Arn, very quietly. "I told you we weren't. We took what we took to help save Southaven and its new king."

"Richard is no longer king?"

"Richard I was five hundred years ago, if that's who you mean. There have been two other Richards since."

"Yes, yes. I have been here a very long time. Longer than it seems." The figure's head bowed low. "I bound myself here by my greed. I now realize that. All these things I valued so much in life have been my undoing."

He looked at Arn. "I had heard rumors of tomb specters here when I bought this vault. I wish I had heeded the warnings." The great shadow stood. He offered his hand to Arn.

Not only did Arn have difficulty moving, he also was noticeably reluctant.

"You needn't worry. I won't harm you." Arn took his old hand and pulled himself to his feet.

"No harm. I had almost devoured all you were when I realized *who* you were. I am so sorry." He did indeed look mournful.

Arn looked at his friends. "But what if you have harmed them?"

"No, I've restored them. They will awaken. What is your name?"

"Arn of Clayhaven. I have descended from no nobility that I know of."

"How did you come across the key? My wife had one, my daughter one, my son. This is my son's key."

Arn explained about the records keeper in Richaver. "He gave it to me."

"Ahh, he's a good man," said the shadow. "My name is Erwin of Clayhaven. How do you not know your lineage, my son?"

It was surreal to be called "son" by this strange creature, surrounded by untold wealth. "I was orphaned, sir, and raised by monks in Clayhaven."

"Well, that would explain it," he said quietly.

Arn went to each of his friends and placed their blanket rolls beneath their heads. The shadow figure watched silently. All three were breathing and seemed asleep. "They will be out for a bit. Tell me of you, Arn of Clayhaven, all that you know. Tell me what happened to the isle. It was once a beautiful place. When I step to the threshold I see only death."

Arn went into the story of all he could tell. Sir Erwin was sorry to hear of Clayhaven's downfall and remembered his home fondly. He was sorry to realize his entire family was gone. Although they were of high blood, he doubted any were still alive. In time Arn chatted with the specter as if he were a long lost friend, and in a way it was strange. This was the only family Arn knew he had.

The contents of most of the treasure chests had been cast all about the chamber, and Arn asked what happened. Sir Erwin said that when he thought he had killed Arn, yet understood that Arn was his descendant, with great anger he had smashed into the treasure he had coveted in his life.

Arn's friends woke in time and were horrified to see Arn's great, great grandfather still standing. Stoneanchor however could tell the difference in the villain. Though he looked frightening, there was not the aura of fear he had had about him.

"Well boy, ye found yer relative at least. I'll be hanged if I've seen a stranger circumstance. Just glad to be alive, I tell ye!"

"As am I," murmured Greygrim.

But Anne actually bowed upon hearing the story and introduced herself as Arn's good friend, which surprised him in a strange way when he heard it.

Over time as Arn talked to the cloaked figure he noticed something. Features of his face had begun to return, almost imperceptibly at first. Now he could see his mouth.

Sir Erwin bowed and said, "It is a long time since I've stood in the presence of a beautiful young lady." He asked forgiveness from each of them for having attacked them. He did explain in his defense that he had thought them tomb robbers.

"Take the blade. Take whatever you want or need. I was wrong to have coveted it in death as I did in life. My family could have used these things, although I did not leave them wanting. There is much evil here. I will escort you back to Stoneanchor's house," he pledged. "I will wait outside your door every night as penance for what I did to you. I will ensure your safety until your ship returns. None will dare stand against me on the Isle of the Dead!"

With that each visitor was allowed their choice of items from the wealth. None took too much. There remained a distaste and distrust for these riches. Greygrim found a fauschlund sword he could not take his eyes from. Anne found a cross inlaid with pearls, not too large, and placed enough gold coin in her pocket to help secure her future. Stoneanchor took a magical, powerful hammer made of dwarven steel and crafted by the dwarves themselves. It was attached to a leather lanyard for ship combat so as not to be lost.

Arn took a few gold coins to pay the Captain Trent for their return trip and to finance the rest of his journey. Sir Erwin insisted Arn take the blade. "That is my most favorite thing," said he with a sad face. "If you give it to the king, it is but a loan to him. Once the champion has defeated the villain Angueth, the blade shall be returned to you, the rightful owner and heir. There is much treasure here, young Arn. It could do much for the needy and for the land of Clayhaven if things are as bad as you say. I give you passage to come and go on this island at need, and let none here stand in your way. I will inform the greedy dead here that you will not take their things, but you have leave to take what you will from my crypt. I bind you to keep the sword and other family weapons in the family line."

With every gift, Sir Erwin seemed to become less frightening, and more visible, more wholesome to view. When they left the tombs they left with a mounted escort. Sir Erwin simply spoke quiet words to the barded steed, and using Arn's powerful blade, he cut the bindings that held the horse to the floor. He also spoke to two warhounds with studded collars, which rose up and stood beside him.

Arn could not resist a canine, even in death. "They are kind of cute."

Stoneanchor guffawed, "That's right, boy, this one is Fluffy, and that one is Fifi!"

"No," said Sir Erwin in a spectral voice. "This is Romulus, and that one is Remus. Let them have the dignity of their names."

Sir Erwin took up a large bag of coins and handed it to Stoneanchor, saying, "I give this to you and ask that you look after my great, great grandson. This should care for your needs and your payment for quite some time. The boy will need armor when he is big enough to wear it. Take my armor and help get it back to him. As a knight, he will need it."

He addressed himself to Arn. "Although you are tall for your age, you have a bit more growing to do before you will fit into this armor."

The turn of events had been strange and overwhelming for Arn. It seemed too much to believe that he could equip himself as a knight, with suitable armor and weapons.

They made their way without incident to Stoneanchor's small home. Sir Erwin and Arn talked the days and nights away. Arn learned a great deal of his family up to the time of the old warrior's death. He learned Sir Erwin had died in the third land invasion of Southaven in the great battle of Terra Fields. The Dark One had been stopped at great cost to the nobility of Southaven. Sir Erwin loved his wife and children very much, and really missed them. He was quite lonely.

Sir Erwin was becoming more real. He was able to touch things, and was becoming quite a distinguished and handsome gentleman. Arn enjoyed playing with the ethereal dogs. They were as friendly as they must have been in life.

The whole aspect of the island changed when Sir Erwin was with them. None dared challenge them, not even the great port ghost.

Finally, two days overdue, the ship returned. Captain Trent and crew were very glad to see Arn, Anne and Greygrim were still alive and well. They were astonished at the treasure they held. The treasure they had not hidden. And equally surprised to see Stoneanchor.

At the last minute, at his grandfather's urging, Arn had added more coins, to care for the people of Clayhaven as he saw fit. He even found a studded collar for Greymist, spiked and jeweled. Perhaps Greymist would even wear it.

He said goodbye to his great-great-grandfather as they stood on the pier. He looked so real now.

Captain Trent asked, "Who was that man, and why didn't he come along?" They explained that Arn was the rightful bearer of the key, and would be able to use it at will. Arn swore he would be back to visit his great-great-grandfather. He had become fond of Sir Erwin during his final days on the island. He prayed for him, that he would be forgiven for his misdeeds, and that heaven would receive him.

Their return to Southaven was completely uneventful. Arn and his friends took turns telling stories to the crew. This time all were curious about what had happened and couldn't get enough of their stories. The lunker proved himself to be a master seaman as well as a master story-teller. Captain Trent offered to keep him on as a full-share crewmember. The dwarf politely declined, finally saying his duty was to watch after the boy, for he needed looking after. The captain agreed with that.

They all enjoyed a couple of meals of pumpkin stew. Stoneanchor had harvested and brought many of his pumpkins. He gave some as gifts to the captain and crew, and the rest were used for cooking.

Upon their return they spoke to several officials in Richaver. After acquiring new but modest apparel, they were welcomed by those with whom they sought an audience. After explaining some of what had happened, the new high king, William, agreed to see Arn.

The story had spread quickly that the boy had returned unscathed from the Isle of the Dead. The new king was young and enjoyed stories. Arn and his friends were invited to meet with King William and the Queen Mother, Elizabeth Pearl.

During the audience one of the knights who survived the battle and had seen Arn being knighted confirmed his knighthood to the court. King William acknowledged this formally, and entered it into the records of Southaven.

He told Arn that a certain Lord Moresfield had died in battle and had left no legitimate successor, so Arn was given the lands of Clayhaven region, complete with a castle home and three villages. The conferring of the property could formally take place three days hence. The court announced an event for the conferring of properties, entitlements and management to Sir Arn of Clayhaven, Steward of Southaven for his deeds in service of the king.

Those who began the tremendous job of succeeding the records keeper discovered on his desk surprisingly open notes taken by the old records keeper himself. Arn was indeed the rightful heir. They also found certain evidence of his betrayal of Southaven and service to the Vagabond.

For it was found that Arn's people, who also by marriage also owned another powerful shire, placed him in control of that shire, of which Clayhaven is only a lesser stewardship.

There was also a dreadful secret discovered. The old records keeper had known all of these things all along and had done nothing to rectify things. He imagined that bringing down a powerful and wholesome house of Southaven would further the work he was doing for the Dark One.

Arn's older brother, Clayven, who would have inherited the main shire and a dukedom was of ill temperament, a drunkard and by some reports, quite mad. His parents had decided he would definitely not inherit the title, which would go to his younger brother, Arnterrius Lee Sutton. So, little Arn had been taken into the woods and left to the wolves in the middle of his first winter.

How the records keeper knew these things was not known. They say he used three polished river stones to see secrets. He had claimed they were given to him by an angel, but some suspect more sinister sources. The king had taken the three stones from him around ten years before, and they had been placed in protection.

Arn and Greygrim relayed the story of the end of the records keeper, his help and his betrayal. In the end, Himmel was given a state funeral after the location of his resting place was revealed.

Arn's frail, cold, baby body had been found by a grey wolf. It was the last in a line of intelligent wolves that had once dwelled in the Silver Dor Valley. She nursed the baby for a time, and watched as the villain child checked the spot where the boy had been left. She was afraid to try to return him because his life was clearly at risk. The great wolf, with some difficulty, made the trek with the baby to a monastery in Clayhaven, where the brothers had always been kind to the wolves of Silver Dor, and given them food when food was scarce.

Brother Kile had been hunting deer and shared the meat with the intelligent wolves. The great grey lass had taken the boy and her youngest son, Greymaw, who had grown fond of the human wee one near the abbey. Arn learned that his friend Greymist had been his brother for almost a month's time and had whelped with him before they made it to the monastery.

The monks had tried to find the child's rightful parents. There had been a lot of raiding that winter, and many had been killed or enslaved. The brothers eventually assumed the family had been killed or enslaved by goor raiders.

On Arn's dirty blanket they could read "Arn" so this became the boy's name.

Arn had been delighted to learn he had a family, but sad that his brother had squandered his fortune, and then either disappeared or died. The dukedom had been taken over by Arn's uncle, a man of great deeds now serving in war.

Greygrim suggested that Arn could seek the dukedom of Sutton, but Arn heard how good a man his uncle was and decided to let him keep what he had. He wanted very much to meet him. His home had always been Clayhaven and now it would be a place he truly belonged.

Arn and his friends actually feasted with the king and stayed in the castle. The view was resplendent with the honor and glory of Southaven. They met the descendents of the fish and crow of ancient legend.

It was a fun time, warm, safe and quite happy for them all. They walked the battlements at night.

The war had not been going well for Southaven. Sometimes in the far distance at night, fires could be seen, and they prayed for their land. Arn prayed for his friends and family in Clayhaven and was anxious to return. He was excited about the title and his newfound ability to actually help those of Clayhaven. He was told most fighting had moved away from Clayhaven, and that it had not been greatly harmed, but he was still anxious.

Near the battlements at the end of the guard day, they watched the changing of the guards. They faithfully repeated a ritual with the keys each and every evening.

The first two relief guards per battlement section approached the duty guards to receive the keys. The approaching guards said, "Hold your step! Who goes there?" with their halberds down in an aggressive stance.

"The keys," would be the reply.

"Whose keys?"

"The keys of the high and ever watchful King of Southaven, whose rich and vibrant lands flow freely with God's blessings, whose lands are no longer scourged by the black blade of the Vagabond. Ever shall we remain vigilant in our duties!"

"You may pass and convey the protected keys of the watch. All is well! God's mighty shield is the only true gate and wall of Southaven. May God save the High King and the free people and protect the sweet lady who is Southaven! These are the keys of our defense. Never again the keys of our shackles."

"Amen!" said all the guards of the night watch.

Arn, Anne and Greygrim really enjoyed watching this ritualistic securing of the new night watch.

Within the confines of the battlements there was very little agriculture. There was mostly administration and military barracks, training areas, armory, heavy defensive siege weapons and also the royal burial sites.

One afternoon of their stay Arn and Anne strolled out to the mausoleum where the last high king was now buried, his body having been recovered at a recent battle. It was very ornate, surrounded by pillars. It was not very large. It was situated on a small hill butting against one of the castle walls. At the middle of the roof squeaked an ornate dwarven silver wind vane.

"That's a strange place for a wind vane," said Arn aloud. The wind would be obscured by the castle wall, and its flow eddied by surrounding hills and buildings.

"I wonder if it truly tells the direction of the wind," wondered Anne.

"I don't know. The wind seems to be blowing north right now."

They walked on for a few minutes and listened to the wind blow off the battlements. This inner part of the defenses was rather quiet at night compared with the busy city sections below, quite a peaceful place, really. Anne carried a few fragrant flowers she had picked at the foot of the knoll.

"Hey look," cried Anne, pointing in response to hearing a small squeak. "It's the wind vane completely flipped around to south."

"I wonder if that is a good omen or a bad one?"

Anne placed her flowers at the door of the crypt, along with the many other fading and wilted ones that had been left by others recently, in memory of their king. Others had left small carvings, drink, even letters from those who could write. These were the outpourings of their hearts after the loss of their beloved ruler.

"I wish I could have talked to him again," said Arn. "He was a wise man."

"He is in God's keeping now, which is far better than this world."

"Maybe some day I will speak to him there." Arn felt he should feel more victorious than he did. He could not help feel sad, and burdened by the rough events he had experienced, and by knowing things that would be to come.

Anne placed her hand on his shoulder. He turned to look at the lovely maid, now clean and clad in a modest fall-patterned dress of red, orange and gold. Her long hair was glistening and clean, and hung down past her shoulders, quite lovely. He smiled at her. She actually seemed to care for him, and she had actually seemed to care for him before any good fortune had befallen them.

Through filth and bad experiences, she and Greygrim had been there, with unfailing support. Theirs was an easy companionship and Arn did not feel as awkward around her as he used to. He looked into her green eyes and she returned his gaze.

Brother Kile had once told him that the eyes were the windows to all of our feelings: love, sorrow, even hate. As he had never done before, he took this moment to gaze into the eyes of a young lady. He wondered at the softness, the depth of her eyes. How could he so easily be drawn into the depths of the beauty of those eyes?

She smelled of lilacs and jasmine, fragrances of the palace.

He understood why so many men went off to war to fight for love and home. If Anne asked him right then, he would go fight the Vagabond himself. He would do it without question. Surely God had placed power in those eyes that a man could never know.

He leaned forward. This time he would surely kiss her on the lips. He knew so well that Anne wanted him to kiss her. His heart wanted to say something, but leaned toward her, watched her close her eyes, and closed his own. He could feel her sweet breath on his face.

"Hey Arn! Anne!" A loud voice yelled from behind them. "What? Do you have something in your eye, Anne?" Arn wondered why Greygrim laughed, and why he would possibly be so cruel, risking his life so frivolously.

He turned around and said, "No. Would you like something for your eye?" he asked angrily, raising his fist.

"Oh Arn, you're so funny!" Anne grabbed his fist with a laugh and pulled it down to his side. To Arn she said, "Thanks."

To Greygrim, "Yes, I did have something in my eye."

Arn managed a chuckle and said, "Let's be off. Just joking, Greygrim. The feast is about to begin."

They headed back towards the castle gates. Arn imagined that Greygrim was knocked in the head, tied up and thrown into the dungeon. Just for a little while. He smiled.

They enjoyed an evening of food and revelry. Arn did not get another chance to kiss Anne, though he thought he would try if he could.

Meanwhile, in another castle, another scene was taking place.

"What did you say to me? With your foul, foolish tongue?" Angueth made his messenger, and right hand man, repeat his information.

"Forgive me, my lord. The last thing I wish to do in your moment of so many triumphs is to bring you such tidings," whined Dragdul. "Again. But I have brought the heads of the commanders who lost the king's body."

"You say a boy of no account, a manure boy, has gone to the Isle of the Dead to secure a weapon with which to kill me?"

"Oh my master, greatest of all assassins, deceiver of such great renown, slayer of his majesty the king of Southaven," said Dragdul, falling to his knees at the feet of the great Angueth. "I am so terribly, terribly sorry to be the bearer of this most grievous of insults. Your blade, my master, may find its mark upon my heart, or perhaps you may remove my head. But I know that you, most magnificent one, never wish anything but a true accounting of a situation, even if it is of this nature."

"The new king whelp, or its mother the old crone, of Southaven ordered this nobody from Clayhaven to acquire a weapon from the vaults of the dead to be given to a champion and used to kill me?" At that Angueth took his great mace from his belt with lightning reflexes and swung at the creature kneeling before him. He did not intend to strike the wretch, but swung just an inch above his head and slammed the mace into a large ornate chair a few feet away. The chair was turned into firewood with one swipe.

After a moment of intense breathing, saying nothing, he spoke. "Dragdul," he offered his black gauntleted hand, "my dear friend, I apologize for my outburst. I did not like that chair." Dragdul stood with his head bowed before his master.

"Tell me where I must find this Arn of Clayhaven now. I want to congratulate him on a job well done. You did say he succeeded, correct?"

"Yes, my master, he did," said Dragdul quietly.

"And it's true you were in Clayhaven, and he was cleaning the privy pots?"

"Yes, master," Dragdul stuttered.

"He must be a powerful knight now, you say?"

"Yes."

"Killed our dear treacherous friend Himmel? You could have handed him, say, a dagger in the throat but instead you handed him your chamber pot?" Angueth loudly snapped out each word and Dragdul began to jump.

"I knew not the future, my master." He bowed his head even lower. "You, my master, are swift to anger, but you cannot hold me responsible for the turn of events with this boy?"

Angueth removed his hand from his spy's shoulder, placed his left finger on the sharp tip of his mace. One quick, frightening motion that horrified Dragdul. He placed the great weapon back into his belt. Dragdul was blinking, horrified at the speed with which he moved.

"After you write down where the manure boy may be found, have that chair fixed exactly as it was."

"Yes, most beneficent one. As you will."

Angueth returned to his great throne, staring at the broken chair. Nobody heard him say, in a very quiet whisper, "I did like that chair. Another injury manure boy will pay for!"

Kari Ann Martin '07

CHAPTER NINETEEN

BATTLE WITH THE PAST

*T*he night before the great parade, Arn and his friends, allowed free rein at the castle, were walking the battlements. The blue crescent moon was quite bright. It was getting late, and they enjoyed looking at the city below and the sky above. All the stars looked brighter than they had back home. During their week in Richaver, it seemed like a magical city.

The parade was to be in honor of Arn, Greygrim, Anne and Stoneanchor for their service to the kingdom. A great banner had been placed bearing his name, Arn of Clayhaven.

For the last two nights, Arn had not dined with his companions. He had actually been seated beside a young baroness named Maria Louise Bellington. At first Arn had been miffed about not being able to sit with his friends, but he had come to know the baroness with long, flowing blonde hair, clear blue eyes and alabaster skin that had never seen much sun or hard work. She had been very attentive to him. Although he undeniably enjoyed Anne's company, it was quite pleasing and flattering to a young man of his former station to be in the company of someone so powerful, beautiful and wealthy. She seemed to actually be interested in him.

Maria Louise was not offended at his lack of knowledge or his rough manners, or if she was, she did not reveal it. Arn endeavored to pattern his manners after those around him, and she was very patient to explain to him the ways of the court.

Supper was to be late this night and Arn was looking forward to seeing the beautiful baroness again. He had been studiously avoiding noticing the daggers Anne had sent him with her eyes each night. After the parade tomorrow, Arn and his friends would be going home, and the king would pass the sword on to someone else, someone qualified to pursue Angueth.

Maria Louise had sent request through her guardian that she be allowed to visit Arn in Clayhaven, and he was looking forward to that.

There on the battlements he and his three friends stared at the large blue moon with a red cast to it, as it always had in autumn, known as the sickle moon. Arn was laughing and trying to make his friends laugh, although he was not very good at it. He had heard a few funny stories. "What is it that a shopmaster with a cart in a cart packing area seeks out vigorously, almost violently, but once he finds it and uses it, he leaves it and doesn't care who gets it?"

Greygrim guessed, "Water for cooking?"

"A good cart parking space!" Arn laughed loudly, a little too loudly at his own joke. A guard nearby grinned and shook his head.

"In a little bit we need to go ready ourselves for the banquet."

"Dining with the baroness again, are you?" asked Greygrim.

Arn answered, rather defensive, "I have to. I have no choice. That's where they put me. I'd rather not."

A guard approached them. "Me lords? Me lady? It's time to change the guard." They had become familiar with the nice chaps who guarded this battlement in their few days of walking it.

"Well, Lloyd, have a good night."

"You too, me lord. I'll remember that funny ye said. I likesed it!" answered Lloyd with a grin. They watched Lloyd and John disappear down the long staircase to meet their relief.

Down at the gates, the guard challenged each arrival. "Who goes there? State your business."

"I bring his lordship, Sir Jeffrey Tollemy, to the feast," came the whispery reply from the coachman.

The guard peered into the dark carriage. "Milord?" Sir Jeffrey stiffly raised his hand and nodded, and the guard waved them forward.

The coachman puppeteer was pleased with his work. Sir Jeffrey could almost talk but not quite. Angueth had left the battles on the frontiers to take care of this important work himself. Two border fortresses had fallen in the past month. It would not be long before the way to the capital itself would open to his army. The second line of defenses was strong, but Angueth had managed to cut supplies to several of them and had also placed a small army of observers nearby to harass retreating forces from the frontier defenses. They prevented the arrival of reinforcements and generally confounded the bad strategic situation of Southaven.

The Red Prince himself had promised Angueth that in time he would sit on the throne of Richaver, after his master was well done with it, of course.

There was one thing Angueth must do, and it was personal. The thought of a mere boy, one of Arn's station, acquiring a weapon intended to kill him! He had lived ten men's lives! The thought boiled in Angueth's brain, like barber's medicine, hurting him.

Of course, Angueth had no need of a barber and had not needed one for many years. His flesh was now dust, his bones still walking, most of them, and he needed no more medical attention.

The black shadow that was Angueth had found out about the night's supper for the new hero. The fat nobleman sitting in the back of the coach had dined each night with his majesty and Arn. It had been easy for Angueth, who in life had been the Vagabond's assassin, to dispatch the coachman, the guards and the dribbling fool now animated in the coach by evil necromancy.

Angueth did like the coachman's disguise. A large-brimmed black hat, black dutch coat with slight red trim, black brechs and riding boots, and thick black gauntlets. The night was chilly and he had pulled his hood up over his head, covering most of his face, while the great hat shadowed the rest. His disguise was no matter now, he was inside and he would find his quarry.

His plan was to kill the boy and his friends before midwatch and be out of the city before dawn. His horse waited not far away in an abandoned mill, where he would hole up for the day and plan to move again at night. He had left a squad of his guards with the steed.

He would make manure boy's head into a trophy. He didn't want to keep the other two, the friends, Anne and Greygrim, nor the dwarf.

Angueth secreted the coach in the stables and wound his way to the battlement wall. To his great joy he could see three figures standing, illuminated by the blue crescent. The guards would be changing. Perfect.

He quietly waited near an abandoned crypt and marveled at the craftsmanship while he waited. He thought he should stay home and do more decorating. A palace should say something about the owner. Angueth waited while Lloyd and John passed by then moved quickly, like a great panther striking, into the night.

The two new watchmen had not yet ascended to their posts. Angueth was upon them before they knew what happened. The first did not even have time to yelp. The second was a young man with good reflexes, and did start drawing his sword before Angueth pinned him against the stone wall, his venomous sword piercing the guard's breastplate.

Angueth took a moment to watch his quarry slump to the ground, and was satisfied with the obvious pain. He smiled and snarled, "You almost drew your blade, didn't you? But you did drop your halberd. That was sloppy. I want you to know, whoever you are, you have been slain by Angueth, the greatest assassin ever. Do you have a family?"

The guard did not answer but the ring on his left hand gave away that he had at least a wife. "Know that you are dead, and you will never see her again," laughed Angueth. Tears welled up in the man's eyes at these words, and with all his might the young guard, whose name was David, raised his fist and punched Angueth full in the face, sending Angueth reeling, almost back over the stone landing.

"You have spirit, I'll give you that," he said, wiping his eye. It was over for the young man in an instant.

Angueth quickly bounded up the stairs. It only took an instant. He was worried the three at the top might have heard the disturbance. As he stood at the top, he saw the three companions had not noticed. He was still as quiet as the mist.

Before they knew anything, Angueth was behind them. "Greetings, peasant children," he loudly hissed. Greygrim was the first to turn, and the first to go off the battlement. With great ease, Angueth picked him up and tossed him off, the boy screaming in pain and shock as he went.

Arn tried to grasp at Angueth but the cloaked figure easily elbowed his throat up against the wall. "Not yet," he said.

Angueth picked up Anne. "What a pretty thing. 'Tis a pity." With the same malice and ease he tossed her too over the front of the battlement.

"I don't have much time, Arn of Clayhaven, but I do want it to hurt," he said with a hiss. "Now, 'tis your time."

Arn was absolutely horrified with what had just happened. He did not know that Greygrim had landed onto a thatched roof and rolled, painfully but safely, to the ground. Anne had landed onto a hay wagon and was injured but Greygrim had gotten to her quickly. He just knew his two best friends in the world had been thrown off this lovely, lonely battlement and there were no guards in sight.

"Where are the two guards who were to be on duty here? Where is David?"

"The guards are gone," answered Angueth. "Just like you soon will be." He tilted his head to the side and regarded Arn. "I remember you from the corridor. My snakes did not kill you or your friends. A pity. It would have saved me the trouble of coming here tonight." He advanced a few paces.

"I am a busy man. I have to destroy this kingdom you value so much. I have to kill this new upstart king and his mother. Perhaps I will do that tonight, before I leave. We have several minutes before a general alarm is raised."

Arn wondered about simply turning and running, how far he could escape down the stairs, or perhaps to the next tower. He considered it but he knew Angueth was very, very fast. The thought of turning his back to him was more than he could bear. If he must die this night, he would die with his face to the enemy.

He thought of his dagger tucked into his belt, made with great care by Gustavus. He wished he had the sword or even the dagger from the champion's belt. Maybe those would improve his chances.

As if reading his thoughts, Angueth said, "I see the shiny pommel of the knife you bear. Go ahead, pull it from its sheath. Deal with me as a man." He smiled, a ghastly revelation of blackened teeth. "After all, I've just killed two of your best friends in the world."

Arn's mind was numb in considering that his friends had just been cast to their deaths. He could feel the cold and evil that poured off of this villain. Somehow he was blocking Arn from thinking clearly.

Slowly something was replacing his fear. Tears stung his eyes, but not tears of sadness. Instead they were tears of anger and frustration.

"Manure boy is going to cry. How sad. Maybe I should leave you to cry in sadness over losing your friends?"

Arn could handle no more and with speed that surprised even Angueth, he pulled his dagger from his belt in one fluid motion. He had practiced this many times on the ship with Slim coaching him. With surprising skill borne of determination he lunged forward, towards Angueth's chest, not so far away.

"Oh good! Manure boy wants to play a man's game!" With even greater speed, Angueth sidestepped the blade, grabbed Arn by the wrist, and in a blinding motion took the blade and sent it clattering to a slate rooftop below. "Ah! That was good! With a little work you might have made a good assassin." Angueth chuckled. "See these weapons here upon me? Any one of them could slice you in half in an instant. But I'm not gong to draw them. I am not. I'm going to squeeze the life out of you, urchin of Clayhaven, until your eyes bulge out and your tongue turns purple. I am going to take the very essence of your life, all that vibrant energy, with my hands. I will feel your very last heartbeat."

Arn was terrified but his anger was still there. With no weapons left, at the very least he would punch Angueth in his hideous face, with all his might. Perhaps he could grab one of the weapons the monster was so proud of. Perhaps they could damage him, as well.

In the distance they both heard the alarm bell ring. Someone yelled, "Eastern battlement is unsecure! Look to the east!"

"Well, my young bumpkin friend, our time is at an end. I must off. The new king and his mother will be less well guarded soon. Sometimes my plans change by the moment!"

Cold vise grip fingers suddenly clasped around his neck! The foul specter smelled of sage, mint and rue, and reminded him of the smell at the Brown Leaf Tavern. Arn took his chance. He slammed his right fist into Angueth as hard as he could, full in the chest.

Angueth's cold eyes regarded the boy in his grasp. "Was that an attempt to hurt me, little sod buster? I have been hit with the finest weapons your little kingdom can make. I've been with the Red Prince, the one you call the Vagabond, almost since the beginning. I've lived tenfold your miserable lives, stinking stall cleaner. Do you really think you could hurt me?"

Arn's vision grew blurry. Perhaps the guards would come soon. He tried to reach the demon's dagger. He felt the pommel in the shape of a skull. He tugged, and amazingly it came free from its scabbard. When he tried to lift the weapon to kill his attacker, he felt a wash of ice cold, like nails piercing his left hand. The pain was intense. He would have gladly shrieked if he could have.

"Well done!" Angueth laughed aloud. "But that blade is not for peasants!"

Arn felt his life literally being drawn from him. Not only was he consumed with the burning need for air, and the burning around his neck, but pain over all his skin as if it was being ripped from his body. Angueth pushed him to the battlement wall. He could no longer even smell the sickly sweet herbs he wore to hide his stench.

He thought but could not speak a prayer of rebuke. It was too late. He felt himself being pulled into the next world and was glad he had done his best. At least he would be with his friends again. The vision of the little pigdog wrapped in its blanket came before him, silly he knew. The little pigdog snout, and Anne exclaiming, "How cute!" The old woman's face he had seen at the gate, and her words, "The key."

The key did have sharp tines and blue glowing runes, some power. Just maybe.

With his last strength, Arn grabbed the key hanging around his neck and jabbed it surprisingly deeply through the coat and through the cloak and deep under it. The chest there did not feel strong as it had when he had punched it. It felt like the chest of an old man.

Just as he passed out, he had the joy of seeing bright blue runes on the key as he activated it, releasing it so as not to be pricked himself.

"What foul work is this?" hissed Angueth, clearly surprised, as what passed for his blood trailed down the shaft of the key into the runes. He released one hand from Arn's neck as he tried desperately to remove the glowing key from his chest. In horror he realized it was a key to the crypts.

Just as his hand grasped the key, his fluid passed through to all of the runes. There was a tremendous clap of lightning and thunder when a shrill, bright bolt of pure energy shot forth from the key.

Angueth shrieked a long animal sound. The key burned at the core of him, where his heart would have been long ago. He howled in agony as he pulled the key from his chest. He threw it down onto Arn's head.

Arn's eyes flickered at the sudden pain on the back of his head, bringing him back to consciousness. The key had obviously hurt his assailant. Curling smoke and blue flame came out of the center of his chest. Angueth was cursing and spitting black bile, wobbling on his feet. He pulled his great sword. Arn could hear guards tramping up the stairs and knew they would never make it in time.

Angueth raised his blade over his head and held it there, swaying to and fro. Arn could not tell if it was dizziness or pain.

"You stinking little nobody." The hissing voice was losing energy and smoke emitted from his mouth. "I give thee regard, Sir Arn of Clayhaven." He raised his blade higher over his head as for a death blow, and in doing so the seriously wounded villain was unbalanced and plummeted backwards over the stone railing, some thirty paces below.

Arn struggled to the edge to see if he lay there or would get back up. If only the guards could get to him in time.

His heart soared when he looked below and saw the great assassin Angueth sprawled perfectly upon the weather vane, pierced completely through his chest. It was the weather vane on the very mausoleum in which the former high king was entombed.

Arn smiled and lapsed into unconsciousness.

It was late into the next day when Arn finally woke and could hold his eyes open. The planned parade had been postponed, he was told. He was glad beyond telling to find Brother Kile at his bedside, his head lolling over a book.

"Brother Kile, is it you?" Arn reached out to touch Kile's shoulder.

"Right you are," he answered, wiping sleep from his eyes. Good to see you awake, Arn. I understand you have had many adventures since we parted?" Kile's kind eyes crinkled with his smile. "Brothers Francis and Clem have been here also, although they are sleeping now. Your friends have been asking for you. I have met Stoneanchor."

"What of Anne? And Greygrim?" Arn was afraid of hearing the reply.

"Faith, and good straw and thatching! Your friend Greygrim the wizard rolled off a thatch roof onto a large pile of compost. He will be all right. He rests beyond that door. And Anne fell upon a straw cart.

Her arm was broken but she is also well, and has been waiting to see you."

As if on cue, beautiful Lady Anne walked through the door, wearing a silken red, purple and grey gown, with her arm secured by a scarf. The fading sun fell through the window upon her and gave her a soft look, like an elven maiden or a fey folk maiden. Arn grinned at the sight of her.

She knelt by his side and stayed there while they talked into the evening.

They were later joined by a host of well-wishers. Stoneanchor kidded Greygrim about compost.

Arn spent several days recovering his strength, and the parade was rescheduled for a time when all three of them should be up to the excitement of the day.

Several times during these days he was visited by the baroness. During these visits Anne made sure to be close by. There seemed to be a great deal of tension, even cross words between the two ladies. Arn did not understand what animosity could possibly exist between them.

The parade was to be in Arn's honor. It would be followed by a great feast and a dance into the night. He bathed and dressed in finery, beautiful clothing he could not have imagined owning. He was to ride in one of the last coaches next to Maria Louise. His friends were to ride in earlier coaches, but he heard from a messenger that the baroness had requested he ride in hers.

He smiled at the thought because he had grown quite fond of Maria Louise. He hoped Anne would not be angry. Considering politics and all.

The monks actually had been involved in battles and were considered heroes, and were assigned carriages to occupy during the parade. They had their own heroic actions to their credit.

He walked down a grand staircase and out a still majestic, but smaller exit of the palace and found Gustavus sitting on the step, waiting for him.

"Come! Ride with me in the parade!" implored Arn.

"Nar, that fangly stuff's not for me. I'll be bootin' it over to the fine fare, and ye can count on seein' me there!"

"We must be off, sir," the coachman said. Arn said farewell to his friend with promises to see each other at the banquet.

As Arn arrived at the coach there sat Maria Louise, resplendent in a white and gold flowing gown and smelling of fresh roses. "Oh, Arn! So good to see you!" She smiled.

Someone else sat in the coach with her, a handsome young man, who smiled in greeting, "My name is Trayor."

"He has just come from the war. Arn, he is a hero. I just knew you would want him to ride with us."

Arn was dismayed to find someone sitting in his very seat and felt like throwing the young nobleman out. The coach was made for two passengers. Anger was welling up inside him.

He did not bother to hide his irritation. "Where am I supposed to sit?"

"Oh, Arn, I had not thought of that!" Maria Louise batted her eyelashes.

"Perhaps you can ride behind," added Trayor. "I believe there is another coming along just for you." Arn recognized the smirk and recognized when someone was talking down to him. His fists clenched, and Maria Louise touched his hand.

"Don't make a scene. Please. There really is another coach coming."

"Yes, I will be along shortly." He felt full of awkwardness and anger and foolishness as he walked away.

"See you at the ball. I will save a dance for you!" waved Maria Louise.

He watched the coach go off with the young lady and the interloper in his spot. He waited a while until finally two street cleaners came.

"Where's the next coach?" he asked them.

"There is no other coach. That's the last one, there," they pointed off into the distance.

He could not believe his bad fortune. His very own parade and he was left out.

One of the street cleaners said, "If you hurry across here, you can catch the beginning of the parade. It's four streets over, before you get to the next wall."

Arn hurried across the streets. The third ring wall, which he was in, the largest and oldest of the rings, had many streets. As he kept walking, it was strange to walk in the city with no one around. They were all at the parade. His parade. *How could I have been so foolish. How could I have thought she really cared?* He felt as if everything he had done was pointless. He would never be anything more than the stall cleaner from Clayhaven. He felt as if his heart had just been ripped out as he walked through empty streets, empty except for a few guards here and there, watching for the Dark One's assassins. He felt entirely worthless and alone.

As he went the buildings became more ramshackle. Due to war and disease the population of Southaven had dwindled in the past hundred years, dramatically. Many of the old buildings were abandoned. It eerily reminded him of Cardith, the port of the dead. He could also hear the revelry of old. He could almost feel silent beings watching him through empty windows. This walk did indeed match his heart, empty, abandoned and alone. The way he had felt all too often.

Some of the buildings had been picked clean for their stone, but some of the larger buildings that were more ornate had been left relatively intact, except for most of their roofs, floors and timber. As he approached a large, dark, three-story building that was particularly beautiful, with most of its roof intact, he wondered what it must have been in its time of former glory. Perhaps it had been a wealthy man's home, or an administrative building of some kind. He realized he had stopped to look at the building and would miss his own parade.

He decided to sprint to the next guardsman, two streets over. He had just started to run, when suddenly he heard a yell from one of the windows that startled him. He stopped cold. Looking up in a third floor window, he saw a man dressed in rags, yelling, "Who are you to come here, rich boy? The fancy parade's that way. Why don't you move along, fancy boy?"

Arn almost looked about, wondering who he was talking to, then realized the fancy clothes he was wearing made him look like a rich boy indeed. He was just about to say that he wasn't rich at all, but was trying to rejoin the parade. He had in his mind to offer the man to come with him to the parade, where he would make sure he had clothes and food. The man screamed, "Get out of here, high dog! I'll not bow to ye!" He stooped and picked something up, and hurled it to Arn, to his shock.

Arn leaped back three paces as the ceramic pot crashed and broke on the paving stones exactly where he had stood. Some of the contents splashed upon his new pants and shoes. He stood dazed, staring at what he knew only too well. It was a chamber pot. The steaming liquid in the cold autumn air he also knew too well. He could barely comprehend what had just happened. This vagrant had thrown his morning liquid at Arn.

He looked down and saw one of the ceramic shards had cut through his pant leg. He slowly lifted his head to the old man, who stood laughing in the window. He knew the mocking laugh all too well. Contempt. His face slowly grew red with rage and hate.

The look on his face, even at a distance, must have surprised the man, because he stopped laughing. Arn said nothing, just pointed his finger, turned and ran up the street towards the guard, rage giving him speed over broken pavement stones and rubble. If he could have thought clearly, it would have reminded him of the time he charged up the hill towards the archers that fall day.

The guard turned toward Arn and said, "May I help you . . ." and before the guard could say anything else, Arn had snatched his bow and pulled a bolt from behind the guard's back. "I saw what happened, sir. Should I arrest . . ."

But Arn turned and was running the other way, as quick as a flash, saying, "No, I will take care of it!" The guard stood still and said nothing else, for it was surely Arn's right to have justice on this lowly criminal in the window. He had insulted the hero of Southaven. The guard knew who he was. He found himself wondering why Arn was not in his own parade.

Arn ran back to the spot where the criminal had been in the window, and he was still there. Arn did not notice that another figure was approaching from the direction of the palace. So focused was he in his rage that he did not hear the short, stocky figure yell, "Wait!"

Arn drew back the bow. The man was high up but clearly visible in the large window. The man did not laugh but stood forth. Arn was sure he could make this shot. He could not have asked for a clearer shot of his chest. The old bearded man did not look at him, but instead looked away into the distance, waiting for death to come through the barb Arn held in his hands. He pulled to the end of the bow. The arrow would sink neatly into the chest of this evil man who had insulted him so.

"Enough," said Arn quietly. "Enough of your kind!" he said louder. "I have had enough of your kind!" he said even louder, and clearer. The man did not move. Tears streamed from Arn's eyes. This had been way too much for him. This vagrant would pay for his insult. He had suffered a lifetime of mockery from people like this, and he now had a chance to make one of them pay. "I hate you!" Arn yelled at the top of his lungs. I didn't even know you! I was going to help you, but now I'm going to kill you!"

He wiped his streaming eyes on his shoulders so that his shot would be true. In his mind he could see the faces of all those who had picked on him most of his life, for being the least of the least in Clayhaven. This will finally bring me some relief from those kind of evil people. He steadied the bow, aimed clearly at his target.

Just then, he felt a hand on his shoulder, which almost caused him to lose the arrow. He recognized the speaker and the words all too clearly. The rough, large hand belonged to his friend Gustavus. "Mercy, lad. He deserves what he gets, though. I can certainly see your point, lad, after all you have done and all you've been through. But what put him in his situation, Arn? What made him the way he is, to cast hurt at you, without even knowing ye?"

Arn shook. Tears streaming from his eyes, "I can't stand these people any more, Gus. No matter what I do, even become a hero, I am still set upon by people like him."

"Arn, lad, look at him. See how he's a-living. You have already won. You were always the winner. They were always the losers. Though they've hurt you over the years, and I'm sure I know they have, you were always better than they were. Because you knew the meaning of the word mercy. Remember the words of the good book. Whoever does good to the least has done it to me. I've never seen anyone be kinder than you, lad, and I've watched ye grow up. You've always had a good heart. No one on this earth will punish you for killing him, except for you. You'll never forgive yourself."

Arn heard the words, though for a time he kept the bow trained on the old man. Tears streamed down his cheeks and his hands began to sweat and shake. He pulled the bowstring full, then let the arrow fly, to the cobblestones where it snapped into two pieces.

Then he fell to his knees. Gustavus's hand was still on his shoulder. Arn cried for a long time. He knew this would not be the end of this fight with his own self-worth, but maybe this was a start.

Gustavus's rough hand rested on his shoulder as gently as a kitten. Finally he said, "As you have had mercy shown to you, you have shown mercy as well. You have done the right thing. It'll come back on ye." It was all he could think of to say.

If Arn had looked up at that moment, he would have seen tears in his friend's eyes also. The tough half-dwarf had never cried in front of anyone. He pulled a handkerchief from his pocket. An apple and several nuts fell to the ground, for he had stuffed his pockets with food, as he always did when he had access to extras. Gus wiped the tears from his eyes quickly so that Arn would not see. Arn did glance up and saw the dwarf's tears, but he would never speak of it. He quickly looked down again.

Arn began to laugh when the apple rolled in front of him. Gustavus handed him the handkerchief and a hulled black walnut and an almond fell. He mumbled something about good eats. Arn began to laugh loudly indeed. The tension fell away as an anchor dropped from a ship. Gustavus, not known for laughter, also began to laugh as he helped the boy to his feet. Neither noticed the old man had left the window and come down. He was staring at them from the corner of the great building.

Arn looked at him and realized that everything Gustavus had said was true. The tear would mend. The stains and smells would come out. No real harm had been done by the old man's words. He did indeed feel pity for him, because he realized as the man had stood in the window he had wanted Arn to end his existence.

What had put the man in such a position? To want a stranger to end his life? The man was bearded, ragged, and smelled from twenty paces. The man then ran to Arn and fell upon his knees in front of him, begging his forgiveness. There was a penetrating stench of spirits and filth on his breath and clothing. Gustavus stooped to pick up the apple and nuts he had dropped and pretended not to notice the somewhat embarrassing turn of events.

The man was almost groveling at Arn's feet. "Mercy, sir. I did not know what I was doing. Please, give me a second chance!"

Arn realized this man was not far down the ladder from where he had spent most of his life. "I forgive you."

"What, sir?"

Arn bid him stand and told him he would not have him arrested, then yelled to the approaching guard that everything was fine. To his own surprise, he reached to his left side and untied the pouch that contained part of the gold and silver that had been given to him as a reward for retrieving the sword and killing Angueth. Without even thinking about it, he handed the man the entire purse, more than he had ever held before in his life. He had never felt such pity for anyone as he did for this old man. He pulled the man to his feet, not wishing anyone to grovel and plead. He eased the old one's heart by saying he would forget, that it was all right.

The old man could not believe that this young prince was not only not having him arrested, but was handing him a purse full of coin. He finally stopped crying, wiping his tears with a coarse sleeve. His left eye had a large scar from cheek to forehead. The man was actually taller than Arn when fully standing. He had a regal bearing with his shoulders squared and his hair pushed back off of his face. His eyes were downcast, though, for he had embarrassed himself. "It has been many, many a tenpassin since anyone has shown me such kindness. Mayhap no one has ever shown me such kindness."

"What is your name," Arn asked.

"My name is Lawrence, good sir."

"Just Lawrence?" Arn said.

The man hesitated, then answered, "Yes, just Lawrence. I will not forget the kindness ye have shown me today, sir."

"That is well," said Arn. "Please, sir, do not buy spirits with this."

"I promise, sir," he answered, looking down. "I promise, good sir."

"I must be off. Do well with the coin, and fare thee well. Find better quarters if you can." He walked to where the broken arrow lay, collected the pieces and tucked them into his belt.

Gustavus growled, "Uh. Here, sir, take these and enjoy." He handed him some coin from his own pockets, as well as the goodies he had hidden there.

Lawrence took an old ratty, white haversack off of his shoulder and placed everything carefully within it. "Thank ye, good sir, thank ye. Ye be dwarf?" he asked tentatively. Usually when people in Clayhaven asked if he was dwarf, or half dwarf, Gustavus took offense. Arn never asked why.

To Arn's shock, he heard Gustavus answered, "Yeah, I be half dwarf." Arn thought Gustavus could have shown no greater mercy to this man, than to utter these words. He looked at his friend in wonder.

He had never known for certain if he was a dwarf, and thought to ask him many questions when the time was right.

Gustavus cleared his throat. "Well, we best be getting' to your parade or you are going to miss it."

"Your parade?" asked Lawrence. "You're the one who slewed Angueth the Assassin?" Arn nodded. Lawrence looked with wonder into the boy's eyes, and could not believe who he had just insulted. He would never have done it if he had known who he was, for Angueth had brought great misery to the people of Southaven, and great misery to him personally. Angueth had killed his one and only love when he had been a young warden in the woods, just one month before they were to be wed. "I cannot take these things from you sirs."

Arn smiled and patted him on the shoulder. "I insist."

"Yep, they be yours. But do as the boy says, stay away from the spirits."

The old man watched them go. All he could get out was a quiet, "Godspeed." He watched them until they passed out of sight, past the guard to whom they returned the bow. The guard scratched his head and shrugged his shoulders, not knowing or understanding just what had transpired.

Lawrence thought better of hanging around the guards and the great people he had just insulted. It would be a long time before Arn learned the rest of Lawrence's story.

He started his way to his favorite tavern, going as quickly as possible. When he was sure no one was looking, he opened the pouch. He was sure he would see a few silver coins, and was shocked that he had a year's wages at least. He immediately proceeded to his favorite tavern, the Dancing Rat. His best friend Marcus would be shocked at his great good fortune. He pulled out two silver from the pouch and placed it carefully inside his haversack.

"My good friend Timothy," he addressed the barkeep. "I'll have me a whole bottle of Black Dog."

"Are ye mad? I told ye last week not to come in here anymore. Where'd you get that silver?" he said, eyeing Lawrence.

"A kind gentleman gave me alms, if it's any of your business, Timothy. Ye said don't come back in here until I had coin, and that's coin. Where's Marcus? I don't see him about."

"Oh, you haven't heard?" he said, pulling a great goblet and a dusty brown bottle with a black dog and a skull on its cloth labeling. "I'm sorry Lawrence. He passed away. Been three nights since."

"He passed away?" Lawrence sat on the tall wooden stool and looked at Timothy. "Are ye joshing me, Tim?"

"Nar!" said the innkeep, placing the bottle with the pulled cork beside the goblet. "Nar, he said his side was a-hurting him. Hurting him bad. He went down to the abbey there. I expected to see him next day, but instead a monk came, looking to see who knew him. I told the monk you was the only friend he had that I knowed of. Guess they didn't find ye, hunh? Told him ye was staying in one of them old houses there."

Timothy patted Lawrence on the shoulder and said, "Just a silver." He took one silver and left the bottle. Lawrence stared a long time at the bottle of Black Dog and the skull upon the label. After a time, he grabbed the bottle and the goblet and retreated to a table in the back corner, where he could watch the door. It was a habit he had gathered when he had been his majesty's chief forest warden. Before the illness of spirits caught up with him. After an untold time of dwelling on his past life, he poured a big draught of the black liquid into the dusty goblet.

He stared a long time more, thinking of the last time he had shared Black Dog with Marcus, his only real friend. It was surely the drink that had killed him, he thought. His liver was surely poisoned.

The night came and went, and Lawrence took not a drop of the drink. Timothy asked many times about him, wondering if old Lawrence too was about to keel over. He even gave him a free bowl of stew. He ate a few bites, but took none of the drink. In time, late in the night, he could hear music playing, revelry down the way, laughter and songs about the death of Angueth. He thought about the boy and the half-dwarf who had been so kind to him earlier, not for the first time that evening.

He picked up the full goblet and walked to the fireplace. All onlookers were shocked when he cast the black liquid into the fire, causing a bright blue flare into the air, and said, "To Marcus!" Then he walked over and handed the goblet and the rest of the Black Dog to Timothy. "You will not see me here again."

Lawrence would long remember Timothy's toothless, gaping, unshaven face. It was very comical and he never saw old Timothy again.

But he would see Arn again. Of that much he was determined. For in the days and weeks that followed, none who knew old Lawrence would have recognized him. His beard shaved, his hair cut, his clothes replaced with fresh, he indeed kept his word. He would never buy spirits again. He even bought himself a fine new blade and two throwing daggers, for it was a long, dark journey to Clayhaven. He would be important in Arn's life as well. He would repay the greatest gift, his life. For his life had been given back to him.

Arn had caught up with the parade near the beginning. He had walked on most of his adventures, so he decided to walk in the parade. He laughed and waved at the people, feeling shy but very happy about the celebration. The grand parade ended with a few words from the young, new king about continuing the fight, and asking for volunteers on the morrow to move to the assistance of Eldross.

The young king asked Arn to return to his realm of Clayhaven and send back as many men as he might come across, and to set a guard upon Moresfield's castle. He had been advised of possible attacks from the northern border watches. He also requested a supply of as many pots as could be made in Clayhaven, for provisions while under siege. He wanted the men and pots as quickly as possible, but advised Arn to stay and make the castle ready for siege before returning. Quite likely Stoneanchor would have made it to Clayhaven by that time.

Arn and Gustavus entered the main feasting hall. There were several buildings about that had been converted into feasting halls so that everyone in Richaver could enjoy a night of feasting before war would surely engulf all of their lives.

They were formally welcomed by the new king. All cheered as he entered. It was all resplendent with tapestries showing heroes and their brave deeds. One of the king's men told Arn that the blank spot on the south wall was to hold a tapestry being made in his honor. From his charge up the lonely hill, to saving the king, to the Isle of the Dead, to slaying Angueth, all would be wrought in fine woven colors to be displayed on the wall.

They soon joined their friends at the great table. The beautiful young baroness sat to Arn's right, along with other dignitaries to the left and right. But his friends waved from the far end of the table. Arn saw the handsome young man who had ridden in the coach with Maria

Louise sitting next to Anne. Arn was not happy to be seated so far from his friends. He was not the only hero.

He walked to the seat of honor and politely nodded to the baroness, then kept walking. He walked to the young man sitting beside Anne, leaned down and whispered something in his ear. The boy smiled, excused himself and proceeded to Arn's place of honor and sat down, which brought many furtive glances and whispers.

Arn just smiled at all those who had noticed the change of place. He simply said, "With your leave, good sirs and ladies, I will sit with my friends, who are just as much heroes as I." He had no desire to sit beside the baroness. The events with the old man earlier had taught him he was still just Arn of Clayhaven, and he would not have any better friends than he had now.

He finally brought himself to look at Anne. He was wondering what her reaction would be to losing the handsome young nobleman. To his relief, she beamed her beautiful warm smile up at him. "I'm so glad you are sitting here, Arn."

"Me as well. I am so sorry for the way I acted earlier. You and Greygrim deserve so much better."

"You see, Anne?" asked Greygrim, leaning over. "I told you he'd come to his senses." He grinned and slapped Arn on the arm. "But don't do that again!"

"Never," answered Arn. "I know who my friends are."

"Hey, why didn't you ask me to sit beside the baroness? She is cute."

"Aw, there are plenty of nicer girls around for a wizard such as yourself."

"You are right." They laughed and relaxed and began to enjoy the feast before them. The king led grace, asking protection for Southaven, for the soldiers and refugees. They all feasted on delicacies such as they had never even dreamed of seeing all at once.

There were roasted chicken, delicious pork, beef of various joints, potatoes, stews, soups, salads, fresh bread, biscuits, gravies, all sorts of vegetables, some of which they had never seen or even heard of. Gustavus especially ate his fill of giant mushrooms, sweet pies, fairy cakes, scones, tarts, all of which he referred to as appetizers. All was accompanied by a big tankard of fresh, sweet milk. Arn had never known Gustavus, or any of them, could put away that much food. But there had never been that much food around before.

After feasting, there was a dance. Maria Louise came to Arn and asked him, "May I have the first dance?"

"You may indeed," winked Arn. He grabbed Greygrim's hand and placed it in hers. "Enjoy the first dance!"

Maria Louise was startled but had no chance to say anything as Greygrim whirled her onto the dance floor. Surprisingly, he was a very good dancer.

"Dear lady," said Arn, bowing to Anne. "I have two left feet and two more spare left feet. But if you would so honor me as to try at this dance, I promise I will do my very best not to hurt you too seriously."

Anne smiled and jumped to her feet. "Let me teach you, Arn," she said.

Tradition was to play a song honoring those who had gone before them as the first dance. So they all danced to the beautiful Waltz Macabre. Arn did the best he could.

He was distracted with how beautiful Anne looked, how lucky he truly was to have a friend as beautiful as she. And by her closeness. She wore an elegant white and pink dress trimmed in gold and silver threads. Her cheeks were red on her fair, freckled skin. Her eyes seemed to dance. Her hair was unbound, long, clean, and smelling of sweet spring flowers. Arn could not help but smell it as many times as he could. They stumbled a bit but enjoyed the dance very much, and clapped as it ended.

He bowed to the lady and she curtsied, as was the custom. As he raised his eyes to her, he focused on her beautiful, full red lips, and caught him staring into her eyes. He could feel her breath close to his face. He could not help himself, but leaned forward and lightly pressed his lips to hers in an honest, sweet kiss.

The fall air was crisper and cleaner after the sweet kiss. Arn had never felt so alive. The music sounded clearer, and his sight was keener than ever. He could smell the sweet air of the last day of fall. Tomorrow winter would begin. He felt so live and happy after that kiss.

They looked around and discovered, to their discomfort, that many were staring at them. They quickly left the dance floor and returned to their seats. A large supply of fairy cakes and tarts had been artistically arranged, so they began to enjoy them.

Greygrim continued to dance with Maria Louise, and after a couple of dances, he returned and slapped Arn on the back. "I didn't think you had it in you!" Arn gulped an entire fairy cake and said nothing. Both Arn and Anne looked a bit sheepish and embarrassed. Despite this, they all enjoyed the evening very much.

Across the hall, Arn thought he recognized a face. He got up and tried to go see the person, but was distracted by so many people wishing to talk with him, that he was unable to find him. He was polite to all who tried to get his attention.

The night wore on to three bells and the revelries came to an end. The soldiers needed some rest for their long march on the morrow. The companions all went back to their fine rooms and said good night. Arn slept better than he ever had. Some of his dreams included silky hair and sweet lips.

When he awoke the next day, it was already eleven. Nobody had prodded him awake since his arrival at the castle, and it was a luxury to sleep until his body was rested. It was a crisp, chill morning, but the fire had been stoked in the huge room he shared with Greygrim. As they breakfasted on cheese, ham and fresh rolls with milk, they spoke of the banquet.

Greygrim told him he was right about Maria Louise, that she wasn't very nice after all. She seemed to defer to anyone who was of a higher station than he was. He wanted to ask Arn about the kiss but thought better of it.

Eventually they went to Anne's doorway and found she was ready for travelling, as was Gustavus. All their gear was ready to go.

Arn and Greygrim gathered their things and met the others downstairs. The brothers were there, ready to travel. They had fine ponies to ride and two pack animals, and were accompanied by two men at arms trusted to help Arn in all things. One guard was tall, of maybe forty summers. The other was perhaps eighteen or nineteen, a bit older than Arn.

On the way out of Richaver, Arn stopped at the metals shop. It seemed forever since they had been there last. He bought each member of his company a lovely gift and for himself, he got the knight from the display window, as well as the dragusin. He added three footknights and a mounted crossbowman that he favored. The shopkeeper threw in three more foot figures, so Arn chose a halberdier, a crossbowman and a longbowman, like he had seen at the battle. The shopkeeper was clearly delighted with the sales, and with discovering Arn and his friends had been successful in their mission.

He reached below a cabinet and pulled out a dusty wooden box, containing an exact replica of the king, mounted and dismounted, looking just like he had on the last day of his life. The set came with two retainers and a miniature tent, in colors as the king's own. "Oh, I can't take that!" exclaimed Arn.

"Oh, yes you can, as long as you wouldn't mind me sayin' that Arn the hero shops here!" grinned the shopkeeper.

"Of course not." He took the gift and promised to make more purchases when he came back through.

"Here's one more thing," said the metal worker excitedly. "A pair of knucklebones and here, a set of rules so you might play a game with these fine miniatures. Arn could not wait to read through the rules and play a new game with his friends. He thanked the man profusely.

They stopped at a couple more shops, then rode on down the road. None of them were used to riding ponies, except for the guards. Arn and his friends dismounted and walked, up a long road towards what? A new adventure? He wondered, for he suspected there would be many more.

As they passed a resting spot not far from the castle, he saw the person again, the one he recognized. The person was reclining on the grass, reading a book, surrounded by a group of people, all resting.

Arn walked towards you, smiling, and extended his hand. "I am so happy to meet you! I remember you at the pier. I have seen you a few times and just was not able to greet you. I wanted to say hello to you at the party last night. I hope you enjoyed it." Arn bowed at you and continued, "I remember the looks of concern and worry on your face and I wanted to thank you so much. I do hope you will join me and my friends again. It is such a great pleasure to have finally met you. I must be off now, but it is my greatest hope we will meet again and have more time to talk.

"Don't be shy Anne, Greygrim, Gustavus! Brothers, come down here and meet these folks. Especially my friend here."

Anne came up with a lovely, freckle-faced, friendly smile. "It's nice to meet you."

Greygrim flashed a magic flower that turned into a butterfly when he gave it to you. "I am Greygrim." Father Kile smiled a dashing greeting, Brother Francis bowed, and Brother Clement said, "Hello, hello!"

"An' I am Gustavus, a smith by trade. It is an honor to meet ye. Arn spoke of ye many a time. I hate to say it, but we had best be off, lad. I hope your friends can join us in Clayhaven."

Arn looked back. "You are right. Farewell, my friend. May your journeys be blessed. Remember you are very important! Without your fond wishes I don't think I would have made it. I am so glad we had a moment to speak." He smiled warmly. "I hope I see you again!"

The company smiled and waved farewell to you as they headed off on their journey.

Godspeed, dear reader. I hope you have enjoyed this chronicle of Arn. Forgive me if I rambled a bit. It is my love for detail. May your blessings be many and your worries be few. May I see you again, reading Arn's book two.

The End

MORE ABOUT
SOUTHAVEN
A BIT OF HISTORY

Greetings, dear reader. As is said by chroniclers whence I came, may you find this humble story not only worthy of your time. May I also open that special doorway which one has been given as a gift from our Creator, that you might come with me and perhaps see a bit of what I have seen and know a small portion of what I know of this humble lad I am blessed to know as Arn of Clayhaven.

If I may formally introduce myself, I am Greyson deSaye. I am a chronicler, not crucial to this story. I am simply the honored narrator of the tragic yet heroic tale of young Arn of Clayhaven. That is all that needs to be said of me.

The story is truly about Arn of Clayhaven, as you might already have guessed. A young man of few talents, plain to look upon in the face, but strong in body. Perhaps if he were not generally quite filthy, you might think he was kind of handsome in a not-so-handsome way, if you get my meaning. A lad of twelve plus summers, who had, I think, when the filth was removed during his yearly bath at mid-summer for the festival, golden brown hair. You would notice, beneath the dark matted locks of hair that had fallen in his face, two piercing grey eyes which were wise for his age.

His story begins in a world of epic strife, a time when men fought other men, or beasts, blade upon blade, and steel upon steel. The land where our young hero lives is a great continent that was once beautiful and peaceful. May I stress the word peaceful to you, dear reader? I don't say this word lightly. For if you have ever seen the light and beauty of creation swallowed by darkness and war, you will know what I mean when I say a blight came upon this fair and wondrous place.

No one to my knowledge has yet spoken of this lad, in writing or song, just me. I have been told not to waste my time writing of this common boy. That he is not worthy of a chronicler who has written of kings. He is no one, so they have said, just lucky.

But I say to you, my reader, that he is a hero. Perhaps I only say that because he once saved my life. Perhaps I only owe him a story. You must make that judgment for yourself. Perhaps I do write this with narrow vision. I am right fond of my life. But this young fellow, just like you, has great value, no matter what anyone else says. His story is most worthy of being told and I will humbly try to do just that.

I should start perhaps a little closer to the beginning. The great continent I mentioned which was swallowed by darkness and war is called Greatcast, where once amid the northern lands five tribes of men lived in peace. They lived with kindness and true brotherly love towards one another. Until—and you surely guessed there would be more—he came.

One desolate, lonely man. Well, maybe I shouldn't say lonely, for he came with servants. Many twisted, gnarled, gaunt creatures, hideous yet pitiful to look upon, and they were his servants and friends. At the beginning he was known by many simply as the Vagabond.

He was the great deceiver from across the dark waters. It is said he came from a continent known as Grimcast. He was also known as the Red Prince, or the Red Traveler. As this dark soul traveled the kingdoms of Greatcast he twisted men's hearts, discovered their desires, then with no magic more than men's greed, he defiled and changed much of the continent to ruin, darkness and despair.

The five great kingdoms of men and all of the lesser kingdoms of men fell to his twisted lies. Jealousy, hatred and greed overcame them. The Vagabond in short time destroyed what was good in the rulers of mankind. It was many a year that most of men were under the oppression of the dark Traveler. He worked very diligently to control most lands except those controlled by other races such as the wily elves of the great woods that dotted the lands here and there, too fast to be easily destroyed, and the dwarves of the Grey Father Mountains deep in their holdings, protected by wise craft and deep delvings. And other races I will not mention here for they were not great in number.

But in time the spirits of men, as always under repression, rose up in revolt. I feel I would not honor the great founders if I did not mention the battle that broke the chains of the Dark One. Humanity fled from the great workhouses, fields and mines. Skirting Grey Father Mountains and heading in a westerly direction, the fleeing host of our ancestors made their way finally to the farthest coast to the southwest and the great jagged black cliffs of Crakeston.

As the heroic leaders of the rebellion had nowhere to go, they moved back towards the plains, debating which course to take, the mountains to the north, or south to the valleyed lands and plains. As they camped and debated their course, the Dark One was not too far behind but did not follow rapidly for his quarry had nowhere to go, and he did so enjoy the hunt. The Dark One being one who liked to turn negative into more positive, as it were, decided to make the hunt more amusing for himself, for he would surely punish all those who had led the rebellion of the foolish sheep that were men. Though this was a disappointing turn of events, he was almost done with his vast black fleet of warships with which he planned to return to those enemies he had on distant shores, which it was said had gathered against him and exiled him from the lands of Grimcast.

The Dark One had planned five great abominations against the five great leaders, each with its own distinct horrors brewed in a great pot of demonic nightmares. The first and greatest of these wicked works was known as War. A horrid effigy to behold, sown from the very corpses of the dead saved from the Great War that had allowed mankind to be imprisoned by the Evil One and his servitor thralls.

The next abomination was Plague, a hideous nightmare brought from the putrid black swamps of the Nothlunds. The humanoid mass stood seven measures tall with puscuous green oozing skin with red sores, fleas swarming about its feet, and corpses of dead rats jutting out here and there. The terror had the head of a rat with great, sharp, broken yellow teeth and sinister rodent eyes. Clouds of mosquitoes and black swamp flies followed him everywhere.

The third of the five was Famine, also known as the Grunken. A thing that even stooped stood ten measures high. It looked as if it were the skeleton of a man draped with tight, jaundiced skin. It could go from a solid state to an ethereal being and emitted a sickening howl that would cause men to drop to their knees, covering their ears, with a hunger in their bellies they had never felt before. Its eye sockets glowed bright yellow with tinges of pink. It was said this monster had been made before to torment the dwarves, and elves would starve and turn to blasphemous ways to fill their bellies, ways we shall not discuss.

The fourth creature was Pestilence, a disgusting insectoid thing, a true abomination to behold, which I shall not describe here. It had swarms of locusts about it and rats and other vermin at its beck and call.

Last was great Tempest, which stood more than twenty measures in height, truly the most frightening of the five. The giant walked shrouded in heavily laden clouds and constantly flashing lightening for eyes, set deep in storm cloud. Its mouth brought forth gales, ice, blizzards, whirlwinds, waterspouts—all manner of fearsome weather elements.

These five loathsome monsters were indeed unimaginably frightening to behold. As if they were not enough, they were accompanied by two earthy hags sent to fight the two great warrior ladies.

Dust was a mass of whirling sand and soil. Her body was of earth and stone, and she was extremely difficult to hurt in any way. It was a challenge to even approach her. One could not breathe for the choking dust about her.

The second was Vulca. She was surprisingly pleasant to behold. She stood about the height of a tall human woman, with goodly proportions. Her skin was of grayish-black, living stone. Beneath it rolled lava for blood. Her eyes were two fiery slits; her mouth spewed forth ash, hot stones and fire. It was said she was married to a great heathen red dragon from high in the Nothlunds, but no one knew for sure. Perhaps the Dark One had made a deal with her for she loved, as her husband did, to torment mortals.

These were the leaders, except for some more mortal sorts. They were numerous. One was named Angueth, when he still held flesh and breath. A tall man, some say handsome to look upon, dressed in great finery, vain, with a heart as black as pitch. But his place was third to the Dark One.

The main soldiers of the Dark One were goor, because they bred quickly. He also employed half-caste goor who were half men, and evil men who had sworn loyalty to him and made deals with him. Within the ranks were also mighty augerhul, tall, grey-skinned, muscular fiends. There were trolls and the mighty tathgul, a monstrous beast of limited intelligence, which stood on two huge, thick legs and had six arms, the snout of a pig, burning, sunken eyes of a demon, large sharp ears, features of an angry ape, and claws as long as sabers. Although stooped, the tathgul stood more than thirty measures high. Nobody knew from where they had originally come, but they were found in the lower part of Greatcast, and had almost been eliminated by the dwarves and elves, for they were hated by all. Only as powerful a wizard as the Vagabond could control these beasts.

The Vagabond himself rode upon his great war wagon called Sorrow, which measured from front to back 25 measures. The front and sides were armored with iron, layered as a fish's scales. Inside the wagon, protected by large iron manlettes and the sides of the wagon, were three archers of the dead, formerly men and elves. They had had evil hearts in life and were now bound in service to their dark master. Any who approached too near Sorrow would indeed feel their four-foot shafts through their throats, for they would protect their master.

A guidesman was placed to the front, for the Vagabond was not a driver. The four beasts which pulled the chariot were of higher intelligence than the guidesman. He merely made clear the master's directions, if there was doubt. He was of great height and girth, had flowing, graying hair, keen eyes, a magic breastplate of bronze, and wore a huge head of a wolf he once defeated on his head. His legs and arms were protected by fine, light armor, while his broad feet were bare. He was one of the wild tribesmen of the north. If you saw under his armor, you would find many tattoos of blue woading on his chest and arms and lower legs. He was an outstanding teamster and known to be one of the best throwers of the javelin. He could hit a running rabbit at fifty paces from his chariot while advancing at full speed. He had two well-stocked banks of magic javelins on each side of his driving pit.

The four massive steeds which pulled Sorrow were, believe it or not, intelligent wolves, with intellect equal to humans. Each had a small kingdom of his own in the Dark Lands. The first was Rend, a beautiful, lithe creature with a grey-black coat and dagger-like white teeth. She was very wise and crafty. Although smaller than her three brothers, she was faster and more cunning. Next was Tear. The smallest of the three brothers, known for toying with his prey, he enjoyed torturing living things. Truly he was a mockery of his canine race. The largest, and the leader, was Gnash. He was as black as obsidian, cold as his heart. He had terrifying, glowing orange eyes. Alpha of the bunch, it was said his howl alone could defeat a battalion of men, because it was terrifying to hear. Last was Gorge, the fattest of the team. Although slower than his littermates, he made up for it with his strength. He could devour a flock of two score sheep in one night. Eating was something he truly enjoyed, especially after a successful fight. The four wolves had been a gift from a mad shaman to the Vagabond when they were pups. They had come from the mountains where the wild men lived.

This was the terror of the Vagabond's favorite transport. When he went into war, sitting on a war tower in the center of Sorrow, he was clad in all black and shining blue armor with two crescent moons on the breastplate, one green and one blue. In between sat the skulls of the original five high kings who were betrayed by the Vagabond. He stood ten measures tall in this form, two arms per side. On his right he carried a huge wheat sickle and his feared tri-staff with many evil spells, made of three great blackwood trees which had grown entwined together. Each staff tip was adorned with a bronze-covered skull of former enemies from the land he came from. One dwarf, one man, one elf, all with magic jewel eyes.

The Dark One himself would not appear at the great battle, for he would be delayed and kept at bay by a host of dwarves and elves, at the cost of their lives. They made a valiant attempt to rid the Cast of the Dark One once and for all. He would not make it to the battle in time, and did suffer several wounds that day that even with his cruel magic he could not heal.

As the great battle began, men found themselves with their backs to the cliffs, their exit cut off by the Dark One. The seven elected leaders, five men and two women, wise and strong, prepared their council of war. With the help of their friends, the elf king and dwarven kings, and with the lethargy of the Dark One creeping slowly on his prey, they managed to prepare positions under the great dwarven engineer, Rile, and with equipping of an archer force by the elves, and a fighting force given iron by the dwarves, and with all praying to the Creator, they managed an army. And three regiments of the strongest men and one mighty dwarven regiment, all of the first three ranks in iron, armed with great steel spears and halberds and beautiful dwarven steel swords, and finely wrought light yet tall arms shields that could be used with two-handed weapons.

To the back of these were three ranks, not as well-equipped, with steel spears and great shields. They had been trained excellently by the elves at catching raining barbs of the Dark One's archers, and could even protect the first three ranks by stepping in and putting the great shields above the heads of their comrades.

At the very back stood two ranks with light or no armor, some were young men, some were young women, some were old, and they would hold a simple weapon that may have been the demise of the Dark One's army. These were river rocks from the rivers nearby, none weighing less than a quarter stone, and some even weighing a full stone, for the stronger throwers. When the battle came on that dark day, so many fell but the four great regiments stood their ground. As the enemy closed, the simple stones of the Creator came crashing down on the heads of their enemy, breaking jaws, smashing shield arms, even breaking weapons. For as the regiment stood behind their hastily made barricades, the surprising rain of stones caused the best regiments of the Vagabond to run and break. And when Angueth's taskmasters managed to whip them back into the assault, they found the ground extremely difficult to walk, for the stones would roll their ankles and snap them like twigs on a crisp, fall day.

At the end, the dwarves arrived riding great bears, and the elves, riding white steeds. The simple concept of throwing stones had won the battle of Star's Tears. It was so named because after the battle, so many tears would fall from the army's widows and children. It is said the Lake of Tears was formed for there were more tears than there were stars in the skies. For three days they mourned their losses but the Dark One and his demon effigies had been defeated, though of the seven leaders, there were left only two. There was Godfrey, the mightiest of the sail-makers, who had led the original sail-makers' revolt, a tall, strong, bearded hero, who would become the first king of Southaven. Also remaining was Anna the Fair, who had been leader of a first revolt of women at a farm in the Nothlunds. She was strong, with long, flowing dark hair and sharp hazel eyes that could charm anyone, and look into one's soul.

The newly elected King Godfrey and Anna the Fair were united in a quiet ceremony, for they had been in love since fleeing the dark lands. Godfrey was amazed by her strength, beauty and resolution. He had never beheld such a wise, strong woman as Anna was, and he deeply fell into the wells that were her eyes. She felt the same. She admired the strong character and forbearance that he evidenced in good times and under trial. Their love grew quickly and strong.

King Godfrey held counsel with his chosen men, the elven leaders and the dwarven leaders, for they knew the people could not remain in this place of great sorrow. They were almost out of food. The counsel was divided on where they should go. No path was clear to the king and queen.

On the fourth day, King Godfrey arose early, with the notice that there was a great white stag seen near the camp. He took up his bow and went in pursuit. As he and his men chased the stag, it bounded over a steep rise and seemed to disappear. But as they went over the rise they observed a great, grey wolf running over the next hill. As he mounted the crest of the hill, the wolf took time to stand and howl. This was strange because it was full daylight, and no pack could be seen about him. The men wished to kill the beast, but the king stayed their bows.

The king wondered to himself if the great beast could be a sign from the Creator. So he sent two men back to gather the people, explaining to his men that a sign had come. The great host slowly moved forth, following the wolf, into the evening. Though the great wolf could have moved fast, he did not. He moved at a walking pace. He would proceed to the next high ground and howl. With the full, autumn moon, they could see his silhouette going forward. When the second moon arose, he stood bathed in the blue-green light of the moons.

The next day the people could not find the wolf, but strangely, though they were not too close to the sea, a sea eagle circled above them, and the queen said, "Look up, husband! There is the sign!"

They followed the great sea eagle by day, rested in the evening, then about midwatch the wolf returned, and the people moved on. Always following the two messengers of the Creator: the sea eagle by day, and the wolf by night.

On the last day of their journey, the king crossed over a rise and saw a land that was lovely to behold, a land none of the travelers had heard of. The grey wolf could be seen in the distance lying on the ground, and the eagle flew lazy circles above the vale. A scout approached to tell the king a huge hive of honey bees had been found, and the people built a fire to smoke the tiny bees away from their treasure.

On this land the fortress of Richaver was established, and from there they built Southaven, thus named because it was south of their former home, and because it was a plentiful and protected land. After the founding of the new kingdom, the Dark One grew angry and sullen, for he had no more army with which to threaten Southaven, and he retreated back to the Nothlunds with a long-range plan to build an even bigger force, and to continue building his fleet.

Frightening stories about the Dark One and his minions had been told throughout Southaven for as long as anyone could remember. As always in the retelling of stories, there was probably some effort made to embellish so as to make the listeners shiver. Still, the true horror of the evil story was hard to imagine when you lived life in relative peace, as did our young hero, Arn, in the small town of Clayhaven.

About Clayhaven, you might get only a couple of good spits out before you passed through the place. It was on a well-traveled road near the border defenses. You wouldn't think this was anywhere of consequence if you saw it. It was typical of the decaying small villages dotted throughout Southaven that had once seen better times. You would not guess, not even for a winning, golden pig tail, that Clayhaven had once been a wealthy place of commerce and artisans had come from all over Southaven to buy and trade Clayhaven's greatest commodity: clay.

Not just any clay, but possibly the finest in the whole world. A fine, white clay, easily worked, extremely strong when dried and fired. It is said that when storage vessels were made from it, the food stored in them remained good for many weeks beyond what was expected with average clay. Many potters, artists and merchants came from all over to purchase this wondrous gift from the ground. Until, in the course of time, this magnificent vein of clay ran out. The population of Clayhaven dwindled, and at the time of Arn's arrival, there were only a few notable businesses in the whole place.

The local inn was old and big. In its past days it had seen many an honored and revered guest, and had been quite beautiful. But in our story, that time had clearly passed. The inn was called the Brown Pipe

Leaf. The patrons now were local peasants, a noble now and again who owned land nearby, and maybe a passing clergyman or an adventurer on his way to some much more interesting place. Like any tavern, the Brown Pipe Leaf had its local riffraff, those not being peasants, but scum. The kind that will catch you in a dark place and will put a knife deep in your back or perhaps if you are lucky, just cut your purse.

The innkeepers of the Brown Pipe Leaf were a big burly man named Asher Cantree, an ex-mercenary, and his wife, Myrtle. She was only slightly surpassed in girth by her husband, but was by far the brains of the operation. It was said she had been pretty once, but time, a hard life and good food had made her plumper and a bit less fair, to be nice to the lady.

Another notable place in Clayhaven was the shop of dreams. I call it that because common folk did dream of being able to buy things there. So this place was their great temptation and joy occasionally, but more often sadness for wanting items found within. The shop was run by a man named Trast. Now, Trast was a man of character. It is said he was once an adventurer, but those days had long passed. Trast was now past his 255th birthday, proof of his being of some high blood.

Down at the bottom end of town was the potter's house, owned by Barston and his wife Lucy. Barston was a potter of notable skill, and he occasionally had buyers from far for his wares. Though he had known the days of the great clay, he no longer had any to sell. He sometimes worked an unusual blue clay. Whence it came, nobody knew. Usually he worked in the common orange clay easily found around Clayhaven.

Gustavus ran the blacksmith's shop. He was a gruff character of unknown age, but an excellent smith. There was a rumor that he was at least half dwarf, and possibly entirely dwarf. You could believe it if you saw him, with his incredible strength, forming metal into useful implements with great skill, in the heat of his great forge. He had a reputation for forging strong and long-lasting blades, and was sought out for that skill on a regular basis.

Oh, and yes, that reminds me of one more place. Perhaps I have forgotten it because most of the villagers had forgotten it. Sad, really. It was a little chapel with a ruined back, which once had been a great cathedral, so they say. The parishioners numbered maybe sixteen or seventeen-odd villagers, and the occasional wanderer, adventurer, or clergyman.

Father Kile was indeed an interesting man. You would not mistake him for a peasant. You might mistake him for a monk if he had the robe on, but you might just have a strong impression that he was noble—though why you would say this, you wouldn't be sure. And I should not forget, or I would do the man dishonor, when he was not tending the abbey or his gardens, he was tending the sick of his village and some nearby villages. He had even been to the local noble's house on occasion and was very successful in healing those he cared for. He was a man of strength, integrity, well spoken, shrewd, some say, but very kind-hearted to those in need.

Father Kile was not alone. Brother Clement worked hard in his gardens and his herbs, and often was seen quite filthy from growing and weeding and tending his small but productive farm of twenty or so goats, four milking cows, and anywhere from twenty to forty chickens. Clement, when not stooped over tending things and whistling hymns and other pretty songs, old songs, was a man of six feet, five inches, with arms like a great bear, and hands as big as a fairly large bowl. He would like that comparison, for Clement's favorite thing was stew and soup, and he made some of the finest in the land. He had even had nobility dine with him on occasion, though discreetly.

Brother Francis' head was not shaven at the top like most monks of his monastic order. He really was a monk, or at least he claimed to be. Oddly, no one argued with him, or maybe not so oddly. He was a powerfully built fellow, but kind. He also knew his herbs, for Kile was also a marvelous instructor. Francis had certainly worked with Kile as long as anyone could remember. You got the feeling that Francis would give his life for Kile and the farm at the drop of a sword, if need be. And you also thought he would be right handy with that sword. He did many other things, including some smithing of his own. He occasionally helped the local smith and enjoyed this hard work immensely.

Well, enough of that. Much more of the story will come clear as you enjoy the truly interesting tale, the adventures of Arn of Clayhaven.

RICHAVER SOUP

4 cups chicken stock
¼ cup pearled barley
1 cup green cabbage, chopped
1 carrot, chopped
2 T walnuts, chopped

Place chicken stock and barley in a pot and bring to a boil. Cover and simmer on low for 30 minutes. Add cabbage and carrots, continue to simmer for 10 more minutes until barley and vegetables are tender. Sprinkle with walnuts before serving. Makes two servings.

BARREL SOUP

4 strips bacon
2 carrots, chopped or sliced
1 large potato, chopped
1 parsnip, chopped
6 cups water or chicken stock

Cook bacon in a skillet until crispy. Remove bacon pieces and leave the bacon fat in the skillet. Add carrots, potato and parsnip. Saute until starting to slightly brown. Add water or chicken stock. Bring to a boil, then lower heat and simmer until all vegetables are tender. Crumble bacon on top before serving.

STONEANCHOR'S PUMPKIN

4 cups pumpkin, cut in small cubes
3 strips bacon
½ onion, chopped
Salt to taste

Cook bacon in skillet until crispy. Remove bacon pieces and crumble; set aside. Saute the onion in bacon fat until translucent. Add pumpkin cubes, salt and crumbled bacon. Add ½ cup water, cover and steam until pumpkin is tender, stirring occasionally. Obviously, Stoneanchor would probably not have had an onion, but this is the way he cooked pumpkin when he returned from his exile.